stars

stars

Original Stories Based on the Songs of Janis Ian

Edited by Janis Ian and Mike Resnick

DAW BOOKS, INC.

DONALD A. WOLLHEIM, FOUNDER

375 Hudson Street, New York, NY 10014

ELIZABETH R. WOLLHEIM
SHEILA E. GILBERT
PUBLISHERS

http://www.dawbooks.com

ACKNOWLEDGMENTS

Introduction © 2003 by Janis Ian.
Come Dance with Me © 2003 by Terry Bisson.
The Scent of Trumpets, the Voices of Smoke © 2003 by Tad Williams.
Finding My Shadow © 2003 by Joe Haldeman.
Ride Me Like a Wave © 2003 by Jane Yolen.
In Fading Suns and Dying Moons © 2003 by John Varley.
On the Other Side © 2003 by Mercedes Lackey.
Nightmare Mountain © 2003 by Kage Baker.
On the Edge © 2003 by Gregory Benford.
Two Faces of Love © 2003 by Tanith Lee.
Immortality © 2003 by Robert J. Sawyer.
Hunger © 2003 by Robert Scheckley.
Society's Stepchild © 2003 by Susan R. Matthews.
Murdering Stravinsky or Two Sit-Downs in Paris © 2003 by Barry N.
    Malzberg.
Society's Goy © 2003 by Mike Resnick.
Second Person Unmasked © 2003 by Janis Ian.
Play Like a Girl © 2003 by Kristine Kathryn Rusch.
All in a Blaze © 2003 by Stephen Baxter.
Cartoons © 2003 by Alexis Gilliland.
Old Photographs © 2003 by Susan Casper.
EJ-ES © 2003 by Nancy Kress.
You Don't Know My Heart © 2003 by Spider Robinson.
Riding Janis © 2003 by David Gerrold.
East of the Sun, West of Acousticville © 2003 by Judith Tarr.
Hopper Painting © 2003 by Diane Duane.
An Indeterminate State © 2003 by Kay Kenyon.
This House © 2003 by Sharon Lee and Steve Miller.
Calling Your Name © 2003 by Howard Waldrop.
Shadow in the City © 2003 by Dean Wesley Smith.
Joe Steele © 2003 by Harry Turtledove.
Inventing Lovers on the Phone © 2003 by Orson Scott Card.

To Anne McCaffrey, who sent me to Worldcon,
and Mike Resnick, who met me there.
—Janis Ian

To Janis Ian, whose enthusiam is contagious,
and whose talent, alas, is not.
—Mike Resnick

CONTENTS

Contents

Introduction

by JANIS IAN

THIS is all Anne McCaffrey's fault, because I was sitting at the kitchen table with Anne and her daughter Gigi when I first heard the word "Worldcon." *What's a Worldcon?* I asked. Annie and Gigi were both horrified; then, with a look of deep concern on her face, Anne patted my hand and said "My dear. . . . You *must* go."

Or maybe it's all Mike Resnick's fault. This book would never have begun had I not written to Mike a few years ago, thanking him for writing *Kirinyaga* and enclosing a copy of one of my CDs. I pointed out the song his story had influenced, and let it go at that.

Much to my surprise, a month later Mike e-mailed me, asking if I wanted to collaborate on a short story with him. *No*, I said, *I don't write stories.* "You write articles, don't you? Speeches? Liner notes?" *Yes, but* . . . "I've read the stuff on your web site. You need to write stories." And to be perfectly blunt, he then badgered and *noodged* until I said all right.

When Mike found out I'd never been to a World Science Fiction Convention (Worldcon. Go figure.), he bemoaned my ignorance, then began an aggressive campaign to get me to go. He is not an easy man to turn down.

Thus it was that I found myself at the 2001 Worldcon (science fiction's largest yearly convention, where they hand out the Hugo Awards, their equivalent of the Oscars). I was terrified; I'd been reading science fiction since I was about seven years old, and here were many of my heroes, along with 5,000 or so fans.

I followed Mike around like a duckling, and he had great fun introducing me to writers I'd admired for years. I stuttered on meeting Nancy Kress, burst into tears as I tried to tell Connie Willis what her work had meant to me, and gaped like the village idiot when I was introduced to Harry Turtledove.

In the course of the week, Mike introduced me to Marty Greenberg, the famous anthologist. The next night, Mike told me he and Marty had a brilliant idea—why not do an entire book of stories based on my work?

I thought they were nuts, and said so. *None of these writers have time for that, none of them would be interested, and no publisher in their right mind would pursue it.*

They already had a publisher interested and ready to commit. They'd spoken to a few writers they knew I loved, and the writers were ready to commit. It only awaited my approval.

What a surprise.

I am not a science fiction editor; I am no editor at all. I'm a songwriter, singer, sometime article- and story-writer who happened to have some hits around the world, beginning with "Society's Child" at the age of fourteen, and continuing through "Jesse," "At Seventeen," and the like. I have nine Grammy nominations and a multitude of platinum and gold albums, which certainly doesn't qualify me for a project of this nature!

But I do have one important qualification—perhaps the most important. I love to read. Throughout my life, books have been my window into another world. I was always terminally unhip in school; the library saved me, hiding me from the cruelty of other children while its books showed me life as it could be.

I left school at fifteen, but I've derived quite a good education from my reading. I've never been to medieval Japan, but I can cheerfully describe the living conditions and hierarchies, thanks to books. I never took physics or chemistry, but, between what I've learned from Stephen Baxter and Greg Benford, I pass as knowledgeable. It is amazing how passive watching television is, and how active reading a story can be.

Many of my own fans don't read this form; they persist in asking me, "Why science fiction?" I can give you a lot of different explanations. First of all, a lot of what you read *is* science fiction, even if you don't realize it. Never mind the spaceships, the lurid covers with terrified women being strangled by seven-armed, bright green Martians. Science fiction incorporates everyone and everything, from Stephen King to Madeleine L'Engle, from *Peter Pan* to *Winnie-the-Pooh* (a talking bear?!).

It doesn't have the boundaries most literary forms have, and since, as a songwriter, my hope is to push the boundaries, it's a perfect form.

Science fiction is a home for the homeless, a place for those of us who have spent our lives on the outside, staring through a plate glass window, watching all the other folks dance while we take notes and turn them into stories about "real life." It's an outsider's form. In my field, contemporary music, looks matter a lot. Are you thin enough? Good-looking enough? Young enough?

In science fiction, we meet young and old, thin and fat, ugly and terrible, with and without the hearts of gold. It's "Snow White" (Witches? People who sleep for decades, then wake at a kiss?) and *Grimm's Fairy Tales* and even *Santa Claus Is Coming to Town*. (Who rides through the air at the speed of light, rearranging their molecular structure so they—and their gifts—can fit through a chimney, covering the entire world in a single night?)

In other words, we *all* grew up on it. We just didn't know it.

For me, science fiction is the jazz of prose.

My criteria for asking writers to participate was simple: their work had to have affected my own work. In some cases, I could even trace a visible line from this story or novel to that song. I can tell you that Jane Yolen's *The Devil's Arithmetic* influenced my song "Tattoo," that Orson Scott Card's *Tales Of Alvin Maker* brought me the fire imagery in "This House," that John Varley's *Press Enter* brought me smack into the computer age. I told each writer how they'd affected me as I invited them, and to my astonishment, many of them said "Yes." Not only that—they said *Yes* with a vengeance. Howard Waldrop pulled out his old Janis Ian records and picked a song I hadn't thought about in years; John Varley did the same. I was immensely flattered to discover how many of my favorite writers counted me among their favorite songwriters.

Many people in the field have been saying, "How on Earth did you get this stellar a cast?" Between them, "my" writers have won dozens of Hugo and Nebula Awards (the equivalent of Oscars and Grammys), and awards from pretty much every other country on Earth, including Japan's Seiun, Germany's Kurd Lasswitz, the British Science Fiction Award . . . well, the list is too long.

I think one thing that helped was my complete naïveté. I approached everyone truthfully, as a fan, and they responded in kind. I had no idea which writers were more successful than others, or which truly needed the pittance they'd be paid for this. I didn't know about awards, or good reviews, or "literary and marketplace viability." I only knew that I loved their work, and hoped they'd be a part of what I was beginning to think of as my Grand Adventure.

Before we began, I heard stories about many of the authors—this one would get it in quickly, but it would be slipshod. That one would never make the deadline. This one would lose interest. Perhaps because I cheerfully confessed to one and all that I had no idea what I was doing, I found 100% of the writers (including those who could not participate) more than helpful, completely professional, and a pleasure to deal with. They got excited by the project, and as I asked each new writer to join us, that writer would pass on suggestions. Orson Scott Card raved about Tanith Lee, who was on my list anyway, so I had the luxury of using his name as a reference. John Varley gave me Spider Robinson's address, and Spider suggested David Gerrold. Frankly, I'd never thought so many of the writers I was asking would say *Yes*, or that all but one already owned my records. In all humility, it's astounding to me that my work has reached so far.

Mike and I decided early on not to impose conditions; not to assign particular songs to certain writers, not to limit their word counts too harshly, not to put any barriers between them and their choices. The writers were given half a dozen or more of my CDs, and left to pick their own songs. With a few, such as Mercedes Lackey, I couldn't restrain myself from asking for something specific (in her case, a Valdemar story). With some, I knew my best bet was to leave them alone, and just hope they picked a song I loved.

What was fascinating to me were the song choices as they began coming in. I half expected all the writers would go for the "famous" songs, but as you will see, there are only a few represented here. People were picking esoteric songs like "This House," and "Hopper Painting." After a few such surprises, I realized that the authors had taken me at my word—they were choosing songs that *moved* them, not songs that had been hits. Nancy Kress chose "Jesse" because something in the lyric moved her, not because it's been recorded by thirty-five different artists.

I am immensely proud of this book, and excited to be a part of it. Not the least because I got to read all the stories "first," before anyone but the author saw them. For a fiction junkie like myself, a new story, a new book, by an author I like, is as good as Christmas and my birthday rolled into one.

The first story to come in was Nancy Kress' "Ej-es." She'd warned me up front, laughing and saying she was turning "Jesse" into a brain virus. I laughed, too, at the time, but when I finished reading her treatment of the song, I realized she'd understood what I was looking for in a way that even I hadn't at the start.

That's the problem with translations, or in this case, transitions. They're never true to the pedantic literality of the words; at their best, they can only be true to the heart.

When I was a very young writer, barely twenty-one, my song "Jesse" was recorded and made a top ten hit by Roberta Flack. When the time came to do a French translation, the great Charles Aznavour offered his services—but only if he could meet with me first. I hesitantly entered his room at the St. Moritz Hotel in New York; it was a beautiful suite, with a fireplace going, and he was so terribly, terribly French that it completely intimidated me.

Aznavour congratulated me on having written a wonderful song, then proceeded to say "Of course, the lyric I write will have very little to do with yours." I was shocked, and wanted to know why? He explained that the nature of a good translation was its fluidity; that, for instance, there was not even a French equivalent to the English word "hearth." In the end, he said "A good translation is not true to the lyric; it is true to the lyric's *intent*."

I've never forgotten those words, but when I read Nancy's story, their meaning hit home. *Her* "Jesse" has nothing to do with hearths, or beds, or empty stairwells, but it has everything to do with the intent. Better still, she'd done exactly what I'd asked for—she'd approached the song without timidity, without reservation.

At one point, my partner asked me what the stories were like. Carried away by my own enthusiasm, I started rambling "Oh, "Jesse's" a brain virus, and "At Seventeen" is a couple of vampire-type kids, "Hunger" is a mermaidish fish-lady, and Dave Gerrold's named a comet after me!" She stared at me for a moment, shook her head, and said, "Okay, I'll ask some other time."

That's the problem with a venture of this nature—can you make it interesting to the lay reader, the person who does *not* normally read science fiction? To tell you the truth, I'm not sure. I do know the variety of stories and ideas in this book is huge, and I do hope everyone will find something to appeal to them—but I really don't know.

I *do* know that the stories are true, in only the way a work of fiction can be true. They have heart. They have life. They have truth. They move me. As an artist, I can ask for nothing more.

To be scrupulously fair, Mike is truly the editor of this volume. I am merely the slack-jawed fan, whose main contribution consisted of writing the invitations, corresponding with the writers about everything but their stories, and squealing every time a new one came in. Mike is the one who made sure deadlines were met, encouraged writers when they became nervous or disheartened, and "edited" when asked. Believe me, with writers of this stature there's not much to be done!

There are writers who could not be here, whether through illness or the constraints of time. The two writers who influenced me most when I began writing songs aren't here: Madeleine L'Engle's *A Wrinkle In Time* taught me more about the light and the darkness than any religious instruction could; she sent me a lovely letter, but pleaded age and health concerns. And Zenna Henderson, who I lived and died by during most of my childhood, and whose light has dimmed forever, is only here in spirit. This book is for them, as surely as it is for anyone else, because they did what every great artist does—they showed me myself, and made me into a better human being.

Thank you to every writer who was able to be a part of this project, and for your faith that it would be a project you'd be proud to participate in. Thanks to Mike and Marty, for the idea, and Betsy and Sheila for running with it. Thanks most of all to the readers, to those of us who keep the libraries and bookstores alive.

It is the luxury of being a semifamous person, these days, that if you are fortunate enough to have a couple of hit records, your name is known to a multitude of people you yourself may admire. To discover that they, in turn, admire *you* is so much icing on the cake.

Come Dance With Me

by TERRY BISSON

. . . who called to say "come dance with me"
and murmured vague obscenities.
It isn't all it seems
at seventeen.
—from "At Seventeen" by Janis Ian

"**N**OT so tight," Billy said. "I can't breathe."

I was like, isn't that the whole idea? But I didn't say anything, I just loosened his rope and straightened it. I never had a boyfriend before, but straightening a tie is something every girl knows how to do, from watching *Friends* and *The Creek*. And this was sort of the same.

"That's better," Billy said. "I still have to do you—Amaranth."

I love it when boys call me Amaranth. Amaranth is my real name, my secret name, the name I chose for myself. I closed my eyes while Billy put my rope around my neck and pulled it tight. It was rougher than the string, that's for sure, but I didn't worry about it leaving a Frankenstein mark. They could do me like they did that other girl and cover it with a high lace collar at my funeral.

"Scared, Amaranth?"

I'm like, No! Billy clickety-clicked the cuffs on my hands behind my back, then ratcheted his own together and dropped the key onto the desk. It rang like a bell when it hit. We were standing on a metal desk in the junked-up office of an abandoned skating rink on New Circle Road, Roller Heaven. There's a joke if jokes are what does it for you.

They say sounds get real loud when you're fixing to die, but you couldn't prove it by me. I listened for a bird, maybe a nightingale, but there weren't any. Maybe they don't like night after all. Maybe it's just another phony name. The best I could do was a dog barking and a horn honking somewhere. Pluto in his little car, picking up his girlfriend. Good-bye, cruel world!

I heard a gagging sound like somebody trying to puke. At first I thought it was Billy trying to say good-bye, so I opened my eyes for one last smile-try, and then I saw he was stretching, trying to use his feet to reach the key. I don't know how he planned to pick it up, unless there was some gum on the bottom of his shoe, and even if he did, then what? Go home to our happy homes? That made me mad, after all my hard work. I kicked the fucking desk over. That's one thing big legs are good for. That and keeping boys away.

Billy was in, right away. As soon as I kicked the desk over, his mouth popped open and his eyes got the look you get when you enter the Realm for the first time. His legs were doing a little dance. My own eyes closed on their own even though they were wide open, which was weird. But okay. I couldn't breathe, but what did I care? I could see the stairs under my feet, and I could see somebody in front of me, running down the steps. I figured it must be Billy—who else? I reached out and grabbed his coat, but it wasn't exactly a coat. It wasn't exactly leather. It was cold and slick, and when I tried to pull him back, it slipped through my fingers, and he went on down, around the corner. Something was hitting the door. BAM then BAM, like those little rams on *Cops.* There was a light, pulling at me, like another rope. It was so bright I closed my eyes, which was like opening them, everything being reversed, which makes sense, if you think about it. I was looking into a flashlight and I felt two hands under my tits, lifting me up. Mommy, I groaned, but it was a black woman.

I heard her say, "This one's breathing," and then she stepped away and somebody else strapped me to a stretcher. Meanwhile EMS came in and cut Billy down. I barely opened my eyes so they wouldn't see that I was seeing. I could tell Billy had made it all the way into the Realm and I was glad, even though I hadn't. It's like in those movies when the guy dies happy because he has saved his girlfriend's life, only reversed. It's gross to see the way they handle people when they are dead. It's not like what you see on TV, believe me. "Can you hear me?" The black woman was back.

I was like, of course I can hear you, you're hollering right in my fucking ear.

"Why did you do it?"

I said, to get out of class, and she goes, "Huh?"

I said, everybody gets out of class when there's a kevorker. Usually there's an assembly. She goes, "Good God, girl," (Have you ever noticed how some people are always calling you girl?) and gives me a shot, which you're not supposed to do without permission, I'm pretty sure. Don't make jokes with cops. Or EMS personnel, which are the same thing. I woke up in jail. You know where you are right away, because of the bars.

I sat up and groaned. There was a fat white lady sitting outside the bars reading a paper. *Suicide watch*. I felt better already. They brought me pancakes for breakfast, with a plastic fork. I acted like I was trying to stab myself with the fork, but the lady reading the paper didn't seem to think that was funny. It was *The Star*. Did you know that *The Star* and *The Enquirer* are put out by the same company? When I found that out, it was like the last straw. After a while two cops wearing suits came and took me upstairs to a little interview room, just like *NYPD Blue*. One cop was black and one was white. Everything at the jail is perfectly integrated. There was another man waiting for them in the room, wearing a less cheap suit.

"I'm your lawyer," he said. "I was engaged by your father."

Congratulations, I said (on his engagement), but he didn't get it. Instead of paying attention to me, he laid a briefcase on the table and unsnapped the two snaps, and they were so loud I thought: maybe I'm dead after all; everything is so loud. But no such luck. The white cop told me I was going be charged with murder, and could possibly face the death penalty if I was tried as an adult. I'm like, Hooray, I feel better already. The black cop pulled out a palmtop, the kind that records onto a flash card, and set it on the table in front of me.

"Eleanor," he said. "Can I call you Eleanor?"

I shrugged and said, Why not. Everybody else does.

"Here." He took a pack of cigarettes out of his cheap generic sport coat.

"You can't give her that," the white cop said. "She's underage."

"So what," said the black cop. They were playing good cop/ bad cop. "You are going to charge her with murder and you won't even give her a fucking cigarette?"

"It's not established yet that they intend to charge her with murder," said the lawyer; "my" lawyer.

The black cop, the good cop, tapped a Marlboro out of the pack and lit it for me with his orange Lakers lighter. I took a drag even though I don't actually smoke. I saw a woman smoke once through a hole in her neck. She was dying of cancer. It was cool. He said, "Can you tell us why you did it?"

I told him so we could have assembly, the same thing I had told the EMS lady. That didn't go over too hot. The white cop looked disgusted. The lawyer looked pissed. The black cop took a drag on his own cigarette, and then squinted at it and put it out. You can always tell when somebody's trying to quit. The lawyer pushed the ashtray as far away as he could without pushing it off the table and said, "Her father tells me she likes to be called Amaranth."

"Amaranth," said the black cop. "Why don't you tell us the truth."

I'm like, Okay. The truth, if that's really what you want. The truth is that there really is a Life after Death. But it's only for teenagers who kill themselves.

★★★

The assembly thing wasn't totally a joke. They call them Healing Assemblies. The first one was in November, right after I transferred to Oakmont. A boy and a girl kevorked in her garage using his dad's car exhaust. They left the radio on and died listening to

WFFV, soft rock, the kind of folky stuff my original mother liked. According to the papers they were "popular," and it was a "mystery" why they had done it, and it was all true, I guess. They were definitely more popular dead than alive. Who isn't? The next two were in January, and they were part of the Goth crowd. They did it at the old skating rink on Outer Loop. They hung themselves with electrical cable. Their names were Gail and Gregory. The two Gs made it easy to remember.

There was another Healing Assembly. Afterward, there were all these girl-hugging clumps in front of the school, like they like to show on TV. I was just about the only girl standing off by myself, as usual, which is maybe why they wanted to interview me. They don't usually interview fat girls. Maybe it was the Goth thing. The TV lady was all set up with a camera guy following her, and a sound guy following him, and a battery guy following them all, like the *Wizard of Oz*. She stuck a mike in my face and said, "Were they friends of yours? Why do you think they did it?"

Well, yes, I think they did it to get out of class, I said. She frowned and switched off her camera and they all stomped off together. By now I was in the middle of a circle of kids. They all walked away, too, looking disgusted, like I had let off an enormous fart. But Billy looked back. I had already noticed him because he was wearing a black string around his neck. Some skinny girl was holding his hand and she pulled him away.

Even though I don't smoke, I can fake it. The next day I went to Marlboro Country outside the lunchroom where the Goth types hang out and bummed a cigarette. Pretty soon there he was. William Winston Lamont was his full name. I had checked it in the Yearbook database during English.

"It's no joke," he said. "There really is a Life After Death."

Cool, I said. Finally my father has put me in a school where I can learn something. I shook out my sleeve so he could see the scars on my wrist.

"What's your name?"

I said, they call me Amaranth, my first actual lie. There wasn't any "they". But I had just moved to Oakmont from Edgefield, all the way on the other side of Columbus, and why not start over?

"Know what this means?" he said, pulling down his collar, like I hadn't already seen the black string tied around his neck.

I said sure, just guessing. But you're not really going to do it.

"What do you mean?"

Guessing again, I said, Your girlfriend won't let you. Miss Teen Queen.

He stepped on his cigarette and said, "Fuck you," and walked away.

Okay, I said.

"What did you say?" he said. He stopped.

I said okay, I said. I said, are you hard of hearing?

★★★

Later that afternoon, my father and my latest mother came to the jail. It was upstairs again to the same interview room. Same two cops, but they waited outside. Same cheap suits. Same lawyer, too.

"She's a minor," my father said. "She's barely seventeen."

The lawyer shook his head. "They say she's going to be tried as an adult." They talked about me like I wasn't there so I pretended I wasn't. The lawyer said the murder charge was because the arresting officer saw me kick the table over. He had watched the whole thing. "He waited to knock the door down so he could catch them in the act."

"Then he's the one who killed that boy, isn't he?" my father said. "Isn't that entrapment?"

"I took the liberty of engaging a psychiatrist," the lawyer said. I said congratulations again, but he didn't get it again.

"We're getting you out of here tomorrow," my father promised.

I'm like, Is that a threat?

"I'm not sure she wants to go home," the good cop said. I hadn't noticed him back in the room

"Is that true?" my father asked. If I closed my eyes, he wasn't there. I could almost see Billy going down the stairs. *Wait!* What happens now, since you can only enter the Realm in twos. Did he make it? Why didn't I?

"Is it a boy, honey?" my latest mother asked.

What's with the honey shit? I'm wondering.

"Damn it, open your eyes," my father said as they led me away in handcuffs.

★★★

I made Billy pick me up at the Kwik Pik since my father has a thing about boys with tattoos. About boys, actually. "Where do you want to go?" he said. I said, second base. He looked at me funny, then parked by this old lake. He started to unbutton my blouse and I cut him off and said, Let's talk.

"Okay." He lit two cigarettes and handed me one. He still hadn't figured out that I don't actually smoke. "What do you want to talk about? If you're talking about Susan, we're sort of broken up, but I'd just as soon she didn't know about this."

I said fuck Miss Teen Queen, I came here to talk about the club. He's like, "What club?"

The Kill-Yourself Club.

"That's not the name of it," Billy said. "The name is a secret. The Kevorkians."

Like my name, I said. Amaranth.

The car had power windows. I hit mine to throw out my cigarette, but it went all the way down. Special setup for tolls. Then I let him get to second base, which boys appreciate. He's like, "Amaranth." I didn't let him go below the waist and after a while he was ready to talk again.

"Tell me about hell first," I said.

"It's not hell," he said. "It's called the Realm. It's like a Web site but you can only get there with the right music. You know Hard Hate?"

Of course, I nodded.

"You know how with really great music you go somewhere, I

mean, really go somewhere? Well, if you do it the right way, with the computer, it takes you somewhere really real. It's like a Web site but it's really real. Another guy in another high school showed it to Greg. He moved here last year from Colorado."

Colorado, I nodded. Of course. This is Ohio. Everything always comes from somewhere else.

"Greg showed it to me, and now Greg is there, so I know it's real. We have two couples in the Realm now. That's the only way it works, we have to do it in twos."

I said, there are rules? I didn't like that. One good reason to be dead is because of all the rules.

"There aren't any rules once you're in the Realm," he said.

How do you know?

"Greg told me. I talked to him last night."

I'm like, Sure you did.

He started the car. Was he taking me home? Buttoning my blouse I said, You have to drop me at the Kwik-Pik. But he said, "I'm not taking you home. I'm taking you to my house, but you have to be quiet."

It was a Volvo, the safest car in the world. A real going-to-hell kind of car.

✸★✸★

The psychiatrist was a nice lady in a nice suit with a nice smile. All nice as hell. The two cops were there, to protect her from me, I guess. We went through the cigarette thing again, and then she said, "Why don't you tell me all about it." I told her what I had told the cop: There is a Life After Death, but it's only for teenagers who kill themselves. I figured the best way to confuse them was to tell the truth. But she was more interested in Billy than in my amazing news. "Do you always sleep with guys on your first date?" she asked.

Only, I said, if they call me by my real name. "What is that?" she said, pecking away on her little laptop, and I said, None of your business. Unless you want to fuck me, too.

She closed her little laptop. "I don't think she's crazy," she told the lawyer. "I think she's just a nasty little bitch." "Amen," said the white cop. The black cop gave me another cigarette. I was beginning to wish he was my boyfriend instead of Billy, who had left me behind, although they were all saying it wasn't his fault. I wasn't so sure. I needed to check with him.

The lawyer came in, and they stood me up to take me back downstairs. I could hear him on his Nokia with my father. They were arguing. I knew my father didn't want me home. The lawyer was telling him that since I was a juvenile they couldn't hold me unless I was a danger to others, or crazy.

What about the murder charge, I said.

"Unfortunately, you are still a minor," said the lawyer.

★★★

Surprise—Billy lived in a big new house in the big new house part of town, only about four blocks from "my" house. Nobody seemed to be home. We went in through the three car garage and down a few steps to the basement without ever going through the house. Billy had his own room with his own door. There was a wooden guitar in the corner. On the walls it was all heavy metal and topless girls, with long, skinny legs.

Billy sat down in front of his computer and put in a CD. The screen saver was fish with skulls for heads, swimming back and forth. The CD was Hard Hate, "Stairway to Hell."

"The music has to be playing," he said. "It does some kind of interactive thing with the processor or something."

Whoever said boys all know all about computers hadn't met many boys. Billy told me to close my eyes while he typed in the secret URL, then got up and gave me his seat. "There, it's ready to go. Just hit RETURN."

I hit RETURN.

The skull-head fish were gone. Now the screen had a picture of stairs. The steps were wide and they curved in from gold banisters on each side. They looked like the casino stairs in Las Vegas that I saw when I went there with my father, right after my original mother died. My father told me she had a heart attack, but I found out later this was a lie. There wasn't any ceiling or any floor. People were standing on the stairs, all couples, holding hands. They were all just outlines. There was a red carpet down the middle of the stairs and everything else was gold. The banisters, the steps, even the shadows were gold.

"See?" said Billy, sounding excited. Hard Hate was playing the same two-guitar intro, over and over. The same four chords. It was like the CD was stuck. "This guy from Colorado found it and showed it to Greg, who showed it to me. That's them, on the stairs, they are all there now. Click on the title."

I clicked on Realm.

Enter User Name

"It doesn't have to be your real name. But it has to be a name you are prepared to use for all eternity." Billy put his hand on my shoulder, under my blouse, on my bra strap, like we were lovers.

I typed in *Amaranth*.

Enter Password

"K-E-V-" Billy began.

I typed in *kevork* without waiting for him to finish.

"Now hit return."

I hit RETURN. All the legs started moving and the couples moved down. But just one step, the same step, over and over. "Click on any one," said Billy.

I'm like, Any one what? Any one couple? How do you click on a couple? Do you click on the space between them? None of them were even holding hands.

"Any one person."

I clicked on a girl outline. A face filled the screen. It was the girl who had killed herself last week. It was the picture that had been in the newspaper. She was wearing a Sunday dress, but she had a black string around her neck, which hadn't been in the paper. I thought that was pretty cool.

"HELLO, AMARANTH," she said. Her lips moved funny like a cartoon. Her voice was whispery under the music—still the two guitars, over and over.

I said Hello.

"No, you have to type it in," said Billy.

I typed in *Hello.*

"Her name is Gail."

I'm like, I know. I read the papers. I typed in *Hello Gail.*

"Ask her a question," said Billy.

I typed: *How the Hell are you?*

"GREAT."

"It's not a joke," Billy said, taking his hand off my shoulder. "Don't you want to know what life after death is like?"

I typed: *What is Life after Death like?*

"IT'S GREAT HERE."

"Click on Greg," Billy said. "Next to her."

I clicked on the boy next to her. Her face went away and his came up. He was wearing a suit and tie. It was the picture that had been in the paper, except for the black string. His lips were moving funny like a cartoon. I started to get up so Billy could sit down but Billy put his hand back on my shoulder.

With his other hand he reached down and typed: *Hey Greg it's me.*

Greg's voice was deep and tinny, under the two guitars: "HELLO, AMARANTH. WOULD YOU LIKE TO JOIN US IN THE STAIRMASTER'S REALM?"

I typed: *I guess.*

"GREAT," he whispered.

I typed: *What's it really like?*

"IT'S REALLY GREAT."

I typed: *Want to talk to Billy?*

"BILLY WHO?"

"I don't want to talk to him anyway," Billy said. "It's late."

We logged off, which was all right with me. I let Billy get to third base on his bed, under the poster girls. He was so proud he walked me home. Sneaking in was easy, since my father and what's her name go to bed right after "Seinfeld."

★★★

My father waited until 3:30 the next day before he came to the jail to take me "home." I guess he thought it was like school. He took me out the side door. He even brought a coat to throw over my head to protect me against the reporters, of which there weren't any.

It was understood that I wasn't supposed to go out. I said, where would I go? I told him I wanted to do some homework. He believed that, even though I hadn't been to school since the week before. As soon as he left, I logged onto the internet and typed in the URL, which I remembered even though I wasn't supposed to have seen it.

http://stairmaster.die

I hit RETURN. Nothing happened. No welcome, no stairs. After a while there was a beep and a box came up.

File not found

I tried a search under kevork, under death, under stairmaster. I got lots of sites but none of them were right. No Stairmaster's Realm. No Billy.

Then I remembered the music. I looked under my desk for my CDs but they were all gone. No Toxic Waste, no Hard Hate, not even Sperm Dogs or Hole. My father had thrown them away! Luckily, there was a box of my mother's old CDs in my closet, with her broken guitar. Bob Dylan, Janis Ian, Joan Baez, Laura Nyro, soft rock. The Beatles. It wasn't the right music, but on a hunch I kept sticking them in and popping them out until I got one that worked.

One guitar but the same four chords, over and over, and there they were: the golden stairs with the red rug.

There were the outline couples, hand in hand.

**Welcome to the Stairmaster's Realm
Enter User Name**

None of the outlines looked familiar. But then how familiar did Billy look to me? I typed in my secret name, *Amaranth*.

Enter Password

I typed in *kevork* and one of the couples in the background moved. I clicked on the boy's face and it was Billy, wearing a suit and tie, just like in his newspaper picture. There was the string. My heart was pounding as I heard his voice, all tinny and small: "HELLO, AMARANTH, HOW ARE YOU?"

I didn't make it. They cut me down.

"IT'S REALLY GREAT HERE."

They put me in jail.

"ARE YOU PLANNING TO JOIN US HERE IN THE STAIRMASTER'S REALM?"

I guess. But how?

"Eleanor? Amaranth!" My father was knocking at the door.

Help.

"COME DANCE WITH ME."

I'm like, huh? But it wasn't Billy, it was the record. And my father at the door, banging and shuffling around.

"Amaranth? Who are you talking to? I thought you were doing homework. Your mother has fixed a nice dinner, to welcome you home. Your favorite, macaroni and cheese."

Macaroni? I thought, hitting PAUSE. Don't think so!

✯✯✯

The kids at school call the corner where the cool kids hang out, Marlboro Country. I waited there, with one black string on my wrist and another on my neck, pretending to inhale. Billy appeared and said, "Now do you believe?"

I always believed, I said. But I told him I didn't understand how the music thing worked.

"It's interactive," he said, as if that explained anything. "You have to go in twos, you have to have the right music—"

Hard Hate, I nodded.

"'Stairway to Hell.' That's the way we got it from Greg, and he got it from Colorado. Now I'm next in line but the question is, who gets to go with me. Not everybody is willing to go all the way."

I'm like, Like your girlfriend?

"She doesn't get it. She thinks they are dead. She doesn't understand that there is eternal life and that they will live forever in a place without rules. There aren't many who are willing to go all the way."

Is this a proposal?

He didn't get it, but that's okay. There's lots of things boys don't get. That night I let him go all the way in his father's Volvo. The next night he picked me up at Kwik Pik and took me to the old roller rink on the north side of town, and you know the rest.

★★★

May I be excused? I asked politely, getting up from the table. Homework, you know.

My father beamed like a fool. I ran back to my room. The stairs were still on the screen, and my mom's music was still playing: soft rock, like before. The same four chords as "Stairway" but not electric. It was spooky.

You have been disconnected.

I logged back on, same music, soft rock, and when the chords started repeating I knew I was there. But this time I couldn't get the outline figures to move. I clicked on Billy. His face came up, but he wouldn't say anything. He looked dead. I clicked on the girl outline next to him, but no face came up. It was spooky, but it made me feel better.

I knew that spot was saved for me.

I put the computer to sleep and crawled under the covers until I heard my father and my latest mom go to bed. As I passed their bedroom, I could hear them talking, or rather, him talking and her listening. "Tomorrow," he was saying, "She will go back to school and see the shrink twice a week," etcetera, etcetera.

I'm like, Sure. As silent as a cat, I went down to the kitchen and got a plastic bag and a flashlight, checked the batteries, and let myself out, clicking the door shut softly behind me.

The garage at Billy's was open. I sneaked in and went down to his room. It was just like the last time I had seen it. There were the girls on the wall. The guitar in the corner was wood, like my mother's before I broke it. The computer was on, but asleep. It was covered with a white sheet, like a veil, or maybe a shroud.

I didn't need the flashlight after all. Hard Hate was still in the computer's CD slot. I popped it out, then popped it back in, thinking, why not? There was no one awake, probably no one home. It was better than "my" house.

While the two-guitar intro was playing I typed in the URL and hit RETURN. Again it was like the CD was stuck, playing the same four chords over and over. Yes! There were the stairs and the welcome logo. I tried to log on, but all I got was

incorrect user name.

I tried *Billy* since it was his computer, and it worked. I pulled the plastic bag over my head and hit RETURN. All the legs started to move. When I clicked on Billy, he looked confused in his suit and tie.

"HELLO, BILLY," he said. His voice sounded whispery under the music.

It's me, Amaranth, I typed in. *I can't breathe.* I thought he would like that.

"THAT'S NICE. WOULD YOU LIKE TO JOIN US IN THE STAIRMASTER'S REALM?"

I can't breathe.

"IT'S REALLY GREAT," he said. The guitars were getting louder and louder.

I can't breathe.

My body kept wanting to breathe, even if I didn't. I touched Billy's face on the screen. I couldn't find his hands.

"I'M FINE," he said. "IT'S REALLY GREAT HERE, BILLY."

I sucked the plastic into my mouth, like a dentist's thing, and all of a sudden there I was, on the steps. I was running down, I had made it through. The music was gone, but I could hear the scraping of my shoes, some new kind of shoes. Leather on stone.

What happened to the rugs? I was on concrete stairs. No gold, no banisters. The walls were gray, rough, and cold. It was like the stairs at the airport parking lot. Suddenly I felt very sad, thinking of my poor fat body laying there like an empty house. I was at the airport when he told me my mother died.

I stopped. I tried to turn around, but I couldn't. I could hear voices down the stairs.

I yelled, BILLY! But it didn't come out as a yell. It came out as a whisper. I must have taken another step down or turned a corner, because he was right there beside me. I was sitting on a landing.

BILLY, I whispered. WE MADE IT. I reached for his hand, but it wasn't exactly there, not so you could hold it.

"WHO IS IT?" he said.

AMARANTH.

"AMARANTH WHO?"

JUST AMARANTH, I said.

"WELCOME TO THE STAIRMASTER'S REALM."

You don't cry when you're dead, even when somebody hurts your feelings. It's just like when you're alive. I looked around. So this was it.

I THOUGHT IT WOULD BE NICER, I said. Sort of said.

"WE ALL DID. WHY ARE YOU PULLING AT YOUR FACE?"

I hated the way my skin felt. WHERE'S THE RUG AND THE . . . THE NICE STAIRS?

"IT DOESN'T LOOK AS NICE FROM THIS SIDE."

WHERE'S THE MUSIC?

"IT DOESN'T LOOK AS NICE FROM THIS SIDE."

I tried to turn around, but I couldn't. "WE GO DOWN BUT NOT UP," some girl said. I hadn't noticed her before. She was sitting two steps down, trying to light a cigarette. The matches wouldn't work.

WHAT ABOUT THE NO RULES?

"IT'S NOT A RULE," said Billy. "IT'S JUST THE WAY IT IS."

I'm like, WHATEVER. There were other girls on the steps below. Some boys, too. They were just sitting. They were not in couples at all. I tried to look up the stairs, but I couldn't.

WHAT HAPPENS NOW?

"NOTHING," said Billy. I sat down beside him. The concrete steps were cold. I was wearing a sort of dress with no back, like a hospital gown.

NOTHING? We sat there for a long time.

NOTHING.

We sat there for a long time.

★★★

Come dance with me.

I'm like, What's that?

"WE'RE FINE," said Billy. "HOW ARE YOU?"

CAN YOU HEAR THAT? I asked. I could hear music, but not Hard Hate. The same four chords, though. How long had I been sitting here, on these concrete steps? It seemed like forever. My hands and my butt were cold.

I stood up. The music was louder. I looked behind me, up. The steps led around a corner that went two ways at once. It was weird. No rug, no gold.

"WE DON'T GO UP," said Billy. He was holding my hand, but my hand was still cold.

Come dance with me.

I JUST WANT TO SEE.

"SHE DOESN'T KNOW ANYTHING," said some girl.

I went up one step. Billy's hand slipped through mine. Around a corner, there was a girl. Sort of a girl. She was young like a girl but old like a teacher at the same time. It was weird. She was singing and I knew the song. It was one of the folky songs my mother had left behind. Soft rock. I suddenly wondered: had she intended to leave them for me?

WELCOME TO THE STAIRMASTER'S REALM, I said. I sounded exactly like Billy. It was not really my real voice.

Come dance with me, she said, and I took another step. She was holding Billy's guitar.

I'm like, THAT'S BILLY'S. Plus, she was too old to be there. This was our place.

I don't think so, she said. It's my place, too. I come here when I sing this one song. I've been coming here for years.

LIKE HARD HATE.

I don't have to kill myself, she said. Sometimes I die on stage. She laughed. That's a joke. Every time I sing this song, I find myself here. Back here. I know this place well. I have known this place for years.

THIS IS HELL.

She's like, Think I don't know that? It's only for kids, but we singers get to come and go. At least I get to play my old D-18. She knocked on the guitar, like knocking on a door.

Music makes space, she said. And since the universe includes every space, every new space is a new universe. No matter how small.

IT'S REALLY GREAT HERE, I said.

She just shook her head. She held out her hand but still played the guitar at the same time, a neat trick. *Come dance with me.*

I followed her up the stairs. One step, two. It felt weird. I'm like, WHERE ARE WE GOING?

I'm not going anywhere. She laughed. Song's over, hear that thunder? I'm outa here, girl. She handed me the guitar and I knocked on it, like knocking on a door. Then she was gone and I heard sirens, pulling me like a rope. I dropped the guitar, but not on purpose. It made a big noise on the steps. "She's still breathing," somebody said.

★★★

I opened my eyes. It was the same black woman as before. A woman was standing behind her with tired sad kind troubled eyes. "Mother?"

"Oh, honey, no, I'm Billy's mother. Was Billy's mother. Now what have you done?"

It was weird; she was holding my hand. I closed my eyes and looked for Billy, but he was gone. It was all gone: the steps, the guitar, the girl singer. It was all gone and the weird thing was, I was sort of glad.

"Here, kid." It was the black cop in the crummy suit. He offered me a Marlboro. "Your dad's on his way."

"Hooray," I said, and I let him light it with his Lakers lighter, even though I don't smoke. And then, for some reason, maybe because he was trying so hard to be nice, I started to cry.

The Scent of Trumpets, the Voices of Smoke

by TAD WILLIAMS

There was a girl, her name was Joan
She heard voices in the air
saying "You are not alone
"All is well. I am here."
      —from "Joan" by Janis Ian

I AM met in the garish Tempix lobby by my "Timeviser"—an artless construction that makes me long for the sensible abbreviations and acronyms of GovHub. She is a plump young woman with an enthusiastic manner, her hair styled in an unbecoming back-thrust.

"You must be M. Aibek." Her own name, she announces (although I did not ask) is Gutrun. Her handclasp is overlong and she stares at me as though I am a much-reported but seldom seen species. At first I think it must be my general dishevelment that has caused her reaction—the long Hydra-S project has left me pale as tank fungus, face blotchy and eyes sunken, thin as a dying breath. In fact, it is the termination of that excruciating, frustrating four-month operation that has brought me to this place, given me this unusual but nevertheless powerful need for a change, to experience something other than the usual white-lights-and-serenity circuit while my body is being cleansed and rebuilt from the cellular level up at the government's ResRehab facility.

As we traverse the short distance to the appointment bay, she chattering about various displays on the walls, I realize there is a simpler explanation for her excessive interest in my person: my former bond-mate Suvinha Chahar-Bose works here at Tempix—may even be this woman's supervisor. Could Suvinha have told her something about me? I despise gossip, and have always done my best to avoid being its subject. When she took early leave from our contract, Suvinha was in an emotionally heightened state, and she is thus likely to have made untrue claims, although my conduct toward her never violated even the slightest word of our agreement. Still, it irritates me more than I like to admit to think this wide-hipped, talkative young woman may think she knows something about me. It goes against every particle of a Manipulator's training. We do not insert ourselves. We do not allow ourselves to be drawn in. We are subtle to the point of invisibility.

I suppose that for those reasons it might seem strange to this Gutrun that I have chosen this particular excursion, but I work hard for my government, and thus I work hard on behalf of all citizens, including her. Do I need to justify my recreation choices to private-sector functionaries?

She explains that she has found, in her words, "just what I need" for my "little vacation." I try to form a polite smile, but it is precisely to experience a life in which I am not impeded at every turn by attention-seekers and condescending obstructionists like this Gutrun person that I have asked Tempix Corporation to find me an antidote, if only for a short while. I am tired of subtlety, for the endless games of what Suvinha once called my "Trust No Human, Especially Yourself" profession. Suddenly a chance to experience the fierce excitements of the ancient Era of Kings, of a setting in which power could be wielded openly and honestly by one person, instead of by the countless quiet manipulations of government operatives like myself, seems very appealing.

True power, swift and pure! It will be like breathing fresh air after months in a dank, windowless cell.

Gutrun says that the destination she has selected is a monarchy in the Terran European Middle Ages, so-called. There was no era of kings as such, she informs me: different cultures moved in and out of monarchy at different times. This kingdom will be the old mid-European country known as France. And I *will* be the king, she assures me.

The self-indulgence of the lobby is fortunately not mirrored in the working areas of Tempix. Behind the loud facade hides the same cool aesthetic that marks virtually any modern operation. The men and women who pass by in the wide, blue-carpeted hallway nod politely to Gutrun as we pass, but show no interest in me at all. I am reassured. In some circles, because of the important but low-profile nature of our work, Manipulators excite a morbid fascination in the public. I wish only to be a customer, to be treated in the manner of all others, efficiently, anonymously. My trip, at least within its bounds, should provide as much notoriety and attention as I can tolerate. I am not Suvinha: I do not enjoy talking about my work to outsiders.

As we pass more Tempix employees, I cannot help wondering if Suvinha—my bond-mate who will now never be wife—began as one of these low-level functionaries. She is a hard-minded woman; I can easily imagine her knifing her way upward through schools of softer, gentler fish, swimming toward the levels of light. Did she make her way there by pure effort, or did she graduate from an academy into a prepared slot? I never asked her.

In the appointment bay I am introduced to three sober young technicians whose names slide gracefully from my mind. I ask if the correct arrangements have been made with ResRehab and they assure me that the bureau's employees will be on the premises to escort my body within minutes after my mind has been connected to the Tempix system. When I have no further questions, they seem puzzled, a little uneasy.

"But you're a new customer," one of them says. "Don't you have any concerns? Aren't you curious about what's going to happen to you?"

I tell them I am more than a little familiar with their operations, owing to previous acquaintance with one of their administrators. When I say this, Gutrun smiles briefly, but wipes the expression clean when she catches my eye. Just such annoying, unfathomable smiles used to flit across Suvinha's face (although there were no smiles the last time I saw her). Is this smug expression an occupational disability peculiar to Tempix employees?

Continuing, I tell the technicians that I understand what the theories are as much as anyone can whose specialization is not Temporal Mechanics. I am aware of the acrimonious debate over whether the experience is objectively real or merely subjectively convincing in the extreme—a debate that has more than once threatened Tempix's legal status. I further assure them that I do not care which is true. I desire only a safe and interesting experience. I would have been just as happy at one of the fantasy factories, which make no pretense to realism. I chose a Tempix trip and that is that.

Despite my careful disclaimer, Gutrun nevertheless insists on explaining things. Although I will be fully aware of my own self at all times during the trip, there are built-in governors to protect me as a time-traveler. I will speak the language fluently—indeed, thanks to the curious mechanics of the host-body methods, I will in some manner even *think* in that language. I will have a certain inherent knowledge of the customs and mores of the setting, as well as complete referral possession of the specific memories of my host-body. These memories, even the likes and dislikes, will in no way impinge on my own personality, Gutrun hastens to assure me, except in those cases where the preferences of the host-body are linked to physical constraints such as allergies or other limitations of the flesh. I can act freely. If this is a true place and a real experience, it is one of an infinite number of quantum pasts, and thus nothing I do will affect reality as I know it, and as I will return to it.

As the shunt is connected and the technicians carefully calibrate their galaxy of instruments, I reflect on these last explanations. Such omniscience toward the host-body's mental substance argues to me against the possibility of true time-travel—against the actual physical existence of the experienced phenomena, but I know the Tempix people will never confirm that suspicion.

I recall that during happier times I had asked Suvinha once to tell me, since she must have known—indeed, for that matter, must know *now*, I abruptly realize. Is she somewhere nearby? Does she know I am here today?—whether the time-travel experience was purely subjective or whether the journey was in some way real, as is so strenuously hinted at in Tempix's exhortations to those weary of the infinite but shallow variations of the fantasy factories. Suvin-ha, amused I suppose by my uncharacteristic interest in her work, teased that she would never violate her geneprinted loyalty oath for a mere man. More seriously, she added that there were certainly many questions still, even among Tempix's top designers, but that she could not tell me the company's official internal stance on the subject. The oath was real, she said; it had to do with the difficulty of programming the governors if the traveler knew too much about the nature of the experience.

Strangely enough, this mundane discussion ended in an argument. I suggested that if the experience were in any way real, even in a quantum, infinite-possibilities sense, the government would never leave it to the vagaries of the private sector. If nothing else, it would be more useful for running simulations than even the best of current generators. How did I know, she demanded angrily, that my beloved government was *not* already using it themselves? And what did I know about real things, anyway?

As I said, an argument ensued. Although we had sexual relations afterward that were strangely satisfying, I think it should be obvious why I did not often inquire about her work.

Gutrun intrudes on my thoughts to inform me that the preparations are nearly finished. She explains that I will experience a few moments of synaesthesia as the transfer begins. I tell her that I have heard of the synaesthetic fugue, the temporary confusion of sensory input, and that I am not concerned. She responds that although it is virtually impossible to predict how much subjective time I will experience, at the end of the three days needed to complete my physical rehabilitation at ResRehab I will be summoned back; that return transfer process will also be signaled by a bout of synaesthesia. She tells me this for my edification only, she explains—there will be nothing I can do to aid or hinder the re-transfer.

As she finishes, favoring me with another smile—this one of the blander, more professional variety—one of the nameless technicians says something to his companions. A number of touchpads are skinned in succession. The room slowly fills with a bland, sweet odor; only moments later do I realize that its source is the bank of light-panels that constitute the ceiling, panels which had been . . . *white?* The word seems suddenly inappropriate. A sharp, tangy smell that ebbs and returns, ebbs and returns, is the sleeve of Gutrun's one-piece passing in and out of my field of vision as she reassuringly strokes my chest. I feel scintillant, blue-sparkling beads of light that must be sweat on my forehead. My unexpected fear is a crackling hiss in my nostrils.

✴★✴

I have been tricked.

If that is too harsh a word, then I will amend it to this: I have been manipulated. Even in my anger I cannot help but appreciate the irony. I suspect I know all too well the author of my manipulation.

Everything becomes clear to me only moments after passing through the synaesthetic state, past a moment of darkness and into growing light. I find that I am lying in a huge, too-soft bed, surrounded by a curtain. I feel air—cool, damp, unprocessed air—on my skin. A vast figure looms, shaking me. I tell him to go away, to let me go back to sleep: my transition has left me feeling limp as a cleaning rag (whatever a cleaning rag might be) and I do not wish to be disturbed. The great, fat man—whose name I suddenly know is Georges de La Tremoille, tells me I may not. *May not!*

Startled into greater wakefulness, I feel the full flood of alien memories wash over me, settling into unexpected cracks and fissures in my own being. The perfidy of Suvinha—or the slipshod nature of Tempix's operation—immediately becomes clear.

I am in the royal bedroom at Chinon. My name is Charles; I

am the seventh king of that name in France. I am also the least powerful monarch in all of Christendom—that is to say, as Aibek sees it, among the nations that worship the same avatar of their one god. How quickly these foreign concepts come shouldering in!

As a king, I am a nonentity. I am not really even Charles the Seventh, since I cannot properly be crowned in the custom of this time. The English and the Burgundians own half my country; even my mad, obese mother has sided with the invaders. My own court titters at my impotence.

As a final fillip, a last slap from unkind chance (or from a vindictive former bond-mate), I am ugly. Aibek the Manipulator never worried about such things, but was not—is not—unpleasant to look at. I had thought that at the very least this time-trip would find me possessor of rude animal health and physical spirits; a warrior-king in his chariot or automobile, leading his pliant minions. Instead, I am short-legged, knock-kneed, long of nose, and sallow of face. I am ill, my new memories tell me, nearly as often as I am not. And my people would not follow me anyway.

So much for the exercise of pure power in a simple, primitive setting. So much for a weary Manipulator's much-needed relaxation. These Tempix people have never dreamed of a storm such as I will bring down on them! At the very least, even if my ex-bond-mate has engineered this all by herself, the company is guilty of negligence on a grossly criminal scale.

But why should Suvinha risk her career to do such a thing to me? What fantasy of wrong has she constructed? It makes no sense.

★★★

It was over half a year ago now, at the end of the final killing week of the Cygnus-B3 fiasco, that I returned home exhausted to my apt to find nothing of Suvinha left but a message on the holo. In my absence she had changed her hairstyle to the mannish topside-and-tails. Her image looked quite different from how I had seen her last, very determined. She was dressed for travel.

The holo-Suvinha said that she understood how difficult my

work was, knew its importance to the government. She said that she knew a Manipulator could never know when an off-world crisis might happen, that these crises had to be dealt with when they happened and that the projects took priority.

She, too, she said, was often called on by Tempix for unpredictable, all-absorbing emergencies. The difference, she said—or her strangely masculine new image did—was that she resented this subsuming of her real life by work, but I did not. I made no contact with her even during the periods when I might have taken time to do so without harming the projects, she said, and when a project was over, I seemed to be waiting impatiently for another crisis as though I needed and wanted to escape from the apt and our bond. As the image of Suvinha said this her eyes—she has very large, deep eyes; they are either black or very dark brown—were hard as windows.

This was a shame, she continued, because it had seemed at times that there might be a real future for us as a bonded couple, if I had only been more willing to connect, to take a chance, to invest myself. There had been moments, she said, and then trailed off without explaining what she meant.

It was true that besides the occasional tension there had also been periods of understanding and peace between us—of happiness, I suppose, and what sometimes seemed even more. I do not tend to trust such ephemera, since it runs counter to both my training and my nature, and as I watched her farewell holo-message I became even more convinced I had been right to withhold that trust. What if I had become more deeply attached and then she had opted out of our contract, as she was doing now? My work would have been devastated and I would no doubt have suffered emotional pain as well.

Then the holo-Suvinha added something which surprised me: she claimed that our sexual life was no longer satisfying. This I was not prepared for. Other women have never complained about my sexual performance—in fact, Suvinha and I have gone many times without synthetics of any type, *skinskinning* as I've heard other Manipulators call the practice when they (on a few rare occasions) discuss their outside lives. I have never been so intimate with *any* woman, casual or bond-mate, and I had understood Suvinha to say the same about the men in her life. Now, against all experience and logic, she was telling me something had been wrong. But not really the *physical* part, her holo carefully added—which, needless to say, mystified me even more. What other aspects might exist and be somehow unattended to, she would not or could not explain.

That night, alone in the empty apt, I had an unsettling dream in which Suvinha was trying to drag me down a long corridor toward something very old and powerful which crouched at the far end. I resisted, but her grip was terrifyingly strong.

Thinking back on all this, trapped now in the unsatisfactory body of Charles, I wonder if I have somehow contributed to this woeful situation myself. It is a disturbing thought, but a Manipulator must never turn from a potentially important truth, no matter how unlikely or how unpalatable. I could have undergone my rehabilitative therapies in peace, drifting in glowing white harmony. Instead I elected to experience a Tempix trip, knowing full well that it was Suvinha's place of business. But who could have dreamed that she would violate her trust in this way, out of something as petty as spite?

No, I decide, it is not my fault. I am the innocent victim of a woman's irrational obsession. I am not to blame.

★★★

La Tremoille insists again that I get up. I realize he has the right, even the power, to insist. He has held what little kingdom I have together. I owe him tens of thousands of livres, a staggering sum of money. I owe *everybody* money. A curse on the house of Tempix!

La Tremoille brings his wide, handsome head down close to me, like a father giving a naughty child final warning.

"The visitor is here," he says. "Do you not remember?"

And I do. A religious maniac of some sort, one who I . . . Charles . . . have been manipulated into meeting, much against my will. What I would rather do, I realize suddenly, or what Charles would rather do, is die. Not painfully or quickly; not even soon—I do find enjoyment in the fleshly pleasures my position permits me—but since my father's death seven years earlier in lunacy and filth and my mother's horrid decline into the worst sort of abasement, life has held nothing larger for me than the next rich meal, the next courtly amusement. I am a small man who is becoming smaller, afraid of things and people I do not know. Being dragged from my bed to meet some crazed, god-struck woman is no answer to any of the problems of Charles or France.

La Tremoille stands by patiently while my manservants dress me. I instruct them to avoid my most ostentatious garb and put on me instead simple clothes. Today, with the gray February light seeping in at the high windows, the weight of brocade and gilt will be too much.

"Did this woman not claim," I ask La Tremoille as we move down the hallway from the residence, "that she would know me from among all men?"

"Girl, Sire, not woman," he corrects me cheerfully. "I have seen her. Yes, she has said this."

"Then take in the Count of Clermont and tell her he is myself; I will follow shortly behind."

La Tremoille hesitates, perhaps fearing that I will disappear altogether, then finally agrees. He, too, is as curious as all the court about this strange young woman and her claims. I am not—or at least Aibek is not. Whether the subject intrigues Charles at all is hard to say. He seems largely ambivalent. We both, as far as I can still find the demarcation between us, hope that she guesses wrongly and is laughed out of the great hall. Then we can go back to bed.

I stop outside one of the side doors. The hall is full of lights and packed with hundreds of courtiers dressed in every color of the spectrum. They are all here to witness this heralded exception to courtly routine, this spectacle of a young woman who claims she is sent by God to have me crowned at last, and to lift the siege of Orleans.

The crowd beyond the doorway hushes and from my place I can feel a poised tension, a rustle of expectation. Above the whispering, then, I hear a high, clear voice, but the words are indiscernible. When the voice stops, an excited murmuring breaks out. Compelled, I step through the doorway, finding myself a place behind the courtiers who line the tapestried walls. I am virtually hidden from anyone in the room's center; even the elegantly gowned ladies before me do not mark their king's entrance, so quiet am I, and so fixed are they on the personage in the middle of the hall . . . a small figure, dressed in rough black, who stands beside Louis, Count of Vendôme. I am astonished.

Suvinha! I try to shout. *What are you doing in this place?* But the words will not pass my lips—something prevents these anachronistic sounds from sullying the virgin air of Chinon. A moment later my astonishment fades. Perhaps it is not Suvinha after all. Still, the girl who stares at the Count of Clermont as he slinks back to the crowd (having evidently failed to fool her) is much like Suvinha. Her hair is different, of course, cut in a masculine bowl and shaved above the ears, black as a raven's tail. As she turns to scan the surrounding faces, I feel sure I see other differences, too. She is far younger than my ex-bond-mate, my will-not-be-wife. The nose, perhaps, is too long, the cheekbones not so high. Still, the resemblance seems too strong for mere coincidence. . . .

Then she sees me, fixes me with those disturbingly deep eyes— gold-flecked brown eyes, like a diffident forest goddess, like a sacred deer surprised at its drinking pool. She walks toward me and her stare never leaves my face. The crowd between us melts away. How can those not be Suvinha's eyes? I am almost terrified when she stops an arm's length away, doffs her black cap, and kneels.

"God give you good life, gentle king." Her voice is calm, but there is subtle music in it.

"It is not I who is king," I stammer. I point to one of the young barons, whose costume indeed far outstrips mine for beauty. "There is the king."

The girl's eyes are locked to mine. "In God's name, gentle prince—" she is smiling as she speaks, "—it is you and no other."

And as I stand transfixed amid the quiet muttering of the court, I remember that her name is Joan, this farm girl with Suvinha's eyes. "If I am the king, what would you have of me, maid?"

Her smile fades, to be replaced by a look of immense solemnity, a look so profound as to resemble almost a child playacting. "Lord Dauphin, I am sent by God to bring succor to you and your kingdom." Her eyes narrow as she stares at me, awaiting my response. When I, suddenly in depths I had not expected, can think of no words to say, her smile returns—a small one that looks as though it accompanies pain.

"My Lord has not yet given you to believe me," she says sadly. "Very well, then, let me tend to you one further sign, to show you that my sweet God knows your secret heart."

She draws near to me, resting one hand lightly on my arm; I flinch. She brings her mouth close to my ear so that others will not know her words. Her cool breath on my cheek smells of apples.

"You feel yourself a lost traveler," she whispers, *"trapped in a world that is not as it should be. Like blessed France, you are divided, weary."* Her hand tightens on my arm. *"Only trust in me, in the power that sends me, and all shall be put right . . . made whole. I bring your happiness—and your completion."*

She steps back and kneels again. Her eyes are indeed deep pools, and the me I seem to see reflected in them is a creature of great beauty. I am enthralled. *Charles* is enthralled would be more accurate, of course. *Enthralled.*

We walk together through the overgrown gardens of Chinon, and she tells me of the voices of Saint Catherine and Saint Michael, the sublime voices that have brought her to me. The dank February is only a backdrop now, a gray jewel cask to set off this sturdy pearl of purity. Courtiers gape from the casements above, watching the King and the Maid in rapt dialogue. I need only trust, she tells me. Because God wills it, she will don armor like a man and go with my armies to break the siege of Orleans. I will be anointed and crowned king at Rheims. To all my objections, my confused questions, this farm girl, this pretty shepherdess with my Suvinha's gaze answers only: "Have faith in me, and the power that I serve."

I am being drawn out into stronger currents, I realize. It is seductive. A part of me longs to let go—a part of Charles, that is. Aibek, naturally, watches calmly and rationally from within, the ghost in the machine. Aibek the Mainpulator, even as he feels the currents swell, will keep an eye on the shore.

But who would ever have dreamed the madnesses of the ancients to be so intricate, so sweet?

★★★

Joan is all she promises. The armorers fit her in shiny steel, a skin of clean, hard metal. Her battle standard of white silk bears upon it the image of Jesus sitting in final judgment of the believers and the unbelieving.

This is her powerful, tempting call, that brings the peasants flocking to her as a living saint, and turns the canniest, most profane old soldiers into grudging converts: *Only believe, and all is possible.* Her bright sword marks off the slender division between the saved and the damned. I wonder, Aibek wonders, how she can have such terrible, beautiful faith in its cutting edge. My world, the world of Manipulators, is the world of increment, of adjustment, of two-steps-forward and nearly-two-steps-back. But here stands the Maid, sword in hand, and makes one bold stroke—*flash!* Stand here and be blessed! Cross to the other side, you are lost.

As she waits with the troops mustered to relieve Orleans, her back spear-straight while the veteran captains like de Loré and de Cúlant gossip and laugh nearby, her gaze lifts from the men at arms to me, and from me to the overarching skies. Her meaning and determination are unmistakable . . . but as I watch the small, clever milkmaid's face, eyes ecstatic and cheeks brushed with the ruddiness of excitement, I cannot help but reflect on the contrast it makes with her bright, masculine armor. She is much like me, I realize—just another ghost in a different machine.

This unexpected linkage warms me, but it saddens me, too. She is only a child. She can be hurt, she can bleed. I suddenly think of Suvinha, of the intense need she sometimes brought to our love-making, her passionate clinging that was not stilled by climax—a riddle I never solved. As I watch the maid I am suddenly aroused. It shames me. I wave my arms and the trumpets blare. The column moves away toward Orleans.

★★★

Helpless in a way I do not like, far more excited than I should be, I attend eagerly to news from the battlefields. At night I lie in my curtained bed and wonder what has been done to me. I curse Tempix and worry, alternately. Could Suvinha, unbalanced in some way by her own emotional nature, truly have constructed this imaginary spectacle, this . . . passion play . . . just to trouble me, to pay me back for imagined wrongs? Is she, in fact, with her privileged position at Tempix, now the leading actress in some incomprehensible drama of revenge? But if so, why has she chosen an avatar of such grace and simple kindness?

And what if these events are just as objectively real as they seem? That is another sort of disturbing thought. Have I become too entangled? Am I risking the very genuine future of these people by allowing my attachment to Joan to grow in this way, trusting the fate of whole armies to a milkmaid? Am I overstepping the boundaries in a way no Manipulator should ever allow himself, even in this strange land of unreason?

Even more frightening, is this all some dream—a hallucination I have forced on myself?

Aibek is in a kind of despair, and every morning La Tremoille finds Charles pale and unrested.

★★★

They have lifted the siege! Orleans is relieved and the Loire is now barred to the Burgundians. There is no other source to be credited for the reversal of my fortunes but the inspiration of the Maid, Joan of Arc. There was at first fearful news that she had taken a wound, a crossbow bolt at her neck, but it is only a minor tear in the flesh. In fact, she had predicted just such an injury, and her calm foreknowledge is noted by all. How can she not be sent from God?

And one of the English called her a whore! My Joan, who hates sin and chases the camp followers away—what grace she must wield, to lead soldiers to whom she has denied the company of whores!—called angrily to the Englishman that he would die unshriven for insulting God and France. Indeed, within the hour the fellow tumbled into the water before the battlements and drowned unconfessed.

I am ecstatic! Still, a small part of me feels a disturbing affinity with the Englishman. I sense the currents growing ever more dangerous, and fear what may lie waiting downstream.

★★★

Jargeau, Meung, Beaugency: one by one, the English-held cities of the Loire fall before the Maid of Orleans. The army of Charles has become the army of Joan—but how can I resist, any more than the now-believing soldiers and the joyful peasants who line the route of God's militant daughter? I travel with them too now, carried helpless but not unwilling toward Rheims and my promised coronation. Joan comes to me often, straight to my side as though we were one flesh. What does she care for my short legs, my corvine beak? She does not see Charles, pigeon-footed would-be king. Clothed in the immaculate armor of her love, she sees in me God's child, her brother in the Lord's work. I am a chaste husband to her passion, as was Joseph to the astonishing enterprise of his own virgin wife.

God's love, she calls it. Love. It is a miraculous, all-changing thing, there is no question. I long to abandon myself to it, but I cannot imagine what would be left of me if I did. It is hard to separate myself from weak, needy Charles at these moments, and Suvinha, strangely, has in my mind almost entirely merged with Joan.

One night in the city of Troyes, which has seen our might and thrown open its gates to us, I dream of Suvinha. She stands before me naked, glorious in her skin, and she is both herself and the Maid. Her beauty is frightening. In her hands she holds Joan's sword. *In truth this is* your *sword*, the dream-Suvinha tells me, and her eyes see a joke I do not understand. *Do not fear that I hold it*, are her next words. *It will be given back to you when you prove you deserve it!* She laughs.

In the morning, as we ride out of Troyes on the road to Rheims, a crowd of white butterflies dances about Joan's pennant.

★★★

Victorious, my power restored, I stand before the altar in the cathedral at Rheims. I am consecrated. I am crowned. The noise of the crowd is around me like a rush of water as I look at Joan, armored, her pennant in her hand. Her eyes are full of tears but her smile is strangely secretive.

I feel a twinge of discomfort. She alone, of all my noble captains, has been allowed to bear her standard into this holy place.

It has borne the burden, she points out; surely it is right that it should have the honor. I must, reluctantly, agree, but I am suddenly troubled that I have given so much to her. How can a Manipulator invest such importance in one person, any person? Is it not precisely such seductions I have spent my entire life learning to resist? Drugged by this strange world and time, am I being even more foolish than I feared?

Later, when the fierce celebration is ending, she approaches me. Where I had hoped to find her face softened by the day's events, instead there is a firm edge of determination. What can the woman want?

Paris, is the answer. Paris, and the English driven from France, Burgundy reconciled to my rule. I have received my boon from God, she claims, so I must allow her to finish her mission. Even after all she has shown me, done for me, I still do not trust in the force that sent her, she says. "You must renounce fear," she tells me. "You must embrace that holy power."

Among the heat of a thousand candles, beneath the heavy brocade and ermine of my coronation garments, I am chilled. Will there be no end to her needs, Charles thinks, I think? The currents grow treacherous.

"Of course," I say. "Of course."

✦★✦✦

I cannot separate my thoughts from her. Even when we are not together, I feel her knowing, judging eyes. I wish I could be what she is, what she thinks I am—bold and truthful, full of faith in the power she serves. There are moments I even think it is possible.

The men are caparisoned and we move against Paris. All around me is the heady confidence of the Maid, reflected in the eyes and voices of ten thousand Frenchmen. But I am silent, turned inward. Have I gone too far? The siege of Paris is bitter. I am certain that I am all Charles now, that Aibek the Manipulator is gone, quite gone. We are repulsed several times by the English, with heavy losses.

"No matter," says Joan, her eyes seemingly on the other world. "So it was at Orleans, also. Only believe."

"No matter," say the common people, "only follow the Maid!" Some of the captains are not so sure, but Joan does not care.

"With only you, me, and God," she proclaims, "my king, France is whole."

One night I sit up, long past the time when silence has fallen on all the camp. Even the sentries are nodding, so quiet it is before the walls of Paris. Charles lowers his uncomfortable body down onto his preposterous knees . . . and I pray.

What shall I do? "Believe" is too simple an answer, is it not? "Trust—" how? Show me a sign!

The next day, in the pulsing heart of the battle, Joan falls with the bolt of a crossbow penetrating her thigh. Beneath the brightly polished armor there is, after all, only the body of a young woman, a girl, full of need. The blood flows wetly down her leg as she cries out. Her herald is struck down and killed with an arrow between his eyes, but I can see only Joan as she trembles, shepherdess cheeks quite pale, eyes dark as wells.

There is nothing in the world so red as blood.

In that moment I stand, delicately poised, between two poles I cannot name or understand. I have pledged myself to believe in Joan, in the power of the holy love, but now she is revealed in her frail humanity and I cannot help drawing away. After all, a Manipulator is distance. A Manipulator is caution.

Some silver thing inside me, some strand of exquisite tension, snaps. I have chosen, without ever quite knowing exactly what that choice was.

"The siege has failed," I announce that night. "We will withdraw. Consolidate our gains."

Joan protests bitterly when she hears, but the Maid's wishes suddenly count for little. Wounded, she is put on a litter as we retreat.

★★★

Now, as though some great, universal movement has been triggered, time begins to telescope—to become compressed. I expect momentarily to feel the rush of synesthesia, to be called back. I begin to lose my grip on Charles, or he on me: my mind touches his and then jumps away, like a stone skipping across the muddy Loire.

Joan's magic is broken, somehow, but although her star is falling, tumbling downward as though something has finally worn through the mysterious traces that held it, still it is her hold that is the strongest on me. Court life is a blur, lights and murmuring voices, a hurrying smear of impressions—but she is not. Whenever the river of Charles' consciousness rises up to greet me, it is her face that swims into focus: Joan, improperly supported, failing at the siege of La Charité; Joan, immaculate but somehow stained, the butt of quiet humor at Chinon; Joan, unable to secure my permission, going virtually unaided to Lagny-sur-Marne, to fight the Burgundians at Compiegne.

I see her on the battlefield there, transfixed in a brilliant arrow of sunlight. Her horse rears, stumbles. Joan topples to the ground. Fallen, she is made prisoner.

My grip is relaxing. Terrified, elated, somewhere in between, I try to slow and catch the visions of Joan that drift by like wind-stirred leaves. The entrenched English buy her from Burgundy. They will try her in Rouen, this madwoman, this "Daughter of God," as a witch.

Their inquisitors demand to know why she said this, why she did that. Joan, my Joan, answers them. Sometimes she is angry, sometimes her words are garbled by tears. She seems confused, defeated, all her certainty eroded. They are relentless, and I, Charles, can do nothing but watch as she sits in her cold cell, her sword shattered, her standard furled away in the vaults of Orleans. I am only an observer now, with no power to rescue the Maid. She has only her faith.

"God and my king have not renounced me," she says, although in my secret heart I suspect she is twice wrong. "How can I do less than remain faithful?"

She will burn as a witch, the English say.

★★★

In the Vieux-Marché they have built a great pile of wood around a crude pole. A sign on the stake proclaims Joan a heretic, an idolater, an apostate. The heralds have blown their shining trumpets and a vast ocean of people, thousands upon thousands, have come crowding into Rouen. I hold tightly to the image of Vieux-Marché, making a backwater of calm in the hastening torrent of images. Joan is coming. Her armor is gone and she wears only a shift of simple black cloth. She has tied a kerchief over her close-cropped hair. The cart bumps over uneven ground and she sways. She is weeping.

The priest-examiners of Rouen rail against the witch as she is chained to the stake. My vision begins to mist as the robed men step away. A man, an English soldier, I think, hands up to Joan a rude cross made from two sticks which she places in the bosom of her dress. Another soldier steps forward, his torch a bright point in my dimming sight, and leans down to the pyre. The flames leap up like hungry children.

It is none of it my fault, I know. I do not even think it is real. And if this is all Suvinha's arcane manipulation, her tormenting of me was pointless. She has not succeeded in changing me. Why should I change? If there was a fault in what happened between us, it was not mine. I am not to blame.

So why then, as Joan's pained ecstatic cries become streaks of bright silver before my eyes, do I fear I have made some terrible mistake? Why is my gaze blurred by the bitter scent of tears?

Now I hear nothing but the satisfied murmur of smoke, and my nostrils are full of the clean, sharp smell of trumpets.

Finding My Shadow

by JOE HALDEMAN

We got canyons of smoke and steel-blue horizons
Our castles explode as the city lays dying
History that once was new
Memories that once were true
No, I can't find my shadow in the city
  —from "Here In the City" by Janis Ian

I USED to love this part of the city. Jain and I had looked at a loft overlooking the park toward Charles Street and the river, dreaming of escaping Roxbury. Not much here now.

My partner, Mason, pointed to the left. "Movement." I jammed the joystick left and up, and the tracks clattered over the curb into dirt, the dry baked ruin that used to be Boston Common.

It was a boy, trying to hide behind the base of a fallen equestrian statue.

I touched my throat mike. "Halt! Put your hands over your head." He took off like a squirrel and I gunned it forward. There was no way he could outrun us.

"Taze or tangle?" Mason said.

"Taze." When we got within range, he scoped the kid and fired. A wire darted out and the jolt knocked him flat. I braked with both feet and we lurched forward into our harnesses.

We both stayed inside, looking around. "This stinks," he said, and I nodded. How did the boy get here without being seen, in the glare of the nightlights? Had to be a rabbit hole nearby.

We waited a couple of minutes, watching. Jain and I used to walk through the Common when it was an island of calm in the middle of the Boston din. Flowers everywhere in the spring and summer, leaves in the fall. But I'd liked the winters best, at least when it snowed. The flakes sifting down in the dark, in the muffled quiet.

Never dark now, but always quiet. With occasional gunfire and explosions.

"The shock might have killed him," I said, "if he's in bad enough shape."

"Skin looks like—" Mason started, when there was a "thud" sound and we were suddenly enveloped in flame. "Fire at will," I said unnecessarily. Mason had the gatling on top screaming as it rotated, traversing blindly. It would probably get the kid.

My rear monitor was clear, so I jammed it into full reverse with the left track locked. We spun around twice in two seconds, harness jamming my cheek. No sign of whoever bombed us.

"Swan Pond?" Mason said.

"That's probably what they want us to do. Not that much fire; I can blow it out." Steering with the monitor, I stomped it in reverse. Braked once as we bumped off the curb, and then backed uphill at howling redline. The windshield cleared except for a smear of soot, and I stopped at the top of the hill, by the ruins of the Capitol.

A female voice from the radio: "Unit Seven, what was that all about? Did you engage the enemy?"

"After a fashion, Lillian," I said. "We were down in the Common, near the parking lot entrance. Kid came up, a decoy, and we tazed him."

"What, a child?" They were rare; the survivors were all sterile.

"Yeah, a boy about ten or twelve. While we were waiting for him to wake up, they popped us with a Molotov."

"I'd say flamer," Mason said. He was scanning the area down there with binoculars.

"Maybe a flamer. Couldn't see forward, so we laid down some

covering fire and backed out. Wasn't enough to hurt the track; we're okay now."

"Kid's not there," Mason said. "Somebody retrieved him."

"Got a fire team zeroed on the coordinates where you started backing up," the radio said. "What do you want?"

I want to go home, I thought. "Sure he's gone?" I whispered to Mason.

He handed me the binoculars. "See for yourself." No kid, no blood trail.

"No one there now, at least on the surface," I said to Lillian. "Drill round, H.E., maybe."

"Roger." I could hear her keyboard. A few seconds later, the round came in with a sound like cloth tearing. It made a puff of dust where we'd been standing, and then a gray cloud of high-explosive smoke billowed out of the entrance to the underground lot, a couple of hundred yards away, the same time we heard the muffled explosion.

"On target," I said. Of course they'd be idiots to stick around right under where they'd hit us. That parking lot had tunnels going everywhere.

"Need more?" she asked.

"No, negative."

"Hold on." She paused. "Command wants you to go take a look. Down below, in the lot."

"Why don't *they* come and take a look?" That was really asking for it. They could pop us from any direction and scuttle back down their tunnels.

"So do you want more arty?"

"Yeah, affirmative. Two drill rounds with gas."

Wipers squeaked, cleaning the soot off the front as we rolled slowly down the hill. "What flavor? We got CS, VA, fog, big H, and little H."

I looked at Mason. "Little H?"

He nodded. "Fog, too." I relayed that to Lillian. Little H was happy gas; it induced euphoria and listlessness. Fog was a persistent but breathable particulate suspension. Not that we'd be breathing it, with little H in the air.

(Big H was horror gas. It brought on such profound depression that the enemy usually suicided. But sometimes they wanted to take you with them.)

The two rounds thumped in while we were fitting the gas masks on. Track's airtight and self-contained, but you never know.

I tuned to infrared, and the ruins around us became even grayer. Spun to the left, and then left again, into the lot's down ramp. "Hold on." I gunned it forward and turned on glare lights all around.

"Jesus!" Mason flinched.

"Go IR," I said. To him it must have looked like I was speeding straight into an opaque wall. I slowed a little as we slid inside, sideways.

If you were looking in visible light, you wouldn't see anything but light, from our glare, in the swirling fog. In IR, it was just a thin mist.

A few derelict cars amid debris. The crater from her first round was still smoking. There were dozens of holes punched through the ceiling from previous drill rounds. I switched off the IR for a moment and saw nothing but blinding white. Clicked it back on and looked for movement.

"What do you see, Seven?"

"What am I looking for?" I said. "No obvious bodies where your HE came in. Nobody walking around in hysterics. No flamers."

"Power down, turn off your lights, and listen." I did. Turned up the ears and heard nothing but creaks and pops from our engine cooling.

In infrared there was enough light to see in, just barely. Faint beams shone down through the arty holes, from the nightlights suspended over the city.

Someone laughed.

"We might have one," I whispered. Little H disperses fast, and it can penetrate deep into a tunnel if the air's moving in that direction.

The laugh continued, not crazy, just like responding to a joke. Except that it went on and on. A husky female voice, echoing.

It sounded like Jain's laugh.

"Sounds like she's in a tunnel," Mark said. "Over there." He pointed ahead and to the right.

"Yeah, good, a tunnel." This was probably the actual trap they'd used the boy as bait for.

Or maybe that is Jain, and she's bait. For me. I shook the notion off. How could they know I was in this track?

"Seven, you have backup coming in. Hold your position."

Hold our position against what, a laugh? "Keep an eye out, Mark. I'm gonna armor up." One of us was going to leave the track, for sure.

"Guess we both better." The armor was restricting and hot, but with it you could survive a flaming or a point-blank hit from a .65 machine gun. That would break a bone or two and knock you down, but you'd live.

Not much room in the track; no room for modesty. I had to stay half in the seat while I stripped down. Mark was watching my reflection. I didn't say anything. If I liked men, he'd be near the top of the list. Enjoy the flash.

The bottom half of the armor wasn't bad, heavy plastic mail, but the top was a bitch for women, if they had any breasts at all. Clamshell snaps along the right rib cage. I grunted at the last one.

"Hurts," Mark said.

"Join the army and have a walking mammogram. Go ahead." He stripped down quickly. I glanced, and was obscurely disappointed that he didn't have an erection. What am I, a toad? No, his partner and immediate superior.

While Mark was armoring up, our reinforcements came down the ramp, subtle as a rolling garbage can. An APC, armored personnel carrier. Here this soon, it must have been the one stationed up by the T entrance at Park.

"That you, Petroski?" I said on the combat scramble freak.

"No, it's Snow White and her fuckin' dwarfs," he said. "Mental dwarves. They said you got movement down here?"

"Just someone laughing after the arty came in." I turned on the green spotting laser and cranked it around to where we'd heard the voice. It looked like an open freight elevator door.

I told him about the boy and the flamer; he'd seen the smoke. "You see the green pointer? The elevator there?" It wasn't bright in IR.

"Yeah, but hang for a second. Got some boys and girls still fuckin' with their breathers."

"What?" APCs are open. "You got guys breathin' this stuff? Didn't they tell you—"

"Yeah, Little H. They've got 'em on, just checking the buddy valves. Command said get right down here, no time for the regular drill."

"Hope it's not that serious," I said. "So far we have the Disappearing Boy and the Laughing Woman. Don't think we have to call in the nukes yet."

The laugh again, and a chill down my spine. I clicked away from the scramble freak. "Mark, I could swear I know that voice."

"Anyone I know?"

"No, from before. Here in Boston."

"That's real likely." Only a fraction of one percent had survived the fever bomb. They were all carriers.

This time the laugh ended in something like a sob. "We lived together more than two years, inseparable. People called her my shadow. She was black."

"Lovers."

"Yeah, don't be shocked." Mark was straight as a ruler, but I thought he knew I wasn't, and didn't seem to care.

"Probably just wishful thinking," he said. "Projecting."

"I don't know. You learn someone's—"

"Ready to ride," Petroski said. "This is a kill, right?"

"No," I said hastily. "Play it by ear. We might want a capture."

"What the fuck for?" The quarantine camp in Newton was full to overflowing. And overflow was obviously what it mustn't do.

"Let's just triangulate on the sound. You go over left about a hundred yards and turn off your engine."

"I've gotta get authorization, not to kill."

"No, you don't," I said, improvising. "I'll go in with the non-lethals. You just back me up with a regular squad."

"In the dark with nonlethals?" Mark said. "You are fuckin' nuts."

"I'm not asking you to come along. Hand me that tangler." It was the size of a pistol but, instead of bullets, it fired a tightly-wound ball of sticky monofilament that blossomed out to become a net. I started to take the Glock 11-mm out of its holster.

"Christ, don't leave your gun behind!"

"I've got a squad backing me up."

"So they can kill whoever gets you, afterward," he said roughly. "I don't want to break in a new partner. Take the fuckin' gun."

Well, that was touching. I left the pistol in place and tucked the tangler inside my web belt. "Satisfied?"

"Yeah, but you're still nuts. Those sickos would just as soon kill you as look at you."

"Yeah, and we'd rather kill them than look at them." I opened the door and swung out into the fog.

The fever virus bomb had sprayed Boston Christmas morning. I was visiting my folks in Washington, or I would have joined the million who were dead before New Year's, bulldozed into mass graves. Or become one of the few who survived to be sickos, carriers.

I'd talked to Jain on Christmas and the next day. She'd gotten the cough a few hours after the bomb, and by the next day her lungs were so full she could hardly talk other than to say good-bye. On the third day, all the phones in Boston were dead.

I couldn't have gone to her. Every American city had been locked down Christmas Eve, when they learned what the bomb was, but not where. "A big city in the East." Soldiers and police running everywhere, in Washington. Our family had piled in a car and tried to get out, but every exit was blocked and guarded. Seemed like typical government nonsense at the time. But they must have known how infectious it was, and how fast it would spread.

Boston was dead by dawn of the third day. Of course when I "joined" the military, I was sent here. Supposedly I knew the city, but without the T, the subway, I was lost. And everything underground belonged to the sickos now.

One half of one percent of a million people meant five thousand carriers—survivors, they called themselves—living off the ruins of the city.

I didn't think Jain could have survived, she'd been so near death when we last talked. Then I found out they all had to go through that stage, and I had some hope that she'd lived. Then I saw what happened to the survivors, and I more than half hoped she hadn't.

Her name hadn't been on the casualty list, but about a third of the bodies hadn't been identified. She always was walking out without her purse.

Petroski came up with a short squad of riflemen, all armored like me. Only one, a sniper, actually had a rifle. The three others had Remington shoot-em-ups, fully automatic shotguns. And I would be between them and their target, a comforting thought.

"What's the call, Lieutenant?"

I thought about the geometry of it. "Put the sniper and one other under that truck there." I pointed. "The other two on the wall, maybe twenty yards left and right of the elevator. Hold fire until I give the order."

"Or you get creamed. You trust that armor?"

"So nuke 'em if I get creamed."

"If it's a flamer, Lieutenant," the sniper said, "get down fast. I'll be shooting straight in. Your armor wouldn't do squat against this." He patted his rifle with affection. It was a 60-mm recoilless.

"Thanks. Try to aim a little high till I can get out of the way." I nodded at their sergeant and he said, "Go."

They scurried off, darting from cover to cover as if it were a training exercise. They'd be safer tiptoeing. If the enemy had IR, they would have fired at us already. They could hear them moving, though, and might fire at the sound.

Nothing happened. I started walking straight toward the elevator. I had an IR flashlight; transferred it to my left hand and drew the tangler.

By the time I was twenty feet away, I could see that what sounded like a "tunnel" was a freight elevator with both front and rear doors open. Corridor beyond.

I chinned the command freak. "Lillian, get me a floor plan of this parking lot, and whatever's north on the same level. Am I walking into another big lot?"

She must have had it up already; it flashed onto my data side almost instantly, my own position a blue circle. "It's a service corridor," she said. "Keep walking straight and you'll wind up in the Big Dig. About a thousand places to hide along the way.

"They're not gonna have much fog in there. You want another round to the north? We can probably get the corridor."

"Not yet. Let me see what's what."

"Okay. Your funeral." Actually, there was a note of relief in her voice. She could shell an old target like the underground lot until Judgement Day, but every time they put a round in a new place, they had to follow up with an assessment team and file a damage report. This was still Boston that they were blowing up, and some day we'd have it back. What was left of it.

Moving as quietly as possible, I inched over to one side of the door and flashed the IR around it. Chinned the scramble freak: "It's an open elevator shaft, like eight feet to the door on the other side. No way I'm gonna try to jump it."

"Want a couple grenades?" the sergeant said.

"Not yet. I—" There was a loud crash and I flattened myself against the wall.

"What the fuck's goin' on?" the sergeant said. "We're gonna lay down some—" There was a loud crack and a 60-mm round screamed down the corridor.

"No! Wait for my command!"

Then a scraping sound. Someone had dropped a metal plate across the shaft, and was pushing it.

The voice that had laughed whispered, "That you, Ardis?"

She knew my name and there was no mistaking the Jamaican lilt. "Jain! Get away from the door!"

"I am. I'm on the floor over on the side. You comin' over?"

"Yeah. Of course." On the freak: "Everybody hold fire until I say otherwise!"

"Or if we lose your carrier wave," the sergeant said.

I popped once for affirmative and stepped toward the metal plate. Then I stopped. "How did you know it was me?"

She laughed, from the little H, then forced herself to stop. "We . . . we're not dumb cavemen, Ardis. Someone monitoring the military web recognized your name and told me. I found out you were in charge of Track Seven and what your duty schedule was. It was pretty easy to set up this meeting."

"Easy! What about the kid?"

"He volunteered. We were afraid you might kill an adult. Your partner, Mark, might. He has twenty-three kills, none of them children."

"How did you know it wouldn't be Mark coming after you here?"

"I know you, Ardis. You wouldn't send him. Come across."

The plate was about a foot wide. I had to look at it to place my feet, and tried not to think about how far down the shaft went. She took my hand for the last couple of steps.

"You be lookin' like Papa Legba," she said. The armor was shiny black and formidable.

The fog was thin in the corridor; I could see her well. She was wearing a shabby jumpsuit that covered most of her body. Her face had some of the hard striations that were the aftermath of the disease, but to me they were like a contour map of her familiar beauty.

I stepped toward her, stepping into a dream; gathered her into my hard breast. Everything blurred. "Alive," I said. "Jain."

"God, my darling," she sobbed and laughed. Then she held me at arm's length and stared into my faceplate. "Look, can anybody else hear what I'm saying?"

"Not unless I click them in."

"Fast, then." She took a deep breath. "Look, I'm not infectious. Nobody is."

"What? What about Newton?"

"Just a prison." She stifled a laugh. "Silly damned stuff. Look, we've had normal people live with us, they don't get no plague."

"Then why not just show them?"

"Once when we tried, they just took everyone to Newton. Second time, they killed everyone. Not sure why; what's goin' on.

"We need you; we need someone in the power loop. Come live with us—come live with me!—for a few months, and then get back in touch with your people."

I had a hundred questions. Then I got one myself: "Lieutenant! What the hell's goin' on in there?"

Without answering, I toed the steel plate and pushed it into the elevator shaft.

"Let's go," Jain said.

"Just a second." I took off the helmet, popped the cuirass and stepped out of the armor. "They can home in on the armor." I kicked off the boots and piled it all up in the corner. "Get out of here fast," I whispered.

We slipped along the wall about fifty yards and Jain lifted a piece of plasterboard that hid a hole big enough to wiggle through. "You first." I crawled into a dark room full of boxes, feeling a little merry and playful from the whiff of little H. She followed me and as she pulled the cover back, I heard a gas grenade rattling down the corridor; heard it pop and hiss. "This way." She took my hand.

We went through a silent door into another corridor, dark except for a cluster of three dim flashlights.

"Mission accomplished," Jain said quietly. "Anybody have something for her to wear?"

"Jacket," someone said, and handed it over, rustling. It was damp and smelled of rancid sweat, but at least it was warm. Sized for a large man, it came down to about six inches above my knees. It would look very fetching, if we ever got to somewhere with light.

We moved swiftly through the dark, too swiftly for barefoot

me, afraid of tripping or stepping on something. But it gave me some time to think.

Jain wouldn't lie to me about this, but that didn't mean that what she told me was true. She might unknowingly be passing on a lie, or she might know the truth and be in denial of it. In which case I was already walking dead.

I put that possibility out of my mind, not because it was un-likely, but because there was nothing I could do about it. And I'd rather be uncertain and with Jain than safe in my track.

We stopped at a tall metal door. While everybody else played their lights on the bottom right corner of it, a big bare chested man—my benefactor?—took a long crowbar to it. After several minutes of grunting and prising, the door popped open.

"This is a good defense," Jain said. "It opens and closes easily from the other side, but nobody's going to just walk through it from here. This'll be a long ladder." I followed the others to step backward onto a metal ladder in the darkness.

It wasn't totally dark, though, looking down. There was a square, the floor, slightly less inky. I had an irrational twinge of modesty, my bare butt right above the stranger below me.

"Almost there," Jain said from over her shoulder above me. "Headquarters."

My foot hit carpeted concrete and I waited for Jain while the others went ahead. "So what's at headquarters?"

"Mostly supplies. Some low-tech communications gear. Every-thing's nine-volt solar power."

It was a large warehouse room with dim lights here and there. Crates of food and water. A child's crib was a grab bag of miscella-neous cans and boxes; Jain rummaged through it and got a Snickers bar. "Hungry?"

"No, more like naked. You got clothes down here?" She walked me down a few yards and there were clothes of all kinds roughly folded and sorted by size. I stepped into some black pants and found a black jersey, a fit combination for my new job as revolu-tionary turncoat, except for the Bergdorf labels. A fancy outfit to be buried in.

A tall, skinny man walked up and offered his hand. "You're Lieutenant Drexel?"

"I don't think I'm Lieutenant anyone anymore. Ardis." He was hard to look at. Besides the skin striations from the virus, a face wound had torn a hole in his cheek, exposing his back teeth.

He nodded. "I'm Wally, more or less in charge of this area. "Has Jain filled you in?"

"Not much. You aren't actually carriers?"

"No. We may have been, right after we recovered. People who came in to help us died. We think it was leftover virus from the attack. But what we think doesn't make any difference.

"It left us weak. Old people who survived the attack all died in the first year; now people in their fifties and sixties are going the same way. Infections, pneumonia, bronchitis."

"Our immune systems are shot," Jain said. "If we don't get medical help, we'll all be dead in a few years."

"We don't really understand what's going on," Wally said. "They've got hundreds of us out at the Newton Center; we've seen them. You'd think by now they'd know that none of us are carrying the disease."

"Maybe they wouldn't know, if they're really strict about quarantine," I said.

"Not all of them are," Jain said. "The guards wear surgical masks, but we've seen some take them off to smoke, even when there were 'carriers' around."

"Could just be carelessness," Wally said. "We're trying to avoid a conspiracy mind-set here."

I nodded. "Hard to see how it's to anybody's advantage to maintain the status quo. All of Boston shut down needlessly? Who profits?"

"Who set off the bomb?" Jain asked.

"Well, we assume—"

"But we don't know, right? Has anybody claimed responsibility?"

"No. Presumably they don't want to be nuked to glowing rubble."

"What if it wasn't 'them'? What if it was us?"

"Jain," Wally said.

"Well, the bomb didn't go off in the business district or Back Bay. It went off in Roxbury, and if it hadn't been for the wind reversing, you wouldn't have had one percent white casualties. You don't like what that implies, Wally, and neither do I, but a fact is a fact."

"I didn't know that," I said.

"Well, they did find what might have been the bomb casing," Wally said, "in the back of a blown-up truck down in Roxbury. Texas license plates. But there was a lot of that kind of damage in the riots, before everybody was too weak to riot."

"I can take you down to see it. Pretty safe. Army doesn't do much down there."

"Nightlights?"

"Go during the day. We only go out at night to attract attention."

★★★

We did go out to see it the next day, and I could have made a case for or against Jain's suspicions. The Texas truck did have a tank in the back that had exploded, but the part that remained attached was identified as LP gas, which it seemed to have been using for fuel. Of course that might have been camouflage for a tank full of the mystery virus; the engine was set up to switch between LP and gasoline.

The driver had died in the explosion. Jain's theory for that wasn't simple suicide, but rather that he had driven around the black neighborhoods for hours, maybe a whole day, releasing the stuff slowly, making sure it would get to its target. He himself would have been one of the first infected. He survived through the initial symptoms, and when he was sure it was working, destroyed the evidence, killing himself.

You would think a nutcase like that would want people to know who had done it, get his name in the history books, but they don't always. The Oklahoma City bombing when I was a kid, and the St. Louis Arch.

Anyhow, my job wasn't to explain anything, but just to demonstrate. For that, I only had to stay alive.

After the first symptomless day, I was pretty sure. They wanted me to stay with them for a couple of weeks, to prove their point beyond a shadow of a doubt, which was no problem. I moved in with Jain, and we sort of picked up where we'd left off. She looked a little different, but it wasn't her looks that had attracted me to her.

And instead of the walk-up in Roxbury, we were living in a $3 million suite overlooking the Charles. We could even have taken the 12th-floor penthouse, but under the circumstances that wouldn't be practical. Without elevators, it was still a walk-up, and we had to carry all our water up from the river.

It was not a typical lovers' reunion. So much of the catching up was about the horrors she had survived and my own less dramatic horror of watching martial law and paranoaic isolationism erode the American way of life.

Or maybe this nightmare was the real America, stripped of cosmetic civilization. What my mother had called the Reaganbush jungle, the moneyed few in control, protecting their fortunes at any social cost. That was Jain's party line, too.

But the people who owned this huge suite would probably like to have it back. The Brahmins who owned Boston would definitely like it back.

And every day I remained uninfected made the situation more mysterious. Who was profiting from this big lie?

We would find out. In a way.

The mechanics of the exposé had to be a little roundabout. We couldn't just go on television and do a tell-all show. There were plenty of stations in Boston, but nobody knew the equipment well enough to jury-rig it to work with our low-voltage sun power, or even knew whether it was possible.

It was easy enough to make a disk, though, a home video of uninfected me surrounded by survivors, telling my story and theirs.

Then we made about a hundred copies of the disk and had them tossed over the fence all around the border of the infected area. Even if no civilians found them, guards would, and it would be easy for them to verify from military records that I was who I said I was.

Four people died in the process of trying to distribute the disks. Well, they were weapons of a sort. Against the status quo.

A couple of days after that, Jain and I were sitting at home reading, when I heard the whining sound of a track decelerating outside. I looked through the dirty window and it was Track Number 7, my old one.

"Let's get out of here," Jain said. There was an escape route through a duct in the basement.

"You go," I said. "I think they want to talk."

"Yeah, they wanna talk." She grabbed my arm. "Go!"

I shook her off. "They know I'm here. If they wanted to hurt me, they could have dropped one artillery round in our lap."

"You trust them?"

"They're just people, Jain." The doors of the track opened and three armored soldiers came out.

"People, shit." I heard her bare feet slapping down the stairs and fought the urge to follow her.

The three came up the outdoor steps and I opened the door for them. They filed inside without a word.

One had captain's bars. When they were all in the living room he said, "This is her?"

"Yeah. That's her."

"Mark," I said. He turned around and left.

The captain grabbed one arm and then the other, and pinioned me. "Let's do it."

The other had red crosses on each shoulder. He or she pulled a syringe out of a web-belt pocket.

There was a huge explosion and the medic went down, hard. The captain let go of me and spun around. Jain was standing at the top of the basement steps with an 11-mm Glock. She and the captain fired at the same time. He hit her in the center of the chest.

Her blood spattered the wall behind her and she was dead before she started to fall.

Her bullet staggered him, but the armor worked, and he recovered before I had time to do more than scream. He punched me in the side of the head, and I collapsed.

He hauled me roughly to my feet. "Medic. Get the fuck up."

He moaned. "Jesus, man." He got up on one elbow. "Think she broke my sternum."

"I'll break more'n that. Do your job."

He got up slowly, painfully. Found the syringe on the floor.

"What's that?" Though I knew. He gave me an injection in the shoulder and threw the needle away.

The captain shoved me toward the door. "Let's go make another video."

★★★

I was in the Newton cell for about eight hours when I started to cough. By then I'd written most of this. Though I don't suppose anyone will ever see it. It will be burned with my clothes, with my body.

I'll never know whether Jain was completely right. She had at least part of the story.

My face is stiffening. The ridges don't show in the cell's dirty metal mirror, but I can feel them under the skin.

It's hard to make my jaw work to close my mouth. Before long it will stay a little bit open, then more, until it's wide as it can go. I know that from the pictures of the corpses. I wonder whether you die before the jaw breaks.

I'm isolated from everybody, but from the small window of my cell I can see the exercise yard, and I can see that Wally was right. There aren't any old people left among the survivors. Nobody over their mid-forties. Next year it might be mid-thirties. In a few years, Newton, like Boston, will be empty.

They can have their city back. Turn off the nightlights, repair the artillery damage. Scrub the dried blood off the walls, pick up the bones and throw them away.

Whenever I move, I can hear the little motors of the camera as it tracks me from the darkness of the corridor. Sometimes I see a glint of light from its lens.

I don't think there was any conspiracy. Just a status quo that perpetuated itself. Us versus them in a waiting game. With insignificant me poised for a few days in the middle: an us who was a them; a them who was an us.

Who lost and found and lost her shadow.

Ride Me Like A Wave

by JANE YOLEN

Hide me in your hollows
Taste the salt that clings to me
shipwrecked your shallows
scented by the sea
Hide me in the wisdom of your thighs
Ride me like a wave . . .
—from "Ride Me Like A Wave" by Janis Ian

THERE is no profit in fishing, less in building boats. Tam knew that. But still he loved the shape of the wood under his hand, rising into a prow, a stern, a long keel. No one could afford the boats he built, no one could pay him what they were worth. So he gave them away to the fishermen of his village, for they made even less than he.

Each boat had an Eye painted on the prow, a red and blue and wide-open Eye, to prosper the catch. Then each boat was blessed by the priest, who gave away his blessings as well.

What they were all after—Tam, the priest, the fisherfolk—was food for the hungry of the village. And as they themselves were the hungry, it was an exchange that was, if not profit, at least something to keep their bellies from crying out, even in the winter after months of dried cod.

Tam did not begrudge the fishermen his boats. Indeed, he often went down to the shore to watch the fleet come in, knowing that every boat riding the whitecaps home was known to his hand.

There was pride in that knowing.

And a full creel of fish for him when they were docked and dry, left by the grateful sailors.

When the spring storms raged, and some of the boats came back bit by bit, board by board, Tam gathered the pieces on the shore below his cottage and shaped coffins for the sailors whose bodies were found, and for the handful of dirt and seafoam for those who were not.

To be honest, Tam was a lonely man, but he did not know it. His love was for the wood and the wave, the one to shape, the one to watch. Strangely, for a man who had always lived by the seaside, he did not go out on the water himself. He feared the cold, green deep. It was enough that the salt clung to him, that he was well scented by its smell.

Can lives that are merely constant be happy?

If you asked Tam how he felt, he would have counted these out: Wood, wind, waves. Not happy, perhaps, but content.

✹✶✹

Now one day, a day of great wind and water the color of flotsam, a day of foam as filthy as the guts of fish, something other than driftwood came to the shore below Tam's cottage.

He found the thing in the dawn, lying on his part of the beach.

Thing. Not human, not fish.

Thing. Not beautiful, not ugly.

Thing. A mer creature.

The hair on its head was a yellow-green, encrusted with broken shells and sea drift. Its breasts stuck up like two small teacups, the nipples inverted. There was a ridge of hard skin, like a scab, running between the breasts and down to a bifurcated gray-green tail. A darker green were the little cuticle-shaped scales that covered the tail. The creature's arms and its chest were scaled, too, but those scales were like feathers, so light-colored they all but disappeared into the green-gold skin.

Tam did not know what to do with it, the dead thing from the sea. He didn't want to touch it, half fish, half human, all horrible.

It smelled, too, a heavy musk, like something pulled up from the great deep. All he could do was stand over it and stare.

Then the mer gave a frothy cough and water and blood spilled out of the gill slits along the neck, slits Tam hadn't even noticed before. The creature's right hand, webbed with a lining like silk, reached up to its mouth. It coughed again and opened its eyes.

They were not a human's eyes, but more fishlike, dark, unfathomable. A shark's eyes. Turning its head, the mer stared at Tam with those black, mirrorless eyes.

He wondered what it saw.

Then drops of water began to fall from the mer's eyes, crawling down its cheeks, mixing with the seawater that puddled in its hair.

Suddenly Tam did not care that it was inhuman, alien, ghastly. She—for the creature was surely a she—was in distress. He took off his shirt, knelt beside her, wrapped her in it, and carried her to his home. There he placed her gently on a pallet by the hearth.

She refused fresh water cold or boiled into tea. She would not eat cress, salted or plain. The fish stew he'd made the night before caused her to moan and look away. She'd already torn off the shirt, once more exposing her tiny breasts with the odd inverted nipples. In the firelight the breasts seemed to shift color, from green to gray to gold.

He picked up the shirt and put it back on himself, buttoning it slowly, aware that it smelled of her, and was wet clear through. Then he squatted by her side and stared.

The problem was, Tam was a doer, and he did not know what to do. They might have stayed that way for hours, days, but she suddenly opened her mouth and began to sing. At least it sounded like a song, though wordless, and without the kind of melody he was used to. Not a reel, not a ballad, not quite a lament.

The song caught him, pulled him to his knees, then propelled him toward her. He could not have stopped then had he wanted to.

And he did not want to.

He lay down by her side, careful not to touch her, as the song went on.

She reached out and rested her strange webbed fingers on his face. The touch was not so much hesitant as searching. She seemed as repelled and as drawn as he.

Suddenly, she pulled at his shirt, so hard the horn buttons broke apart. The wet linen ripped.

"Hey!" he cried, but it did not frighten her.

Then she grabbed at his trousers, her touch oddly frantic, as if she had only now understood the clothes were not his skin. Her fingers raced across his waist, his thighs.

He pushed the trousers down to his ankles, taking no time to get out of his boots.

She made a funny, gasping sound, then cupped him between her hands, her touch both gentle and electric. He shuddered as if chilled, as if in cold water, as if shocked by an eel, then closed his eyes.

When he opened them again, she had spread herself, the tail forked as if two limbs, and then she reeled him in.

Not having done any such thing but once before, with a whore from the town, who had lain under him like a beached whale, he let himself come into her, riding her like a wave. It was a rising and a falling, a swelling and a cresting. When he put his mouth on hers, her lips were soft and slippery. Then he put his head in her hair and smelled the seaweed there.

He was, at last, more than content.

***

When Tam woke, the mer was gone, a trail of jingle shells out the door where she must have struggled alone. Pulling his pants up, he rose from the pallet, grabbed his Sunday shirt from the cupboard. He could see in the dirt floor where her tail had left a serpentine path and he followed it all the way down to the sea.

He wondered suddenly why she had come. A gift from some sea god for all the boats he had made? For all the sailors he had helped? For the ones he had buried?

Or was she instead a sea god's curse? He touched himself, fearing he would find himself diseased, changed. There was no electricity in his touch, and no comfort either.

Wading into the sea, up to his knees, he strained to see out across the now placid water for some sign of her.

"Come back. Come back," he called.

But no one—no thing—answered his cry.

★

Every few weeks there were gifts of fish left at his door. Not the kind of fish that the sailors gave him after a good catch—cod and ling and halibut. These were large-eyed, deep sea, hideous creatures he was afraid to eat. He used them to fertilize his vegetable garden.

After a while the gifts stopped.

★

The years passed. If he remembered the mer and the night he rode her like a wave, he thought it but a dream. Or a nightmare. Or a bit of both. He never spoke of it to anyone, except once in his cups after a long night gathering the bits of broken boats from the sea.

The sailors thought he was yarning, telling a tall tale, and they dragged him back to his house where, with grateful thanks, they put him to bed.

He never spoke of it again.

Nor did they.

★

One day, when Tam was very old, and the pain in his chest too strong to be ignored, he did what many of the sailors of that village did when they could no longer put out to sea. He got into his best clothes, left a note on the table, held down with his carving knife, and walked into the sea.

The sea wrapped him in its cold arms.

At first he trembled, like a boy with his first lover. Then he smiled for the cold had pushed away the pain. So, taking in a last gulp of air, he walked even farther in.

The sea took away his breath and cradled him in green. Memories rushed in like a wave.

In the last moments, he saw the mer again, holding her hand out to him, drawing him in.

He went to her gladly, letting her touch him again, letting her kiss him with her slippery mouth until he died, content, surrounded by the green world and his dozens of mourning children.

In Fading Suns and Dying Moons

By John Varley

Within the memories of our lives gone by,
afraid to die, we learn to lie
and measure out the time in coffee spoons
In fading suns, and dying moons
  —from "Aftertones" by Janis Ian

THE first time they came through the neighborhood there really wasn't much neighborhood to speak of. Widely dispersed hydrogen molecules, only two or three per cubic meter. Traces of heavier elements from long-ago supernovas. The usual assortment of dust particles, at a density of one particle every cubic mile or so. The "dust" was mostly ammonia, methane, and water ice, with some more complex molecules like benzene. Here and there these thin ingredients were pushed into eddies by light pressure from neighboring stars.

Somehow they set forces in motion. I picture it as a Cosmic Finger stirring the mix, out in the interstellar wastes where space is really flat, in the Einsteinian sense, making a whirlpool in the unimaginable cold. Then they went away.

Four billion years later they returned. Things were brewing nicely. The space debris had congealed into a big, burning central mass and a series of rocky or gaseous globes, all sterile, in orbit around it.

They made a few adjustments and planted their seeds, and saw that it was good. They left a small observer/recorder behind, along with a thing that would call them when everything was ripe. Then they went away again.

★★★

A billion years later the timer went off, and they came back.

★★★

I had a position at the American Museum of Natural History in New York City, but of course I had not gone to work that day. I was sitting at home watching the news, as frightened as anyone else. Martial law had been declared a few hours earlier. Things had been getting chaotic. I'd heard gunfire from the streets outside.

Someone pounded on my door.

"United States Army!" someone shouted. "Open the door immediately!"

I went to the door, which had four locks on it.

"How do I know you're not a looter?" I shouted.

"Sir, I am authorized to break your door down. Open the door, or stand clear."

I put my eye to the old-fashioned peephole. They were certainly dressed like soldiers. One of them raised his rifle and slammed the butt down on my doorknob. I shouted that I would let them in, and in a few seconds I had all the locks open. Six men in full combat gear hustled into my kitchen. They split up and quickly explored all three rooms of the apartment, shouting out, "All clear!" in brisk, military voices. One man, a bit older than the rest, stood facing me with a clipboard in his hand.

"Sir, are you Doctor Andrew Richard Lewis?"

"There's been some mistake," I said. "I'm not a medical doctor."

"Sir, are you Doctor—"

"Yes, yes, I'm Andy Lewis. What can I do for you?"

"Sir, I am Captain Edgar and I am ordered to induct you into the United States Army Special Invasion Corps effective immediately, at the rank of Second Lieutenant. Please raise your right hand and repeat after me."

I knew from the news that this was now legal, and I had the choice of enlisting or facing a long prison term. I raised my hand and in no time at all I was a soldier.

"Lieutenant, your orders are to come with me. You have fifteen minutes to pack what essentials you may need, such as prescription medicine and personal items. My men will help you assemble your gear."

I nodded, not trusting myself to speak.

"You may bring any items relating to your specialty. Laptop computer, reference books . . ." He paused, apparently unable to imagine what a man like me would want to bring along to do battle with space aliens.

"Captain, do you know what my specialty is?"

"My understanding is that you are a bug specialist."

"An entomologist, Captain. Not an exterminator. Could you give me . . . any clue as to why I'm needed?"

For the first time he looked less than totally self-assured.

"Lieutenant, all I know is . . . they're collecting butterflies."

✦★★✦

They hustled me to a helicopter. We flew low over Manhattan. Every street was gridlocked. All the bridges were completely jammed with mostly abandoned cars.

I was taken to an air base in New Jersey and hurried onto a military jet transport that stood idling on the runway. There were a few others already on board. I knew most of them; entomology is not a crowded field.

The plane took off at once.

✦★★✦

There was a colonel aboard whose job was to brief us on our mission, and on what was thus far known about the aliens: not much was really known that I hadn't already seen on television.

They had appeared simultaneously on seacoasts worldwide. One moment there was nothing, the next moment there was a line of aliens as far as the eye could see. In the western hemisphere the line stretched from Point Barrow in Alaska to Tierra del Fuego in Chile. Africa was lined from Tunis to the Cape of Good Hope. So were the western shores of Europe, from Norway to Gibraltar. Australia, Japan, Sri Lanka, the Philippines, and every other island thus far contacted reported the same thing: a solid line of aliens appearing in the west, moving east.

Aliens? No one knew what else to call them. They were clearly not of Planet Earth, though if you ran into a single one, there would be little reason to think them very odd. Just millions and millions of perfectly ordinary people dressed in white coveralls, blue baseball caps, and brown boots, within arm's reach of each other.

Walking slowly toward the east.

Within a few hours of their appearance someone on the news had started calling it the Line, and the creatures who were in it Linemen. From the pictures on the television they appeared rather average and androgynous.

"They're not human," the colonel said. "Those coveralls, it looks like they don't come off. The hats, either. You get close enough, you can see it's all part of their skin."

"Protective coloration," said Watkins, a colleague of mine from the Museum. "Many insects adapt colors or shapes to blend with their environment."

"But what's the point of blending in," I asked, "If you are made so conspicuous by your actions?"

"Perhaps the 'fitting in' is simply to look more like us. It seems unlikely, doesn't it, that evolution would have made them look like . . ."

"Janitors," somebody piped up.

The colonel was frowning at us.

"You think they're insects?"

"Not by any definition I've ever heard," Watkins said. "Of course, other animals adapt to their surroundings, too. Arctic foxes in winter coats, tigers with their stripes. Chameleons."

The colonel mulled this for a moment, then resumed his pacing.

"Whatever they are, bullets don't bother them. There have been many instances of civilians shooting at the aliens."

Soldiers, too, I thought. I'd seen film of it on television, a National Guard unit in Oregon cutting loose with their rifles. The aliens hadn't reacted at all, not visibly . . . until all the troops and all their weapons just vanished, without the least bit of fuss.

And the Line moved on.

★★★

We landed at a disused-looking airstrip somewhere in northern California. We were taken to a big motel, which the Army had taken over. In no time I was hustled aboard a large Coast Guard helicopter with a group of soldiers—a squad? a platoon?—led by a young lieutenant who looked even more terrified than I felt. On the way to the Line I learned that his name was Evans, and that he was in the National Guard.

It had been made clear to me that I was in charge of the overall mission and Evans was in charge of the soldiers. Evans said his orders were to protect me. How he was to protect me from aliens who were immune to his weapons hadn't been spelled out.

My own orders were equally vague. I was to land close behind the Line, catch up, and find out everything I could.

"They speak better English than I do," the colonel had said. "We must know their intentions. Above all, you must find out why they're collecting . . ." and here his composure almost broke down, but he took a deep breath and steadied himself.

"Collecting butterflies," he finished.

★★★

We passed over the Line at a few hundred feet. Directly below us individual aliens could be made out, blue hats and white shoulders. But off to the north and south it quickly blurred into a solid white line vanishing in the distance, as if one of those devices that make chalk lines on football fields had gone mad.

Evans and I watched it. None of the Linemen looked up at the noise. They were walking slowly, all of them, never getting more than a few feet apart. The terrain was grassy, rolling hills, dotted here and there with clumps of trees. No man-made structures were in sight.

The pilot put us down a hundred yards behind the Line.

"I want you to keep your men at least fifty yards away from me," I told Evans. "Are those guns loaded? Do they have those safety things on them? Good. Please keep them on. I'm almost as afraid of being shot by one of those guys as I am of . . . whatever they are."

And I started off, alone, toward the Line.

★★★

How does one address a line of marching alien creatures? *Take me to your leader* seemed a bit peremptory. *Hey, bro, what's happening . . .* perhaps overly familiar. In the end, after following for fifteen minutes at a distance of about ten yards, I had settled on *Excuse me,* so I moved closer and cleared my throat. Turns out that was enough. One of the Linemen stopped walking and turned to me.

This close, one could see that his features were rudimentary. His head was like a mannequin, or a wig stand: a nose, hollows for eyes, bulges for cheeks. All the rest seemed to be painted on.

I could only stand there idiotically for a moment. I noticed a peculiar thing. There was no gap in the Line.

I suddenly remembered why it was me and not some diplomat standing there.

"Why are you collecting butterflies?" I asked.

"Why not?" he said, and I figured it was going to be a long, long day. "*You* should have no trouble understanding," he said.

"Butterflies are the most beautiful things on your planet, aren't they?"

"I've always thought so." Wondering, *did he know I was a lepidopterist?*

"Then there you are." Now he began to move. The Line was about twenty yards away, and through our whole conversation he never let it get more distant than that. We walked at a leisurely one mile per hour.

Okay, I told myself. Try to keep it to butterflies. Leave it to the military types to get to the tough questions: *When do you start kidnapping our children, raping our women, and frying us for lunch?*

"What are you doing with them?"

"Harvesting them." He extended a hand toward the Line, and as if summoned, a lovely specimen of *Adelpha bredowii* fluttered toward him. He did something with his fingers and a pale blue sphere formed around the butterfly.

"Isn't it lovely?" he asked, and I moved in for a closer look. He seemed to treasure these wonderful creatures I'd spent my life studying.

He made another gesture, and the blue ball with the *Adelpha* disappeared. "What happens to them?" I asked him.

"There is a collector," he said.

"A lepidopterist?"

"No, it's a storage device. You can't see it because it is . . . off to one side."

Off to one side of what? I wondered, but didn't ask.

"And what happens to them in the collector?"

"They are put in storage in a place where . . . time does not move. Where time does not pass. Where they do not move through time as they do here." He paused for a few seconds. "It is difficult to explain."

"Off to one side?" I suggested.

"Exactly. Excellent. Off to one side of time. You've got it."

I had nothing, actually. But I plowed on.

"What will become of them?"

"We are building a . . . place. Our leader wishes it to be a very special place. Therefore, we are making it of these beautiful creatures."

"Of butterfly wings?"

"They will not be harmed. We know ways of making . . . walls in a manner that will allow them to fly freely."

I wished someone had given me a list of questions.

"How did you get here? How long will you stay?"

"A certain . . . length of time, not a great length by your standards."

"What about your standards?"

"By our standards . . . no time at all. As to how we got here . . . have you read a book entitled *Flatland*?"

"I'm afraid not."

"Pity," he said, and turned away, and vanished.

★★★

Our operation in Northern California was not the only group trying desperately to find out more about the Linemen, of course. There were Lines on every continent, and soon they would be present in every nation. They had covered many small Pacific islands in only a day, and when they reached the Eastern shores, they simply vanished, as my guide had.

News media were doing their best to pool information. I believe I got a lot of those facts before the general population, since I had been shanghaied into the forefront, but our information was often as garbled and inaccurate as what the rest of the world was getting. The military was scrambling around in the dark, just like everyone else.

But we learned some things:

They were collecting moths as well as butterflies, from the drabbest specimen to the most gloriously colored. The entire order Lepidoptera.

They could appear and vanish at will. It was impossible to get a count of them. Wherever one stopped to commune with the natives, as mine had, the Line remained solid, with no gaps. When they were through talking to you, they simply went where the Cheshire Cat went, leaving behind not even a grin.

Wherever they appeared, they spoke the local language, fluently and idiomatically. This was true even in isolated villages in China or Turkey or Nigeria, where some dialects were used by only a few hundred people.

They didn't seem to weigh anything at all. Moving through forests, the Line became more of a wall, Linemen appearing in literally every tree, on every limb, walking on branches obviously too thin to bear their weight and not even causing them to bend. When the tree had been combed for butterflies, the crews vanished, and appeared in another tree.

Walls meant nothing to them. In cities and towns nothing was missed, not even closed bank vaults, attic spaces, closets. They didn't come through the door, they simply appeared in a room and searched it. If you were on the toilet, that was just too bad.

Any time they were asked about where they came from, they mentioned that book, *Flatland*. Within hours the book was available on hundreds of Web sites. Downloads ran to the millions.

★★★

The full title of the book was *Flatland: A Romance of Many Dimensions*. It was supposedly written by one Mr. A Square, a resident of Flatland, but its actual author was Edwin Abbott, a nineteenth century cleric and amateur mathematician. A copy was waiting for me when we got back to camp after that first frustrating day.

The book is an allegory and a satire, but also an ingenious way to explain the concept of multidimensional worlds to the layman, like me. Mr. Square lives in a world of only two dimensions. For him, there is no such thing as up or down, only forward, backward, and side to side. It is impossible for us to really *see* from Square's point of view: A single line that extends all around him, with nothing above it or below it. *Nothing*. Not empty space, not a black or white void . . . nothing.

But humans, being three-dimensional, can stand outside Flatland, look up or down at it, see its inhabitants from an angle they can never have. In fact, we could see *inside* them, examine their internal organs, reach down and touch a Flatlander's heart or brain with our fingers.

In the course of the book Mr. Square is visited by a being from the third dimension, a Sphere. He can move from one place to another without apparently traversing the space between point A and point B. There was also discussion of the possibilities of even higher dimensions, worlds as inscrutable to us as the 3-D world was to Mr. Square.

I'm no mathematician, but it didn't take an Einstein to infer that the Line, and the Linemen, came from one of those theoretical higher planes.

The people running the show were not Einstein either, but when they needed expertise they knew where to go to draft it.

★ ★

Our mathematician's name was Larry Ward. He looked as baffled as I must have looked the day before and he got no more time to adjust to his new situation than I did. We were all hustled aboard another helicopter and hurried out to the Line. I filled him in, as best I could, on the way out.

Again, as soon as we approached the Line, a spokesman appeared. He asked us if we'd read the book, though I suspect he already knew we had. It was a creepy feeling to realize he, or something like him, could have been standing . . . or existing, in some direction I couldn't imagine, only inches away from me in my motel bedroom, looking at me read the book just as the Sphere looked down on Mr. A. Square.

A flat, white plane appeared in the air between us and geometrical shapes and equations began drawing themselves on it. It just hung there, unsupported. Larry wasn't too flustered by it, nor was I. Against the background of the Line an antigravity blackboard seemed almost mundane.

The Lineman began talking to Larry, and I caught maybe one

word in three. Larry seemed to have little trouble with it at first, but after an hour he was sweating, frowning, clearly getting out of his depth.

By that time I was feeling quite superfluous, and it was even worse for Lieutenant Evans and his men. We were reduced to following Larry and the Line at its glacial but relentless pace. Some of the men took to slipping between the gaps in the Line to get in front, then doing all sorts of stupid antics to get a reaction, like tourists trying to rattle the guards at the Tower of London. The Linemen took absolutely no notice. Evans didn't seem to care. I suspected he was badly hung over.

"Look at this, Doctor Lewis."

I turned around and saw that a Lineman had appeared behind me, in that disconcerting way they had. He had a pale blue sphere cupped in his hands, and in it was a lovely specimen of *Papilio zelicaon*, the Anise Swallowtail, with one blue wing and one orange wing.

"A gynandromorph," I said, immediately, with the spooky feeling that I was back in the lecture hall. "An anomaly that sometimes arises during gametogenesis. One side is male and the other is female."

"How extraordinary. Our . . . leader will be happy to have this creature existing in his . . . palace."

I had no idea how far to believe him. I had been told that at least a dozen motives had been put forward by Line spokesmen, to various exploratory groups, as the rationale for the butterfly harvest. A group in Mexico had been told some substance was to be extracted—harmlessly, so they said—from the specimens. In France, a lepidopterist swore a Lineman told her the captives were to be given to fourth-dimension children, as pets. It didn't seem all the stories could be true. Or maybe they could. Step One in dealing with the Linemen was to bear in mind that *our* minds could not contain many concepts that, to them, were as basic as *up* and *down* to us. We had to assume they were speaking baby talk to us.

But for an hour we talked butterflies, as Larry got more and more bogged down in a sea of equations and the troops got progressively more bored. The creature knew the names of every Lepidopteran we encountered that afternoon, something I could not claim. That fact had never made me feel inadequate before. There were around 170,000 species of moth and butterfly so far cataloged, including several thousand in dispute. Nobody could be expected to know them all . . . but I was sure the Linemen did. Remember, every book in every library was available to them, and they did not have to open them to read them. And time, which I had been told was the fourth dimension but now learned was only *a* fourth dimension, almost surely did not pass for them in the same way as it passed for us. Larry told me later that a billion years was not a formidable . . . distance for them. They were masters of space, masters of time, and who knew what else?

★★★

The only emotion any of them had ever expressed was delight at the beauty of the butterflies. They showed no anger or annoyance when shot at with rifles; the bullets went through them harmlessly. Even when assaulted with bombs or artillery rounds they didn't register any emotion, they simply made the assailants and weapons disappear. It was surmised by those in charge, whoever they were, that these big, noisy displays were dealt with only because they harmed butterflies.

The troops had been warned, but there's always some clown . . .

So when an *Antheraea polyphemus* fluttered into the air in front of a private named Paulson, he reached out and grabbed it in his fist. Or tried to; while his hand was still an inch away, he vanished.

I don't think any of us quite credited our senses at first. I didn't, and I'd been looking right at him, wondering if I should say something. There was nothing but the Polyphemus moth fluttering in the sunshine. But soon enough there were angry shouts. Many of the soldiers unslung their rifles and pointed them at the Line.

Evans was frantically shouting at them, but now they were angry and frustrated. Several rounds were fired. Larry and I hit the deck as a machine gun started chattering. Looking up carefully, I saw Evans punch the machine gunner and grab the weapon. The firing stopped.

There was a moment of stunned silence. I got to my knees and looked at the Line. Larry was okay, but the "blackboard" was gone. And the Line moved placidly on.

I thought it was all over, and then the screaming began, close behind me. I nearly wet myself and turned around quickly.

Paulson was behind me, on his knees, hands pressed to his face, screaming his lungs out. But he was changed. His hair was all white and he'd grown a white beard. He looked thirty years older, maybe forty. I knelt beside him, unsure what to do. His eyes were full of madness . . . and the name patch sewn on the front of his shirt now read:

ИОꙄ⅃UⱯꟼ

"They reversed him," Larry said.

He couldn't stop pacing. Myself, I'd settled into a fatalistic calm. In the face of what the Linemen could do, it seemed pointless to worry much. If I did something to piss them off, *then* I'd worry.

Our Northern California headquarters had completely filled the big Holiday Inn. The Army had taken over the whole thing, this bizarre operation gradually getting the encrustation of barnacles any government operation soon acquires, literally hundreds of people bustling about as if they had something important to do. For the life of me, I couldn't see how any of us were needed, except for Larry and a helicopter pilot to get him to the Line and back. It seemed obvious that any answers we got would come from him, or someone like him. They certainly wouldn't come from the troops, the tanks, the nuclear missiles I'm sure were targeted on the Line, and certainly not from me. But they kept me on, probably because they hadn't yet evolved a procedure to send anybody home. I didn't mind. I could be terrified here just as well as in New York. In the meantime, I was bunking with Larry . . . who now reached into his pocket and produced a penny. He looked at it, and tossed it to me.

"I grabbed that when they were going through his pockets," he said. I looked at it. As I expected, Lincoln was looking to the left and all the inscriptions were reversed.

"How can they do that?" I asked.

He looked confused for a moment, then grabbed a sheet of motel stationery and attacked it with one of the pens in his pocket. I looked over his shoulder as he made a sketch of a man, writing L by one hand and R by the other. Then he folded the sheet without creasing it, touching the stick figure to the opposite surface.

"Flatland doesn't have to be flat," he said. He traced the stick man onto the new surface, and I saw it was now reversed. "Flat-landers can move through the third dimension without knowing they're doing it. They slide around this curve in their universe. Or, a third-dimensional being can lift them up *here*, and set them down *here*. They've moved, without traveling the distance between the two points."

We both studied the drawing solemnly for a moment.

"How is Paulson?" I asked.

"Catatonic. Reversed. He's left-handed now, his appendectomy scar is on the left, the tattoo on his left shoulder is on the right now."

"He looked older."

"Who can say? Some are saying he was scared gray. I'm pretty sure he saw things the human eye just isn't meant to see . . . but I think he's actually older, too. The doctors are still looking him over. It wouldn't be hard for a fourth-dimensional creature to do, age him many years in seconds."

"But why?"

"They didn't hire me to find out 'why.' I'm having enough trouble understanding the 'how.' I figure the why is your depart-ment." He looked at me, but I didn't have anything helpful to offer. But I had a question.

"How is it they're shaped like men?"

"Coincidence?" he said, and shook his head. "I don't even know if 'they' is the right pronoun. There might be just one of them, and I don't think it looks *anything* like us." He saw my confusion, and groped again for an explanation. He picked up another piece of paper, set it on the desk, drew a square on it, put the fingertips of his hand to the paper.

"A Flatlander, Mr. Square, perceives this as five separate entities. See, I can surround him with what he'd see as five circles. Now, imagine my hand moving down, *through* the plane of the paper. Four circles soon join together into an elliptical shape, then the fifth one joins, too, and he sees a cross section of my wrist: another circle. Now extend that . . ." He looked thoughtful, then pulled a comb from his back pocket and touched the teeth to the paper surface.

"The comb moves through the plane, and each tooth becomes a little circle. I draw the comb through Flatland, Mr. Square sees a row of circles coming toward him."

It was making my head hurt, but I thought I grasped it.

"So they . . . or it, or whatever, is combing the planet . . ."

"Combing out all the butterflies. Like a fine-tooth comb going through hair, pulling out . . . whaddayou call 'em . . . lice eggs . . ."

"Nits." I realized I was scratching my head. I stopped. "But these aren't circles, they're solid, they look like people . . ."

"If they're solid, why don't they break tree branches when they go out on them?" He grabbed the gooseneck lamp on the desk and pointed the light at the wall. Then he laced his hands together. "You see it? On the wall? This isn't the best light . . ."

Then I did see it. He was making a shadow image of a flying bird. Larry was on a roll; he whipped a grease pencil from his pocket and drew a square on the beige wall above the desk. He made the shadow-bird again.

"Mr. Square sees a pretty complex shape. But he doesn't know the half of it. Look at my hands. Just my hands. Do you see a bird?"

"No," I admitted.

"That's because only one of many possible cross sections resembles a bird." He made a dog's head, and a monkey. He'd done this before, probably in a lecture hall.

"What I'm saying, whatever it's using, hands, fingers, whatever shapes its actual body can assume in four-space, all we'd ever see is a three-dimensional cross section of it."

"And that cross section looks like a man?"

"Could be." But his hands were on his hips now, regarding the square he'd drawn on the wall. "How can I be sure? I can't. The guys running this show, they want answers, and all we can offer them is possibilities."

***

By the end of the next day, he couldn't even offer them that.

I could see he was having tough sledding right from the first. The floating blackboard covered itself with equations again, and the . . . Instructor? Tutor? Translator? . . . stood patiently beside it, waiting for Larry to get it. And, increasingly, he was not.

The troops had been kept back, almost a quarter mile behind the Line. They were on their best behavior, as that day there was some brass with them. I could see them back there, holding binoculars, a few generals and admirals and such.

Since no one had told me to do differently, I stayed up at the Line near Larry. I wasn't sure why. I was no longer very afraid of the Linemen, though the camp had been awash in awful rumors that morning. It was said that Paulson was not the first man to be returned in a reversed state, but it had been hushed up to prevent panic. I could believe it. The initial panics and riots had died down quite a bit, we'd been told, but millions around the globe were still fleeing before the advancing Line. In some places around the globe, feeding these migrant masses was getting to be a problem. And in some places, the moving mob had solved the problem by looting every town they passed through.

Some said that Paulson was not the worst that could happen. It was whispered that men had been "vanished" by the Line and returned everted. Turned inside out. And still alive, though not for long. . . .

Larry wouldn't deny it was possible.

But today Larry wasn't saying much of anything. I watched him for a while, sweating in the sun, writing on the blackboard with a grease pencil, wiping it out, writing again, watching the Lineman patiently writing new stuff in symbols that might as well have been Swahili.

Then I remembered I had thought of something to ask the night before, lying there listening to Larry snoring in the other king-size bed.

"Excuse me," I said, and instantly a Lineman was standing beside me. The same one? I knew the question had little meaning.

"Before, I asked, 'Why butterflies?' You said because they are beautiful."

"The most beautiful things on your planet," he corrected.

"Right. But . . . isn't there a second best? Isn't there anything else, anything at all, that you're interested in?" I floundered, trying to think of something else that might be worth collecting to an aesthetic sense I could not possibly imagine. "Scarab beetles," I said, sticking to entomology. "Some of them are fabulously beautiful, to humans anyway."

"They are quite beautiful," he agreed. "However, we do not collect them. Our reasons would be difficult to explain." A diplomatic way of saying humans were blind, deaf, and ignorant, I supposed. "But yes, in a sense. Things are grown on other planets in this solar system, too. We are harvesting them now, in a temporal way of speaking."

Well, this was new. Maybe I could justify my presence here in some small way after all. Maybe I'd finally asked an intelligent question.

"Can you tell me about them?"

"Certainly. Deep in the atmospheres of your four gas giant planets, Jupiter, Saturn, Uranus, and Neptune, beautiful beings have evolved that . . . our leader treasures. On Mercury, creatures of quicksilver inhabit deep caves near the poles. These are being gathered as well. And there are life-forms we admire that thrive on very cold planets."

Gathering cryogenic butterflies on Pluto? Since he showed me no visual aids, the image would do until something better came along.

The Lineman didn't elaborate beyond that, and I couldn't think of another question that might be useful. I reported what I had learned at the end of the day. None of the team of expert analysts could think of a reason why this should concern us, but they assured me my findings would be bucked up the chain of command.

Nothing ever came of it.

***

The next day they said I could go home, and I was hustled out of California almost as fast as I'd arrived. On my way I met Larry, who looked haunted. We shook hands.

"Funny thing," he said. "All our answers, over thousands of years. Myths, gods, philosophers . . . What's it all about? Why are we here? Where do we come from, where do we go, what are we supposed to do while we're here? What's the meaning of life? So now we find out, and it was never about us at all. The meaning of life is . . . butterflies." He gave me a lopsided grin. "But you knew that all along, didn't you?"

***

Of all the people on the planet, I and a handful of others could make the case that we were most directly affected. Sure, lives were uprooted, many people died before order was restored. But the Linemen were as unobtrusive as they could possibly be, given their mind-numbing task, and things eventually got back to a semblance of normalcy. Some people lost their religious faith, but even more rejected out of hand the proposition that there was no God but the Line, so the holy men of the world registered a net gain.

But lepidopterists . . . let's face it, we were out of a job.

I spent my days haunting the dusty back rooms and narrow corridors of the museum, opening cases and drawers, some of which might not have been disturbed for decades. I would stare for hours at the thousands and thousands of preserved moths and butterflies, trying to connect with the childhood fascination that had led to my choice of career. I remembered expeditions to remote corners of the world, miserable, mosquito-bitten, and exhilarated at the same time. I recalled conversations, arguments about this or that taxonomic point. I tried to relive my elation at my first new species, *Hypolimnes lewisii.*

All ashes now. They didn't even look very pretty anymore.

***

On the twenty-eighth day of the invasion, a second Line appeared on the world's western coasts. By then the North American Line stretched from a point far in the Canadian north through Saskatchewan, Montana, Wyoming, Colorado, and New Mexico, reaching the Gulf of Mexico somewhere south of Corpus Christi, Texas. The second Line began marching east, finding very few butterflies but not seeming to mind.

It is not in the nature of the governmental mind to simply do nothing when faced with a situation. But most people agreed there was little or nothing to be done. To save face, the military maintained a presence following the Line, but they knew better than to do anything.

***

On the fifty-sixth day the third Line appeared.

Lunar cycle? It appeared so. A famous mathematician claimed he had found an equation describing the Earth-Moon orbital pair in six dimensions, or was it seven? No one cared very much.

***

When the first Line reached New York, I was in the specimen halls, looking at moths under glass. A handful of Linemen appeared, took a quick look around. One looked over my shoulder at the displays for a moment. Then they all went away, in their multidimensional way.

★★★

And there it is.

I don't recall who it was that first suggested we write it all down, nor can I recall the reason put forward. Like most literate people of the Earth, though, I dutifully sat down and wrote my story. I understand many are writing entire biographies, possibly an attempt to shout out *"I was here!"* to an indifferent universe. I have limited myself to events from Day One to the present.

Perhaps someone else will come by, some distant day, and read these accounts. Yes, and perhaps the Moon is made of green butterflies.

★★★

It turned out that my question, that last day of my military career, was the key question, but I didn't realize I had been given the answer.

The Lineman never said they were growing creatures on Pluto.

He said there were things they grew on cold planets.

After one year of combing the Earth, the Linemen went away as quickly as they appeared.

On the way out, they switched off the light.

It was night in New York. From the other side of the planet the reports came in quickly, and I climbed up to the roof of my building. The moon, which should have been nearing full phase, was a pale ghost and soon became nothing but a black hole in the sky.

Another tenant had brought a small TV. An obviously frightened astronomer and a confused news anchor were counting seconds. When they reached zero, a bit over twenty minutes after the events at the antipodes, Mars began to dim. In thirty seconds it was invisible.

He never mentioned Pluto as their cold-planet nursery. . . .

In an hour and a half Jupiter's light failed, then Saturn.

When the sun came up in America that day, it looked like a charcoal briquette, red flickerings here and there, and soon not even that. When the clocks and church bells struck noon, the Sun was gone.

Presently, it began to get cold.

On The Other Side

by MERCEDES LACKEY

Oh, but all that I remember
is the children were in danger
on the other side
—from "On the Other Side" by Janis Ian

I DIDN'T want to come here; I really did not want to see this town ever again. There was nothing to bring me back to Cheverford, after all—my parents were gone, my brothers all with the Guard or dead, and as for friends, the less said about them, the better.

But I didn't have any choice. A Herald goes where she's sent, especially now, when we've lost so many. Truth to tell, I thought that even though I didn't want to come back, I could handle it. I thought I had my emotions neatly tied up and stuffed down into a box.

But when I topped that last hill and looked down into the river valley where Cheverford lay, I could feel my stomach knotting. And nothing that Keria said to me made it any different; this was the place where my life had begun and ended and begun again, and I still wasn't sure that the choices I'd made to end that first life were the right ones. Oh, certainly, I had Keria, I was a Herald now, and had all that went with it—but all of the might-have-beens broke the bonds I'd put on them and reared up like accusing ghosts to surround me.

We trotted down the hill, Keria and I, trailing a cloud of invisible regrets and heartaches. Poor Keria; she didn't deserve to be saddled and bridled with my troubles.

:*Your troubles are mine*,: she said smoothly, sounding serene, quite as if nothing ever troubled *her*. Well, I always was the emotional one in our partnership. Nothing much ever seemed to upset Keria—not that she wasn't sympathetic and deeply empathic, it's just that she never let emotions rule her the way they ruled me.

Just as well, really; we wouldn't be an effective partnership if *both* of us were ruled by our emotions.

It's a funny sort of partnership to most people, though—at least to those who don't know that a Companion is really another person and not just an unusually intelligent white horse. Horse! As if that word could even come close to defining a Companion! *They* Choose *us* for starters, usually when we're between thirteen and seventeen (though I'd been a year later than that) and not the other way around. We Heralds might be the ones that people see, dispensing the Queen's Justice, explaining the law, doing what needs to be done—but we couldn't do all that without the Companions. Adviser, friend, assistant, closer than kin, they're *people*, they just happen to be in a horse's body, I suppose.

The town had changed quite a bit since I'd left, and not just because I'd left in the spring, and now it was autumn. A dozen houses stood on the side of the river that had once been untenanted, there was a new wheel on the mill, which turned silently as we trotted over the arched stone bridge. The old wheel had been about to shake itself to pieces when I left, so it wasn't surprising that it had been replaced—the wonder was that stingy Old Man Mullien had been willing to replace it rather than trying to rebuild it one more time.

But the biggest change was the reason why I was here—up the hill above the town on the farther side of the bridge—a huge, new building that could have passed for a wing of the Collegium, except that there was no sign of age about it. This building, modeled on the original of the Collegium, was something new for Valdemar—but never before had there been a need for such a place.

But never before had there been so many children left parentless in Valdemar either. A village could always absorb one or two orphans; it was unheard-of for there to be no relatives to whom an orphaned child could be sent.

But the Tedrel Wars had changed all that; the Tedrel Wars had changed everything. Now we had these places called "Orphanages;" now we had entire villages where the only creatures that had been left alive were the children. In that last, hideous flood of death, when the Tedrels had assumed that Valdemar had been weakened enough to conquer with one final push, they had laid waste to every settlement in their path. For some reason, they'd left children under the age of seven alive, but no one else.

I'd heard speculation that the Tedrels had intended to round up the ones that survived, bring them in, and raise the younglings as their own. It was as good a theory as any, since the Tedrels had intended to take all of Valdemar for themselves, or at the very least, as much of it as they could gobble up, but they didn't have, or encourage, families of their own.

Not surprisingly, the littles were traumatized and in need of someone who had enough Empathy to tell exactly what would help them the most. Furthermore, *some* of them were showing signs of Gifts, though it was very hard to tell *which* ones, sometimes. And that was where I came into the picture.

Well, it was more accurate to say that Keria and I came into the picture. *She* was an Empath and, more to the point, just like an Empathic Mindhealer, of which we had exactly none to spare; with any luck and my help in speaking to them, she would be able to help the children over the worst of their troubles. And I (like the legendary Herald Pol of Lavan Firestorm's time) had that special little Gift of being able to sense virtually all of the Gifts at work. I should be able to pick out who was doing what, when it came to things like plates being flung across the room, or everyone waking up with exactly the same nightmare. At that point, well, either Keria would be able to sort the child out so that he (or she) would *stop* doing things, or Keria would determine if the child ought to be Chosen, at which point it was out of our hands and presumably a Companion would arrive to carry the little one away. True enough, they were *far* too young to go into the Collegium, but that wasn't our problem; the Collegium would have to adapt, or some other provision would be made. We didn't make decisions, Keria and I; we just implemented them.

So there it was. This would be the second such Orphanage we'd been sent to since they were set up. Each one held about thirty children, that being the number that was deemed manageable by a residential staff of four, two couples, with the cleaning and cooking being helped out by a couple of day-servants from the village, if needed.

We were far from the Border of Karse, where all the troubles had been. My old village was *nothing* like the high, heavily-wooded hills and mountain forests that these children had grown up among. My country was gentle, long-settled, farms that had been in families for two and three hundred years, pastures supporting fat black-and-white milch-cattle and plump, slow white sheep, not rangy red hill-cattle and long-haired goats. We had rolling hills intersected by tame, chuckling streams, not slopes that plunged down to meet rivers that ran shallow one moment, and raging the next. There were woods, but they were populated with oak and ash and beech, not firs and pines that reached green-black fingers to point at the moon, nor birch and aspen that showed white skeletons when winter came and their leaves were gone.

There was little here to remind these children of their lost homes, although *if* they wanted to go back when they were older, no one was going to stop them. There was no telling what they'd want later; for now, we were mostly concerned with keeping them cushioned by unfamiliarity, as if we were bandaging their wounded spirits.

But as I said, that was none of my business. I was here to help them in a small, immediate way. I was actually grateful for that; there was so little anyone could do to help them, and the fact that I could do anything at all made me feel less helpless in the face of all of the monumental losses. There were plenty of Heralds, especially those who (like me) hadn't so much as gotten farther south than Haven during the Wars that were going about with a sense of peculiar guilt because they hadn't done anything other than "ordinary" Herald's duties then, and weren't doing anything other than that now. I was lucky; I had a real feeling that I was contributing something.

The only problem, of course, was that I had to come back *here* as part of doing that job.

As usual, there were children—not the orphans, you could tell that by their clothing, just ordinary village children—who were playing in the river and along the bank, keeping an eye on the road for anything interesting that might happen by. Well, I was interesting enough to send them all splashing up out of the shallows and pelting barefoot and bare-legged up the dusty road, across the bridge and into the village, yelling shrilly that "Herald's comin'!" Keria's hooves chimed merrily on the stone of the bridge, and her bridle bells rang along with them; warning enough to anyone with an ear, even if the children hadn't started up like hounds on a scent at the first sight of us. Now capped or bare heads poked out of windows and kitchen doors, curious and eager, and I winced inside, seeing familiar faces, waiting to see the expressions of interest turn to recognition, then pity. Except that they didn't.

:*They don't know you, Chosen,*: Keria said. :*Most won't recognize you unless you remind them of who you were. Partly it's the uniform, partly it's the years, but mostly it's that you have had experiences they only hear about in news and tales, while they have stayed at home and changed very little from the people you knew.*:

I couldn't argue with the evidence of my own eyes, but it seemed very strange. :*Have I changed that much?*:

I felt her amusement. :*Well, my dear, think! In the time since you left, you have lived through* how *many floods,* how *many fires, arbitrated* how *many feuds, not to mention all of the other disasters and near-disasters you've coped with? That is more experience in even five years than most of these folk will see in a lifetime.*:

I was feeling particularly mordant, I suppose. :*So, now that I've turned into a care-ridden hag*—:

:*Oh, Havens, if you're going to go on like that, there's no use talking to you!*: she exclaimed, but in a teasing tone, so that I should know

that nothing was meant by it. She had to cosset me like that sometimes; I could be as touchy now as I had been as an adolescent—

Which was, of course, the time in my life I most particularly
didn't want to think about.

He wouldn't be there, of course. He couldn't be. He'd only
stayed for as long as he had because of me.

Because of me. . . .

And I knew he'd moved on once I was gone, once he knew that
I wasn't coming back. I knew, because I had asked. Oh, yes, I had
asked; it was easy enough to do after Keria came for me and took
me to Herald's Collegium, with Bardic Collegium just over the
way, and all the records of which Bard was wandering where easy
to get at. Nobody even asked me *why* I wanted to know, though I
fell all over myself with the explanation, "He was from my village,
and he came back once he was in full Scarlets," I said, knowing
that my face matched those Scarlets in intensity, if not hue. "I—I
wondered if he moved on," I concluded, lamely enough, face so
hot the Bardic Chronicler could have warmed her hands at it.

But "Bard Jordie Ambersen, was it?" was all she said, all tact
and diplomacy, and not a hint that there was anything out of the
commonplace, like any Bard, really. Even Jordie was that way, or
perhaps he had just been oblivious to the fact that he had been
eating me alive with his love, and I had to run from him or lose
myself and become nothing more than his shadow. And *he* was
being eaten by staying, in our little village that thought him
"clever" and "amusing" and had no notion of what sort of a treasure was sitting in the Black Swan, night after night, playing "one
o'them old tunes, young Jordie, none o'that newfangled nonsense."
He wouldn't leave—for my sake, he'd have said; that a wandering
life was no life for a woman, much less a young girl like me—that
it was too hard, with no home of her own, and often as not, no
place to lay her head, even. And if ever there was to be a child
coming—well! Now, he said, we had to stay here where I would
have a home when we married, and everything would be stable.
Even though I didn't *want* "stability" and neither did he. Even
though I didn't know who and what I was yet, and he was turning

me into a picture of what *he* wanted. Even though his voice was being stifled "for my sake" and I was being sucked dry for his. Would he have believed it if I'd told him?

"Ah. Up north he's gone. Last reported at Berrybay, dear." She smiled slightly. I fled. It was all I needed to know. The rabbit had run, and the bird had flown free of the cage that had been too small to contain it, if only it had known.

I returned only once in all the time since, when a winter-fever carried off both my mother and father together. I came back in Trainee Grays, but not to bury them, for the village already had, but to say whatever good-bye I could. Poor things, they had been so proud I had been Chosen, but so bewildered when I wrote that no, I hadn't heard from Jordie, and no, I didn't expect to. Purest accident that on the road, fleeing from Jordie, I had met with Keria, but they were not to know that. My brothers couldn't come home, the ones that were still alive—they were on the front lines of the Wars. I did duty for the family, sold the house and land, and fled back to the Collegium to have the money sent to them. I didn't need it, and soldiers always need money.

I went to the Black Swan, for there was no Waystation here, and at any rate, I was not on circuit to be making use of it. "Herald Enna," I said, and got no second looks, for Enna was a common enough name. "Here for the Orphanage."

"And a mercy," said Maggy Chokan from behind the bar, as her husband nodded and presented me with the Herald's Book to sign. "Not that I grudge the poor wee mites their shelter nor blame 'em for their griefs," she added hastily. "But the way things keep flyin' about up there, and them storms that hev been springing up, they're not *natural*."

I nodded gravely. "That's what we're here to sort out," I replied, taking the room key that her husband handed to me, quite as if I hadn't known them at all. Well enough to know that the few cases of "things flyin' about" had probably been multiplied a thousandfold in her mouth, and that there was nothing at all unnatural about the summer storms that were as familiar a memory to me as the old stone bridge.

Well, why should they remember *me* if it came to it? Except as the unaccountable girl who everyone thought would marry Bard Jordie, but got Chosen instead? And my face had probably gotten blurred in their memories, confused with the round, vague, unformed faces of half the other adolescent girls in this place—all of us dreaming, most of us unwilling to make the sacrifices to force the dreams to come true. And one of us not willing to have a dream that meant becoming less than we were.

No matter how much love came with it.

I took my key—a cumbersome thing it was, too, and utterly unnecessary, even if I *hadn't* been a Herald, since no one had ever, in anyone's memory, stolen so much as a wooden spoon from a room in the Black Swan. But there—supposedly someone, back in Maggy's grandfather's time, had taken a purse from a room, so there must needs be keys now.

:On the other hand, with all the strangers on the roads now, perhaps keys will be needed,: said Keria. *:The Tedrel Wars left some strange flotsam floating about the Kingdom.:*

I unlocked the door to my room; it creaked. *:True enough, and what are we to do? Demand a certificate of virtue from every stranger? Are you comfortable, my love?:*

:Tolerably,: she said, by which I knew that she was not, but she had her own ways of making sure that her comforts were supplied. I had no doubt that before too long, she would have the situation taken care of. *:Going up to the Orphanage?:*

:I think so; I need to let them know we're here, and what we're going to do. I can have a look at the children now, perhaps while they're playing, and we can start the real work tomorrow when I know what Gifts we're dealing with. Or not,: I added, for there had been at least one case of a very clever little sleight-of-hand artist who had everyone convinced that there was a haunting going on in the first place.

:Or not,: she agreed, and so, once I saw my packs safely brought up by the man-of-all-work, I locked the door, put that ponderous key in my belt pouch, and began the walk up the hill to that raw, new building.

Someone had been at work trying to make the place less stark,

I saw as I neared it. There were flower beds and young trees, all of them recent plantings, all around it. There were swings of rope and leather, the kind that you ordinarily saw hanging from the limbs of old trees, set up in wooden frames since there were no trees big enough near the building. Someone had gone to extraordinary length to build a sand pit, full of clean sand, with small sized pails and tiny shovels in it. Yet none of this looked played with.

I sighed. I wasn't at all surprised, since this was pretty much what I had come to expect at these Orphanages. The children seldom felt safe outside of four walls, for many of them had been outdoors when the Tedrels descended on their villages, and had been chased away from the security of their homes by armed and threatening men. That this had been done so that those men could kill their parents and older siblings without them witnessing the fact was something that didn't get into the part of their minds where fear lived.

It was early in the afternoon; the children should be at their lessons for the moment. It would be a good time to speak to their guardians.

I went around back to the kitchen, where I was sure of finding at least one of them.

In fact, I found two, both of the women, plus a couple of young women from the village acting as kitchenmaids, all hard at work on the preparation of food for thirty growing children. I watched them for a little, until I was satisfied that there was no skimping going on—not that I *expected* it, but it was good to be sure.

But no, the rabbit being chopped up for the stew was as good as anything I'd get in the inn, the bread coming out of the oven was crusty and golden and there was plenty of it, and one of the two women was filling a berry pie with a lavish hand. I cleared my throat ostentatiously.

A candlemark later, I was satisfied with the guardians as well as the physical surroundings, and in fact, it turned out I knew them, though they didn't recognize me. Not that they should have; they were older than I as well as more than a touch above my social station, and even in a village there is a line between "gentleman's daughter" and "market-farmer's girl" that is seldom crossed. Strange to see them being deferential to me now. It was a change in my status that I never even noticed until now, when I *knew* the two couples in question. But perhaps that had as much to do with the Wars as anything else. The Wars changed life in Valdemar for everyone, whether or not they were directly affected. Or perhaps I was being unfair, for here were Gemma and Lara, the Squire's girls, who I last saw "setting their caps" at Harl and Berd, Guild-master's and landed Knight's sons respectively, yet they were married to Lame Tam the miller's third boy and half-blind Hadal, a mere clerk (who wore a pair of thick glass lenses in a wire frame just so he could see), and both seemed happy enough.

Perhaps Harl and Berd had gone to the Wars and not come back . . . I wasn't about to ask.

Just as I was about to ask to see the children themselves, I heard something that made me freeze in my tracks—a lilting tenor voice lifted in song. A voice I knew only too well.

I've learned how to control my expression, but something must have struck Gemma as odd, for she said immediately, "Oh, that's only my husband's cousin, Bard Jordie Ambersen; he came when he heard from Tam about the children, and we've been having ever so much less trouble with them since he arrived."

She peered at me anxiously, as if afraid that I wouldn't approve, but of course, it was perfectly obvious why the children would be doing better and how could I possibly object? Bardic Gift included a sort of MindHealing and a variant of Projective Empathy. It made perfect sense for him to come and help—

"I think it's fine," I hastened to assure her. "But I'll need to see the children when he is *not* around, or his Gift will muddle up what I'm looking for. It just rather startled me, no one told me that a Bard had kindly volunteered his services."

"Ah," she said, and smiled, and we went on to make arrangements for the morrow, while Jordie sang on, oblivious, over our heads. One of the history songs, but he was projecting (oh, *how* he was projecting) and while he was teaching them history, he was soothing them, or trying to.

As for me, well—coward that I was, I fled as soon as I could, back to the inn, back to Keria. I didn't want to meet him. I didn't want his questions, his reproaches, or his pity. I especially did not want to see love looking out of his eyes, calling me, calling me back.

Keria said nothing that wasn't commonplace; *she* knew. She didn't even mention him.

I don't know what woke me. I *do* know that it couldn't have been more than a heartbeat later that the village alarm bell began to hammer out the tocsin for "Fire." And it would have taken a completely Mind-deaf Herald not to have known, *known*, that the fire was at the Orphanage.

I don't remember dressing or leaving my room, or (most importantly) snatching up the coil of rope I always had with Keria's saddle. The next thing I recalled was vaulting off Keria's back, the rope over my shoulder, a soaking-wet blanket under one arm *(you have lived through* how *many floods,* how *many fires?),* and dashing into a building that was already aflame.

All these Orphanages were built to the same plan; the children were housed in rooms on the third floor, under the attics, their classrooms were on the second, and the domestic arrangements as well as the rooms of the guardians were on the first floor. The staircase—the only staircase—was fully involved, but I pulled the wetted blanket (had it come from my bed? Grabbing one and wetting it down was second nature, no thought to me now when the danger was fire) over me, held my breath, and made a dash up it. The flames scorched me, but I got through somehow with nothing worse than a few holes burned in the wool.

And now I heard it; felt it, more than heard it. A song, whose only burden, impelling and compelling, was *come to me, come to me. . . .*

Jordie. No one else. But in this case, it wasn't meant for me to hear, for he didn't even know I was there. It was meant for the children.

But I followed it. Up the stairs, up past the schoolrooms where flames were licking up behind me, up to the children's rooms, filling with smoke, to the one corner of the building where smoke and flames hadn't yet reached. Stumbling in behind a coughing, sobbing child, to where Jordie stood at a window, surrounded by other children; I couldn't count them, it was dark, too full of smoke, and at any rate there was no time.

But *he* knew me; knew me before I spoke. I felt it; felt the recognition, but I ignored it. There was no time for him, no time for anything but the escape plan that every Trainee at the Collegia knew, that surely *he* knew, for it was one we Trainees rehearsed three and four times a year. It had never been used, to my knowledge. Until now, it had never been needed.

He grabbed a sheet off the bed near him—I handed him my belt knife (when had I put on my belt?) and he began tearing strips off the sheet while I made the rope fast to a ceiling beam and threw the rest of the coil out the window.

It went taut almost immediately. *:I have it,:* Keria said, *:and—good, I've got four men on it. Five.:*

:Back it up as far as you can,: I told her, and the rope began to slant. *:And get more people on it.:*

Meanwhile Jordie had knotted a strip of cloth around a child's wrist, and was looping it over the rope, singing all the while, projecting calm as hard as I had ever felt it. He tied the other end around the child's opposite wrist, sat her on the window ledge, and before she could think what was happening, pushed her out the window.

For that was the escape plan, of course; ropes slanted out the window, and what we called the "slide for life" down them, hanging onto towels, scarves, anything we could find to loop over the rope. Best if it was the metal rings we kept in our rooms for the purpose, of course, but anything would do. . . .

While the first child was on the rope, screaming bloody murder, I already had the next on the rope and Jordie the third half tied. They were already in such a panic despite his projection that honestly they didn't know what we were doing, and they were howling so badly that they never even heard the ones outside screaming.

We could see perfectly well now, though . . . the flames were getting close.

And worse than that, was the smoke. It was making a thick layer near the ceiling so we had to crouch to keep our heads out of it. And the heat—

Worst of all somehow was the voice of the fire, a howl, a roar, the sound of a hungry beast that had every intention of devouring us. I've never heard anything like that before, and it echoes in my nightmares nearly every night.

I tried to count littles as we shoved them out the window and came up two short; that was when I saw them, on the floor of the hallway, not moving, where they'd dropped in their tracks trying to get to us. We hadn't been able to see them until this moment.

Maybe they were dead—but maybe they weren't. And I knew if I could get them out the window there would be *someone* out there who would at least try to breathe life into them—

I draped the steaming blanket over me again while Jordie shouted, and dashed out into the hall. Thank the gods they were small—I grabbed both of them and dragged them into the room; Jordie shook his head, but I tied them on and shoved the limp bodies out the window, one, two—but the smoke was roiling, looking like a live thing, with little flamelets starting to lick over the surface of it. I had never been in a fire like this one, this bad, but I had a horrible, sick feeling about this. Something bad, something *very* bad, was about to happen. . . .

I had my strip of cloth; I *think* Jordie had his. I had mine up over the rope—I'd *just* grabbed the other end—

I can't really describe what happened next; it just seemed as if one moment there was only that thick pall of black, roiling smoke behind us, trying to get out the window—

—and the next moment, there was nothing but flame, flame that *shoved* me out the window. I was on fire as I screamed down the rope, in agony with the pain of my burning skin, my hair streaming out behind me like the fiery tail of a comet, and the rope itself parted before I was halfway to the ground.

Down I came, and I remember being smothered in a blanket,

someone, a lot of someones, beating out the flames, and I remember screaming Jordie's name until I couldn't scream for anything but pain. . . .

Thank the gods the human frame can only take so much. Eventually, it all went to black, interrupted now and again by voices and orders, orders which I followed dutifully, because they came from Keria, voices which I mostly ignored. More than once, I prayed for an end to it. Most of the time, when I wasn't too drugged to think, I reckoned I would probably die. There was sharp regret at leaving Keria alone; aching regret that it hadn't been Jordie down that line first. Heralds were expected to die heroically. Bards were supposed to go live and sing about it, after.

Then, at some point, the blackness faded, and I was somewhere else. Not anywhere I recognized, though.

I was sitting on a grassy hillside; pleasant and warm, but for some reason, there was a sort of pearly fog over everything. While I tried to puzzle out where I was, that familiar voice said, as if taking up a conversation I didn't recall, "They're calling us heroes, on the other side."

"Yes," I agreed calmly. "But—"

I turned, and there was Jordie, lounging beside me as he used to do when we went out on picnics. He smiled. "Yes, but. Heroism isn't something we intended, was it? It was just, the children were in danger, and we knew how to save them, so we didn't think. We just *did* it."

"Maybe that's the essence of being heroes," I said slowly.

He shook his head at me. "Bards aren't heroes. *Heralds*, now—that's another story, but who is going to believe a Bard as a hero?"

Since that was just what I'd been thinking, I kept silent out of guilt.

But he wasn't done with me, and wasn't about to let me have a word in yet. "When were you Chosen? Was it after you ran away from me, or was that the *reason* you left?"

"After," I said, shame flooding over me. "I had to run; I think I had some vague idea of getting a job in an inn somewhere, but if I'd stayed—I couldn't have resisted you, all of you, friends and parents and all, but *especially* you. You all were so sure what I should do. I tried to tell you, Jordie, but—but—"

"But I was eating you alive, sucking you dry, I *see* that now," he interrupted gently, so gently. "I see it now, but I couldn't then, and I wouldn't if—if I were still on the other side. You were right to run, I know that now."

I wanted to cry, I wanted to, but I couldn't. I was held in calm despite what I wanted to do. "Jordie—it wasn't just that. It wasn't just *me*. You were turning into something *tame*. I felt—I felt as if I was watching a racehorse being hitched to a farm cart. As if I was making a gryphon catch mice for a living, just so that I could have a steady livelihood—"

"It's all right," he said, and gave me one of those smiles. "It's all right. We'll do better next time. I just—I'm glad I saw you again. I'm glad we were together at the last. And the children are safe, all of them, even the last two."

He looked up, out into the mist, as if he could see something I couldn't, and nodded. "Next time," he repeated. "Next time, we'll do better by each other. Now—you have to go."

"Go?" I said. Now I was completely confused. Surely this was a—a sort of waiting place before you went to the Havens? Or wherever you went when you were dead. "But—aren't we—aren't I—"

"Oh, no. You don't belong here," he said, with that sweet, sweet smile. "You belong on the other side, my love. I stay here. *You* have to go—"

All the while he was speaking, the mist got thicker and thicker, and brighter and brighter, and his voice grew more and more distant, as if he was drawing away from me. "Good-bye, my love," he said, from leagues away, a whisper in the brightness. "Take wing and fly, on the other side."

And the brightness faded, and I found myself here, in this bed, in this room, in a House of Healing.

On the other side. And somehow, although my face and hair were drenched with tears, under the grief was comfort—the certainty of forgiveness and forgiving, that healing had begun from wounds I hadn't acknowledged even to myself. And a knowledge that some day, whether that day came soon or late, I would find myself in that brightness again, and pass through it.

And we'd do better, next time, on the other side.

Nightmare Mountain

by KAGE BAKER

*Now there's only Nightmare Mountain
grown too high to climb
Never would have done it if I'd known
it meant losing home
—from "Nightmare Mountain" by Janis Ian*

THERE was once a poor man, and he had a daughter.

He wouldn't for a second have admitted he was poor. He owned a fifty-acre almond ranch in San Jose, after all. He came of fine stock from the South, and all his people on both sides had owned property before the War. It was true their circumstances had been somewhat reduced in the days following the capitulation at Appamattox; it was true he and all his kin had been obliged to flee persecution and head West. But they were people of account, make no mistake about it.

Great-Aunt Merrion would sit on the front porch and look out over the lion-yellow hills, and recollect: "My daddy once owned three-fifths of Prince County, and the farm proper was seven miles to a side. Nothing like *this*." And she would sniff disdainfully at the dry rows of little almond trees.

And Aunt Pugh, who sat on the other side of the porch and who hated Great-Aunt Merrion only slightly less than she hated the Yankees, would wave her arm at the creaking Aeromotor pump and say: "My daddy once owned a thousand acres of the finest bottomland on the Mississippi River, as verdant as the gardens of

Paradise before the fall. How happy I am he cannot see the extent to which we are reduced, in this desert Purgatory!"

Then they would commence to rock again, in their separate chairs, and little Annimae would sigh and wonder why they didn't like California. She liked it fine. She didn't care much for the ranch house, which was creaking and shabby and sad, and full of interminable talk about the Waw, which she took to be some hideous monster, since it had chased her family clear across the country.

But Annimae could always escape from the house and run through the almond trees, far and far along the rows, in spring when they were all pink and white blossoms. Or she might wander down to the edge by the dry creek, and walk barefoot in the cool soft sand under the cottonwoods. Or she might climb high into the cottonwood branches and cling, swaying with the wind in the green leaves, pretending she was a sailor way high in the rigging of a ship.

But as she grew up, Annimae was told she mustn't do such things anymore. Running and climbing was not proper deportment for a lady. By this time there were two mortgages on the ranch, and Annimae's father went about with a hunted look in his eyes, and drank heavily after dinner, bourbon out of the fine crystal that had been brought from Charleston. As a consequence, Annimae very much regretted that she could no longer escape from the house and sought her escape in the various books that had been her mother's. They were mostly such romances and fairy tales as had been thought proper for genteel young ladies a generation previous.

To make matters worse, the money that had been set aside to send her to a finishing school had gone somehow, so there was no way out there either; worse yet, Great-Aunt Merrion and Aunt Pugh took it upon themselves to train her up in the manner of a gentlewoman, her dear mamma (whose sacred duty it would have been) having passed away in the hour of Annimae's birth. They had between them nearly a century's worth of knowledge of what was expected of a fine planter's lady in charge of a great estate, but they so bitterly contradicted each other that Annimae found it next to impossible to please either of them.

When Annimae was fifteen, her father sold off some of the property to the county, though Great-Aunt Merrion and Aunt Pugh warned that this was the beginning of the end. He bought Annimae a pianoforte with some of the money, that she might learn to play. The rest of the money would have paid off the mortgages, if he hadn't speculated in stocks.

By the time Annimae was seventeen she played the pianoforte exquisitely, and across the sold-off fields the new Monterey Road cut straight past the ranch house, within a stone's throw of the window before which she sat as she played. Great-Aunt Merrion and Aunt Pugh were mortified, and thenceforth withdrew from the porch to the parlor, rather than be exposed to the public gaze on the common highway.

One night Annimae came to the end of an air by Donizetti, and fell silent, gazing out into the summer darkness.

"Do play on, child," said Aunt Pugh irritably. "The young have no excuse to sit woolgathering. A graceful melody will ease your father's cares."

Annimae's father had already eased his cares considerably with bourbon, upstairs at his desk, but ladies did not acknowledge such things.

"I was just wondering, Aunt Pugh," said Annimae, "Who is it that drives by so late?"

"Why, child, what do you mean?" said Great-Aunt Merrion.

"There's a carriage goes by every night, just about half past nine," said Annimae. "It's very big, quite a fine carriage, and the driver wears a high silk hat. The strangest thing is, the carriage-lamps are all set with *purple* glass, purple as plums! So they throw very little light to see by. I wonder that they are lit at all.

"The horses' hooves make almost no sound, just gliding by. And lately, it goes by so slow! Quite slow past the house, as though they're looking up at us. Who could they be?"

Great-Aunt Merrion and Aunt Pugh exchanged a significant glance.

"Purple glass, you say," said Great-Aunt Merrion. "And a driver in a top hat. Is he an old buck—" and I am afraid Great-

Aunt Merrion used a word no true lady ever uses when referring to a member of the Negro race, and Aunt Pugh smiled spitefully at her lapse behind a fan.

"I think so, yes," said Annimae.

"I expect that must be poor crazy Mrs. Nightingale," said Aunt Pugh.

"Poor!" exclaimed Great-Aunt Merrion, with what in anyone less august would have been a snort. "Poor as Croesus, I'd say. *Nouveau Riche*, child; no good breeding at all. Do you know how Talleyrand Nightingale made his money? Selling powder and ball to the Yankees! For which he most deservedly died young, of the consumption (they *said*), and left that bloodstained and ill-gotten fortune to his wife."

"*I* heard he shot himself in a fit of drunken despondency and shame," asserted Aunt Pugh. "And *she's* nobody. Some storekeeper's daughter from New Orleans. And there was a child, they say; but it was a puny little thing, and I believe she had to put it into a sanatorium—"

"I heard it died," stated Great-Aunt Merrion, and Aunt Pugh glared at her.

"I believe you are misinformed, Miss Merrion. So what should this foolish woman do but take herself off to the Spiritualists' meetings, and venture into the dens of fortune-tellers, like the low-bred and credulous creature she was."

"And what should that foolish woman come to believe," said Great-Aunt Merrion, cutting in with a scowl at Aunt Pugh, "But that all her misfortunes were caused by the unquiet spirits of those who perished due to Northern aggression supplied by Nightingale Munitions! And one evening when she was table-rapping, or some such diabolical nonsense, her departed husband *supposedly* informed her that she had to run clean across the country to California to be safe."

"Nor is that all!" cried Aunt Pugh, leaning forward to outshout Great-Aunt Merrion. "She believed that if she built herself a house, *and never let the work stop on it*, she would not only escape the predations of the outraged shades of the Confederacy, but would herself be granted life everlasting, apparently in some manner other than that promised by our dear Lord and Savior."

"I do wish," said Great-Aunt Merrion, "Miss Pugh, that you would not raise your voice in that manner. People will think you lack gentility. In any case, child—the Widow Nightingale has built herself a mansion west of town. It is a vile and vulgar thing. *She* calls it Nightingale Manor; but the common children of the street refer to it as Nightmare Mountain. I do hear it has more than a hundred rooms now; and night and day the hammers never cease falling. One wonders that a lady could endure such appalling clamor—"

"But they do say she shuts herself up in there all day, and only ventures forth by night, in that purple carriage of hers," said Aunt Pugh. "Or goes occasionally to make purchases from shopkeepers; yet she never sets a foot to the ground, but they come out to her as though she were the Queen of Sheba, and she picks and chooses from their wares."

"It never ceases to amaze me how common folk will abase themselves before the almighty dollar," said Great-Aunt Merrion with contempt, and Aunt Pugh nodded her head in rare agreement.

But on the very next evening, as Annimae's father was lighting the fire in the parlor himself—for the Chinese servants had all been discharged, and were owed back wages at that—Annimae looked out the window and saw the strange carriage coming up the drive.

"Why, Daddy, we have callers," she exclaimed.

Annimae's father rose up swiftly, white as a sheet, for he was expecting the Marshal. When the gentle knock came, his mouth was too dry to bid Annimae stay, so she got up to open the door; though Great-Aunt Merrion hissed, "Child, mention that our house boy just died, and you do not yourself customarily—"

But Annimae had opened the door, and it was too late.

There on the porch stood an old, old man, leaning on a stick. His hair was snow-white with age, his skin black as Annimae's pianoforte. Though it was a moonless night, he wore smoked spectacles that hid his eyes. He was dressed in a black suit of formal cut, and was just drawing off his tall silk hat. Holding it before him, he bowed. On the drive behind him was the carriage, indeed painted a deep violet, with two great black horses hitched to it. Visible within the carriage was a tiny woman, swathed in a purple lap robe. Perhaps there was something behind her, huddled up in the shadows.

And Annimae felt a wave of summer heat blow in from the night, and it seemed the perfume of strange flowers was on that wind, and the music of insects creaking loud in the darkness.

"Good evening, Miss. Is Mr. Devereaux Loveland at home?" the old man inquired, in a nasal voice.

"What do you want here, boy?" demanded Great-Aunt Merrion.

"I do beg your pardon, Ma'am, but my mistress is crippled with the rheumatism and hopes you will excuse her if she don't get out of the carriage to speak to you herself," said the old man. "She wishes to know if Mr. Loveland would be so kind as to call on her at Nightingale Manor, at any convenient hour tomorrow."

Annimae's father started forward, and stared past the old man at the carriage.

"You may tell her I would be delighted to do so, boy," he said hoarsely. "What is it your mistress wishes to discuss with me?"

"Matters of mutual advantage, sir," said the old man, and bowed again.

"Then I shall call on her at one o'clock in the afternoon," said Annimae's father.

When Annimae had closed the door, Aunt Pugh said scornfully: "A *lady* would have left a calling card."

But the next day Annimae's father dressed in his finest clothes, saddled his white horse and rode away down Monterey Road, well ahead of the hour so as not to be late. It was seven in the evening before he came riding back.

When he had led his horse to the stable himself (for the Mexican groom had been discharged) he returned and came straight into the house, and standing before his hearth he said to Annimae: "Daughter, I have arranged your marriage. You are to become the wife of Daniel Nightingale."

Annimae stood there stunned. Great-Aunt Merrion gasped, and Aunt Pugh sputtered, and then the pair of them raised twenty concerted objections, as her father ignored them and poured himself a glass of brandy from the parlor decanter. But Annimae felt again the strange warm wind, and a reckless joy rising in her heart.

"What d'you mean, that woman has a son?" roared Great-Aunt Merrion. "A *marriageable* son?"

"I am given to understand he is an invalid," said Annimae's father, with a significant look at the old women.

A certain silence fell.

"And he is the only child and heir?" said Aunt Pugh delicately.

"He is, madam," replied Annimae's father.

"Mm-*hm*," said Great-Aunt Merrion. Adamant was not so hard and bright as the speculative gaze she turned on Annimae. "Well, child, you have indeed been favored by fortune."

Annimae said: "Is he handsome, Daddy?"

"I did not see him," said Annimae's father, studying the ceiling beams. Taking a drink of the brandy, he went on: "The, ah, the young gentleman is unable to receive visitors. Mrs. Nightingale offered his proposal."

"But—how did he fall in love with me, then?" asked Annimae.

The two aunts pursed their old lips tight. Annimae's father lowered his head, met his child's eyes and said:

"I was informed he goes out riding a'nights in the carriage, and has glimpsed you seated at the window, and was entranced by the vision of beauty and gentility you presented. And he burns for love of you, or so his dear mamma says."

"Why then, I will surely love him!" said Annimae with firm conviction.

"That is your duty, child," said Great-Aunt Merrion.

But neither Great-Aunt Merrion nor Aunt Pugh were pleased with the conditions set on the match: which were, that there was to be no grand church wedding, blazoned in the Society Pages, no public ceremony or indeed a church ceremony at all, but one conducted in Mrs. Nightingale's private chapel, and that within the next three days. And they were in agonies of mixed emotions about the small trunkful of twenty-dollar gold pieces Mrs. Nightingale had sent to pay for Annimae's trousseau.

"Charity? Who *does* she think we are? How dare she!" said Great-Aunt Merrion.

"Imagine having to buy a wedding dress ready-made! Such a shame!" said Aunt Pugh.

But they spent the gold lavishly, and as a result Annimae looked exquisite, a very magnolia in ivory lace, when she mounted into the hired carriage with her father. They set off in state, with the aunts following in another carriage behind, and rolled away down dusty commonplace Monterey Road.

As they rode along, Annimae's father cleared his throat and said:

"I expect the old ladies have explained to you your duty to your husband, Daughter?"

"Oh, yes," said Annimae, assuming he meant the selection of suitable house servants and how to entertain guests.

Annimae's father was silent a moment, and at last said:

"I expect any child of mine to be able to withstand adversity with courage. You may find married life a trial. Consider yourself a soldier on the battlefield, Daughter; for the fortunes of our family all depend upon this match. Do not fail us."

"Of course I won't, Daddy," said Annimae, wondering what on Earth that had to do with Valentine hearts and white doves.

So they came to Nightingale Manor.

Annimae had expected it would be a lofty castle on a crag, and of course this was not so, for it sat on the flat yellow orchard plain of San Jose. But it did rise like a mountain in its way. She glimpsed it out the window a long way off, and caught her breath. High turrets and spires, cupolas, gables, balconies, corbels, cornices, finials, and weathercocks, with its walls scaled in every shape of gingerbread shingle and painted all the colors of a fruit bowl! And all rising from a grand park miles long.

They drew up before the gate at last, and Annimae cried out in delight. It was a wildly lush garden, for that dry country. Lawns green as emerald, formal rose beds edged by boxwood hedges planted in circles, in stars, in crescent moons, and diamonds. A double row of palms and oleanders lined the carriage drive. Annimae counted at least three fountains sending up fine sprays through the heavy air. The house itself seemed to spread out in all directions; nowhere could one look, however far out into the park, without catching a glimpse of roofline or a tower somewhere among the trees. Annimae heard the sound of hammering. It seemed far away and muffled, but it was continuous.

As the carriages drew up before the porch (a fretwork fantasy of spindlewood, scrolls, and stained glass), the front door was already being opened by the old black man. He smiled, with fine white teeth, and bowed low.

"Welcome to Nightingale Manor, sir and ladies. My mistress is expecting you all in the chapel. If you'll please to follow me?"

They stepped across the threshold, and Annimae heard her aunts breathing heavily, keeping their lips tight together for fear lest they should exclaim aloud. The old man led them through a succession of the most beautiful rooms Annimae had ever seen. Fine carpets, polished paneling of rare inlaid woods, stained glass windows set with crystals that sent rainbows dancing everywhere. Golden rooms, green rooms, red rooms, rooms blue with every color of the sea, and the deeper they went into the house, the more dimly lit it all was. But after they had been walking for fifteen minutes, Aunt Pugh exclaimed:

"Boy, you have been leading us in circles! I declare I have walked five miles!"

"It's a long way to the chapel," said the old man, in tones of sincerest apology. "And the house is designed like a maze, you see. If I was to leave you now, I don't reckon you folks could find your way back. I do beg your pardon. We're nearly there."

And only three rooms and a staircase later they were there, too. They entered a chamber vaulted like a church, set all around with more stained glass, though a curious cold light shone through the panes that was not like daylight at all. Before a little altar of black and porphyry marble stood just three people, two of them looking ill at ease.

One was the Reverend Mr. Stevens, clutching his Book of Common Prayer. The other was clearly a workman, middle-aged, dressed in heavy overalls. He was sweating, twisting his cap between his hands. He smelled of sawdust and glue.

The third was the woman Annimae had glimpsed in the carriage. She was merely a plain, plump, middle-aged little lady, all in purple bombazine, who had been pretty once. Her eyes were still remarkable, though at the moment their stare was rather fixed and hostile.

"Miss Annimae Loveland; Mr. Devereaux Loveland; the Misses Merrion and Pugh," announced the old man, with proper solemnity. The mistress of the house inclined her head in acknowledgment.

"Reverend, you may commence," she said.

"I beg your pardon, but where is the groom?" demanded Great-Aunt Merrion, whose feet were hurting her a great deal.

"Great-Aunt, hush," said Annimae's father. Mrs. Nightingale merely said:

"My son's condition does not permit him to venture from his room at present. The marriage will be conducted with Mr. Hansen standing proxy."

"Why, I never heard of such a thing!" squealed Aunt Pugh.

"Hold your tongue!" said Annimae's father, in a tone of such venom Aunt Pugh went pale.

Annimae scarcely knew what to think, and was further troubled when the Reverend Mr. Stevens leaned forward and said quietly: "My child, do you freely consent to this marriage?"

"Of course I do," she said, "I'd just like to meet my husband, is all."

"Then let us proceed," said Mrs. Nightingale.

The service was brief, and swiftly spoken. Bewildered and disappointed, Annimae spent most of the ceremony staring up at the inscriptions in the two stained glass windows above the altar. One read: *WIDE UNCLASP THE TABLES OF THEIR THOUGHTS*, and the other read, *THESE SAME THOUGHTS PEOPLE THIS LITTLE WORLD.*

Mr. Hansen's hands were shaking as he fitted the wedding band on Annimae's finger, and he mumbled his responses. She in her turn was puzzled at how to put the ring on his hand, for it was much too small for his big thick fingers; but she settled for putting it on the little finger, and as soon as the ceremony was concluded he slipped it off and handed it to the old man, who received it on a velvet cushion and bore it away into the depths of the house.

Then he returned, and with the utmost punctiliousness and grace ushered Annimae's father and aunts away to a cold collation in a room much nearer to the front door than seemed possible, after all the distance they had traveled coming in. Immediately after a glass of champagne and a sandwich apiece, the father and aunts were escorted to their carriages, again with such courtesy that they were halfway back to the ranch before they realized they'd been thrown out.

But Annimae was shown to a splendid dining room, all crystal. Though there were no windows in any of the walls, a domed skylight let in the sun. Mirrors lined every wall and shone inlaid from most other surfaces, so that a hundred thousand Annimaes looked back at her.

Mr. Hansen and the Reverend having been dismissed, she found herself seated at the far end of a table empty but for Mrs. Nightingale, who sat at the other end. The old man wheeled in a serving cart, deftly removed the silver epergne from the middle of the table so the two women could see each other, and served them luncheon.

Annimae racked her memory, desperately trying to recall what she had been taught about Light and Gracious Conversation Appropriate to Dining. Mrs. Nightingale, however, spoke first, shaking out her napkin. The faraway pounding of hammers counterpointed her words, never ceasing once during the ensuing conversation.

"I have something of importance to tell you, girl."

Annimae nearly said, "Yes, Ma'am," but recollected herself in time and replied instead: "Certainly, Mother Nightingale."

Mrs. Nightingale stared at her, and then said: "We labor under a curse. I do not use the term in a figurative sense. As you are now one of us, you will be affected. Attend carefully, Daughter-in-Law. Only in this room may we speak of it; for *they* are fascinated by their own reflections, and will pay us no mind."

"Yes, Mother Nightingale," Annimae replied, watching the old man as he ladled soup into her plate, but by neither wink nor smile did he indicate he was hearing anything in the least strange.

"Are you familiar with Spiritualism?" Mrs. Nightingale inquired.

"I—I don't believe so, no," Annimae replied.

"Well, it is simply founded on the discovery that it is possible to converse with the dead," said Mrs. Nightingale in a matter-of-fact way, tasting her soup. "The spirit world is quite real, and sages and ancient mystics have always been aware of it; but in these modern times its existence has at last been accepted by Science."

"I did not know that," said Annimae. "How interesting."

"The thing is," said Mrs. Nightingale, frowning, "that a great many credulous people think that those who have passed over to the other side are just naturally in possession of great truth, and wisdom, and benevolence toward all mankind. And, as anyone who has ever experienced a commonplace haunting knows, that is a lot of fool nonsense."

"Is it really?" said Annimae, cautiously buttering a roll.

"It is, girl. The dead in their ranks are exactly as they were in life. Some are wise and well-intentioned, but others are wicked. Wrathful. Spiteful, and inclined to remorseless persecution of the living," said Mrs. Nightingale sadly. "As I know to my cost, this many a weary year. You see, certain malignant entities are bent upon the destruction of all whom I love."

"Goodness, what a terrible thing," said Annimae.

"They hounded my late husband to an early grave. And both I, and my dear son, have been so fenced and crossed with subtle maledictions that, were we living in an ignorant age, I think we should have perished miserably long ago," said Mrs. Nightingale. "Fortunately, I do have friends in the spirit world, who were able to advise me; and so we are able to take protective measures."

"I am very glad to hear that, Mother Nightingale," said Annimae.

"For example," said Mrs. Nightingale, "I am cursed in such a way that I will die the very moment my feet come into contact with the earth. Dust blown in on the floor of the carriage does me no harm, apparently; but were I ever to step out into the garden, you would see me wither and expire before your eyes. And there are a host of lesser evils, but the wearing of colors with strong vibrational power—purple works the best, you see—helps to ward them off."

"How fascinating," said Annimae, who was running out of pleasant and noncommittal remarks.

"Alas, poor Daniel is not as fortunate," said Mrs. Nightingale. She set her hand on a locket about her neck. "When he was a baby, I despaired of saving his life. It has been only by the most extreme measures that I have preserved him."

So saying, she opened the locket and gazed for a moment on its contents, and for the first time her expression softened.

"I–is that a portrait of Daniel?" Annimae inquired.

Mrs. Nightingale closed the locket with a snap. Then, apparently thinking better of her gesture, she removed the locket and handed it to the old man.

"Sam, please pass this to my daughter-in-law."

The old man obliged, and after fumbling a moment with the clasp Annimae got the locket open. Within was an oval photographic portrait of a baby, perfect as a little angel, staring out at the camera with wide eyes. In the concavity of the lid was a single curl of fine golden hair, enclosed behind crystal.

"How beautiful!" said Annimae.

Mrs. Nightingale held out her hand for the locket. "That was taken before our troubled times," she said, slipping it back about her throat.

"And is Daniel's health very bad?" said Annimae anxiously.

"Why, no, girl; his health is now excellent," said Mrs. Nightingale. "And he owes his survival entirely to the prescription of my spirit friends. His curse is that he must hide from all eyes. To be seen by a living soul, or a dead one for that matter, would be fatal to the poor boy."

"But how does he do anything?" Annimae stammered.

"In utter darkness," said Mrs. Nightingale. "Unrelieved by any ray of light. I have had chambers built for him in the center of this house, without windows or doors, reached only by certain secret means. The wicked dead never find him, for the whole of the house is designed as a maze to confuse them. They are seduced by bright colors and ornamentation, and so they go round and round but never find the dark center."

"But . . . I was told he saw me, and fell in love with me," said Annimae pitifully.

"And so he did," said Mrs. Nightingale. "Did you think I could keep my boy in eternal darkness? No indeed; the good spirits told me that he might come and go by means of a ruse, though it must be only on moonless nights. He wraps himself in a black shroud, and climbs into a box made to resemble a coffin.

"When he signals, the servants carry it out to where I wait with the carriage. They load his coffin into the back; Sam drives us away; and the foolish dead never follow. Then Daniel climbs out and sits behind me, where he cannot be seen. He is greatly refreshed by the night air, and the chance to see something of the world."

"Oh! You drove past our house every night," exclaimed Annimae.

"So we did," said Mrs. Nightingale, looking grim. "And so he fell under the spell of an image glimpsed through a pane of glass, and would not rest until you became his bride. I must admit to you, Daughter-in-Law, that I was against it. Any disturbance of our domestic arrangements represents a peril to his life. But so taken was he with your beauty, that he threatened to destroy himself unless I spoke with your father. The rest you know."

And Annimae was flattered, and felt beautiful indeed, to have won a man's love at such cost. She warmed with compassion for him, too.

"I promise you, Mother Nightingale, I will be a faithful and loving wife to dear Daniel," she said.

"You will need to be more than that," said Mrs. Nightingale. "You will need to be a comrade-in-arms to *me*, Daughter-in-Law. We must wage a constant battle against the dead, if Daniel is to live." And she pressed her fingertips to her temples, as if in sudden pain.

"What must I do?"

"You will learn," said Mrs. Nightingale, a little distractedly. "Sam and Bridget will explain the arrangements. Oh, my migraine is returning; all these strangers in the house admitted malign influence, as I feared. Sam, I must retire to the thirteenth room. See to the girl."

So saying she rose, dropping her napkin, and walked straight to a wall. Annimae, watching in astonishment with spoon halfway to her mouth, thought her mother-in-law was about to collide with the mirrored surface; but at the last minute a panel opened and Mrs. Nightingale stepped through, to vanish as it slid smoothly into place behind her.

"How did she do that?" Annie exclaimed.

"It was a mechanism concealed in the floor, Ma'am," Sam told her, retrieving Mrs. Nightingale's napkin. "Triggered counterweights behind the paneling. There's secret passages all over this house! She designed them herself, you know. My mistress is a most ingenious lady."

"What happens now?" asked Annimae, looking about herself forlornly.

"Why, I'll serve you the rest of your luncheon, Ma'am," said Sam. "And then I'll just clear away the mistress' place, and take myself off to the kitchen. You want anything, you just ring."

"Please—" said Annimae, suddenly afraid to be left alone in this glittering room full of unseen presences. "Won't you stay and talk to me? I need to know things—" And she almost called him *boy*, but it did seem to her ridiculous, as august and white-haired as he was. And, mindful of his bent back, she added: "You can sit down while we speak, if you like. And you can have some dinner, too. I mean—luncheon!"

He smiled at her, and the white flash from his teeth winked in every mirrored surface in the room.

"Thank you, Ma'am, I surely will."

He served out filet of sole to her, then drew up a chair and helped himself to a cup of coffee. Settling back with a sigh, he explained the complex system by which the house ran.

On no account must any room ever be approached in the same way twice. There were a dozen different ways to reach any single destination in the house, and until she memorized them all, either he or another of the servants would guide her. There was no map, lest the dead see it and find their way where they weren't wanted; in any case no map would remain accurate for long, because rooms were continuously being remodeled in order to confuse the dead. Doors and windows were put in and taken out at the direction of the good spirits. Chambers were sealed off and reopened. Some doors opened on blank walls, or into space, even three stories up, so she must be careful; stairs might lead nowhere, or take a dozen turns and landings to go up only one floor.

"I never knew there were such things," said Annimae, feeling as though her head were spinning.

"Oh, folk have always protected themselves from haunts, Ma'am," said Sam, leaning over to serve her a slice of coconut pie. He took a slice of bread for himself. "Horseshoes over the door for good luck, eh? And the red thread, and the witchball, and the clover with the four leaves? They keep away all harm, so people say. Mistress just has the money to do it on a big scale, all modern and scientific, too."

"Scientific," Annimae repeated, impressed.

He looked at her a long moment, over his smoked spectacles.

"Don't you be afraid," he said at last. "Just you do like you been told, and it will all fall out pretty as any fairy tale. Romance and a happy ending, yes indeed."

"Can you tell me more about Daniel?" asked Annimae. "Is he handsome?"

Sam shrugged.

"I reckon he is, Ma'am. I haven't laid eyes on the master since he was a baby. But he has a beautiful voice, now. How he sings for love of you!"

"When may I go see—that is, when may I meet him?" Annimae set down her napkin. "Can you take me there now?"

Sam coughed slightly, and rose to his feet. "That would be my old woman's business, Ma'am. You wait; I'll send her."

He left the room, and Annimae shivered. She looked about and met her own timid gaze everywhere. For the first time, she noticed the motif that was repeated on the fine china, in the carpet pattern, in the mosaic arrangement of the mirrored bits and even in the panes of glass that made up the skylight: spiderwebs, perfect geometric cells radiating out from an empty center.

She scarce had time to contemplate the meaning of all this before a door opened and a woman all in black strode in briskly, upright though she, too, was very old. Her hair must have been red as fire when she'd been a girl, for a few strands of that color trailed still through the rest, which was white as smoke; and her eyes behind their dark spectacles were the hot blue of candle flames.

"I'm to take you to himself, now, Ma'am, am I?" she inquired, politely enough; but her eyes flashed dangerously when Annimae put her hands to her mouth in horror.

"*You're* Sam's wife? But—!"

The old woman looked scornful as she curtsied. "Bridget Lacroix. Bless you, Ma'am, you needn't be surprised. There's no scandal at all in me marrying Sam Lacroix. Don't you know how many of us Irish came to Ameri-kay as slaves? White chimpanzees, that's all we are; or so that fine Mr. Kingsley said. And if the mistress don't mind it, I'm sure you shouldn't."

"I am so sorry!" said Annimae, much distressed. "I never meant offense."

Bridget looked her over shrewdly. "No, I don't suppose you did. Sam told me you was innocent as a little baby. But it's time you grew up, me dear." She grinned. "Especially as it's your wedding day."

She led Annimae out of the dining room and through another, where jets of flame burned brilliantly in wall-mounted glass globes. The globes were all colors, hung with prisms that threw swaying rainbows everywhere. And there were more windows set in the walls, stained glass repeating the spiderweb pattern Annimae had noticed before. They, too, were lit from behind by the strange cold light she had wondered at in the chapel. Annimae, who had only ever seen candles and kerosene lamps after dark, exclaimed:

"What is this place?"

"Oh, this is just the Room of Eternal Day," said Bridget. "The dead don't like passing through a place so bright, and it shows up that they haven't any shadows besides, and that embarrasses 'em, don't you know. All very up-to-date in here! That's gaslight, of course, but for the windows she's laid on that new electrical light. Clever, isn't it?"

They went on through that room, and came to another that was lined floor to ceiling with clocks, and nothing else. Great inlaid grandfather clocks stood in the corners and ticked solemnly; French bisque clocks sat on shelves and ticked elegantly, as painted Harlequins and Columbines revolved atop them; old wooden regulator clocks thumped along wearily; and little cheap brass clocks beat away the seconds brightly. But no two clocks were set to the same time.

"How strange!" cried Annimae, and Bridget chuckled and said:

"Oh, this is the Room of All Time and None. It's just to confound the dead. They work very particular shifts, what with midnight being the witching hour and all. If one of 'em strays in to see what o'clock it is, he'll be stuck here guessing with all his might and main."

They left that room and soon came to another, no less curious. There was no spiderweb motif here; rather the recurring image was of a tiny white moth or butterfly, but it was repeated everywhere. It figured in the wallpaper pattern like so many snowflakes, it was woven into the design of the carpet, and into the brocade of the chairs and the inlay of the tables and cabinets, and etched into the very window glass. The curio cabinets held nothing but pressed specimens of white moths, displayed against a blue velvet background.

"What on earth are all these butterflies for?" asked Annimae.

"Oh, it's only the Soul Trap," said Bridget. "Because, you see, the nasty dead are a bit stupid, and they have a compulsion to count things. Any haunt comes through here, here he must stay until he's numbered every blessed one of the little creatures. Generally by then the ghost will have forgot whatever wickedness he was up to."

"What a good idea," said Annimae, because she could not imagine what else to say.

They proceeded deeper into the house, and as they did it grew dimmer and dimmer, for there were no windows nor light fixtures here, and the corridors turned and turned again ever inward. At last Bridget was only a shadow beside her, that cleared its throat and said:

"Now then, Sam told me you might want a little learning. You know, don't you, what it is a bride does with her husband?"

"Well," said Annimae, "As nearly as I recollect, we're supposed to fall on each other with kisses of passion."

"Hm. Yes, me dear, that's how it starts."

As far as Annimae had been aware, there was nothing more; and in some panic, she racked her brains for what else happened in books and poems.

"I believe that then I'm supposed to swoon away in a transport of love," she said.

"So you must," said Bridget, sounding exasperated. "But there's a great deal goes on between the kissing and swooning, sure. Think of what the stallion does with the mare."

"Oh," said Annimae, who had seen *that* many a time. She walked on in thoughtful silence, drawing certain conclusions, so intent that she scarcely noticed when it became pitch-dark at last. Bridget had to take her hand and lead her through the fathomless gloom.

Soon they heard glorious music, close by but muffled. Someone was playing a Spanish guitar with great virtuosity, each note chiming like a bell even through the wall's thickness.

"Why, who's that?" asked Annimae.

"Oh, the jewel, the darling! He's serenading his bride," Bridget exclaimed with great tenderness. There was a sound suggesting that she had put out her hand and was sliding it along the wall as they walked. Presently she stopped, and rapped twice.

The music halted at once. An eager voice said:

"Annimae?"

"She's here, charming boy," said Bridget. "Hurry now, while it's safe."

There was a click, and then a rush of air that smelled of gentlemen's cologne. Annimae felt herself prodded gently forward, closer to the scent, into a warmer darkness. Something clicked again, behind her now. She fought back a moment of wild terror, realizing she had been locked in; but at once warm hands took her own, and they felt so live and steady that her fear melted away. She touched the wedding ring on his finger.

"I'm here, Daniel Nightingale," she said. "Your own true love—"

"Oh, my own Annimae," said the new voice, breaking on a hoarse sob. And Annimae, feeling brave now, leaned forward in the darkness and sought her husband's lips. She encountered his chin instead, for he was a little taller than she was. He bent to her and they kissed, and the kiss was nicer than anything Annimae had ever known in her whole life. The face of the baby angel in the locket came before her mind's eye; in the table of her thoughts it grew, became the face of a handsome man.

She had compiled a list of rapturous phrases to murmur in his ear, but somehow she couldn't stop kissing, nor could he. Their arms went around each other, they grappled and swayed. Annimae felt once again the dizzy happiness she had known high up in the cottonwood tree, when she seemed about to lift free of the dry earth and soar away, into a green paradise.

The whole time, her young fingers were exploring, touching, tracing out the strange new shape of a man. Such broad shoulders, under his linen shirt! And such smooth skin! Such fine regular features! His hands were exploring too, feverish and fast, and fever woke in her own blood. She thought about mares and stallions. He lifted his mouth from hers and gasped,

"Please, let's lie on the bed—" and she was making sounds of agreement, though she hadn't any idea where his bed or anything else in the room might be. He half-carried her a few yards, and they collapsed together on what must be the counterpane. She understood what he wanted and, remarkably quickly considering how much effort and care had gone into putting on her wedding dress, she writhed out of it.

Then the smooth counterpane was cool under her and he embraced her so close, and, and, and . . .

Long afterward she recollected the rapturous phrases, and duly murmured them in his ear. Now, however, she knew what they meant.

Now she believed them.

★★

So began Annimae's married life. She was as happy as any new bride in any of her books, even with the strange constraints upon her life. There was no question that she loved Daniel Nightingale with her whole heart, and that he loved her.

"You were the most beautiful thing I'd ever seen in all my life," he sighed, as they lay close together in the dark. "The window shining out across the darkness, and you framed there bright as an angel. I loved you so! You were the very image of everything I'd ever wanted, in the life I'd never be allowed to live. And I thought, I *will* live it! I will marry that girl!"

"Your mamma said you threatened to die for love of me," said Annimae.

"I would have," he said, with a trace of sullenness. "Just opened that door and walked out through the house, and I'd have kept walking until I found the sunlight."

"Oh, but that would be a terrible thing!" said Annimae. "With so many folks who love you? You mustn't ever do it, my dearest."

"I never will, now that you're here," he conceded, and kissed her.

"And after all," she said, "It's not really so awfully bad, like this. You're no worse off than a blind man would be. Much better, really! You needn't beg for your dinner on a street corner, like poor old Mr. Johnson in town. Instead you're my handsome prince, under a spell. And, who knows? Maybe someday we'll find a way to break the spell."

"If only there were a way!" he said. Then, hesitantly, he asked: "Do you think my mother is crazy?"

"Well, I did wonder at first," she admitted. "But I guess she isn't. Spiritualism is a big religion, I hear, and they wouldn't let all those people run around loose if they were crazy, would they? And everything in the house is so modern and scientifical!"

He sighed, and said he guessed she was right.

Their days began around ten o'clock in the morning, when a gentle rap at the panel signified that Sam had brought a wheeled cart with their breakfasts. Annimae would scramble through the heavy velvet curtains that cloaked the bed—only there in case of emergency, for the room was black as ink at all hours—and, finding her dressing gown by touch, slip it on and open the secret panel. Sam would enter along with Gideon, who was Sam's son and Daniel's valet. She became quite skilled at pouring coffee and buttering toast in the dark, as Daniel was shaved and dressed sight unseen, and Sam made the bed and collected their linen, all by touch alone.

The four of them often conversed pleasantly together, for Gideon would bring the news culled from the morning's *Mercury*, and Daniel was eager to hear what was going on in the world. They might have been ordinary people in an ordinary household, Annimae thought; and the reassuring domestic details comforted her, and further convinced her that her life wasn't so strange, after all.

After breakfast she would leave Daniel's suite for a little while, to take the sun. It appeared painfully bright to her now; she saw why all the servants wore smoked spectacles, and begged a pair of her own from Bridget. Then she could wander the gardens, feeding the fish in the reflecting pools, admiring the exotic flowers, picking fruit from the bushes and trees. She brought back bouquets of roses for Daniel, or apron-pockets full of blackberries warm from the sun.

She seldom met the gardeners, the twins Godfrey and Godwin, who were also Sam's sons. Most of the servants had adjusted to a nocturnal schedule over the years, for the mistress of the house kept late hours, too. Annimae did wander out now and then to the perimeters of the house, where the workmen were always busy hammering, sawing, extending the vast and gorgeous edifice with raw new redwood that still smelled of the wilderness. They were always too busy to speak, though they doffed their caps to her, blushing.

Sensing that she made them uncomfortable, Annimae stopped coming by to watch their progress. The house would never be finished anyway; and after a week or so her heart beat to the rhythm of the ceaseless hammers. It was a comforting sound. It meant that Daniel was safe, and all was right with the world.

After her morning walks, she was summoned to luncheon with Mrs. Nightingale, which was like having an audience with a gloomy and severe queen. Mrs. Nightingale questioned her in great detail on Daniel's continuing health, though she refrained from asking about the most intimate matters.

"Daniel *seems* to be thriving with your companionship," was the closest she came to a compliment. "Though the good spirits are still concerned for him. You must not grow careless, Daughter-in-Law."

"I do assure you, Mother Nightingale, his life is as precious to me as it must be to you," said Annimae. Mrs. Nightingale regarded her in a chilly kind of way, and then winced and shut her eyes.

"Is it your headache again?" Annimae inquired in sympathy. "Perhaps it's the sun, don't you think? I am sure you would be much more comfortable if you wore dark spectacles, too."

"They are not for me," replied Mrs. Nightingale, getting stiffly to her feet. "I gaze into a far brighter light than mortal eyes can imagine, when I commune with the spirits. You'll excuse me, now. I am wanted in the thirteenth room."

So saying, she walked through a wall and vanished.

Annimae went also to the mansion's library each day, once she learned the various routes to get there. It was not really such a big room, relative to the rest of the house. It contained a Bible, and the collected works of Shakespeare, though neither one seemed to have been read much. There were several volumes of fairy stories, for Mrs. Nightingale had used to sit in the corridor outside Daniel's room and read to him, when he had been small. There were many, many other books, principally by one Andrew Jackson Davis, and both they and the books by Emanuel Swedenborg had pride of place, though there were others by a Countess Blavatsky.

These all treated of the mystical world. Annimae made it a point to sit and read a chapter from one of them each day, in order that she might better understand her husband's plight. She tried very hard to make sense of esoteric wisdom, but it bewildered her.

All the books claimed a great universal truth, simple and pure, revealed by spirit messengers from Almighty God; yet its proponents contradicted one another, sometimes angrily, and not one seemed to be able to state convincingly what the truth *was*. Every time Annimae thought she was coming to a revelation, so that her heart beat faster and she turned the pages eagerly, the promised answers failed to materialize. The great mysteries remained impenetrable.

So with a sigh she would leave the books, and find a way back through the black labyrinth at the house's heart. The deeper the shadows grew, the lighter was her step dancing home to her beloved. And what great truth was there, after all, but that it was sweet delight to pull off all her clothes and leap into bed with Daniel Nightingale?

And when they'd tumbled, when they'd had so much fun they were tired, Daniel would lie beside her and beg her to relate everything she'd seen that day. It was difficult to tell him of the glories of the garden, for he knew very little of colors. Black and purple, midnight blue and the shades of stars or windows were all he could summon to his mind. Red and pink to him were smells, or tastes.

But she could tell him about the swallows that made their nests under the eaves of the carriage house, queer daubed things like clay jars stuck up there, with the little sharp faces peering out; she could tell him about the squirrel that had tried to climb the monkey-puzzle tree. He wanted to know everything, was hungry for the least detail.

Afterward they would rise in the dark, answerable to no sun or moon, and find their way together into the splendid bathroom, as magnificent in its appointments as any Roman chamber. The spirits had devised ingenious systems to heat the room with jets of warmed air, piped in from below, and to fill the marble tub with torrents of hot water from a spigot. There were silver vessels of scent for the water; there was scented oil, too.

When they had luxuriated together they returned to the central room, where Daniel played the guitar for her, as she sprawled in bed with him. And it seemed to Annimae this must be just the way princes and princesses had lived long ago, perhaps even in the days of the Bible: young flesh oiled and perfumed, a silken nest and endless easeful night in which to make sweet music.

It never occurred to her to wonder what the future might hold. Daniel raged against his confinement, and she comforted him, as she felt it was her duty to do. Sometimes they discussed ways in which he might gain more freedom, in the years to come: perhaps a portable room, or even a suit of leather and canvas like a deep-sea diver's, with a sealed helmet fronted in smoked glass? Perhaps Daniel might walk in the sunlight. Perhaps he might go to Europe and see all the sights to be seen. Whatever he did, Annimae knew she would always be there beside him; for that was how true lovers behaved, in all the stories in the wide world.

There was no fear in the dark for Annimae, now, ever. Only one thing still made her startle, when it woke her twice each night: the tolling of a vast deep-throated bell somewhere high in the house. Mrs. Nightingale had it struck at midnight, for that was the hour when the good spirits arrived. Mrs. Nightingale, having retired to the thirteenth room and donned one of thirteen ceremonial robes, would commune there with the spirits for two hours, receiving their advice and instruction. At two o'clock the bell would toll again, and the spirits would depart.

"And then she comes out with a great sheaf of blueprints for the carpenters, you know," said Bridget, sprinkling starch on one of Daniel's shirts and passing it to her daughter, who ironed it briskly. "And whether it's orders to tear out an old room or start a new one, they set to smartly, you may be sure."

"Don't they ever get tired of it?" asked Annimae, gazing about the handsomely appointed washroom—so many modern conveniences!—in wonder. Bridget and Gardenia exchanged amused glances.

"They're paid in gold, Ma'am," Gardenia explained. "And at twice the wage they'd be earning from anybody else. You can bet they just go home at night and fall on their knees to pray old Mrs. Nightingale never finishes her house!"

"Why is it called the thirteenth room?" Annimae asked.

"To confuse the spirits, Ma'am," replied Gardenia. "It's the seventeenth along that corridor, if you count."

"Why does Mother Nightingale spend so much time there?"

"It's by way of being her house of mysteries, isn't it?" said Bridget, sorting through the linen hamper. "Her command post, if you like, where she plans the battle against the wicked dead every night. There's strange things goes on in there! Chanting all hours, and flashes of light, and sometimes screams to freeze the blood in you! She's a brave lady, the mistress. All for our Danny's sake, just to keep his dear heart beating."

"I'm afraid he gets a little restless now and then," said Annimae uncomfortably. "He says that sometimes he doubts that there's any spirits at all."

The mother and daughter were silent a moment, going about their tasks.

"Poor boy," said Bridget at last. "It's to be expected, with him growing up the way he has. Seeing is believing, sure, and he's never seen danger."

"Do *you* believe in the spirits?" Annimae asked.

"Oh, yes, Ma'am," said Gardenia quietly. "Without a doubt."

So the brief bright days blinked past, like images on nickel-odeon screens, and the long fevered nights passed in lazy ecstasy. The last of the summer fruit was garnered away in the vast cellars, with Bridget and her daughters carrying down tray after tray of glass jars full of preserves. The orchards were golden. When the leaves began to fall, Godfrey and Godwin raked great red-and-yellow heaps that were set to smolder in the twilight, like incense.

There came an evening when Annimae was awakened at midnight, as she always was, by the summoning bell. Yet as its last reverberation died away, no customary calm flowed back like black water; instead there came a drumming, ten times louder than the desultory beat of hammers, a thundering music, and faint voices raised in song.

As she lay wondering why anyone would be drumming at this hour of the night, she felt Daniel sit up beside her.

"Listen!" he said eagerly. "Don't you hear? They're dancing!"

"Is that all it is?" said Annimae, a little cross. The sound frightened her for some reason.

"It's their holiday. We must go watch," said Daniel, and she felt him getting out of bed.

"We mustn't!" she cried. "It's not safe for you, honey."

"Oh, there's a safe way," he said, sounding sly. She heard him open a cabinet and take something from a hanger. "I go watch them every year. This year will be the best of all, because you're with me now. Don't be afraid, my darling."

She heard him walk around to her side of the bed. "Now, get up and come with me. I've put my shroud on, and I'll walk behind you all the way; and no one will see us, where we're going."

So she slid from the bed and reached out, encountering a drape of gauze cloth. His hand came up through it and took hers reassuringly, tugged her impatiently to the secret panel. So quickly they left the room that she had no time to pull on even a stitch, and she blushed hot to find herself out in the corridor naked. Yet it was a hot night, and in any case much too dark to be seen.

"Fifty paces straight ahead, Annimae, and then turn left," Daniel told her.

"Left? But I've never gone that way," said Annimae.

"It's all right," Daniel said, so for love's sake she followed his direction. She walked before him the whole way, though she kept tight hold of his hand through the shroud. Left and right and right again he directed her, through so many turns and up and down so many stairs she knew she'd never find her way back alone, even when they reached a place with windows where milky starlight glimmered through. The house was silent, the corridors all deserted. The drumming, however, grew louder, and the clapping and chanting more distinct.

"This is the earliest thing I can remember," Annimae heard Daniel say. "I woke up in the dark and was scared, and I tried to get out. How I stumbled over everything, in my shroud! I must have found the catch in the panel by accident, because the next thing I knew, there was the corridor stretching out ahead of me. It seemed as bright as stars, then. I followed after the music, just as we're doing now. And, look! This is the window I found."

They had come around a corner and entered a narrow passage ending in a wall, wherein was set one little window in the shape of a keyhole. Daniel urged her toward it, pushing gently. She could see something bright flickering, reflecting from below along the beveled edges of the glass.

"My true love, I do believe somebody's lit a fire outside," said Annimae.

"Yes! Don't be afraid. Look out, and I'll look over your shoulder," said Daniel.

So Annimae bent and put her face to the glass, and peered down into a courtyard she had never before seen. There was indeed a fire, a bright bonfire in the center, with a column of smoke rising from it like a ghostly tree. Gathered all around it, swaying and writhing and tossing their heads, were all the servants. Godfrey and Godwin sat to one side, pounding out the beat of the dance on drums, and all their brothers and sisters kept time with their clapping hands, with their stamping feet. They were singing in a language Annimae had never heard, wild, joyful. Now and again someone would catch up an armful of autumn leaves and fling them on the blaze, and the column of smoke churned and seemed to grow solid for a moment.

The beat was infectious, enchanting. It roused desires in Annimae, and for the first time she felt shame and confusion. *This* was neither in fairy tales nor in the Bible. It did not seem right to feel her body moving so, almost against her will. Daniel, pressing hot behind her, was moving, too.

"Oh, how I stared and stared," said Daniel. "And how I wanted to be down there with them! They never have to live in fear, as I do. They can dance in the light. How can I dance, in a shroud like this? Oh, Annimae, I want so badly to be free! Watch now, watch what happens."

Annimae saw Gardenia filling her apron with leaves, to pitch a bushel of them on the fire. The flames dimmed momentarily, and when they roared up again she saw that two new dancers had joined the party.

Who was that black man, bigger than all the rest, waving his carved walking stick? How well he danced! The others fell back to the edges and he strutted, twirled, undulated around the fire. Now he was sinuous as a great snake, powerful as a river; now he was comic and suggestive. Annimae blushed to see him thrust his stick between his legs and rock his hips, and the stick rose up, and up, and he waved and waggled in it such a lewd way there were screams of laughter from the crowd. Even Daniel, behind her, chuckled.

Shocked as she was by that, Annimae was astounded to see a white girl down there at the edge of the fire, joining the black man in his dance. Who could she be? What kind of hoydenish creature would pull her skirt up like that and leap over the fire itself? Her hair was as bright as the flame, her face was fierce, her deportment mad as though she had never, ever had elderly aunts to tell her what ladies mustn't do. Oh! Now she had seized a bottle from one of the onlookers, and was drinking from it recklessly; now she spat, she sprayed liquor into the fire, and when the others all applauded she turned and sprayed them, too.

Then the black man had slipped his arm around her. He pulled her in and the pace of the dance quickened. Round and round they went, orbiting the fire and each other, and the drumming of their heels drove Annimae almost to guilty frenzy. Rough and tender and insistent, the music pulsed. As she stared, she felt Daniel's hands move over her, and even through the shroud his touch drove her mad. She backed to him like a mare. He rose up like a stallion.

"You're my fire, Annimae," moaned Daniel. "You're my music, you're my dance. You're my eyes in the sunlight and my fever in the dark. We *will* escape this house, someday, my soul!"

It was all Annimae could do to cling to the windowsill, sobbing in pleasure and shame, and the drumbeats never slowed. . . .

Though they did cease, much later. Annimae and Daniel made their unsteady way back through the black labyrinth, and slept very late the next day.

The next afternoon, Gardenia came to Annimae as she walked in the garden and said: "If you please, Ma'am, there's two old ladies come to call on you."

Annimae went at once inside, back through chambers she hadn't entered in months, out to the front of the house. There in a front parlor alarmingly full of the cold light of day sat Great-Aunt Merrion and Aunt Pugh, inspecting the underside of a vase through a pair of lorgnettes.

"Why, child, how pale you are!" cried Aunt Pugh, as Annimae kissed her cheek.

"How you do peer out of those spectacles, child!" said Great-Aunt Merrion, giving her a good long stare through her lorgnette. "Far too much reading in sickrooms, I'll wager. Wifely duty is all very well, but you must think of yourself now and then."

Annimae apologized for being pale, explaining that she had a headache, and wore the glasses against brightness. She bid Gardenia bring coffee for three, and poured as gracefully as she could when it came, though she still spilled a little.

The aunts graciously overlooked this and told her all the news from the almond ranch. Her father's investments had suddenly prospered, it seemed; the mortgages were all paid off, the servants all hired on again. Her father had once more the means to dress as a gentleman, and had bought a fine stable of racehorses. Why, they themselves had come to visit Annimae in a grand new coach-and-four! And all the merchants in town were once again respectful, deferential, as they ought always to have been to ladies of gentle birth.

But Great-Aunt Merrion and Aunt Pugh had heard certain loose talk in town, it seemed; and so they had known it was their duty to call on Annimae, and to inquire after her health and well-being.

They asked all manner of questions about Annimae's daily life, which Annimae fended off as best she might, for she knew it was dangerous to speak much of Daniel. Detecting this, the old ladies looked sidelong at each other and fell to a kind of indirect questioning that had never failed to produce results before.

Annimae was tired, she was still a little shaken and, perhaps, frightened by the violent delight of the previous evening. Her aunts, when all was said and done, had known her all her life. Somehow she let slip certain details, and the aunts pressed her for explanations, and so—

"Do you tell me you've never so much as *seen* your husband, child?" said Aunt Pugh, clutching at her heart.

"Good God Almighty!" Great-Aunt Merrion shook with horror. "Miss Pugh, do you recollect what that Mrs. Delano said outside the milliner's?"

Aunt Pugh recollected, and promptly fainted dead away.

Annimae, terrified, would have rung for a servant at once; but Great-Aunt Merrion shot out a lace-mittened fist and caught her hand.

"Don't you ring for one of *them*," she whispered. She got up and closed the parlor door; then produced a vial of smelling salts from her handbag. Aunt Pugh came around remarkably quickly, and sat bolt upright.

"Child, we must break your heart, but it is for your own sake," said Great-Aunt Merrion, leaning forward. "I fear you have been obscenely deceived."

She proceeded to relate what a Mrs. Delano had told her, which was: that she had a cousin who had known Mrs. Nightingale in

Louisiana right after the Waw, when all her cares were first beset-
ting her. This cousin, who had an excellent memory, was pretty
sure that Mrs. Nightingale's baby had not merely been sick, it had
in fact died. Moreover, there were stories that Mrs. Nightingale
was much too familiar with her household staff, especially her
coachman.

"If you know what I mean," Great-Aunt Merrion added.

Annimae protested tearfully, and gave her aunts many examples
of Daniel's liveliness. Aunt Pugh wept like a spigot, rocking to and
fro and moaning about the shame of it all, until Great-Aunt Merrion told her to cease acting like a fool.

"Now, you listen to me, child," she said to Annimae. "There's
only one reason that woman would concoct such a cock-and-bull
story. I'll tell you why you can't look on the face of that son of
hers! *He is a mulatto.*"

"That's not true!" said Annimae. "I saw his baby picture."

"You saw a picture of the baby that died, I expect," said Aunt
Pugh, blowing her nose. "Oh, Annimae!"

"There used to be plenty of old families got themselves a little
foundling to replace a dead boy, when the estate was entailed," said
Great-Aunt Merrion. "So long as there was a male heir, decent
folk held their tongues about it. Money kept the nursemaids from
telling the truth.

"Well, hasn't she plenty of money? And didn't she move clear
out here to the West so there'd be nobody around who knew the
truth? And who'll see the color of her sin, if he's kept out of sight?"

"What's his hair like, child? Oh, Annimae, how you have been
fooled!" said Aunt Pugh.

"Likely enough he's her *son*," sneered Great-Aunt Merrion.
"But he's not the one who ought to have inherited."

Annimae was so horrified and angry she nearly stood up to her
aunts, and as it was she told them they had better leave. The old
women rose up to go; but Great-Aunt Merrion got in a parting
shot.

"Ghosts and goblins, my foot," she said. "If you're not a fool,
child, you'll sneak a penny candle and a match into that bedroom,

next time you go in there. Just you get yourself a good look at that Daniel Nightingale, once he's asleep. You'd better be sure than be a lasting disgrace to your father."

Annimae fled to the darkness to weep, that none might see her. Two hours she fought with her heart. All the fond embraces, all the words of love, all the undoubted wisdom of the Spiritualists and her own wedding vows were on her heart's side. But the little quailing child who lived within her breast too thought of the aunts' grim faces as they had spoken, backed up by the dead certainties of all grandmothers and aunts from the beginning of time.

In the end she decided that their dark suspicions were utterly base and unfounded. But she would slip a candle and a match in her apron pocket, all the same, so as to prove them wrong.

And when she came in to Daniel at last, when his glad voice greeted her and his warm hands reached out, she knew her heart was right, and silenced all doubt. Sam came in and served them supper, and she listened and compared the two voices, straining for any similarity of accent. Surely there was none!

And when the supper dishes had been taken away and Daniel took her in his arms and kissed her, she ran her hands through his thick hair. Surely it was golden!

And when they lay together in bed, there was none of the drum-driven madness of the night before, no animal hunger; only Daniel gentle and chivalrous, sane and reasonable, teasing her about what they'd do when he could go to Paris or Rome at last. Surely he was a gentleman!

But she had slipped the candle and the match under her pillow, and they lay there like wise serpents, who wheedled: *Wouldn't you like just a glimpse of his face?*

At last, when he had fallen asleep and lay dreaming beside her, she reached under the pillow and brought out the match. No need to light the candle, she had decided; all she wanted was one look at his dear face. One look only, in a flash no evil ghost would have time to notice. And who would dare harm her darling, if she lay beside him to keep him safe? One look only, to bear in her mind down all the long years they'd have together, one tiny secret for her to keep like a pressed flower. . . .

Annimae touched his face, ran her fingers over his stubbly cheek, and set her hand on his brow to shade his eyes from the light. He sighed and murmured something in his sleep. With her other hand, she reached up and struck the match against the bedpost.

The light bloomed yellow.

Daniel was not there. Nobody was there. Annimae was alone in the bed.

Unbelieving, she felt with her hand that had been touching his cheek, his brow, that very second. There was nothing there.

That was when Annimae dropped the match, and the room was gone in darkness, and she could feel her throat contracting for a scream. But there was a high shriek beginning already, an inhuman whine as though the whole room were lamenting, and that was Daniel's voice rising now in a wail of grief, somewhere far above, as though he were being pulled away from her, receding and receding through the darkness.

"ANNIMAE!"

The bed began to shudder. The room itself, the very house began to shake. She heard a ringing impact from the bathroom, as the silver pitchers were thrown to the tiled floor. The table by the bed fell with a crash. A rending crack, a boom, the sound of plaster falling; a rectangle full of hectic blue-white light, and she realized that the secret panel had been forced open.

Annimae's mind, numb-shocked as it was, registered *Earthquake* with a certain calm. She grabbed her robe and fled over the tilting floor, squeezed through the doorway and ran down the long corridor. Tiny globes of ball lightning crackled, spat, skittered before her, lighting her way at least. But she could see the walls cracking, too, she could see the plaster dropping away and the bare laths. The carpet flexed under her feet like an animal's back. The shaking would not stop.

She rounded a corner and saw Mrs. Nightingale flying toward her, hair streaming back and disheveled, hands out as though to claw the slow air. Her face was like a Greek mask of horror and rage, her mouth wide in a cry that Annimae could not hear over the roar of the falling house. She sped past Annimae without so much as a glance, vanishing in the direction of Daniel's rooms.

Annimae ran on, half-falling down a flight of stairs that was beginning to fold up even as she reached the bottom, and then there was a noise louder than any she'd heard yet, loud as an explosion, louder than the cannons must have been at Gettysburg. To her left there was an avalanche of bricks, mortar, splinters and wire, as a tower came down through three floors and carried all before it. It knocked out a wall and Annimae saw flowers glimmering pale through the plaster-dust, and dim stars above them.

She staggered forth into the night and fled, sobbing now, for her heart was beginning to go like the house. On bleeding feet she ran; when she could run no farther she fell, and lay still, and wept and knew there was no possible consolation.

Some while later Annimae raised her head, and saw that the sky was just beginning to get light in the east. She looked around. She was lying in a drift of yellow leaves. All around her were the black trunks and arching branches of the orchard, in a silence so profound she might have gone deaf. Turning her head uncertainly, looking for the house, she saw them coming for her.

A throng of shadows, empty-eyed but not expressionless, and at their head walked the dancers from the fire: the black man with his stick, the red-headed hoyden. Beyond them, dust still rising against the dawn, was the nightmare mountain of rubble that had been the home of true love.

Annimae lay whimpering at their approach. With each step they took the figures altered, changed, aged. They became Sam and Bridget Lacroix. The sullen shades in their train began to mutter threateningly, seemed about to surge forward at Annimae; but Sam stopped, and raised his cane in a gesture that halted them. His sad stern face seemed chiseled from black stone.

"Shame on you, girl," he said. "Love and Suspicion can't live together in the same house, no matter how many rooms it has."

Annimae scrambled to her feet and ran again. They did not follow her.

She forgot who she was, or why she was traveling, and she had no destination in mind. By day she huddled in barns or empty sheds, for the sunlight hurt her eyes unbearably. By night she walked on, ducking out of sight when a horseman or a carriage would come along her road. For some days she wandered up a bay shore, following the tideline. The mud felt cool on her cut feet.

At length she came to a great city, that whirred and clattered and towered to the sky. She regarded it in wonder, hiding among the reeds until nightfall, hoping to pass through in the dark. Alas! It was lit bright even after midnight. Annimae edged as close as she dared, creeping through the shadows, and then turned to stare; for she found herself outside a lovely garden, planted all in roses, shaded by high dark cypresses, and the wrought-iron gate was unlocked. It seemed as though it would be a comforting place to rest.

She slipped in, and stretched out on one of the cool white marble beds. Angels mourned, all around her.

When the pastor at Mission Dolores found her, she was unable to speak. He had his housekeeper feed her, bathe her, and tend to her feet; he sent out inquiries. No one came forward to claim Annimae, however, and the sisters at the Sacred Heart Convent agreed to take her in.

In the peace, in the silence punctuated only by matins and evensong, gently bullied by well-meaning maternal women, still she remained mute; but her memory, if not her voice, began to come back to her. There was still too much horror and confusion to absorb, though one fact rose clear and bleak above the rest: she had lost her true love.

He had been dead. He had been imaginary. He had been real, but she had betrayed him. She would never hear his voice again.

She would be alone the rest of her life.

And it seemed a grimly appropriate fate that she should come full circle to end up here, a child in a house full of aunts, confined to the nursery where she clearly belonged, having failed so badly at being a grown woman. Perhaps she would take the veil, though she had always been told to distrust Catholics as minions of the Pope. Perhaps she would take Jesus as her new husband.

But one morning Annimae woke to a welling nausea, and barely made it to the little bathroom at the end of the dormitory hall before vomiting. Afterward, she bolted the door, and ran water for a bath.

Stepping into the water, she caught a glimpse of herself in the mirror.

She stared, and stared unbelieving at her swollen body.

Nightmare Mountain
by JANIS IAN

Wish you would have told me
what was wrong with you
Made mountains out of valleys
and took away the view
Wish you would have told me
Told me there and then
I never would have done it if I knew
it meant losing you

So many dreams forgotten
in the twinkling of an eye
Dreams of unborn children
used to glitter in our sky
Now there's only Nightmare Mountain
grown too high to climb
Never would have done it if I'd known
that it meant losing home

There's lots of other chances
now that I've got lots of time
to search out these romances
that once occupied my mind

I wish you would have told me
before this mountain grew
I never would have built it if I knew
that it meant losing you
It meant losing you

On the Edge

by GREGORY BENFORD

In the summer of our youth . . .
We were gonna make the whole world honest
—from "Guess You Had to Be There" by Janis Ian

L ENIN is working night shift, but not for extra pay. He's a sala-ried supervisor and can't get overtime. Mostly he needs some-thing to do.

The restlessness won't go away. He ducks a personnel issue and slips into his eighth floor office. His thirtieth birthday is coming up soon, and it's riding at the back of his mind. At least, he thinks that's what's bothering him. He turns out the lights so he can watch the silvery sprawl of Greater L.A. stretching into the dis-tance like some kind of electrical cancer.

He has been thinking about the Revolution a lot lately and somehow this neon consumer gumbo going on forever is at the heart of his terror, but he does not quite know why. So he presses his balding forehead against the cold windowpane and looks at the endless twinkling glitter in the cool spring night. Abstractly, he wonders if this bland mall splendor will stand eternally. And on what foundation? Time and a half for overtime? Even he doesn't believe it, even if the workers under him are benefiting from the boom in business that seems like it will go on forever.

Babes in Blandland, he thinks, but it's easier to come up with a quick put-down than to frame an idea, and he knows it.

The cleaning lady comes in. A little early, she explains, because her son is sick and she has to get home. Stooped, weary, her Latino face manages a creased smile. Lenin feels a red rage at the very sight of her sad, suffering eyes. He gives her a twenty.

The infinite city still looms outside. He picks up the phone and calls his ex, but she has blocked his number. It has been two years since the divorce but he still harbors some dusty hope that it could all work out right after all. Months ago she had told him to move on. But to what?

★★

Washington is on his way home when his damn cell phone rings. He reaches to answer, stops.

Probably it's a headhunter trying to interest him in coming aboard some hot new company. Word has already spread that he turned around his present firm, HighUpTech, big time. It's going on the AMEX next week with a net value over one-fifty mil when the starting gun goes off. Not bad for just two years of ruthless trimming, innovative product design, and some poker-faced cunning.

Does he want to do that number again? He lets the phone ring.

He leaves the 405 for the run uphill into Palos Verdes and stops for a light. A woman standing on the center divider is selling flowers. Her gaudy spring blossoms are well arranged. He hands her a twenty and waves off the change. She is in the usual dingy uniform of jeans and a rough man's shirt and smiles at him, her hair an oily tangle. He wonders how many wrong turns she had to make to get this far down.

When he gets home, his wife loves the flowers. Her obvious surprise reminds him that he's been distracted a lot lately, not paying attention to the personal basics. She hands him a chilled Esplanade glass filled with his favorite Sauvignon Blanc. He prefers that now to a Chardonnay. Starting to feel the acid in the stomach, maybe a sign of age? But he's only 31. He throws some honey-roasted almonds into his mouth and goes out onto the deck to take in the diamond-sprinkled avenues pointing away toward the Holly-wood Hills.

Somehow he no longer finds this view impressive. *Great wealth, but where's it going?*

His wife comes out to him, slips an arm around his waist, and he says something suddenly about how *big* the city is and what the hell it's all about. He has surprised himself and before he can figure out what he meant she kisses him meaningfully and he thinks about bed. Bucks in the day, bed at night, maybe catch some basketball in between the two on the digital cable. He tries to think if there's anything else, maybe something that starts with a B.

★★★

Goldman arrives early to meet the Trotsky guy. She likes the place. It's a homey clapboard coffee place on the beach, but the coffee's strictly chain knockoff product. At least it's cheaper than the spotless places the chain usually throws up, and here you can read the newspapers as long as you like without ordering another drink. She has a bagel anyway with her mocha supreme grande and has to count out the pennies left at the bottom of her jeans pockets to get the change together. That's it, she's flat busted again.

And Trotsky doesn't show up on time. She finishes the News-pap on the table's screen and sips the mocha with extra cinnamon on top, a real perversion, while outside the sunny dusk turns to a crystal night in Venice. A rollerblader comes in, a wiry woman in cutoffs despite the chill. Long hair, kinda dirty-blonde in the way she likes.

The woman gives her a glance and there's a little something going on right away. Goldman has been trying to go straight for a while to see what it's like. Not Father Knows Best or anything, but to get the flavor back in her mouth, was the way she thought of it.

The woman sits at the next table and they do some eye stuff. That gets Goldman's pulse up, like always, but then Trotsky comes lumbering through the door and looks around with his jerky head movements and darting eyes, like an eagle on the hunt. That gets to her even more, something electrically predatory. Women don't have that pointed energy.

He comes over to her table and plunks his bony body down. Right off, he starts talking about some news stuff, not even saying hello. The owner stands glowering by the cash register, a black guy who makes a point about every customer having to order something. Trotsky catches the look and makes a show of ignoring it, keeps right on talking. The black guy puts on his apron, some kind of territorial signal maybe. Some quick eye and shoulder stuff passes between the two men. Trotsky gets up and orders an herbal tea.

While he's over at the counter, Goldman catches a sidelong from the woman still in her roller blades. Her soft green eyes mingle sympathy and an eyebrow-arching *whassup?* Goldman feels herself getting wet.

Trotsky comes back with his tea. He's angry that they don't have brown sugar and says that if the owner wasn't black Trotsky would write a letter to the chain management about it. Goldman has always liked how he sticks to the straight and narrow, even on little things. And he was good in bed those three times, she reminds herself. Wolfish, intense, talked all the way through it, even the oral part. None of the talk was dirty either. Kinda weird.

Then he has to go to the john and the woman gives her the look again. Decision time. Lots of options here.

The rollerblader would be pretty squishy. Soft, warm, predictable. Playing to her short-term self.

Trotsky was a ferret-faced irk sometimes, sure, but he thought ahead, saw horizons. Which should she go for this time? Maybe a threesome? No, he wasn't the type. Big ideas but tight-wound inside. She stirs her coffee and reaches for more cinnamon.

★★*

Jefferson walks into the board meeting the next morning with a solid, confident stride. The satellite company he consults for has sent him to push the new networking scenarios to these biz types. No sweat, he's done it all before. Which is the problem.

People crowd in around him the moment he's in the room. He sees his friend Washington at the middle of a similar jam. The two of them have joked about this effect. A bio-business analyst from UCLA told them it had something to do with chimpanzee tribalism. People need direction and they flock to people who give off the right signals, the musk of power.

Halfway through his PowerPoint presentation he feels the carpet seem to slide away. He keeps talking, practically knows the lines by heart now. But his Self, as he likes to think of it, is elsewhere. Out there.

He talks on about a big real estate deal along the Mexican border, water rights and pollution guarantees and the rest of it, but the zest is gone. Instead he's thinking about virgin lands and windswept forests and big skies. Somewhere.

A raised hand in the audience. "Mr. Jefferson, what's the ten-year rollout on convertible trust deeds here?"

—and the room swims away into deep moist green, towering trunks, rippling waters, dizzy desires all around him.

✦★✦

Lenin wears a big floppy hat to the demonstration. He tells himself it's to keep down his sun exposure; a man with a premature bald spot at age 29 has got to watch that. But a woman in his affinity group smirks at the hat, guessing that he wants to make it a little harder to identify his face. There's plenty of TV around and there will be footage on tonight's news. That's the point, after all. But he doesn't figure to get him in trouble at work either.

They form their lines, keep discipline, shout their slogans. Eco stuff, mostly, with a demand for a Global Minimum Wage. As an economist, he wonders what the hell that would mean but keeps his mouth shut.

Pretty soon there's some shoving and chanting and yelling and he gets into it, shoving back. A cop trips him and laughs. All the power of private capital comes rushing up into Lenin's face and slams him in the nose. He rolls over and gets some blood on his black suit, the standard uniform with vest he always wears to these things. A woman runs over and hands him a towelette for the blood and the cop kicks him in the butt. Lenin backs away but catches the cop's eye.

"You can kiss my ass," he mouths clearly enough for the cop to hear but nobody else. The cop's face is a quick study in surprise-irritation-rage, coming just that fast.

The kids around Lenin are all in jeans or sweats, and he feels out of place in his suit. They use tactics borrowed from punk rock, warmed over Spanish anarchism, rave culture. Amazon folk songs blend with obscenities. Overexposure has long ago robbed both of any impact on him.

A call went out well before this demo, all about defining principles and goals, skimpy on theory and long on rhetoric. So for weeks he had dutifully spent time with affinity groups fighting for microscopically narrow causes, using consensus-based decision making that took forever. He had thought a lot about their "ways of being"—methods that ranged from the strictly legal, through the iffy quasi-pacifist, in practice which meant tripping cops or throwing paint. He disliked all the phony-talk euphemisms like "diversity of tactics" that really meant old-fashioned street fighting. That negative finger-pointing stuff wasn't the way to go now, somehow.

He walks away from the scramble, confused. His nose hurts and he wonders if the hat looks silly with the suit. Maybe that's why the woman laughed.

★ ★

Goldman wakes up early and finds some coffee in a tin. She gets some hot water going, but it's a battle in this strange kitchen. The woman with dirty-blonde hair, what's her name, is a messy housekeeper.

With a biologist's eye Goldman inspects the scummy dishes in the sink and scrawny plants on the windowsill. Sunlight slants into the kitchen bright and clean, like a reproach.

Her mental cobwebs are just clearing as she fetches the *L.A. Times* from the driveway. A Santa Ana is blowing, unfurling her hair and making her skin jump. There's the usual mercantile news on the front page, so she takes refuge in the comics. There's the one about a woman bio prof that's always good; she identifies with the strip's surreal logic. After she's sucked the juice out of those, there's the ritual skimming of the bookshelves, only there aren't many. She picks up *A Primer of Soto Zen* and reads the first entry from Zen Master Dogen (1200–1253). It's about a monk who carried around Buddhist relics in a box until Dogen told him to give them up. The monk refused and next time he opened the box there was "a poisonous snake coiled within." A pretty good joke, she thought, a symbol of the folly of worshiping mere signs instead of the essence.

Just then the dirty-blonde woman comes shuffling in, naked and yawning. The breasts that so fascinated Goldman last night, after she ditched the Trotsky guy, show some sensual sag and big brown nipples.

Without a word the woman slurps up some of the Colombian coffee, hooks a hand around Goldman's shoulder and cups her breast. A warmth climbs up into Goldman's mind, a mingling of sweaty musks from last night and the savory zest of the coffee scent in this cluttered, moist apartment. Then hands sliding over soft skin, sniffs and savors, murmurs, her mouth somehow salty on a nipple.

It stops her thinking, which she supposes is a good thing. Live in the moment, that's what it will be like when the Revolution comes.

★★★

Washington gets out of his Mercedes to see what the crowd is all about. Turns out it's a demonstration against free trade. "Against free traffic, too," he mutters irritably.

A thin guy passing in an old black suit gives him a sharp, pinched-eye look. "We're against exploitation, man," the guy says and Washington recognizes him.

"Say, did you go to Cal?"

"Uh, yeah."

Washington recalls. They were in the same year and argued with each other in economics classes. There's blood on the man's old-style black suit and a kind of desperate glaze in the guy's eyes. Val, that's the name. Washington always remembers names, had drilled himself to, it was essential in networking.

Val's nose starts trickling blood again. Washington sees that his Mercedes is going nowhere because masses of people are streaming in both directions. Ragtag types running from the cops a block away, and media hounds closing in on the scene, hungry for it. Yet somehow Washington doesn't want to turn his back on all this, senses a humming of promise.

He takes Val into a bar to use the john to clean up. Washington sits in a booth and orders them both Irish coffees. It's uncharacteristic for him, no booze before five P.M. has been his rule, but he's not feeling like hitting the office today anyway. The same-old same-old won't cut it for him anymore. Time to move on.

Val comes back, bloodstains gone from the suit. He is embarrassingly grateful for the Irish coffee waiting. Suddenly Washington is telling Val about how pointless it seems to him, all the deals and perks. "No *scale* to it, you know?" he concludes. Even though he's been in on the birth of two Fortune 500 companies in ten years.

"Been there, done that," Val says heavily. The phrase has called up some private demons for him, too, Washington can see that. "Things looked great for us at Cal, y'know? Then first thing you know, you're running up your frequent flyer plastic and buying a Grass Hog weed whacker at Home Depot and it's all over."

They have three more rounds of Irish coffees and then a sandwich lunch with arugula salad. It's almost like the old Cal days, disagreeing on nearly everything but enjoying it. Washington asks what line of work Val is in and gets a story he's heard before. Econ degree, some grad work, fooled around with politics until the same old games got boring, pointless. Part-time professor at some state school, then some start-ups to learn about *real* economics. "But not at the *center*, you know?" Val says with an almost tearful tone.

They stare at each other for a long moment. "Going nowhere," Lenin says and Washington knows that he doesn't mean himself, but the world.

Washington sighs. "Back then, we were busy searching after truth and beauty . . ."

"And now they turn it into late night movies."

"Guess you had to be there."

Rueful chuckles. They watch a basketball game for a while on the TV. Neither had noticed this is a sports bar. Guys are starting to trickle in, it's early afternoon. Some are in jeans and others in three-pieces. They're all there for the game, getting away from whatever reality they're living in.

He and Val talk over the basketball game, not really interested. They get excited about something and then guys nearby are shushing them—*Hey, you don't wanna hear the game why you here?*—so soon enough they're out on the street.

The demo is over, the TV vans packing up their antennae on their roofs. Washington should get on to his office. But there's an electricity between them, sparks from the collisions of frustrations, dreams, ideas. He hasn't felt like this in years.

His cell phone's been ringing all the time. He's been getting offers for absurd chunks of cash. He turns it off and goes for a walk with Val instead.

✦✦✦

Franklin uses his new tunnel phone to make the call. It's a beautifully made gizmo he just had to take apart as soon as it came in from shipping. He tries it out by walking around his office and having his secretary listen to how the mike tracks him and adjusts its acoustic feed. Her voice comes back good and clear on the five-speaker input, too.

He walks over to his view, straight down the barrel of the Sunset strip. His company's media-mogul logo dominates even the big studio signs in view. He ordered it positioned there, so he could glance out and see their latest big deal show looming over the tourist crowds.

The pleasure fades, the way it does a lot lately. *All this talent, just to amuse.* He taps his fingers, makes a decision. His second call on the new phone is to an old girlfriend from back in business school. One night they had a hot-'n-heavy after a big group report was done. Just one, but he has found himself thinking about her lately.

Her voice shifts from office-official to warm and soft when she recognizes him. "Wow, all these years! Great . . . Dinner? Tonight? I'd love to, but . . ." Long pause and he finds himself holding his breath. "I've been on the road a lot, and I'd planned to just stay in tonight. Why don't you come over? 7:30?"

Bingo! He brings a bottle of Aussie Shiraz and a couple of pictures of one of his inventions. He thinks it's good to be up front about his sideline interests, so women don't think he's just another media pirate, though he is that, too.

She's lovelier than he remembers, a little too thin for his taste now. Instead of the severe black business suits she always wore then, she's in a soft blue blouse and willowy skirt with flowers on it. Her mouth is as tough looking as ever, she's some kind of lawyer, but she has on one of those cable music channels, wispy atmospheric stuff. One of the new scent gizmos has flavored the air like a pine forest and her auburn hair shimmers in the recessed lighting. He drones on about his work while she draws him out, standing in her sandals and stirring vegetables and ostrich meat in a wok. He gets an erection just talking and finds it hard to think. He pours the wine and does the usual number about the Australians being overrated. That leads to some conventional talk about the troubles in Malaysia. She sips the wine and tells him she really tries to use only American products. The World Trade Organization is trying to flatten out the whole planet, she says, and he decides to just nod and move on to something else.

He tells her about some of his inventions, especially the one to electrocute his Thanksgiving turkey as an act of kindness. For his trouble he got stunned, not the turkey. When he regained consciousness he had said, "I meant to kill a turkey, and instead I nearly killed a goose." She laughs at the right places and it's going well.

They talk until it's late. She's devoted to a variant of the usual twelve-step program. There is a picture on the wall of her standing next to a guy in a white suit, beaming self-confidence. He can't follow what it's all about.

His usual game plan, directing the soulful talk after dinner to more intimate areas, keeps sliding away. Maybe his heart isn't in it. He makes some moves and she responds with a breathless ardor, but his erection doesn't come back. That's a first and he doesn't understand what it means. She works on him, a little too hurried, but it's no use.

Contrary to his absolutely solid pattern, he starts making his good-byes. She seems reluctant to let him go. At the door she tells him that she always wanted to get back in touch again, that she has thought about him for years. There is a note of desperation in this that Franklin recognizes, he hears it a lot these days. It probably isn't about him and her at all but something else, something they both sense. But he doesn't think climbing into the sack with her is going to help either of them this time.

He leaves, gunning his sports car on the freeway, and gets a ticket. This really ticks him off and to cool down he stops at a frond bar he remembers from years before. This late it's nearly deserted and he sits at the bar and orders from the wine menu. A woman two stools away looks at him and turns a certain way so he can see the outline of her breasts, which are ample, in her silky blouse. He gives her the full 100-Amp smile and in a few minutes they're in a booth ordering some of the new Jaipur appetizers. Her name is Emma Goldman and he gets an erection right away.

★★★

Trotsky decided to move to California because he was just too tight-wound in Manhattan.

So he keeps trying the Venice scene, making himself sit in those coffee shops. He even goes roller-blading and throws a Frisbee on the beach, getting a tan in cutoffs. He works as an accountant, some of it under the table for some tech companies to keep the taxes down. Maybe not completely ethical but what is, these days?

He thinks he's mellowed out some since New York, but there's the old dissatisfaction simmering behind his eyes. Nothing will make it go away. During one of his frustrating walks on the beach he runs into Kropotkin from the old gang on the East Side. Kropotkin is wearing a baseball cap on backward, real out of date, and says he's trying to break into screenwriting. Working as a waiter right now, but he's got plans.

Kropotkin gets e-mail from Stalin, who's still trying to find a shady angle in politics back East, something in New Jersey. Trotsky tells Kropotkin to stay away from Stalin, the man is a control freak. They say the usual about getting together real soon now. Each is wearing the new clip-on ID pens that picks up digital info on who you talked to, all automatic over infrared. So they have each other's contact info and all, but as they look at each other Trotsky realizes neither will use it. He still thinks Kropotkin's a pleasant dreamer but, face it, a loser.

The thing with Emma Goldman didn't work out and he can't figure why. He thought he was coming over pretty well. The sex was good. Things started to go sour at that coffee shop meeting and he took her out a week later for dinner at a fish taco joint.

They just didn't click anymore. Maybe he wasn't upscale enough. Or maybe, he thinks, he still talks about his ideas too much. About Siberia and all.

He tries getting high, an area he has always scorned. Dope was okay but made him go to sleep. Ecstasy just made him hear stuff in the music of those mixer clubs, themes and resonances that he knew the next day could not possibly have been there. Those meat-rack clubs got to him, too. Everybody wore that retro look, 1940s sleek or the Latino peacock thing. Trotsky was still in black jeans and shades.

So he goes out to a seminar on The Human Prospect. A pretentious title, sure, but he has always been tempted by the big perspectives, things beyond the present. There's a thick folder of handouts, three-color pie charts and dimensional projections.

The meeting is full of the usual futurology elements. Here comes overpopulation, greenhouse climate change, bioengineering, cloning, the whole menu. Everybody nods and an old leftie gets up and somehow ties this to the execution of the Rosenbergs. There's a verbal slugfest over anti-Semitism and racism and Israel.

He gets up and leaves. On the way out he exchanges sour disappointed looks with a guy wearing all black, the usual business signature. The guy makes a sardonic wisecrack and Trotsky comes back with one that makes them both laugh in a wry, sad way.

They stop at a bar to trash the "seminar" they've just been in. Right away they hit it off. Trotsky has his ideas about a genuine Revolution from below, based on people getting as part of their pay some shares in their company.

"Self-ownership, that's it," the guy agrees, name of Jefferson. "Every man a capital owner."

"And woman," Trotsky adds automatically. Jefferson nods and they have another round of some dark African beer. Trotsky unloads his idea then, a plan so odd that Jefferson at first can't see it. "Take Siberia? How? Why?"

"It's the biggest virgin territory on Earth."

"Virgin? But people are there, left over from the Soviets."

"Okay, call it California virgin. The girls around here, by the time they're in junior high school they know plenty, have done some. But still essentially intact."

Jefferson smiles. "You should have been a lawyer." He is a big guy with an easy smile, the kind people warm to right away. Not like himself, Trotsky realizes ruefully. Jefferson is the sort of figure the Revolution needs.

So he reels off the numbers. Siberia has a tenth of the total land area of the planet. It has big reserves of timber, metals, oil. Two crappy railroads, a few airports. The Russians abused it for four centuries and now the Chinese are infiltrating it, grabbing at the water supplies already.

"The Communists never knew how to open a frontier right," Jefferson says thoughtfully.

Trotsky pounces. "Magic word—frontier. Who owns the imagery? Us! Westerns!"

"You want there to be . . . Easterns?"

Trotsky laughs, liking this guy even more. "In time, sure. Rough and ready. There are thirty million people living there, tough people."

"Let's not treat them the way we did the Indians," Jefferson says archly.

"Exactly! This will be a frontier with social justice."

Jefferson frowns. "That phrase usually means income transfers."

Trotsky sees he has to be careful here. Time to show he's not some warmed-over socialist, he's ahead of that, sure. But Jefferson in his black take-me-serious suit and that every-man-a-capitalist idea is going to want economic freedoms. "Okay, got you. We give everybody in Siberia, native or immigrant, shares in the profits."

"Immigrants?"

Trotsky is getting wild-eyed, he knows that, the look that puts people off, maybe that did him in with Goldman. But he can't stop. "Sure, immigrants. From around here, even. Gals who work in factories, guys who thought they'd never do more than pump gas. From everywhere."

"What America used to be," Jefferson says with a distant look in his eyes.

"So these corporate fascist regimes—China, nearly all of southeast Asia—they'll have some real, close-up competition. A solid, worked-out example of another way to uplift people. An alternative, sitting due north of them. On the mainland, not some idea from 'way over the horizon." Trotsky stops, realizing that he may have gone too far. But what the hell, this is the Revolution.

Jefferson looks both dreamy and shrewd, an expression Trotsky has never seen before. "So . . . how do we get Siberia?"

"See, that's the free market glory of the thing. We buy it."

★★★

Emma Goldman fumes as she leaves her yearly evaluation session. On overall effort she got a ninety-eight percentile and a pay raise. But now the company says to shut down the research work she's doing on the contraceptive and join a team doing "more likely market oriented tasks." And she's just finished the prelim field trials!

She remembers the long hours in the lab, the part of the work she liked best. The nifty ideas that didn't pan out and some that finally did. All that, gone?

She calls her assistant in and tells him to assemble the task group, twenty-three good people. They're waiting in the conference room when she finally gets her head around what she has to do.

"I'm sorry to tell you that our program is discontinued, as of Friday," she opens. Gasps. "And I resign."

Out the door she goes, not looking back.

★★★

Franklin brings along Emma Goldman to the dinner with Washington. She's been pretty down lately with the resignation, but tonight she says she's got some venture capital guys behind her at last, and the work can go forward again. She's still mysterious about just what the work is, even though the corporate proprietary rules don't apply.

He forgets about that because she's rubbing against him at discreet moments, giving him the eyes. All in good taste, though. She's just a very sexy lady. Washington has no woman with him, just this funny guy in a black suit. Emma mistakes his name for Lennon.

Washington is at his best, holding forth about this guy Lenin's ideas. The main one seems to be "horizons." Lenin thinks they should be expanding human horizons and uplifting the bulk of humanity—all at the same time. "You can't do one without the other," Washington says.

"Not by bread alone, I know all that," Lenin says. "But you've got to have bread to say that in the first place. Otherwise, you're too busy."

Franklin is hungry and the bread here is very good. It's a retro-TwenCen restaurant, red meat and martinis, and show business people don't come here.

Washington nods. "A way to unite humanity, that's what we need."

Franklin decides to bring up his agenda, since everybody else is. "Do something *big*, then. Go to Mars."

They all blink over their appetizers. Emma Goldman is the first to speak. "How's that help people?"'

"By giving them a focus." Franklin waves his hands. "A huge drama, running three years. Life or death, every day, on prime time."

It takes them a while to get it. Of course it will cost money. Plenty. "Maybe as much as another carrier group for the U.S. Navy," Lenin says sardonically. "Instead of cruising around the Third World, we can cruise to Mars?"

Franklin thinks going to Mars with a manned expedition— Emma says, "Womanned, too," and they all laugh—would pull the whole planet together.

"Why?" Lenin probes.

"Because they'll go to settle a real, important scientific point," Franklin says. "Did life ever arise there? Does it still hold out, under the dried-out surface? We *all* gain a little stature by answering that."

There are looks around the table. Somebody mentions social justice and somebody else says *Why does it have to be either/or?* and Emma smiles at him. *Why can't far horizons and up-close justice work together?*

There's plenty of talk, endless talk, and some joking. But unlike all the gossip and tit-for-tat talk he's heard for decades now, this dinner party discussion is *about* something.

Franklin can see that Washington is waiting until the people around the restaurant table have ridden their individual hobby horses as far as they will go. When the momentum is spent, Washington says, "Y'know, for years now I've had a restless feeling. I thought I was living in the long plateau of an empire. That there was no place to go. But now . . . you feel it too, don't you?"

They did. A woman comes in selling flowers, playing to one of the high-priced mannerisms that makes Lenin curl his lip. But tonight Franklin buys roses for Emma and somehow it's just fine. She beams. Lenin goes along with it without making a fuss. "Gotta keep perspective," he admits.

Emma reminds them all that if they're going to promote big ideas, they should remember that people have to stay grounded in their own selves, their bodies. If they don't, it will get all abstract and theoretical. Like the TwenCen. "That's how big dreams turn into nightmares," she says.

"We're practical people," Washington says, "not ideology idiots. Sure, you're in a car, you need to know the general direction—but then it's up to people who know how to steer."

★★★

There's some arguing over that, while they cut into thick steaks and have another martini. Emma has had two and she gets a bit giddy. Washington's speech—and he always seems to be making a speech, too, a macho thing, quite unconscious—has put her off. But you have to use the energies flowing in the moment. She notes how the other men look up to him—literally, except maybe for Jefferson in some Taiwan lifters. Physical presence had to count if you were going to change the world; we are primates, after all. No politics could do without a salting of biology. Evolution and economics had to work together.

Under probing she tells them that the product her new company is going to make is a male contraceptive. "That's not new," Franklin says.

She leans forward, her dress sliding smoothly over her body, and argues back. Macho these guys might be, but she could handle that. There were other skills, honed back in Africa. Evolution, yes.

★★★

Franklin smiles, his nose reddening from the drink. Her silky grace, her fetching dress belying the steel-sharp argument—none of this came by accident, of course. One of the things Franklin loves about her is her direct sensuality, intellect unashamed. She is completely at ease within herself. Nobody else at the table can match her for that.

She says, "Gentlemen, this contraceptive is the answer to population growth in the Third World. It'll sell for pennies, because we'll price it low. No research overhead on it, so my new company can lowball market it. I got the patent rights as part of my separation agreement from my old company. They thought there was no money in it! No demand from guys."

Washington begins, "It's going to sell cheaply? But price isn't enough with most men in the tropical nations, I thought. There was a piece in the *Economist* about it just a few weeks ago."

Emma Goldman nails Washington with a jabbing finger to make her point. "Right! Most men think it isn't their problem, right?"

Around the table there come reluctant nods. "So I designed the tricky part of this product myself. It's a chewing gum. Easy to take."

Washington persists. "Even that's probably not going to make a big dent in the demographics—"

"*And*—" She jabs at Washington again. "—it's addictive. Not harmful, not even narcotic. Just addictive."

The men sit, stunned. Between them passes a very rare event: silence.

Just then the waiter arrives for dessert orders. Still a bit dazed,

Washington beckons toward the shadows—and there, coming in for the ending, is an old buddy, Jefferson. With him is a sleek black beauty named Sally, and Jefferson seems a little embarrassed about it. They've been seeing each other a long time, it seems, but not in public until now. He's also got in tow a skinny fellow, underdressed for this restaurant and with hot, darting eyes: Trotsky. They have an idea they want to discuss, they say.

Franklin gets up to go to the bathroom and Emma goes, too. The restaurant has those new unisex johns and they go in together. A matron outside looks scandalized. There was a time when they'd have taken advantage of the moment, maybe just to irk the matron, and actually have sex.

Not now. There is something about this night. A heady sensation *of gathering energy, of living on the edge, the very limit of who you could be.*

They don't want to disturb it, because in the air there seems to hang a certain crystalline note, like a bell that has rung in a distant steeple, the tone lingering on, clear and long.

Franklin notices on his way back to the table that he has an erection. Ahead, the gang is making a lot of noise, arguing and joking, disagreeing and planning. Behind is Emma, a smoldering center of his world. Somehow it all comes together in mind and body for him, soft surges of the heart. He looks out the window. Diamonds sprawl across the San Fernando Valley. Somewhere out there somebody is bleeding to death and somebody else is giving birth. He leans against the cool windowpane *brimming with distant luminous promise,* and feels the whole vast moment seep through him and knows it is the Revolution.

Two Faces of Love

by TANITH LEE

1

When the Silence Calls Your Name

I dreamed the sky was falling
I heard the planets end
I heard the voices calling
Never again
Never again
—from "When the Silence Falls" by Janis Ian

2002

SO you're going up into the mountains? A woman of twenty-seven in your beat-up car, speed blowing your hair, and the hurt of the world on your back, pain big as one of those boulders.

She drives through the golden-leaf light of dying afternoon. Off the highway now, those tracks will still, she supposes, take her to the cabin before nightfall. Years ago she'd had to get used to American roads, American cars. Now she's used to everything.

Long shadows of pines stripe the roadway. The low sun flashes between. It's almost strobelike, hallucinatory. Above, the mountains rise from the lower decks of the land, carved out of sky, catching sun mysteriously on things that sparkle—quartz, knives, tears.

The last gas station is a hundred miles in the past. The old man who shambled out had glared at Hester as if she were an ancient enemy, not a human being needing to fill the tank of her car. He was surly and rude, like everyone else she'd met along the roads, the drunk jackasses in their convertible, the kids who slung rocks presumably just because she dared drive by, the cop who'd pulled her over—such a minor infringement—made a sneering comment on her English accent: "You a Brit?" and then lectured her from the superiority of being six-foot-three, with a gun. Even the gas station dog had snarled, red-eyed, on the length of cruel, crude chain.

The dirt road turns a corner, around the brown flank of the slope. Forest closes in. How much farther? Had they lied to her about the cabin? People lie, don't they?

About thirty feet ahead a deer, propelled as if in flight, leaps across the road. She curses the deer. She might have hit it. Everything is against her.

Look at the sunset, Hester. You used to like those, like you liked deer and other animals, like you liked people and new places, landscapes, cities. Just as you loved—once.

Blue shade going to purple, but coming up out of the trees, you find this sky like the translucent wing of a fire-butterfly.

Hester remembers sundown outside the crowded restaurant where Drew shouted at her, left her, and the girl he'd been flirting with all night had seemed to smile an unhidden secret smile of contempt.

No, the sunset's lost on Hester.

When she reaches the cabin, it's as it was described. It sits at the head of its own track, up on the ridge, with a loosely strung-out bodyguard of pines, and over all the top-lit mountains' colossal backdrop.

Sun almost down now. In the light-struck forest, she glimpses squirrels, gophers darting to their lairs. Here the pool of shadow gathers, out of which a streamlet races glittering for the vanishing light, and tumbles for its troubles right over the ridgeside.

Log-and-stone built, the cabin is far less rustic than it seems. Inside are big rooms, windows with views, cleverly piped-in clean water, a heating system, generator, microwave, TV, a freezer stacked with delicacies. There are oil lamps too, for fun.

She distrusts, however, the sympathetic New York friends who have loaned her the cabin. ("You need to get out of the City, Hes.") And anyway, the cabin-couple were too happy together. The Earth was populated by pairs holding hands, locked in a public embrace.

Night falls when she's inside. She switches on electric lamps, organizes the percolator and drinks some coffee. She takes a hot shower.

Outside, birds sing, stop.

Below on the road she can see from a window, far, far down, cars still pass now and then, with a snakelike hiss. They said wolves herd into the valleys in winter, but now it's only early fall. Instead an owl laments in the pines. Lying awake for hours, the liquid mercury of stars sears holes in the drapes, her lids, the moon drives over to gleam its flashlight in her eyes, and she hates the owl. The world, once so possible and fine, has shrunk to a pip at the kernel of her bitter heart.

She sees no reason in anything, for she has been shut out, she and her kind.

What wakes her from her foray into sleep is—*nothing*. That is, the *silence*. Silence wakes her like the ringing of a mighty bell.

Half comatose, sitting up in darkness, panicked, she tries the portable radio she had left on to counteract the owl. But the radio is silent, too. None of the stations of the world will speak to her now.

Hester receives an intimation of fear.

Then she realizes, the battery is dead.

When she pads into the main room, the TV answers at a touch, milling with persons, laughing in their seamless perfections. Envious and despising, she turns down the sound after all, but leaves them there, stupidly performing to an empty room.

Why get scared like some child? The world won't end—isn't that what they say? Oh, well, it isn't the end of the world . . . and if it did—why should it happen now? The eternal nightmare of apocalypse anyway couldn't be missed. She thinks of a terrible brightness in the heavens, the rush of thunders like an express. Two more hours pass before she sleeps again.

Hester dreams.

A car is driving through the sky (a Cadillac? a Rolls?), perhaps a modern version of the Chariot of the Sun—it is scalding bright. There is, isn't there, something awesome and frightful about this car, though perhaps it's only made of clouds or flames.

A voice speaks in Hester's ear, one word only:
Now.
She doesn't wake. The radio and the owl are silent. In the main room the TV murmurs. Has anything changed?

※★※

In the morning, the TV has gone quiet. Dumb and accusing it stands there, blank-faced and inert.

Hester feels angry now. It never takes much, for the solid gray grief to tip over into rage. She swears at the TV. She gets dressed, eats a pancake she hasn't sufficiently heated through, despite the warnings on the box, and goes out to the car. There's a town, they've told her this. According to her happy, sympathetic, success-fully-still-in-love friends, the town is located only a few miles along the road. Her portable CD player is acting up, too. The CDs jump, voices hiccuping in demented treble.

Why does every fucking thing go wrong at once?

Hester drives. Light now is clear and sharp. Rocky vistas soar above.

Nothing passes on the road. That's good.

Sometimes she thinks she sees birds or animals moving, a sort of flutter on-off-on in the sunlit woods. Twice she spots, indifferently, what might be an eagle, hugely outspread on the sky, static as if pasted there. It's looking for something to kill below. That's what they do.

Despite the map she's been given, and the described directions, Hester doesn't find any town. She drives for nearly two hours. She keeps expecting it—this road goes through it, they'd said. Must be farther off than they said, or is she somehow on the wrong road? Not even a shack, a store, a gas station goes by, though there must be some. In the end, it seems wise to head back while there is fuel left in the tank.

No wonder there's no other traffic on this road. Nowhere to go.

Like me.

The car radio won't work either. What is this, *The X-Files*?

On the way back, she glances up occasionally, after the eagle, but it must have come unstuck and hurtled down into the pines. The woods are caught in a motionless noon hush.

In the cabin again, she makes lunch, being more careful now to heat the burger meat through. She drinks half a glass of red wine. But alcohol doesn't lift her mood. Get used to that.

What am I going to do?

Frankly, now she's here, Hester is actually afraid of being all alone, the very thing that frightened her most when Drew began to talk of their splitting up. She'd clung to him, not bodily, but with her words, her heart. And in the end he started to hurt her with *his* words, to deliberately dislodge her by his actions, till finally he was gone.

She's brought some books with her. She sets them out, chooses, tries to read. She reads the same sentences over and over. The wine has made her leaden. She falls asleep.

Hester dreams of a cloud on fire, nuclear perhaps? No, more beautiful, more—far more—*terrible*—

By evening, when she wakes up, the blue-violet shadows are gathering, and the sun beyond the ridge makes everything into raw topaz, and the CD machine won't play at all.

Hester stands out on the deck, craning to see gophers and squirrels darting around in their preslumber rituals. She can't detect any tonight.

The pines rustle. You have to strain to hear. No birds now, nothing sings. Her presence must have disturbed them all.

Tomorrow I'll walk through the woods, she thinks, a nature ramble. I'll see plenty of things then. Critters, maybe people strayed from the cabins further up.

Somehow she knows she won't.

Hester sits on the deck, and the sun goes and evening descends. The world is sapphire, then indigo. Stars appear.

Perhaps this aloneness is what, anyway, she truly needs. She'd craved solitude from all but one person. When he was gone, no one else could help her. Soon she longed to get away from them all, and from the hubbub of the city, too, their nest. Get away from everything. Now, though . . . Well, she's here. If she didn't need this, still she's got this, like all the rest she hadn't needed. She would have to face up to it.

All evening, night, she moves around the cabin, out on the deck, circles the house, and slides back in again.

How entirely voiceless is this world on the ridge, only the rough silk barely-audible shiver of the pines, the clucking of the stream over its stones, her own footsteps, her breathing.

Eventually she goes back in and gets ready for bed. Hester lies, waiting for the owl to begin its eerie hoots. But the owl doesn't make a sound.

Does she sleep now? Perhaps. It's all confused, dreams washed over wakefulness, sleep dropping dull lacunae through her conscious mind. The clock's stopped. Why's the damn clock stopped? That happens when someone dies—childhood's there, in London, a grandmother looking pale with a no longer functioning alarm clock in her hands—"No, Gran, it's only because the battery's dead—"

What are you going to do?

Sleep, I'll sleep now.

I *can* hear a voice—

(Oh, it's me, I'm crying. It's me crying.)

A wind blows along the edges of the earth, full of gathered sighs, and ebbs away.

★★★

Next day, you're up so early. Showered, dressed, scrubbed, and ready for the world. You make a holiday breakfast: hash browns, eggs, orange juice. Then on with the walking shoes and out.

Hester swings through the woods.

The trees stand so tall and still. There are only the pines, though she was told there were other kinds of trees. Nothing, aside from Hester, moves. The sunlight showers profligate on the ground. Surely—just one single noise somewhere—some chattering bird alarm-call at her approach? A song? All right, then, a distant car? None of the above.

No cars pass now along the road below. Yes, you've watched, haven't you, Hester, *timed* the time during which no car has gone by, when that first evening they had annoyed you so by passing three or four in an hour.

Another stream slips between ferns. She can hardly hear it, muffled in its own depths. She bends over the water and looks for fish, or insects. Nothing is there.

A faint sound makes her imagine a plane is traveling overhead, but craning up so fast her neck gives a snapping note, there isn't anything at all. Except, in the east, the sky blazes with erupting clouds, gold-white. *Not* like the dreams. Oh, no.

What you gonna do?

"Drew—don't leave me—we can work something out—I don't care about anyone but you—nobody—nothing—"

When the silence—

When the silence . . .

In her head she's screaming there's no silence louder than the bomb-blast aftershock when love runs out the door.

Hester strides back the way she's come. Desiccated needles crunch under her sneakers. In the cabin she prepares lunch. Why does the microwave work, and the generator, when the TV and radio and the CD player don't? Superstitiously, she won't consider this.

Instead she tries the cabin phone. The cheerful polite message plays back to her the voices of her successful-lover friends. Okay, she'll call them. Tell them how wonderful it all is and ask them where is the bloody town she hasn't been able to find.

She hears the phone ring. The sound of this—she goes on listening to it, maybe for ten minutes. No one picks up. They're out. No. They never go out before the afternoon, working in the apartment. What's happened? Don't be ridiculous. Probably they're making love, that's why the phone won't answer. They just forgot to unplug it. They wanted the world to know what they're at—

Phones don't ring if something happens. It would be robot

voices telling her the lines are down, or some sort of sinister whistling—or utter—*silence*.

Hester calls up numbers at random. Some she invents. All ring. None answers. Once she tries to replay the recorded message on the cabin phone, but now it, too, refuses to reply. As she always knew, everything is a conspiracy against her.

★★★

The next morning Hester goes to the car and checks the gas. The tank is still nearly full, though how can it be? The gauge too must be faulty. She wonders if she should drive back along the highway to the previous gas station, the one with the animosity of the man and the chained dog. Why do that, Hester? To see—if they are still there?

Hester makes a roster for herself. She even writes it down. Once on the hour, every hour, she will call various numbers of friends scattered over the vast continent of the USA. (Not Drew's number, of course, never that.) She'll even call her family in London, England. Won't that startle them, after a whole year?

When she's finished lunch, she'll walk. She will actively seek out cabins and shacks in the woods, and that trout stream the New York friends told her, along with a fruit farm, had been hacked out of the skirts of the mountains. She knows roughly where they are. They'd shown her photos, hadn't they.

If nothing—if she doesn't get anywhere, though she will, then tomorrow she must risk the gas and drive back along the road onto the highway. For one thing, the lights, look at them, keep blinking. The generator—failing? If it does, pragmatically she thinks, the freezer and fridge will go, and the heating. And then she'll just have to—well she'll have to—

Has something happened out there? A great hush of nothing, of vacancy—or only the battery of the busy world finally going—*dead*—

Now Hester has a phase of immaculately grooming herself again. She puts on a face-pack, manicures and pedicures and paints her nails. She washes and conditions her hair and applies makeup carefully to her fresh, stripped face. All dressed up—

In the fridge the light blinks, too, on and off, then diminishes. The fridge is full of moist dimness. A little spill of water creeps from under the freezer.

Part of the roster for this day stipulates keeping watch for any animal activity in the pine forests, any birds heard or seen. Once she's sure there *is* something—she rushes out onto the veranda deck, and sees a small bough has fallen from a pine, its abrupt movement deceiving her.

There's another moment of deception, too. The call signaling through the phone is suddenly interrupted, and Hester waits breathless for a voice—any voice—to speak to her. But all that speaks to Hester is the silence.

Hester, says the silence, on and on. After she throws back into the car the mobile she's been using in desperation, Hester tries to eat lunch. Then she walks in the woods.

She walks all afternoon, climbing up and down vague tracks, over outcrops and slopes where the powdery soil rushes away in front of her. Everything is so large. The trees are giants. Between them the undergrowth is sparse. The mountains, the largest things of all, bar the sky, hang disembodied. She sees no one. No animal life. No cabins, shacks, not even the residue of any old camping places. From the exact high-pitched area she's had described to her as offering a view of the town, the one she tried to reach earlier, she looks over and around. There is no town there, only valleys full of pines. She's discovered, too, or *not* discovered, rather, there is also no fruit farm in the other direction.

The sun goes. Tramping back, she notices the ending bars of brassy light, how flat they are, and everything they fall on seems, for a moment, two-dimensional.

Approaching, but not yet seeing the cabin, Hester has a horror it won't any longer be there. So she runs, tripping and jumping through the last trees, and finds the cabin still standing. But inside, the water from the freezer has become a pool. The lights are out, unresponsive to everything she tries to trick them to come on.

Hester lights oil lamps. Tomorrow she'll drive back along the highway. Whatever has happened out there has now, like an uncurling, noiseless wave, reached here. She seems positioned at its center, the eye of a storm that is *not*.

★ ★

Why aren't you afraid, Hester? Oh, but you are. You are sick and crazed with terror. It's only—you'd already learned how to be always afraid. It's become your everyday life, this empty panic that goes continually on. Ever since he left you alone and everything else was made meaningless, and alien.

"Honey, you really do have to try—" "Baby, he's not worth it—" Worth *what?* Try *what?* To pull herself together, push the pain out of herself, out of this her of whom he's unworthy, and who wants only him. The kind, despairing friends, their chatter, their *condolences*—as if Drew had died. He had, for her—but no. It was Hester who was deceased.

What are you dreaming? It's about the girl in the restaurant, long hair down her back, so much more attractive than Hester, so much less available. Hester dreams she herself is in a teeming city, whose glass towers soar into the upper air, but no one teems there after all, and the glass scrapers-of-sky are really mountains, hollow, and also of glass.

Hester wakes up, gets up, goes to stand on the deck. The black-blue night is massed with blazing planets and the misty milk of stars. It's not cold anymore, not warm. There's no breeze, the scent of the pines is slight. Nothing moves or stirs or makes a sound.

Hesst—ahhh breathes the silence into both her ears.

Somehow, before she knows it will happen, she is seeing a shadow multitude of figures descending all the hills and the mountain edges all around. They're not *there*, these shades, nothing is there. They are tall, with long hair down their backs, these peoples of the past, these memories. They glide down all the slopes the way water runs off, and then, as water does, they're gone, sinking into the earth.

Hester can't hear the stream. She picks across the hard floor of the land on her bare feet and stares into the streambed. Like water runs off—

The stream has vanished from its bed. Nothing is there either, to glimmer, or make a sound.

✯★✯

It's fall—that's English autumn. But more than that. *Fall.* Call it fall. Things call and fall. Skies fall down. They come away in huge masonry sections, crashing noiseless on the crushed world.

High above, pitiless, the planets sing and spin. Can you hear them?

Is this a dream now? Or *real* now?

Hester stares up at the sky. Cloud must be invisibly passing. One bright star has winked out, gone like the light inside the fridge.

She retreats into the cabin. She puts her hand on the wall. Solid, it's solid.

Through the windows, clouds cover more stars. The night darkens.

All the oil lamps are alight now, and no moths come to them.

Hesst-ahh calls the silence, *Hessz-tahrr.*

She falls (falling) asleep at the bar in the kitchen area, sitting on the stool, head propped on her manicured hand.

Something is going through heaven, not an angel, not anything that has wings, or a form, but, like the lamplighters of old, it's putting out the lights.

Instead, daybreak somehow arrives. A dull morning, as if rain were expected, yet cloudless. The sky's blue—but dead. Battery expired.

Hester, waking up, removes her stiff numbed hand from under her neck-twisted head. It takes a while to restore circulation. Only then does she really see out of the windows.

She runs to the bathroom, voids herself. She sits there, crying now, telling herself, but only in whispers, that she's lost her mind, that's all it is.

But you're brave, aren't you, Hester? You were brave before. When he left you, you didn't just lie down on your face in the dirt, and you don't now. You attend to yourself, wash your hands carefully at the faucet which will barely play a trickle of water. Then you go out again and take another look.

"It's *me*. That's all. I've gone off my head. It has to be me."

It isn't you.

During the fall of the fall night, something has also visited the Earth. It's rubbed out all the trees. Every one. They're gone, the pines on the ridge, the woods, the forests that spread their shaggy miles of pelt below for deer, bears, and wolves, gophers and yellow jacks. Gone.

There are no trees. There are no forests.

The ridge stands bald as a desert rock with its cargo of car and cabin, solitary above the bare slopes. And behind, the mountains, nailed on the dead sky, unclothed and ephemeral as no mountains *ever* are. But now, they *are*.

So this is how it's to be. Proverbially without any explosion, screamless and unvocalized. Not even the predicted whimper, for who would dare accost this torrent of nosound—

When the silence falls.

★★★

That night's sunset is the last one. She knows this. She watches. The sky flushes a lifeless red and folds away. A kind of twilight comes, resembling the twilight the day had been. No stars, no planets remain.

Once she thinks she hears a wind blowing, but it's some noise of her own breathing, and Hester sits listening to it.

She has no way to mark the hours. What would be the point of marking them?

She lies down.

She listens to the silence, and it calls out *Hess-staar* over and over again. This continues. How long? She doesn't know. No one could.

She dreams the car is driving again across the sky.

Then she's up and running. Hester flies through the cabin, flings open the door, flings herself down the steps, then stands frozen, petrified. One more rock. She's awake. The car isn't in the nothing-sky above. It's on the track. Gradually it pulls itself nearer. It creeps up the ridge and moves in beside her own vehicle, quite naturally, as if in a crowded parking lot. The car door comes undone, and he gets out.

Standing there, she can see him so plainly, because there's really nothing else left to look at. Is *he* a shadow? No, solid like the cabin, made of flesh and blood.

"Drew," she says, somehow says, or some voice in her body says it.

It's Drew. He comes toward her at a stumbling run. He takes hold of her, and she can feel his hands gripping her, and smell the electric smell of him, heightened by adrenaline.

"You're here," he says. He holds her, holds on to her. She puts her arms about him, experimentally. "You're here," he says again. "I've driven three nights. I think, nights. Can't tell. The car ran out of gas—empty—no gas station. Car just kept going anyhow. Christ knows. The sun went. It just went away like every other goddamn thing."

"Yes," Hester murmurs.

Their voices hang there in vast silence, lost, tangled up together.

"It's something they did—that great governmental They." This is what he says next. They are sitting in the cabin, sipping water from the bottles, eating cookies. Although the stores have deteriorated, there are still lots of things to sustain them. "What?" he questions, not her, but something, someone else. She recalls, it was his habit to do that. "We thought it'd be a war, right?" (Still not to her.) "Or some accident—or terrorism. We had some cause to think it might be that. But not—this. What'll they do now, those blind, self-righteous bastards? Those great generals? They're gone, too. Every single one, maybe, with the rest." He looks at her. She, staring back at him, tries to relearn his features, tries to feel all the seething of her love. "Where did it go, Hester?"

"I don't know. I don't know where it went."

Like love, she thinks. It's what you said to me, back then. You didn't know where love had gone—

"I guess," he says. "Maybe there could—be others like us? I knew I'd find you here."

"Why?"

In her head, her voice adds drearily, why find *me?* Surely there were all those others you preferred. Shouldn't you have found *them?* Perhaps you tried. I'm all, this time, you could get. Poor Drew, she thinks unkindly. But she doesn't feel unkind. She doesn't feel—anything much.

He doesn't answer her anyway.

He says, finally, "I guess you're real?"

"Are you?"

"I don't know," he says.

They sit in the twilight, a little apart,

★★★

Later, they eat something else.

Sometimes they talk, not very much. What can they say? He keeps telling her how glad he is to find her. She says the same. She feels—only faintly surprised—*surprised?* Is *that* what she feels?

The horrible movie scenario of their situation begins to offend her. They are, perhaps, the last man and woman left in a compulsorily evacuated world. The last *things*—for this world will have very little else. Possibly they could survive. Possibly . . . Had she, long,

long ago, ever fantasized about such an idea? Alone with him, and no other to intrude or lure away? Drew has to want her now, she's all there is. And for her, how many times she had cried out, *he* was all she wanted. Fuck all the rest. Now see—*now* see what you've done.

Somewhere on the roads, while the kids threw stones and the dogs snarled and she hated them all, and the sunsets flamed un-loved—somewhere, had there been some kind of eldritch crone, who took note. Atropos, maybe. *You shall have what you desire.*

She had it. All was gone, and Drew was with her, for the rest of their lives.

They sleep a while, side by side, on the two beds, not touching. She had suggested doing it like this. They don't make love. Does love have any role in this? Or does it have the *only* role?

When she wakes, and sees Drew still there, sleeping, a gush of fury, like poison, goes through Hester.

She turns on her side, away from him. She remembers places they've been, the cities bright with lights and lives. Even lying close then, lost in each other, beyond them the murmur of the highways, the passage of the sun, the moon and the planets over the sky. Had being with him made the world more beautiful—or—Oh, Christ, Christ—the beauty of the world reflected back on Drew, changing him into the god he never was. The world. The first love. Mightier than mother or father, mightier even than oneself. Not backdrop— the wellspring of life—

"What are you seeing?" he asks her, waking as she does her sentry duty at one of the windows.

"The mountains," Hester says. She no longer whispers. "They're starting to go."

He leaps up. He stands panting by the window in terror. But her terror has darkened and grown still.

"I suppose," she says, "it will all go eventually."

"Then—what about us?"

"No," she says. "I think not us."

How do you *know*, Hester?

Hester moves slightly away from Drew.

"At least, we're together now," he says. He sounds smug, even in his fear. Of course, he can rely on her wanting him. Hadn't she told him often enough? He puts his arm around her. Presently she moves away. She thinks how men are said to call out, when dying, for their mothers. . . .

She hears the intake of his breath and sees, too, what he is seeing, another mountain dissolving like a pillar of salt.

★★★

All that day, if it's day, or night, if it is, they stand or sit, watching the mountains vanish one by one, into the now visible silence.

Drew sobs.

Hester thinks how she cried for Drew, night after night when nights were nights and days, days.

She doesn't cry now.

Time, if there is time, passes.

The mountains sail off into nothingness.

In the end, there's only one mountain left, balancing there in the void that isn't dark or light. This is the hour Drew wants to make love to her.

They had found a bottle of bourbon, they'd drunk some. With the last mountain still there, he had gently pulled her to him.

She doesn't want this.

What she wants—

What are you going to do, Hester?

She goes outside and sits on the barren earth, and observes the last mountain, as, like a glacier, it melts.

Does she want Drew, or the mountain? Drew or the world? Today, or forever? Well?

That's when some other voice, calling wild and low within the silence, too absolute, as usual, to be heard, becomes known to her. She doesn't know what it says. It doesn't matter what it says—only that it's there.

Then the silence is there again instead, hissing in her ears *Hsstrr, Hssrr*—

When she walks from the cabin, down the path, gets in her car, Drew appears, charging across the ridge. Behind him, the cabin looks like a stage set. He acts badly, waving the whiskey, shouting, as she did when he left *her*. She sees his dislike of her, even now, all he really has to offer her. The car jumps forward down the track.

Turning her back on the melting mountain, does she sense it hesitate? Hester, don't look behind you to see. She isn't looking back. She's driving headlong forward, away from Drew, away into the emptiness which is all that's left—or all there ever was.

★★★

Atropos is not sitting by the road. No good-bad fairy waves her wand. Nevertheless.

★★★

The world returns somewhere on the highway. It's like—what's it like?—like driving straight out of the skin of a bursting gray balloon.

The light and sound, the sunlight, daylight, trees, the harsh hard surface of the road, reel about her. She careens straight off the highway, almost wraps the car around a pine. Around a *pine*.

Hester sits laughing. She's probably there, doing that off and on, for hours. The sun (the *sun*) sails over, and now and then, cars—*cars*—monotonously pass. Bird and animal scrambling, shining like sunflakes, through undergrowth, rummage through leaves and needles, swing from boughs, hilarious acrobats, sometimes alarmed by her applauding cries. A squirrel, seriously miffed, sits staring at her, out on a limb. It's as though she never saw a squirrel in her life. Did she? The play of its muscles, every sun-tipped hair on its back.

When the blood-gold sky begins to cool, Hester calls Drew's number on her mobile without difficulty. He answers. "Good evening, sir. Can I acquaint you with our new Three Minute Pizza

Service?" "No, thanks," says Drew. He cuts the line away from her. He didn't know her. But then, she no longer knows him either. After this she rings the cabin. The answerphone message comes on, spic and span. She listens to the recorded voices of her friends. Which is a perfect prologue to calling them in New York. "Hi! How *are* you? Oh, honey, I'm glad—sure—see you then."

Mountains crowd around the road, above the woods, and as the light goes out, they alter to opaque lilac marble, good for another million years, and crowned by immortal stars.

When Hester drives into the neon-lit gas station, the dog lurks with its evil head wagging. She sees it as if never before had she seen a dog. Then she drops the unwrapped chocolate bar between its paws. As the dog snaps it up, the old man shoulders out on her. "Hey, what you doing?" he bellows. Filling the tank, she laughs at him. "Crazy bitch," he tells her, and the choco-salivating dog snarls. Music—it's music to her ears.

2

The Fiddle Plays Until It Aches

Can you hear the wind begin to howl
Too late, too late to turn back now
And the fiddle plays until it aches
and fills her resting place
—from "Forever Young" by Janis Ian

1890

I KILLED her. I will tell you why.

✦✦✦

The day I first met her, my future wife, I thought her fallen from the sun above—her golden hair, her eyes of dark amber and skin clear as clean water, her rose-red mouth. Our courtship was swift. She loved me and I her. I have heard other men complain that they found no passion in their wives, but in her was all the passion of Woman. I daresay, the passion of angels, if angels lived in mortal guise.

Did I mention, we were both young? I was, as is often the case, a little older than she, but not so much. I am a tall man, straight and strong. I could lift her up in my arms, she weighed so little, her heavy golden hair the heaviest part of her, I think. I asked her if, like the birds, her bones were hollow. We were happy, gladsome, like the First Two in the Garden. It seems from all Gardens we are, at last pushed forth, for some transgression we do not understand.

Ten years went by. I paid them little heed. We lived well and had no wants, save for each other. That no children had come to us was by our own design. I had no wish to remake myself in that way, and she had told me, early on, she was afraid to submit to the processes of pregnancy and labor. I did not mean to put her in harm's way, and took the best care, since I have seen plenty of women lost in that fashion. Death is jealous of the living. But— there is another more jealous even than death.

It was that very night she confessed to me her fear of becoming a mother, that she confided also the other terror in her heart. "You'll think me foolish, as I am yet quite young—but oh, how I fear growing old!"

"Dearest, is it dying you mean to say?"

"Oh, no," she cried, smiling at me in the candledim, "death is nothing. There is a shining world beyond that gate. I have always known it. Partly, sometimes, it seems to me I *remember* it. There, there's nothing ever bad, only joy everlasting. That is why it is a sin to throw away one's life here. One must wait for this reward."

What she said did not surprise me. I have told you, I thought her fallen from the sun. Perhaps she had dropped farther, from Heaven itself.

But she continued, "I am only afraid of age. I've seen so often what it does. It wrecks and ruins and spoils, it takes away our vitality and our beauty, making us unrecognizable to ourselves and others. It cripples and deforms. We are instruments, well-tuned. We play so sweetly, but then the wood warps, the strings break. Pain and misery and humiliation end our songs. Age is a torturer," she added with an awful sadness, resigned even in her distress, "and time is jealous and rushes us where we dread to go."

I safeguarded her then from her first fear, that of childbirth, but from the second I could not, of course. I hoped, I think, she would grow less to mind her fate, which is the fate of all who persist in life.

She did not.

The ten years elapsed, then another six. Had I noticed by that time any of those changes and spoilings she had mooted? No, not in her. In myself maybe, but one shrugs off these unavoidable affronts. There is no choice.

I began, however, to find my wife, who, like certain of the most beautiful women, had no vanity at all, spending long hours before her mirror. Indeed, she requested a better one, that she might chart more ably the process, as she now began to term it, of the Disease of Time—old age.

She was not yet old. Her years were less than five and thirty. But I, too, seeing her at her pitiless, frightened self-regard, I, too, began to be afraid.

I tried to tempt her from her apprehensions. We took trips here and there, traveled even into foreign places, where always she was feted and adored, as she deserved. It was in Italy, that peach-warm, languid clime, that the initial and real barb was thrust into her. At our hotel, an American girl of about seventeen or eighteen was looking for her mother and, misunderstanding, some Italian gentlemen escorted her to my wife. The girl laughed and explained that, although all of us were from the same country, we were not related. My wife behaved charmingly, as always she did. When they were gone again, I saw the shadow dark as a blush of shame across her face. "What is it, my dearest?" I thought, I believe, for one moment, she had come to regret the fact that she might *not* genuinely claim some young woman as her child. But my love replied slowly, in a little voice, "I am now seen to be old enough to have a full-grown daughter. Now they see what you will not." Then, before I could speak, she rose and went away. It was in Italy, too, after that first barb had been thrust home, that she took her first lover. She made no secret of what she did. He was younger than she. She was embarrassed by it, made worse afraid, yet every night she went to him. And when this lover tired of her, she said, "He sees I'm too old." And then she took another.

So it went on. On our return, my wife was able always to find for herself young men. It came to my notice presently that she paid for them—yes, paid, in dreadful "proper" ways, by "lending" them money and giving them extravagant gifts.

And I, what do you think of me, who permitted himself to be so used and cuckolded, and, by her, made banker to these reprobates? Think what you will. I do not tell you this to ask for judgment, for already I am judged, and soon enough a higher Judge will look into my crime. I tell you only that you may know the truth.

More years passed. Each one brought, for her, further physical catastrophes. I, too, now saw—she *made* me see—the gray hairs that she ripped from her gold, the dye she had recourse to, that was never good enough to match her own wondrous hair, the tonics, pills, cosmetics. She made me note the stiffness that now settled in her back, she spoke of the pains in her feet, and on and on of a tooth which had decayed, and another which broke and had to be pulled. She was never angry. Oh, God—she never railed against this destiny as many do. No, she *cowered*. She lay down, a victim, trembling in abject horror. She, who did not even fear death and hoped for Heaven. It was *this* she feared, and fear was on her now, day and night.

So arrived that evening, a month ago. Winter was flying low above the land, lighting white lamps of frost. That day we drove to dine in town. She had made of herself the best, as she saw it, although to me she seemed older, a painted caricature of all she had been—was. But we made merry and drank wine, and she flirted with other men. When we came home, I held her in my arms. "I have been a poor and unworthy wife to you," she said. I answered, "You have been my only love and always you will be that, to and beyond the gates of eternity." She slept soon from the draught I had added to her tea. And as she slept, I smothered her with the pillow. It did not take long. Our last embrace, when she was dead, was sharper than the razor's edge. I cut her free of chains with it, and it is I that bleed.

I was tried and found guilty of her murder, committed, they said, out of rank jealousy at her unfaithfulness, but it is time who is jealous, and death who garners all.

You will see me sent into the dark as her body is lowered into the dark and frosty ground. She buried under the hill, I buried alive within my prison cell, till death the lover remits me, too. Then I must face the verdict of One who, understanding all, will yet judge me mercilessly in His mercy. Thus, perhaps, even in the lands beyond the world, never again shall I see her. But this I know, and shall know always, through my act she is now fearless, and forever young.

Immortality

by Robert J. Sawyer

Baby, I'm only society's child
When we're older, things may change
But for now this is the way they must remain
—from "Society's Child" by Janis Ian

SIXTY years.

Sweet Jesus, had it been that long?

But of course it had. The year was now 2023, and then—

Then it had been 1963.

The year of the march on Washington.

The year JFK had been assassinated.

The year I—

No, no, I didn't want to think about that. After all, I'm sure *he* never thinks about it . . . or about me.

I'd been seventeen in 1963. And I'd thought of myself as ugly, an unpardonable sin for a young woman.

Now, though . . .

Now, I was seventy-seven. And I was no longer homely. Not that I'd had any work done, but there was no such thing as a homely—or a beautiful—woman of seventy-seven, at least not one who had never had treatments. The only adjective people applied to an unmodified woman of seventy-seven was *old*.

My sixtieth high school reunion.

For some, there would be a seventieth, and an eightieth, a nine-tieth, and doubtless a mega-bash for the hundredth. For those who had money—real money, the kind of money I'd once had at the height of my career—there were pharmaceuticals and gene therapies and cloned organs and bodily implants, all granting the gift of synthetic youth, the gift of time.

I'd skipped the previous reunions, and I wasn't fool enough to think I'd be alive for the next one. This would be it, my one, my only, my last. Although I'd once, briefly, been rich, I didn't have the kind of money anymore that could buy literal immortality. I would have to be content knowing that my songs would exist after I was gone.

And yet, today's young people, children of the third millennium, couldn't relate to socially conscious lyrics written so long ago. Still, the recordings would exist, although . . .

Although if a tree falls in a forest, and no one is around to hear it, does it make a sound? If a recording—digitized, copied from medium to medium as technologies and standards endlessly change—isn't listened to, does the song still exist? Does the pain it chronicled still continue?

I sighed.

Sixty years since high school graduation.

Sixty years since all those swirling hormones and clashing emotions.

Sixty years since Devon.

★

It wasn't the high school I remembered. My Cedar Valley High had been a brown-and-red-brick structure, two stories tall, with large fields to the east and north, and a tiny staff parking lot.

That building had long since been torn down—asbestos in its walls, poor insulation, no fiber-optic infrastructure. The replacement, larger, beige, thermally efficient, bore the same name but that was its only resemblance. And the field to the east had become a parking lot, since every seventeen-year-old had his or her own car these days.

Things change.

Walls come down.
Time passes.
I went inside.

★★★

"Hello," I said. "My name is . . ." and I spoke it, then spelled
the last name—the one I'd had back when I'd been a student here,
the one that had been my stage name, the one that predated my
ex-husbands.

The man sitting behind the desk was in his late forties; other
classes were celebrating their whole-decade anniversaries as well. I
suspected he had no trouble guessing to which year each arrival
belonged, but I supplied it anyway: "Class of Sixty-Three."

The man consulted a tablet computer. "Ah, yes," he said.
"Come a long way, have we? Well, it's good to see you." A badge
appeared, printed instantly and silently, bearing my name. He
handed it to me, along with two drink tickets. "Your class is meeting in Gymnasium Four. It's down that corridor. Just follow everyone else."

★★★

They'd done their best to capture the spirit of the era. There
was a US flag with just fifty stars—easy to recognize because of the
staggered rows. And there were photos on the walls of Jack and
Jackie Kennedy, and Martin Luther King, and a *Mercury* space cap-
sule bobbing in the Pacific, and Sandy Koufax with the Los Angeles
Dodgers. Someone had even dug up movie posters for the hits of
that year, *Dr. No* and *Cleopatra*. Two video monitors were silently
playing *The Beverly Hillbillies* and *Bonanza*. And "Easier Said Than
Done" was coming softly out of the detachable speakers belonging
to a portable stereo.

I looked around the large room at the dozens of people. I had
no idea who most of them were—not at a glance. They were just

old folks, like me: wrinkled, with gray or white hair, some notice-ably stooped, one using a walker.

But that man, over there . . .

There had only been one black person in my class. I hadn't seen Devon Smith in the sixty years since, but this had to be him. Back then, he'd had a full head of curly hair, buzzed short. Now, most of it was gone, and his face was deeply lined.

My heart was pounding harder than it had in years; indeed, I hadn't thought the old thing had that much life left in it.

Devon Smith.

We hadn't talked, not since that hot June evening in '63 when I'd told him I couldn't see him anymore. Our senior prom had only been a week away, but my parents had demanded I break up with him. They'd seen Governor George Wallace on the news, person-ally blocking black students—"coloreds," we called them back then—from enrolling at the University of Alabama. Mom and Dad said their edict was for my own safety, and I went along with it, doing what society wanted.

Truth be told, part of me was relieved. I'd grown tired of the stares, the whispered comments. I'd even overheard two of our teachers making jokes about us, despite all their posturing about the changing times during class.

Of course, those teachers must long since be dead. And as Devon looked my way, for a moment I envied them.

He had a glass of red wine in his hand, and he was wearing a dark gray suit. There was no sign of recognition on his face. Still, he came over. "Hello," he said. "I'm Devon Smith."

I was too flustered to speak, and, after a moment, he went on. "You're not wearing your name tag."

He was right; it was still in my hand, along with the drink chits. I thought about just turning and walking away. But no, no—I couldn't do that. Not to him. Not again.

"Sorry," I said, and that one word embarrassed me further. I lifted my hand, opened my palm, showing the name tag held within.

He stared at it as though I'd shown him a crucifixion wound.

"It's you," he said, and his gaze came up to my face, his brown eyes wide.

"Hello, Devon," I said. I'd been a singer; I still had good breath control. My voice did not crack.

He was silent for a time, and then he lifted his shoulders, a small shrug, as if he'd decided not to make a big thing of it. "Hello," he replied. And then he added, presumably because politeness demanded it, "It's good to see you." But his words were flat.

"How have you been?" I asked.

He shrugged again, this time as if acknowledging the impossibility of my question. How has anyone been for six decades? How does one sum up the bulk of a lifetime in a few words?

"Fine," he said at last. "I've had . . ." But whatever it was he'd had remained unsaid. He looked away and took a sip of his wine. Finally, he spoke again. "I used to follow your career."

"It had its ups and downs," I said, trying to keep my tone light.

"That song . . ." he began, but didn't finish.

There was no need to specify which song. The one I'd written about him. The one I'd written about what I *did* to him. It was one of my few really big hits, but I'd never intended to grow rich off my—off *our*—pain.

"They still play it from time to time," I said.

Devon nodded. "I heard it on an oldies station last month."

Oldies. I shuddered.

"So, tell me," I said, "do you have kids?"

"Three," said Devon. "Two boys and a girl."

"And grandkids?"

"Eight," said Devon. "Ages two through ten."

"Immortality." I hadn't intended to say it out loud, but there it was, the word floating between us. Devon had his immortality through his genes. And, I suppose, he had a piece of mine, too, for every time someone listened to that song, he or she would wonder if it was autobiographical, and, if so, who the beautiful young black man in my past had been.

"Your wife?" I asked.

"She passed away five years ago." He was holding his wineglass in his left hand; he still wore a ring.

"I'm sorry."

"What about you?" asked Devon. "Any family?"

I shook my head. We were quiet a while. I was wondering what color his wife had been.

"A lot has changed in sixty years," I said, breaking the silence.

He looked over toward the entrance, perhaps hoping somebody else would arrive so he could beg off. "A lot," he agreed. "And yet . . ."

I nodded. And yet, there still hadn't been a black president or vice president.

And yet, the standard of living of African-Americans was still lower than that of whites—not only meaning a shorter natural life expectancy, but also that far fewer of them could afford the array of treatments available to the rich.

And yet, just last week, they'd picked the person who would be the first to set foot on Mars. *Of course, it was a man*, I'd thought bitterly when the announcement was made. Perhaps Devon had greeted the news with equal dismay, thinking, *Of course, he's white*.

Suddenly I heard my name being called. I turned around, and there was Madeline Green. She was easy to recognize; she'd clearly had all sorts of treatments. Her face was smooth, her hair the same reddish-brown I remembered from her genuine youth. How she'd recognized me, though, I didn't know. Perhaps she'd overheard me talking to Devon, and had identified me by my voice, or perhaps just the fact that I *was* talking to Devon had been clue enough.

"Why, Madeline!" I said, forcing a smile. "How good to see you!" I turned to Devon. "You remember Devon Smith?"

"How could I forget?" said Madeline. He was proffering his hand, and, after a moment, she took it.

"Hello, Madeline," said Devon. "You look fabulous."

It had been what Madeline had wanted to hear, but I'd been too niggardly to offer up.

Niggardly. A perfectly legitimate word—from the Scandinavian for "stingy," if I remembered correctly. But also a word I never normally used, even in my thoughts. And yet it had come to mind just now, recalling, I supposed, what Madeline had called Devon behind his back all those years ago.

Devon lifted his wineglass. "I need a refill," he said.

The last time I'd looked, he'd still had half a glass; I wondered if he'd quickly drained it when he saw Madeline approaching, giving him a way to exit gracefully, although whether it was me or Madeline he wanted to escape, I couldn't say. In any event, Devon was now moving off, heading toward the cafeteria table that had been set up as a makeshift bar.

"I bought your albums," said Madeline, now squeezing my hand. "Of course, they were all on vinyl. I don't have a record player anymore."

"They're available on CD," I said. "And for download."

"Are they now?" replied Madeline, sounding surprised. I guess she thought of my songs as artifacts of the distant past.

And perhaps they were—although, as I looked over at Devon's broad back, it sure didn't feel that way.

★★★

"Welcome back, class of Nineteen Sixty-Three!"

We were all facing the podium, next to the table with the portable stereo. Behind the podium, of course, was Pinky Spenser—although I doubt anyone had called him "Pinky" for half a century. He'd been student council president, and editor of the school paper, and valedictorian, and on and on, so he was the natural emcee for the evening. Still, I was glad to see that for all his early success, he, too, looked old.

There were now perhaps seventy-five people present, including twenty like Madeline who had been able to afford rejuvenation treatments. I'd had a chance to chat briefly with many of them. They'd all greeted me like an old friend, although I couldn't remember ever being invited to their parties or along on their group outings. But now, because I'd once been famous, they all wanted to say hello. They hadn't had the time of day for me back when we'd been teenagers, but doubtless, years later, had gone around saying to people, "You'll never guess who *I* went to school with!"

"We have a bunch of prizes to give away," said Pinky, leaning into the mike, distorting his own voice; part of me wanted to show him how to use it properly. *"First, for the person who has come the farthest . . ."*

Pinky presented a half dozen little trophies. I'd had awards enough in my life, and didn't expect to get one tonight—nor did I. Neither did Devon.

"And now," said Pinky, *"although it's not from 1963, I think you'll all agree that this is appropriate . . ."*

He leaned over and put a new disk in the portable stereo. I could see it from here; it was a CD-ROM that someone had burned at home. Pinky pushed the play button, and . . .

And one of my songs started coming from the speakers. I recognized it by the second note, of course, but the others didn't until the recorded version of me started singing, and then Madeline Green clapped her hands together. "Oh, listen!" she said, turning toward me. "It's you!"

And it was—from half a century ago, with my song that had become the anthem for a generation of ugly-duckling girls like me. How could Pinky possibly think I wanted to hear that now, here, at the place where all the heartbreak the song chronicled had been experienced?

Why the hell had I come back, anyway? I'd skipped even the fiftieth reunion; what had driven me to want to attend my sixtieth? Was it loneliness?

No. I had friends enough.

Was it morbid curiosity? Wondering who of the old gang had survived?

But, no, that wasn't it, either. That wasn't why I'd come.

The song continued to play. I was doing my guitar solo now. No singing; just me, strumming away. But soon enough the words began again. It was my most famous song, the one I'm sure they'll mention in my obituary.

To my surprise, Madeline was singing along softly. She looked at me, as if expecting me to join in, but I just forced a smile and looked away.

The song played on. The chorus repeated.

This wasn't the same gymnasium, of course—the one where my school dances had been held, the ones where I'd been a wallflower, waiting for even the boys I couldn't stand to ask me to dance. That gym had been bulldozed along with the rest of the old Cedar Valley High.

I looked around. Several people had gone back to their conversations while my music still played. Those who had won the little trophies were showing them off. But Devon, I saw, was listening intently, as if straining to make out the lyrics.

We hadn't dated long—just until my parents found out he was black and insisted I break up with him. This wasn't the song I'd written about us, but, in a way, I suppose it was similar. Both of them, my two biggest hits, were about the pain of being dismissed because of the way you look. In this song, it was me—homely, lonely. And in that other song . . .

I had been a white girl, and he'd been the only black—not *boy*, you can't say boy—anywhere near my age at our school. Devon had no choice: if he were going to date anyone from Cedar Valley, she would have had to be white.

Back then, few could tell that Devon was good-looking; all they saw was the color of his skin. But he had been *fine*. Handsome, well muscled, a dazzling smile. And yet he had chosen me.

I had wondered about that back then, and I still wondered about it now. I'd wondered if he'd thought appearances couldn't possibly matter to someone who looked like me.

The song stopped, and—

No.

No.

I had a repertoire of almost a hundred songs. If Pinky was going to pick a second one by me, what were the chances that it would be *that* song?

But it was. Of course it was

Devon didn't recognize it at first, but when he did, I saw him take a half step backward, as if he'd been pushed by an invisible hand.

After a moment, though, he recovered. He looked around the gym and quickly found me. I turned away, only to see Madeline softly singing this one, too, *la-la-ing* over those lyrics she didn't remember.

A moment later, there was a hand on my shoulder. I turned. Devon was standing there, looking at me, his face a mask. "We have some unfinished business," he said, softly but firmly.

I swallowed. My eyes were stinging. "I am so sorry, Devon," I said. "It was the times. The era." I shrugged. "Society."

He looked at me for a while, then reached out and took my pale hand in his brown one. My heart began to pound. "We never got to do this back in '63," he said. He paused, perhaps wondering whether he wanted to go on. But, after a moment, he did, and there was no reluctance in his voice. "Would you like to dance?"

I looked around. Nobody else was dancing. Nobody had danced all evening. But I let him lead me out into the center of the gym.

And he held me in his arms.

And I held him.

And as we danced, I thought of the future that Devon's grandchildren would grow up in, a world I would never see, and, for the first time, I found myself hoping my songs wouldn't be immortal.

Author's Note: **Janis Ian dropped out of Manhattan's High School of Music and Art in 1966—so whoever the heck graduated from Cedar Valley High in 1963, it certainly wasn't her.**

Hunger

by ROBERT SHECKLEY

I hunger for you like the sky
for the weight of the sun
I hunger for you like the tide
for the moon to come
I hunger for you like the skin
of a doe for the blade
—from "Hunger" by Janis Ian

I WAS sitting in my tub in the window seat. It was one of those hot, slow-moving summer days that seemed like it would go on forever. The flowers in the little garden outside were drooping. In a corner of the darkened parlor, a spider was spinning his web. He barely moved. I was heat-dazed, and the water in my little tin tub, which had started out as cool, was already lukewarm.

I saw several childen come into the field alongside our house. They were carrying a soccer ball. I couldn't imagine how they found the energy to play. But I wanted to play, too.

I leaned out the open window and called, "Throw it to me!"

They didn't, of course. They ignored me. I was the plump little mermaid freak. They didn't know that you needed a good layer of fat to live in the ocean. It's cold there. (So I had been told.) But I had never seen the ocean. It was a hundred or more miles away, to the east. I was afraid I never would see it. I hadn't even seen a real river. All I knew was this dusty little town of Piney Butte, North Carolina. There was a river just a few miles away, but Meg had never brought me to it. She always had an excuse. I guess she loved me in her own way, and didn't want to see me go.

In this town, it wasn't any fun being a mermaid. There wasn't even a swimming pool to practice in, though I'd been told I'd take to the water naturally.

Back in those days I dreamed all the time about the ocean. And I dreamed of escaping from this place, getting to the sea, and finding others of my kind.

When I complained about a mermaid's life, Meg, my stepmother, always advised me to be patient, to ask for little, and to be grateful for what God had given me. I couldn't see that he had given me much except for gills and a tail. Which I had no use for on land. Meg always said there was a secret plan to these things, and that in time the plan would be revealed.

Meg had once been a scientist at Wood's Hole before the fire storms of '62 destroyed it and she went back to where she had been born. She had gotten pretty religious since returning to North Carolina. Our country's present series of catastrophes hadn't shaken her faith.

Once upon a time, so she told me, she had believed that science would save the human race. Now she thought that God would do the trick.

Meg was not a comforting woman, but she could be nice sometimes, like when she told me stories about how people had once thought it would be fun to be a mermaid. But for me it had no benefit, not in Piney Butte, and that was the only place I knew.

I wondered why Allison and Greg, my real parents, had allowed the scientists to do this to me. It was cruel. I imagined my parents saying, "Go ahead, make her a mermaid, it's the coming thing." And then they died when the smallpox came to New England, and I got placed with Meg, and she and Les moved to this stupid town far from the sea.

As it turned out, that afternoon I watched the soccer game marked the beginning of the next catastrophe.

It began to rain. It rained for the rest of the day, and all night, and all the next day, and the day after that. A hard, relentless rain, driven by a summer storm. It must have been brewing down in the horse latitudes, and after that circling in the Sargasso Sea until it built up strength. Then it moved inland, crossed the Outer Banks, and came to us in Piney Butte.

Everyone got out and went to work to shore up the dikes that protected our low-lying land. And that's when the next catastrophe struck.

I was alone in the house. There's nothing much a young mermaid can do to fix a wall on land. I heard the sound of a rifle shot. The next thing I knew, the front door was pushed open and men came in. Five or six of them. Strangers. Hard-looking unshaven men with long hair, wearing ragged clothing. They came in, holding rifles, shaking the water out of their long hair. They saw me and gathered around my tub.

"Well, what in the world have we here?" one of them asked.

"She's got a tail," another said, peering into the tub. "Damned if we haven't got ourselves a mermaid."

They made some jokes I didn't understand. Then one of them said, "What are we going to do with her?"

"Sell her in Raleigh!"

"No market, the country's running over with freaks."

"She's half fish, ain't she? Let's roll her in flour and pan-fry her!"

"Take her along with us! It's about time Davis' Raiders had some fun!"

I begged them to leave me alone, but they just laughed, and two of them pulled me out of my tub. They made a lot of jokes I didn't understand. There were more of them outside the house. They were all mounted on horses. They slung me up to one of the riders.

"What have you got here?" a big older man asked. He wore a slouch hat pulled down over his bearded face, and there was a lot of blood on one leg of his overalls.

"We got us a mermaid, Cap'n."

"And what do you propose to do with her?"

"Have a little fun once we get a chance to camp again."

The Cap'n frowned. "You boys ain't got no sense. Half the county militia coming after us, and you want to play with a little fish girl!"

"We got needs, just like everybody else! And besides, the militia won't be out looking for us in this rain."

The Cap'n was a serious man. He looked like he might order them to put me down. But he wasn't looking too good, not with that wound in his leg, and the man he was talking to looked feisty and ready for a fight.

"You find any food?" the Cap'n asked.

One of the men said, "A sack of corn and a couple of chickens is all."

"Then let's get out of here!"

★★★

They threw me across the saddle like a sack of corn, and they galloped away. I had no idea what they were going to do to me, but I feared the worst. We rode for a long time through the rain, and I got sick, bouncing on my belly across the saddle. We passed through small forested hills and valleys. The rain stopped. By late afternoon the sun was out and we came to a brook.

The Cap'n—his name was Dan—held up his hand, everyone stopped, and they made camp. They tied a rope around my waist, with the other end fastened to a tree. They seemed to be in very good spirits, even Dan, even with his wound, which made walking difficult, but didn't stop him from riding. They took out a jug— whiskey, I suppose—and passed it around. They offered it to me, but I didn't want any.

They got pretty hilarious. They started talking about food after a while. None of them had eaten all day. Their raid on Piney Butte hadn't yielded them much, and I learned that one of them called Otis had been shot dead the day before, and Dan had been wounded.

At some point in this discussion Dan said, "I sure could eat me a mess of fried fish."

That got a lot of response. There was a lot of talk about fishing, and some wild-sounding claims as to expertise. But it turned out they didn't have any hooks, having lost their last one a few days ago.

They were pretty glum, thinking about that, but then Dan said, "Hell, we don't need no hooks, we got a fish woman. Stands to reason she can catch fish."

They all looked at me. I was about to say I had never caught fish in my life, when Dan gave me a big wink and he said, "You can do that, can't you, darlin'?"

I don't know why I trusted Dan. Maybe because he was wounded. But I had a feeling he was on my side. So I said, "I used to catch fish for the town."

One of the men, Jake, I think he was, said, "This is the craziest thing I ever heard. She's going to catch fish for us and bring them back of her own free will?"

"She'll have no choice," said Dan. He held up a coil of rope. "She'll be our captive fish catcher. If she doesn't do good, we'll just pull her in and spank her. You can do that yourself, Jake."

Jake looked puzzled for a moment, then said, "Don't sound too bad. Either I get to eat fish or spank a mermaid. And spanking's not all I'll do to her."

Some of the others had some ideas as to what they'd do to me, too. Dan winked at me again and tied the rope around my waist, and cinched it tight.

"That'll hold her," he said. Then he grabbed me by one arm and pulled me over to the edge of the stream.

"Do a good job, girl, and maybe we won't be too hard on you." He pushed me into the water. As he pushed me, he slipped something into my hand. It wasn't until I was underwater that I saw it was a knife.

"Get to work, girl!" he shouted, and played out line. I dove. It felt natural and wonderful to be in the water. The knife was dull, but by prying with the point I managed to get the knot undone. And then I was swimming free, following the flow of the stream, knowing it would lead me at last to the sea.

I didn't think about anything but escape for the next few hours, swimming as hard as I could, and staying low in the stream. I couldn't figure why Dan had given me the knife. I finally decided maybe he had a sister, or even a wife, or maybe a girl-child of his own. Maybe he had loved her, once upon a time before the world turned crazy.

The stream fed into a river, and there I was at last, swimming toward the sea, because that's where all rivers wind up.

The river was wide and deep, and swimming in it was not much effort. It was like walking must be for regular people, with the added advantage of a current to keep me on my way when I wanted a little rest.

At one point I caught a fish, and ate it, all except for the head and spine. It tasted good. Later I caught and ate another one, and my appetite was satisfied.

★★★

After a while I just let the current carry me, making only an occasional correction to stay in the middle. I calmed down after a while. My experience with the raiders seemed now like a half-forgotten nightmare. Even Piney Butte was fading from my memory.

But other, older thoughts and memories were returning. I remembered a dream I had a long time ago, back when I lived with Allison, my real mother. In my dream, Allison had just given birth to my baby brother. I saw him lying in a white bassinet. He was very tiny, no bigger than a little bird. In fact he was a bird, with gray- and brown-feathered wings. But his face was human.

He was saying something to me in a chirping little voice, but I couldn't understand his words.

"I don't understand," I told him.

He chirped again. Then he stood up. I thought he was saying, "I'll see you again, Lena." And then he flapped his wings and flew away.

I felt very blue, watching him go. He had been so nice. And

so pretty. I wished he had stayed. I was sure we could have been friends.

★★★

Years later I told Meg my dream, and asked her if I really had a litle bird brother.

Meg was a no-nonsense person. "You have no brother, bird or otherwise," she said. "Not by Allison and not by me."

"But I do!" I insisted. "I saw him in a dream. A tiny feathered manikin with wings."

Meg shook her head. "It was only a dream."

"And he was a bird, a tiny bird."

"Not possible," Meg said, and that was the end of it for her.

★★★

Some time later I remembered telling my dream to someone else, a scientist, I think. A big man with a square gray face and thinning white hair.

He told me, "No, my dear, the authorities would never have let the scientists develop such an experiment. No sane person would have attempted it. The brain in a skull such as you describe would have had far too little room for computational capacity. Enough for a small animal, perhaps, but not enough for a human being. It was only a dream, Lena. Your little brother does not exist."

I wanted to ask him, how much brain does it take to make a person happy? But his expertise and air of certainty frightened me and I didn't say anything.

★★★

The river had widened, and the shorelines on either side were low and dim. The sun was almost down, and it was cool.

Maybe I did say something about happiness, because I could hear that man's voice in my dream saying to me, "Happiness is not everything, you know. A human being needs the capacity to cope with the changes this world of ours is undergoing. Our developers are working with several different alternatives for the human race. To pick the wrong one would put ourselves in an evolutionary dead end. With our world crumbling around us, it would be unwise to put any effort into unworkable solutions such as your bird boy."

"So creating a fish girl like me is a better answer?"

"That's how it seemed a few years ago. The oceans make up seven-tenths of the surface of the Earth. They are relatively unexplored territory. And unlike the planets that we presently know of, they are capable of supporting life like ours."

"So why aren't there more like me?"

He shrugged. "Maybe there are. The undersea experiment was discontinued a few years ago. Funding was withheld. People in the government decided that the new underwater species wasn't developing to hoped-for specifications. You see, it's not challenging enough to live in the ocean. All drive is lost in the relative ease of underwater life. Living in the ocean is too easy. Just swim around, eat fish, do no real work, do nothing to enhance and improve the race and its environment. It smacked too much of a romantic idealism. You must be one of the last of the sea people to be created. In terms of the future of the human race, the prospects for you and your kind are poor, at best."

I felt he was wrong, but I had no words with which to argue my conviction.

✦✦✦

And then I heard another voice, a familiar voice. It was saying, "Yes, the project is possible. But not likely to happen until nanotechnology is developed beyond the point it's at now."

It was Mr. Slater's voice. Mr. Slater taught science in our school in Piney Butte, and he was into nanotechnology and miniaturization. He wanted passionately to breed a race of smaller people. A creature the size of my dream brother would have delighted him.

"There need be no loss of quality in a change of scale," he used to tell us. "And the advantages would be immense. Imagine how much longer the Earth's resources would last if we were smaller! The way to achieve this is clear. Take a nanofactory programmed to produce an exact copy of itself. Set your controls so that each succeeding generation produces a size smaller than itself. Combine that with what we know of the human genome. Soon enough you'd have a factory capable of producing miniature humans. From there it's an easy step to microminiaturization. In theory, at least, there's no limit. Or the limit is only bounded by the size of the protein molecule. Or maybe the only real limit is the size of the atom!"

Someone asked, "But how would these tiny people protect themselves from the dangers of the world?"

Mr. Slater shrugged. "Insects make out all right. They are a far more successful species than we are. And bacteria are even more successful."

"Bacteria don't write history," someone objected.

"Bacteria are history!" Mr. Slater said. "If you have the real thing, why write about it?"

Mr. Slater was crazy, of course. But he was the only science teacher in a little town like Piney Butte.

☆★★

So I drifted and dreamed, and after a while I noticed that the river was growing shallow. I wondered if while I was dreaming I had drifted out of the main current. I swam to the banks, but they were shallow, too. After a while I was trying to swim through water no more than a foot or so deep, and it kept on shallowing, until I had to hop and pull myself through soft mud. The deepest part was still in the middle, though it wasn't deep enough for swimming.

I pulled myself along, squirming and hopping on my tail. Then I noticed that there were little islands in the river, some of them with trees. I could see something flashing on one of the islands. I studied it for a while, but couldn't make out what it was. I was afraid of encountering more raiders, but the island looked too small for people. I finally decided to investigate. I dragged and hopped over to it.

At first all I saw was a fallen tree. Then I noticed something shiny and metallic half-covered by the tree. That's when I met Mr. Spider. His body was about the size of a flattened football, and it glinted in the sunlight. He had six or eight metallic legs. He also had eyestalks growing out of his shell, and there were little black eyes at the end of them.

"Hello, Mr. Spider," I said.

The eyestalks twitched. The spider said, "You seem to be a standard model human creature, except for the tail and gills. Your secondary sexual characteristics argue that you are a female. Your tail tells me you have been considerably modified from the original human model. Am I correct?"

"You are, Mr. Spider."

That was the start of our conversation. I was pleased that Mr. Spider didn't seem to consider me a child. He just talked to me like one intelligence to another.

"What happened to you, Mr. Spider?"

"I was crossing the river, and when the storm came up, I took refuge here for the night. Lightning inconveniently collapsed the tree I was sheltering under, and it pinned me to the ground. That was over a day ago. I've been trapped ever since, trying to dig myself out. Unfortunately, one of my flippers has been damaged. It will self-repair when I get unpinned, but for the present I am as you see me."

"Let me see if I can help," I said, and succeeded, with a great deal of effort, in lifting the trunk high enough so he could scramble out.

"And now," I said, "let me take you ashore on my back."

"It is uncommonly good of you," said Mr. Spider. "I have an appointment to meet my friend Flash downstream from here, and, what with my damaged flipper . . ."

"Say no more, I'd be delighted," I told him. "I've been longing for some company, and you seem to know your way around these parts." I hesitated, then said, "You don't look much like a human, Mr. Spider."

"Not all humans are created in the human, homo sapiens model. I am one of a new generation of pseudo-human thinking/feeling machines. The feeling part is very important, you understand, because without feeling, how can you think? And to what purpose?"

"So you can think and feel?"

"Yes, and on my own. It used to be that I and others like me had our thinking done for us at a central point to which we all were attached. But microminiaturization made that no longer necessary."

"Are you what your makers intended?"

"Probably not, but it doesn't matter. Why should I accept one human's conception of how I ought to be? I approve of myself, and that is enough."

We continued across the river, and Mr. Spider showed me where he wanted me to take him. It was a nice spot, with old cypress trees near the water. "Flash should be along any time now. I dreamed last night that he was coming here."

"You dreamed him? Is that a reliable way to meet somebody?"

"It's the only sure way. You haven't learned about dreams yet, have you, Lena?"

"I dreamed once of my baby brother. He was a bird. He said I would see him again."

"Then you will."

"Then he does exist?"

"I have never met him. But if you dreamed him, I'm sure he does exist." He hesitated, then said, "This is a time of changes, you know."

★★

I must have dozed off, because the next thing I remember is Mr. Spider saying to me, "This is my friend, Flash, an example of photo-syntheticus man."

I opened my eyes and looked. Flash was about five feet tall and shaped like a man. But you'd never mistake him for one. His body seemed to be made of vines and gourds, and he had an array of strange, pale plants on the top of his head.

"He takes in sunlight through his head plants," Mr. Spider said, "and converts it inside himself into what he needs. He doesn't talk. But he can make a few sounds. Those he's making now mean that he likes you."

"I like him, too," I said.

Lights danced on and off on Flash's head and body, in a pattern I could make no sense of.

"Yes," Spider said, perhaps reading my mind, "he can communicate through light signals. But I can assure you, it's not Morse code! I haven't deciphered his light-language yet. I don't need to. Flash speaks to me in dreams."

From Spider I learned that Flash took in his nutrition from sun and rain. He did not have appetite in the usual sense. All food was the same to him, since there was no better or worse sunshine. Nor was his passion sex, since he seeded himself.

"Are there others like him?" I asked.

"Flash buds prototypes of himself. But there are no new Flashes being created. It was decided by the human powers who decide these things that homo photo-syntheticus was too passive, didn't have to work for a living like a human. This didn't seem a good model for a new human, so it was discontinued."

"But they let Flash himself live?"

"Well, actually he was thrown out. They thought he was dead and they consigned him to the junk heap. But it takes a lot to kill someone who is mainly plant. There was a mild winter with plenty of rain, and Flash recovered. I met him in the dumps of human-town and brought him away from there. He's been doing fine ever since."

"That was good of you, Mr. Spider."

"We new humans have to help each other. Flash has a place in life, and a passion."

"What is his passion, Mr. Spider?"

"Some spiritual thing, I think," Mr Spider said. "His bodily passions are few, if they exist at all. This frees up his love, his taste for a certain measure of fairness."

"He seems to me an ideal sort of man," I said.

"He's not a man at all. Don't let Flash's human look persuade you. His human form is no more than anthropomorphic sentimentalism on the part of his creators. Actually he's the most alien and strange of us all. Flash is not actuated by passions, which he does not have. Such a creature has no particular love of food, since he takes in sunlight. He has no sexual passion, since he is self-propagating. He has no aesthetic sense, since he is incapable of crafting objects, and if you can't craft it, you can't experience it, or love it."

"So what does he love?"

"It seems to me," Mr. Spider said, "that Flash has freed his mentality to where he can entertain and enjoy himself with thoughts of a high ethical, moral, and aesthetic nature. His love is the play of life. And he is sentimental enough to favor the victory of the living. Unlike real men, he does not require death for an aesthetic outcome. Flash himself is to all intents and purposes immortal. He gardens himself, and the plants that he gives birth to arc just like him. His only human quality might be called love of the play. And the play he and others are producing now demands that you live, mermaid girl, and get to the sea and find your intended."

"I'd like that myself," I said. "What about you, Mr. Spider?"

"As for me," Mr. Spider said, "I am not much like regular humans either. My body takes in nourishment but does not rejoice in feeding. Sex is with me, but it is a mild drive, and not necessarily a pleasure. The metallic and mechanical nature of my body divorces me from the pleasures and pains of the flesh."

Not long after that, Mr. Spider and Flash were gone, and I was alone again in the river.

✦★✦

I was musing on what I had learned, and thinking to myself that I had entered into a new age, an age of miracles. It was a time of new life, taking over from the old life-forms that had had their chance and failed. And I was one of those new life-forms.

I struggled on through the shallow water, flipping myself forward with my tail. I was growing very tired. The water stank from the sewage floating in it. I knew I was near a human settlement.

I stopped and dozed for a while, there in the shallow water. And I dreamed again.

★★★

I saw my brother again in a dream. This time I heard him speak. He said, "Sis, I've been trying to get in touch with you. But I can do it only in your dreams, and I'm still learning. It's very hard, though. The Dreamer says I'm a natural, and I want to learn. There are difficulties ahead for you, and danger. You need to be ready for all that. I'll talk to the Dreamer, see if he can help."

"What sort of difficulty? What kind of danger? Who is this Dreamer?"

My brother didn't answer at once. At last he said, "Sis, I can't explain. But I'll bring help. Just go on as you are, don't detour, there'll be help."

Then I woke up. I had never felt so alone.

★★★

I continued to make my way down the river. Suddenly, from out of nowhere, there was a great splashing of water, and a loud, angry voice. I wanted to dive and conceal myself, but the water level was too shallow. Something was coming at me, a horse, galloping very rapidly. At first I thought it was a horse and rider, but then I saw that the human head was on the horse's neck, broad and bearded. The face was twisted in an angry passion. I thought it looked insane.

At first I thought it was the raiders again, in some nightmare disguise. I screamed, "Leave me alone, raiders!"

The horse-man pulled himself to a halt and said, "I'll show you a raider. Stand up! Let me look at you!"

I stood up on my tail. The horse-man was amazed. "What in hell are you?"

"A mermaid." When he didn't seem to understand, I added, "A fish person."

"I never heard of those."

"Well, I never heard of horse-people."

He shook his head and frowned. He had a broad face. He could have looked nice if he'd only stopped frowning and grimacing.

"Yes, I'm a horse person. Do you know what that makes me in their eyes?"

"A centaur?" I asked timidly.

"No such luck," he said. "They said I was a freak horse, and they whipped me when I wouldn't pull their plow any faster. But not even that was the worst of it. Do you want to know what was?"

"Please tell me," I said, although I really didn't want to know.

"It was when they tried to mate me with a mare. Can you imagine the stupidity?"

"It's difficult," I said.

"I said to them, 'Bring me a horse woman like myself.' They said, 'There are no horse women. No female centaurs.' I said to them, 'How can that be? If you can create a male centaur, why not a female?' They said, 'Money ran out before Phil could get to it.' Can you imagine that?"

"It was bad," I said. "Very bad." Because that is what I thought he wanted to hear, and I didn't want to get him angry.

"Well, I got even when I got ahold of the Winchester." He had two arms growing out of his sides, and in one of them he held a rifle, and there was a bandolier of ammunition around his neck. "I don't like to spend too much time down here in the river. It's not my element. I'm going away now—back to the hills and mountains. That's the proper element for a centaur. Good-bye, fish woman."

★★★

I don't want to remember the final part of journey down the river, but I have sworn to myself to tell everything.

✦✦✦

The river continued to widen, and it became even more shallow. I never imagined before that a river could run out of water, but this one did. Oh, you could see a little movement on the surface, but this was no more than an inch deep. Below that was mud, sand, and rock. Mostly mud where I was. I no longer looked like a girl or a mermaid. I was plastered with mud from head to tail. I must have looked like a statue of a mermaid, or an effigy of one.

I thought I was near the sea when the mud became mostly sand and rock, and water started flowing again. I guess it had filtered itself through all that mud. But it was still pretty foul, and I tried to breathe as little as possible as soon as I was able to swim again.

The river now narrowed suddenly, and turned into a channel. The sides were paved with cement, and now the water was rushing. It carried me along at a healthy clip, I can tell you. I was trying to keep my head above the surface so as not to have to taste that noxious water, and I kept dodging tree trunks and bodies.

Then I heard a voice on the shore bellowing, "Hello there, fish girl!"

I swam toward the shore. There was the centaur again, standing on the bank. I cautiously stopped thirty feet from him.

"Hell, girl," he said. "I didn't come here to harm you."

"Then why did you come?"

"To warn you."

"About what?"

"Well, fish girl, I guess you were born unlucky. You've gotten yourself to the one place on the Carolina coast where you can't get through to the sea."

"Why are you lying to me?" I shouted at him.

"No lie! God's honest truth! Maybe you were too young to remember, about fifteen years ago, the big sea monster scare in these parts?"

"No, I never heard of it."

So he told me. I can't reproduce his words. I had to ask him to repeat parts of it over and over, and clarify other parts. But what he told me came to this:

About fifteen years ago, there was a big invasion scare in these parts. Stories of weird underwater monsters coming up on the shore, dragging off men and women to their underwater lairs, storing them like alligators, to eat later, when they were ripe enough. Whether they believed it or not, the State government had to do something about it. So, with some Federal aid, they created a Zone of Interdiction. This part of the coast, for fifty miles in either direction, was barricaded and mined. Barbed wire, self-firing guns on watch towers, keyed to respond to movement. Other stuff.

But the worst of it was, just downstream from where we were, there was the gigantic blockhouse. At first it had been a fortress, with weapons facing out to sea. But when no invasion came, it was changed into a sewage plant, and made to operate on the polluted river. Everything the river brought to it was chewed up and fumigated and sterilized. And through the plant was the only way to the sea!

***

"Thanks for nothing," I told him. "Why did you go so far out of your way to tell me this?"

"Well, fish girl, I thought I'd offer to take you another way. You can ride on my back. I'll find a safe way for you."

"And why would you do that?" I was beginning to take a dim view of the motives of men. And something in this crazy horseman frightened me and put me on my guard.

"I thought we could team up," the centaur said. "Two freaks without anywhere to go . . . I'd be good to you, fish girl. Come out of the water, get on my back."

It was tempting, even though I found the centaur hateful. He had a crazy mind full of terrible thoughts. But I was in a desperate situation, and I needed help badly.

But I remembered my brother had told me not to deviate. I didn't know quite what that meant, but I thought it meant just go on by myself.

"No," I shouted, "I'm going on!"

"Then you're a damn fool and to hell with you!" And with that the centaur wheeled and galloped away.

***

And so I continued down the river, now a narrow rushing channel. I stayed near the surface so I could see what was coming up. The water was half solid with waste. Plants and dead animals floated in it.

***

And then I saw, ahead of me, a gigantic concrete structure. It looked like a fortress. The river ran under it, and it was moving faster and faster. Where the water disappeared there was a dirty froth, and I could see that the water was running under the structure.

As I approached, I saw that there was a huge steel cylinder in the middle of the factory, half in the water. It was toothed, and it was pulling flotsam from the river. As I approached, I could hear a mixture of terrible grinding noises and rolling sounds.

I knew then a ghastly fear. I didn't want to be killed, and certainly not like that. As I came into the final stretch, I could see the rolling cylinder turning, reaching for me. I tried to swim away from it, but I could make hardly any progress against the current. I knew I was finished.

And then I saw a bright light just above me. I blinked and resolved it into a tiny winged shape that seemed to be made of light. My brother!

It was too loud to talk in the crashing and thundering and grinding of that giant cylinder. But I could hear a voice in my head, saying, "Hang on there, sis. Help is on the way. Swim to your right . . ."

Somehow I managed to do that. The current seemed just as powerful.

But suddenly I felt a strong hand grab my right wrist. I blinked and made out a shape—a merman—six or seven feet long—powerful-looking.

Again, I couldn't hear him, but his thought was, "Okay, mermaid, I've got you. Now swim with me. We'll get you out of this."

My body didn't want to respond. I was experiencing the greatest fatigue I had ever known. But somehow I kept my tail working, and I made my way with the merman to the right bank.

"It's a narrow channel," he thought. "Keep hold of my hand. I'll get you through."

And we plunged then into the dark tunnel he had told me about, or dreamed at me.

"Flatten yourself against the wall!"

I did as he said. We passed through in a rush, going by way of this channel that the sea must have dug, bypassing the cylinder by inches. We continued, I don't know for how long. And then, all of a sudden, we were in the ocean. I tasted salt water for the first time, coughed for a while, then became used to it.

After a while he led me up to the surface. I lay there, resting. He said, "I am Hans. The Dreamer sent me. When you have rested, I will lead you to where we live."

***

All of that was a long time ago. Hans is my mate now, and we have two little mermaid girls. Hans swam here all the way from Denmark, can you imagine? Looking for a mate and a better life, and he says he's found both with me.

Once I went down to the freezing, crushing depths where the Dreamer lives. The Dreamer is huge and slow-moving. I didn't stay long, but he sent me friendly dreams after that.

I think the Bible was wrong. We didn't start with the Word,

but with something more powerful. Before the Word there was the Dream. Everything good and bad follows from that.

We people of the sea and air are not good fabricators. But we get things done when they are necessary to us. No, we don't want to invade and conquer the land. That's a fantasy on the part of the land-based humans, the large, brainy meat eaters, who think they have something valuable to steal. We keep away from them. We keep to ourselves, in our own element, and year by year our numbers increase. We know that all life may vanish from this planet due to some unavoidable cataclysm. But we have always known that life ends.

Maybe we can get somewhere else in dreams. The Dreamer is trying to teach us.

Life ends, but the Dreaming goes on.

Society's Stepchild

by Susan R. Matthews

When we're older, things may change—
But for now this is the way they must remain
They say I can't see you any more, baby,
can't see you any more
No, I don't want to see you any more, baby . . .
—from "Society's Child" by Janis Ian

T HE public-car dropped them off on the corner of the street. Walking arm in arm with Cilance to the little old-fashioned house, Nebrunne stood silent for a moment, remembering childhood visits. "You're going to love Aunt Marnissey," Nebrunne promised Cilance yet again.

She loved him so much that it made her heart ache just to look at him. Understanding how uncomfortable he must feel to be in this unfamiliar place gave her so much anxiety she almost wished she'd never spoken to her aunt in the first place. There were things he might not know about her aunt, that might have reassured him—"I should have told you the whole story much earlier, Cilance. It'll have to wait now, we're here."

This tree-shaded and white-paved suburb of Orachin was an older area of the city. Great-Aunt Marnissey lived in a neighborhood that had stayed almost purely Telchik, while the population of the city as a whole had blended with many different races of Dolgorukij—even Sarvaw—over the years since Aunt Marnissey had been Nebrunne's age. The only Sarvaw people who lived here would normally expect to see were maintenance workers or casual laborers, and few enough of those.

Elsewhere in the city a Sarvaw didn't need to feel alone—there were plenty of dockworkers, freight handlers, food-service workers needed to run Orachin's industrial machine, and Sarvaw were well accepted where hard physical labor was to be done. Cilance wasn't a dockworker, though. Cilance was a medical technician. Nebrunne had met him at work.

"Nebbie, my skin's crawling," Cilance whispered, standing on the front step, waiting for an answer to Nebrunne's signal at the door. "Are you sure she knows who I am?"

There was no getting around the fact that Cilance was what some souls still called the wrong sort of Dolgorukij, especially the older folk. His Sarvaw heritage was there to see, the space between his eyes, the color of his hair, the complexion of his skin, the size of his hands relative to his body.

"It'll be all right," Nebrunne whispered. "Someone's coming. Don't worry. Just be yourself. She'll love you."

There were things about Great-Aunt Marnissey that made Nebrunne confident that the oldest surviving female member of her family would understand: but in light of family history there was no question but that Aunt Marnissey had to be consulted first, to bless the match.

★★★

When the signal came at the door, Marnissey was still upstairs in her bedroom plaiting a creamy-yellow blossom into her hair. Its fragrance was sweet in the air and evocative of dreams and romance. Yes, it was a courting-token, but what of that? Those were old practices, nowadays no more than a wink and a nod to things that no longer mattered; and she'd bought it herself. Camm hadn't sent it to her. She'd saved the receipt in her accounts, in case her mother asked her any questions.

She'd wanted to be the one to get the door. Now she tied her plait off hastily—leaving the handspan tail undone, because after all that was the way one wore a courting-token—and snatched her jacket up from the back of the chair, rushing down the stairs, riding the hurry she was in over her uncertainties about the wisdom of what she was doing.

Her mother was at the door. Marnissey could hear her. That was better than if it'd been her father, but bad enough. Well, her mother had to learn, didn't she? This was a new age. Sarvaw were just as good as Telchik. They were all Dolgorukij under the skin. Prejudice had no place in the modern world.

Marnissey's mother was turning from the door with an expression of confusion and distress. "Wait here, you. Marnissey. Marnissey, there's a—person—here to see you, you're going out with *him* tonight?"

Yes, she was, and her mother could stare white-faced at her courting-braid all she liked. It was just fashion, that was all. "Why not, Mam?" Marnissey said boldly, in the face of her mother's shock. "It's just the guest lecture. It's Camm! You know about Camm, I've been talking about him for weeks." The door was half-open, her mother's hand flat to the old-fashioned wooden edge of it. Intolerable. Marnissey called out to the man she knew was waiting on the step. "Come on in, Camm, I'm just finishing up here."

But her mother pushed the door closed firmly. "You didn't tell us enough about Camm, daughter. You should be ashamed. What if your father had answered the door?" Now, this made no sense; how was it her fault if her parents couldn't behave decently to her friends? "And courting-flowers. We'll talk about this later. You'd better be sure you're home in good time. Go on with you."

Shaking her head sadly over her mother's insensitivity, Marnissey opened the door firmly enough to back her mother off, and went outside. If that was the way they were going to be about Camm, she wasn't going to expose Camm to their rudeness by asking him in. Yes, they'd talk about this later; her parents were going to have to learn to accept things as they were, and Camm was her friend, her really much closer than just friend, even if he was Sarvaw.

"I'm sorry about that," she shrugged. Camm was waiting patiently for her on the step, his hands in his pockets; she could smell his shaving lotion. He looked her up and down and smiled; nodded—at the courting-flower in her hair, maybe?—and shrugged in his own turn. He was so beautiful. No, his features were not so fine or elegant as those of a Telchik Dolgorukij; but why should they be? She loved his nose for its weight, his cheekbones for their strength, the warmth of his dark eyes for their tenderness, the size of his hands for their gentleness. Yes, he was Sarvaw. Beautiful. "Parents. Let's go?"

"Got tickets," Camm said. "Up front, center. I'm a little worried, though. No question that Parmenter's the champion, but lately I've heard some of her remarks about breaking down barriers, I'm not sure whether she's trying to push too fast." He held out his arm for Marnissey as he spoke, and turned down the little walkway between the house and the street. "Because, I mean, well, we're talking about history that runs octaves deep. If we want to really communicate with people, we've got to be a little sensitive to their insecurities, don't you think?"

Marnissey gave her beautiful friend Camm a little shove, loving the feel of the hard muscle of his upper arm under her hand. Sarvaw had been the victims for so long that it was part of their thinking. There was so much healing to be done, there; but she had the strength for it, she knew she did. "I think we'd better hurry."

The public-carrier ran on a restricted schedule in the evening. Camm preferred to walk when he could anyway, because of the way people treated him when he rode the public-carrier, especially when he rode the public-carrier with her. The lecture hall for tonight's event was within walking distance, yes, but it was still a good hike. "We'll solve the rest of the Combine's problems after the lecture, Camm. Come on."

Arm in arm with Camm, Marnissey went happily down the hill to hear Parmenter speak about the issues surrounding the integration of Sarvaw more fully into the government and economy of the Dolgorukij Combine.

★

The tea shops had been full, after the lecture. Marnissey suspected that Camm was just as happy about that; not because he grudged the expense—even Camm had enough money to buy a flask of rhyti and a pastry or two—but because he hadn't fit in well since he'd arrived at the city's university to take an advanced degree in commercial law. Some tension was unavoidable, but he'd had little choice—no Sarvaw university offered any equivalent expertise in commercial law.

He'd never shown her the slightest sign of bitterness. That had been one of the first things she'd noticed about him, one of the first things she'd come to love. He was so courageous and so understanding, five times the man of any of her Telchik peers.

There was no getting around the fact that people she'd known all her life turned their backs on her when they saw her with Camm, and declined to wave her over to join a table where there were two vacant seats for fear she might actually expect Camm to come and sit down with them as though he were Telchik rather than Sarvaw. She could be strong, for Camm's sake; she would be an example to them all. It wasn't self-righteousness on her part: she would have loved him had he not been Sarvaw, so how could she love him less for being exactly who he was?

Less time spent talking in the tea shops meant more time to walk home with him, his arm around her shoulders, talking as they went. "Of course there'll be issues," Camm warned. "Listen, Marnissey, it's not just *your* parents, I'm sorry to say. I'll have explaining to do at home as well."

It had been dark for hours now. The streetlights had come on as the sunlight faded, yes, but with the trees that lined the pavements still in leaf they were as private as if they were alone in all the world. Marnissey couldn't remember a time when she'd been so happy.

Reaching up for Camm's face in the dark she kissed him tenderly, and stood in the warm embrace of his arms for a long moment before she shook herself free and walked on. "I don't expect to be welcomed into your family, Camm, except as your wife. I mean I won't be expecting any special treatment. All I ask for is a chance to show that I love you, and I'll be happy."

This was her block; it was just three houses down, now, to her house, where the light at the door was still turned up brightly. Waiting for her. The rest of the lights in the house were already down, so her parents had gone to bed. She felt a little rush of grateful relief for that: no confrontations would ruin her memories of tonight's perfect romance. "If there's anyone could overcome their reservations, it'd be you, Mar," Camm said with humorous resignation in his voice, slowing his steps as they got nearer the house. "I've never met anyone with so much determination—"

Something was wrong.

The small hairs at the back of Marnissey's neck prickled in a nervous rush of reaction to something she could not quite sense: and the shadows exploded, the darkness on either side of the pavement rising up and rushing at her screaming unintelligible curses. Something hit her, struck her in the stomach, she fell down backward onto the pavement but something warm broke her fall—Camm.

She knew that it was Camm, though she could not recognize his voice. They were hitting him. Kicking him. She couldn't breathe, and just as she began to gasp for air something cold and viscous and heavy struck her in the face and filled her mouth. Her nose. Her eyes, her ears, it stank, her head was stuck in something horrible; struggling to free herself Marnissey heard the final taunts from her attackers as they fled—"Blood-soiler. Watch the shit between your legs!"

Blood-soiler. It was a bucket, over her head. Marnissey pushed it the rest of the way off and tried to clear her mouth and nose of filth, desperate for air. A bucket filled with mud and excrement, she was covered with it, and collapsed over Camm's slowly struggling body in despair. Why weren't people coming to help them? Hadn't anybody heard? How could they not have heard, she was sure she must have screamed, she'd heard Camm yell when they'd started hitting him, a shout of outraged fury mixed with pain—

It seemed to take forever for the police to come. There was

blood all over Camm's face; she couldn't stop retching. They helped her up and into the ground-car, and took her down to the police station.

✹✹✹

The priest from the university chapel had come, Uncle Danitsch, the wrong priest—the young one, the sincere one, the strict one. Marnissey went to Uncle Birsle when she went to chapel at all because Birsle was much more tolerant of the compromises that daily life demanded, but Birsle wasn't on duty at this time of night. The matron had brought Marnissey a dampened towel so that she could wipe her face, but she stank, and she could taste the obscene mix of hatred and contempt with which she'd been assaulted in her mouth still.

"Thank you for your statement," the policeman said. "We take these things very seriously indeed, Miss. We'll be investigating as aggressively as we can. We won't tolerate this sort of ugliness in our city."

It was comforting and it was nice to hear, but Marnissey wasn't sure she could believe it, because ever since she'd gotten to the station she'd had an uncomfortable suspicion that they were laughing at her. That they were sorry she was hurt, but believed that she'd been asking for it, as though she was to blame in some way for having been assaulted. "You haven't gotten anywhere with any of the other incidents, though, have you?"

Her accusation came out sounding a bit more savage than she'd intended. Uncle Danitsch shifted uncomfortably where he stood leaning up against the heavy table in the interview room, but held his peace. He hadn't been at the school for very long. She hadn't heard much about him, but if she put her mind to it, she remembered that Danitsch was pledged to Spotless Purity.

She didn't like that thought. Spotless Purity was one of the Nine Filial Saints, and his Order maintained the genealogies of the Dolgorukij—especially the great houses, yes, but also of all the rest of the Holy Mother's children. Spotless Purity could tell if you'd ever had a Sarvaw amongst your ancestors, and would, too, if there was a risk that you might marry into an unsoiled family line and compromise the purity of its Aznir or Arakcheyek or Telchik blood with that of slaves.

"'Other incidents,' Miss, I'm not quite sure I follow," the policeman said, very bland-voiced, very professional. Down at the foot of the table Camm was shaking his head; she could see him, out of the corner of her eye, but she refused to notice. It wasn't the first time someone had assaulted Camm since he'd come here. This had to be added to the reports, to construct a case, to build a dossier.

"You know perfectly well. Camm was attacked in the library three months ago. They hurt his arm, his leg, his knee." It had been the beginning of their relationship, in a sense. She'd noticed him before, of course; she could hardly not have noticed a Sarvaw among the other students on campus.

Still, it hadn't been until he'd disappeared for a few days—and then reappeared with a limp and a bandaged face—that she'd started to pay attention to who he really was. She'd wondered what he'd done to have deserved a beating. Then she'd realized that he hadn't done anything, anything at all, except be Sarvaw in a Telchik school.

"I'm sorry, Miss, but we ran a check when you came in. This is the first report of any such blood-soil incident all year, excusing your presence, Uncle."

She couldn't believe that. The people who'd attacked Camm had told him to stay away from Telchik women; Camm had described the whole horrible thing to her—what he remembered of it. How could that not have been reported as a blood-soil crime?

She turned her head to stare at Camm in confused consternation, but Camm had turned his head away, and there was something in the ashamed angle of his bent neck that explained it all to her. He hadn't reported it. He hadn't wanted to make trouble, he'd always told her he knew he had to put up with a certain amount of mischief because he was an outsider, but she hadn't realized he was as determined as that. He hadn't reported the beating; had he reported any of the other incidents?

Uncle Danitsch intervened before she could confront Camm, demand he tell the police about the earlier assaults. "If you're satisfied with her statement, Officer, I'll take this young lady home. The doctor's coming for her friend, I understand?"

For whatever reason this simple question was too much for Marnissey to bear, and why it should be so after everything else that had happened to her tonight Marnissey couldn't say—but it was. "He's not my friend," she said, and began to cry at last. "He's my fiancé."

Camm rose stiffly from where he was and came to her, embracing her to comfort her. She wept. This hadn't been the way she'd wanted to announce her engagement; was it to be the pattern of her future?

★★★

Now that the news was out she spent each available moment with sweet Camm, as much because no one else would have anything to do with her as that she loved him desperately. Only three days and the school had turned against her, against them both—yet oddly enough it seemed she bore the brunt of it; she was the one who was lowering herself, she was the one who planned to commit the blood-soil crime against her ancestors.

There seemed to be less blame assigned to a Sarvaw for aspiring to a Telchik wife than to a Telchik woman, the guardian of the purity of the blood, for electing to debase herself with a Sarvaw husband. It was as if all of the hostility previously directed against them both had focused on her alone.

It wasn't easy. Camm was subdued and quiet, and though he did the best he could to support her Marnissey began to realize—slowly, painfully—how difficult the task that she had taken on so thoughtlessly really was. The complications of her life were not fully revealed to her, however, until the moment—three days and counting after the attack—when Marnissey on her way from her study group to her academic counselor noticed her friend Abythia talking to Uncle Danitsch, beside the chapel arch, noticed at first because Uncle Danitsch was not usually about so late in the afternoon, but then caught a fragment of what Abythia was saying and froze in her tracks.

"Blood-soiler," Abythia said, her voice cold and heavy with poison. "To think that my own prayers might be contaminated— isn't there some penance I can do, for having ever known such a person? Ugh."

The concept was one she'd heard before from other people, sneering at other targets. The Holy Mother, so the theory went, would sniff suspiciously at devotions offered by honest Telchik unfortunate enough to be tainted by association with an unfilial daughter; and what could be more grotesquely unfilial than degrading the purity of one's genetic heritage by giving oneself to a Sarvaw?

It had been octaves since the Sarvaw had been reintegrated into the Dolgorukij Combine by force of arms. There was still no word in High Aznir for "female Sarvaw hominid" that didn't mean the same thing as "property" or "whore," nor any word for "adult male Sarvaw hominid" that didn't also mean "slave" or "beast of burden." Her own parents were no help to her, and Marnissey was miserably aware of having failed them in a real sense. She should have waited until she could at least have told them. She should have given them some time to become accustomed to the fact before she had published it to the whole world.

And still it wasn't any of those things that truly stunned her. Not the things Abythia said; just the one phrase. Blood-soiler. She'd heard Abythia say those words before. It had been Abythia who had assaulted her.

Uncle Danitsch took Abythia's hands in his own, turning away from Marnissey when he saw that they were observed. The gesture was telling—and terrible.

Abythia had assaulted her. Abythia had been a part of that obscene ambush, Abythia, Abythia had dumped a bucketful of filth and mud over her head and called her names. Her own friend Abythia. Worse than that—Uncle Danitsch was a part of it; the picture that he made with Abythia was too overtly conspiratorial for any other interpretation, no matter how Marnissey's horrified mind sought to place it in another light.

She'd grown up with Abythia. She'd gone to school with Abythia. She'd celebrated saints' days, complained about the politics of girlish cliques and cabals, pored over courses of study, dreamed about the future, agonized over admission tests with Abythia.

She hadn't been close to Abythia since she'd started her degree studies at the university—they were in different programs—but it was so much worse that Abythia should despise her than her own parents. She expected her parents not to understand, but she would have trusted Abythia with the deepest secrets of her heart. Abythia, Abythia, Abythia had assaulted her; how was she to live?

The shock left her numb all the rest of the day. She sat through her appointment with her academic counselor almost not caring that her interim grades were very much reduced from expectation or that her counseling team had serious doubts about her fitness for a job in the education of young children, but was willing to acknowledge that perhaps it would be all right—the standards in Sarvaw schools being so much less stringent, due to the correspondingly reduced ability of the children.

They assumed that she'd move off-world once she was married; there seemed no possible future for her here, in her own home, and she'd always supposed that she'd join the academic establishment in Orachin where she'd been born, and live out her life respected—valued—cherished—as a teacher. She would never teach in Orachin if she married Camm. What was she to do?

She didn't have the heart to see Camm and share the things she'd learned today with him. She went to chapel instead, to see Uncle Birsle and ask for his help. She hadn't spoken to him since before the attack; she'd lost track of time—her world had ended that night, when she'd thought it was just beginning.

"Well, it is too bad that Danitsch was called," Uncle Birsle agreed, carrying a flask of rhyti from the warmer-service near the door to his office to set it down in front of her. "A bit of a fanatic,

I'm afraid, I've spoken to our superiors about it. I'd have suggested you love your Camm in private for a while longer, myself. A long while longer. Until you were graduated longer. There's just no getting around the fact that there's ugliness out there, but I'm sorry that you couldn't be spared. Both of you."

Birsle's office was small and dark, but warm. Dennish, in a sense, a haven for a wounded spirit, but the icon of the Holy Mother on the wall behind his desk still seemed to look at her accusingly, for all of his gentle reassurances. "Is that the way it has to be?" Marnissey demanded, struggling with tears of loss and shame. "It can't be so great a crime to love. How can it be so horrible a sin as that? He's the best—the most beautiful—the man I want, as I've never wanted any other—"

He shrugged, but kindly, with sorrow of an impersonal sort in his gentle smile. "Don't be naïve, Marnissey, look at what you're doing to yourself and him and your family. What happened to you the other night is only the beginning, and what do you expect for your children? His family will be no happier to have a Telchik woman in their midst than yours is to find itself related to a Sarvaw. But you told the police that you meant to be married, so there's nothing to be done about it. Except perhaps withdraw from attending classes, and petition to complete your degree program on remote."

Uncle Danitsch was collaborating with her attackers; Birsle gave her no comfort, only hard unromantic strategies. "The Holy Mother would be ashamed to hear you," Marnissey accused bitterly, through her tears. "She loves the Sarvaw just as much as she loves any other Dolgorukij. It says so. In the text."

From the small pained smile on Birsle's face it almost seemed he had expected the attack. "Equally well," he agreed. "But separately, Marnissey, remember? Now go home. Don't make any more trouble for your family than you already have."

Even the Church was to be denied her, then. She had nowhere to turn, nowhere but Camm. She didn't want to see Camm just now. How could she complain to him of all the snubs and shunning that she was being made to suffer? It would seem as though she was blaming him for it all.

She went home. Her mother had gone into the city today and wouldn't be home until much later. Her father had prepared a quick stew, she could smell it as she came into the house, and she knew without being told that he hadn't wanted to go to the grocer's today to buy fresh food.

She liked her father's quick stew, but she couldn't face the dish now knowing why her father had made that choice for third-meal. Marnissey went up the stairs to her bedroom alone and lay on her back on her bed long after the sun had gone down, staring at the ceiling in the dark.

✳✳✳

She had study groups for the next few days and didn't go. Camm came to the door; she heard him, and she wanted to see him, but she stuffed her pillow into her mouth and let her mother send him away. The school sent a message that her absence had to be excused, or it would reflect against her academic record—a bit of petty administrative bullying that was almost as much funny as infuriating, it was that obvious. That stupid.

She went to her study groups the next day following. No one would speak to her, and she sat in the back, disheartened. She tried to participate, but the group leader wouldn't acknowledge her presence; when she got home there was another note from the administration, saying that she shouldn't come to study group unless she was prepared to join the discussion. It was too much. She needed to see Camm. She put on an old jacket and crept out of her house by the bedroom window to go down to the student dormitories.

She didn't make eye contact with the people that she passed in the street, in the halls. She'd lived in the city of Orachin all her life, some of those people had been as close to her as members of her own family, and it was as though they had all of them been bewitched and turned into monsters, jeering harpies speaking in faery tongues. She could hardly bear it.

Camm, beautiful Camm, Camm whom she needed so much was in his room sitting at his workstation reading a text. He frowned when he saw her. She closed the door; he got up and opened it again. "You don't want to be behind closed doors with me," he warned. "People will talk. We've got to be a little more careful for a while, Mar, I'm afraid."

She was tired of *afraid.* Had it only been two weeks since their engagement, and the attack? How could she live with any more "afraid" than this? "Don't let them govern our behavior, Camm," she said. "People who would take it wrong aren't worth being concerned about. And I need you to hold me. It's been awful without you."

But she could guess the problem. If they couldn't be behind closed doors together, still less could they embrace in his bedroom, even with the door open. There was to be no comfort for her. None. Camm sat back down at his workstation, slowly, and shook his head. "We have to be strong," he said. "It's too bad we were startled into letting our secret out too soon."

Secret, what did he mean, secret? They hadn't discussed keeping it a secret. She felt completely overwhelmed: now even Camm was deserting her, denying her comfort and support. "Are you sorry?" she challenged him, with cold fury in her voice. "Maybe you've changed your mind about marrying me. Is a Telchik wife more than you can handle after all? You don't seem to be doing very well with a Telchik fiancée."

It was a horrible thing to say. She knew that the moment she heard the words come out of her mouth. More horrible still was the fact that Camm didn't get angry, Camm didn't leap to his feet and reproach her, Camm just sat at his workstation looking up into her eyes with the one lone tear fleeing down his cheek.

"You're right," he said. "It doesn't seem so. But, Mar, we're under a lot of pressure we hadn't really anticipated. I want to marry you, I want to spend the rest of my life with you, but maybe we made a decision a little ahead of time. Maybe we should be unengaged, we have to get through our schooling, after all. That'll be another year. We can't get through it like this."

He didn't want her. Or, he wanted her, but he wanted his credentials more than he wanted her. How could he even suggest such a thing? Did he think she would abandon him just because she'd been attacked—and her friends had turned their backs on her—and the administration was harassing her—and her family wasn't speaking to her—

"But I love you, Camm." She did. She loved his courage and his wit, his wisdom, his cheerful optimistic nature. His beautiful Sarvaw face. His beautiful Sarvaw body, that was so different from that of the people with whom she had grown up.

"Oh, I love you as well, Mar." If that was true, why wouldn't he look at her? "And we should maybe take a step back, here. Start again from the beginning. Talk to your parents, for one thing."

What kind of courage failed so readily in the face of adversity? Marnissey stepped back and away from him, horrified. He didn't raise his head, he didn't look at her, she backed out of his room and went back to her house, too confused and benumbed to be afraid of walking alone in the dark this time.

★ ★

Things got quieter, they settled down. She tried her best not to see Camm, not to be too greedy for him, not to admit that she was still seeing him—that she loved him so desperately that only her anguish at the injustice of the situation she was in could be compared. When she was with Camm, she was invisible. When she kept away from Camm, people would sit with her, would walk with her, talk to her, even eat with her, but she couldn't trust them any longer.

Who knew whether her once-friend Abythia was being sweet and loving with her in order to encourage her to stay away from Camm, in order to show her that all could be forgiven—or in order to keep track of her, spy on her, report on her to some secret cabal? And it wasn't fair to Camm. Marnissey didn't ask what went on in his life when she wasn't there. She could hope it wasn't much different than before, but she knew that was probably an unrealistic wish on her part.

She was crossing the school's quadrangle one day going from her lab meeting to class when she heard the sound of running feet behind her and tensed despite herself. It was Camm. She knew the sound of his footfall. He slowed as he approached her and she clutched her graphscreen-reader to her, her stomach twisting into a knot.

She didn't know whether she wanted to see him—because she loved him, she needed him, she missed him, he was right there with her every day and he might as well have been worlds away—or wished that he would stay away from her. So long as they had no contact, it was almost possible to pretend that things hadn't changed forever the night Abythia had emptied a bucketful of excrement over Marnissey's head, and called her a blood-soiler.

"Hello," Camm said; Marnissey nodded, and kept walking. "How have you been, Mar? I haven't seen you." Of course not. He'd told her they should be discreet. She'd given up her parents' peace of mind, the company of her friends, for him, for him; and all he'd offered her in return was to say that they'd been incautious.

She didn't know how to respond. "As you suggested," she replied. "Taking a step back. Giving people a chance to adjust. Taking it slowly. Careful. Quiet. Prudent."

Camm nodded, looking past her to where some of her friends stood talking amongst themselves in front of the technical library. "You're angry at me," Camm said. "My poor Mar. It's been a lot rougher than it had to be. I'm sorry. I wish I could change it all for you."

That wasn't what she wanted to hear; but perhaps that in itself was a message. No *I love you and I miss you and I can't wait until you are mine forever.* No *I dream of you, I want you, the world must be made to know how proud I am that such a beautiful—talented— admirable woman would consent to be my bride.* Nothing. *You've had a rough time, I'm sorry. That's the way it's going to be, though, rough.*

Suddenly it seemed to Marnissey that she was not up to facing so much rough. She hadn't understood what she'd been in for. Camm had tried to tell her, but he'd put the best face on it always. Had he been afraid of discouraging her?

How much hadn't he told her because he'd wanted her, because he knew she'd think twice about a life that could have something as shocking as a bucketful of excrement in it? How loving could it truly be to ask the woman who would be his wife to take the stink of shit in her nostrils, the taste of manure in her mouth, as part of the everyday price of being his?

She'd read of Dasidar and Dyraine in literature studies; she'd been taught from childhood to admire Dyraine as the type of heroic endurance—suffering years of abandonment, ill-use, hardship and want, true ever and always to Dasidar who would come for her one day in the end and vindicate her patience in triumph. It was the great romance of the Dolgorukij-speaking peoples, even Sarvaw.

Now in a moment of sickening self-realization Marnissey suddenly understood that although she'd cherished a fantasy of herself as Dyraine and Camm her Dasidar, she didn't have the strength of a Dyraine. She was not a heroine. She was only an ordinary young woman from a well-to-do Telchik family who'd lost herself in a delusion of romantic heroism that she could not sustain.

If she'd been Dyraine, she'd have been able to smile at Camm bravely and tell him he was loved, and that no hardship was too great if only it meant she could be by his side. She wasn't Dyraine of the Weavers. So she said something else instead.

"It's been rough enough to show me my mistake." She couldn't fault him for not having the soul of a Dasidar. Dasidar was a mythic hero, a perfect type; and not Sarvaw. Camm was as ordinary as she was, with almost as few resources at hand to deal with the ferocious pressures that oppressed them.

He'd been right, those weeks ago, when he'd suggested they step back a bit. More right than he'd known, perhaps. "I've wronged you, Camm, I'm sorry, but this has been a mistake. No. I won't marry you. And we already know we can't be friends. They won't let us."

They were almost clear to the other side of the quadrangle,

where she had her class—the class that she might yet pass, that she had no hope of passing as Camm's fiancée or his sweetheart. That class. One of several of those classes. Camm stopped to stare down at her; his face was ugly with hurt.

"You don't mean that," he said. It was the wrong thing; it made her angry—didn't she know whether she meant it or not? "You can't mean that, Marnissey, I know it's been horrible for you, but we love each other. I love you, Mar, I want you to be part of my life forever, please don't let the prejudice of these—Telchik—stand in our way."

She was Telchik. She, herself. Pointing that out would do no good and only increase the stress of this already unhappy conversation, however. Marnissey suddenly sensed a feeling in her heart that she hadn't known for weeks, something she didn't want to let go: relief. Joy. Happiness. It was so easy. It had been a mistake. Yes, she was fond of him and he was beautiful, but how could she ever have been so immature as to imagine that they had any chance of happiness together, any chance at all? Hadn't she known all her life what people thought about Telchik women who went with Sarvaw men, whether or not they came right out and said it?

She needed the giddy sense of freedom, that intoxicating feeling of awakening at the last possible moment from a horrible nightmare and realizing that it was just a dream. An error. She had misjudged. No. She was not going to marry Camm. She would beg her parents' forgiveness. She'd gained knowledge and wisdom from the ordeal, but she didn't have to compound her juvenile error by following through on it just because she'd said that she was going to. She didn't have to marry him. She could have her life back, not the same, but not irrevocably ruined either.

"I do mean it, Camm." She sounded very calm to herself, admirably firm. "I'm quite clear. And I'm sorry. Uncle Birsle will give me penance for a false promise, but we should both be glad that I figured it out before it was too late. Good-bye, Camm. Marry someone who loves you better than I can. I won't."

She started to move forward toward the building—she didn't want to be late to class—but Camm reached out suddenly and grabbed her arm. She dropped her reader; the display screen cracked. It would have to be repaired, and her notes were there, as well as the assignment log and the text selections.

"Mar, don't do this, you're discouraged, I don't believe you weren't as sure of yourself as I was—as I am—"

Too many people had seen them having an argument, too many people saw her reader fall. Five or six of her classmates were coming, hurrying across the quadrangle toward them. To her defense, Marnissey realized, and the idea gave her a sudden rush of warm feeling even while it made her anxious for Camm's sake—and her own—that an incident be avoided.

"I can't see you anymore, Camm," she said, plainly and firmly, so that her once-friends would know she'd made her decision. "I don't want to see you anymore. That's all there is to it. And I have nothing more to say to you."

One of her classmates picked up her reader, handing it to her with a somber respectful expression on his face. Camm backed away a step, and then another; turned his back and walked away with his shoulders slumped and his hands in his pockets—but as Marnissey hurried into the building to go to class her heart was singing. It had been a mistake, that was all. How could she ever have imagined she could turn her back on her family, her friends, her whole community, to be Camm's lover?

A mistake. She was so lucky she had seen it for what it was in time. She could hardly wait for the period to be over so that she could go home and explain to her parents, and beg to be accepted back as their filial and loving daughter once again.

✦✦✦

"It's not so easy as that, is it, young lady?" her mother asked, sharp reproach in her words. "You've changed your mind, you've come to your senses, all to the good. But you've made ill-considered decisions before, that's how we got into this mess, after all. No. Your father and I will be happy to embrace you as our daughter, but not until you've spoken to the priest and done your penance. It will give us time to open our hearts to the Holy Mother, and pray for understanding."

It was a setback and it lay heavily upon the joy of freedom in Marnissey's heart, but she couldn't blame her mother. Her mother was right. Her mother had been right all along. She couldn't protest, not really; she knew that she owed penance for the error she'd committed—for making a sacred promise that she couldn't keep, for exposing her family to so much ugliness.

"I'll go first thing," she promised, and her mother accepted a dutiful daughter's filial kiss for the first time in weeks. It was a start. Marnissey went up the stairs to her room to close herself in and think about how she could explain to Uncle Birsle. The priest would understand; he would approve. He would not exact too heavy a penance from her, surely.

Camm came to the house and stood outside her bedroom window and called out to her, but her father called the police, and Camm ran away. She was angry with Camm for trying to see her. It called the sincerity of her decision into question, it increased the anguish in her heart over what she owed for going back on her promise, it sharpened her desire to open up her soul before the Holy Mother and receive the blessing of penance with reconciliation at its end.

She couldn't sleep. Her whole family was up much later than usual—her father had to give a report to the police, she heard him saying that the prowler was a stranger—but even when the house was quiet at last she stayed awake, kneeling at her bedside with her face buried in the bedclothes, desperate for morning to come so that she could go and see the priest.

She couldn't wait for midmorning, when Uncle Birsle would be on duty. She could not. It had already been an eternity since yesterday afternoon, when she'd had her final talk with Camm. Uncle Danitsch would give her more strict a penance, perhaps, but that would be all to the good, it would emphasize the sincerity of her repentance if she went to Danitsch knowing that he would be more severe with her.

As soon as the sun began to lighten the horizon she changed

her clothes and rinsed her mouth and ran into the city, onto campus, to the chapel; found Uncle Danitsch at prayer and told him everything, her mistake, her awakening, her profound regret, her thirst to be forgiven and reconciled, her determination to maintain the separation she'd begun to make between herself and Camm. Everything.

He questioned her strictly—whether they had been intimate, how intimate had they been, how often had they been intimate, who had initiated the relationship in the beginning, which one of them had suggested that they marry—but in the end he seemed to be satisfied that her repentance was genuine. He assessed a basic set of penance-exercises and told her to go home and come back the following day to learn what her complete penance was to be.

She took her assignment into her heart willingly and gratefully and carried the promise of penance home with joy. Her mother met her at the door; when Marnissey explained what she had done, her mother kissed her on the forehead and sent her into the kitchen for breakfast.

She went to class with prayerful repentance in her heart. She worked on her lab exercises with keen interest and attention, full of gratitude to Danitsch for his understanding. She went to chapel at midday to pray, her mind too full to stop and speak to Uncle Birsle, whose expression when he looked at her on her way past seemed to be one of curiosity; surely Danitsch had spoken to him— but she'd make an appointment and explain herself in full once Danitsch had given her full penance. That would be good. She'd see whether Birsle had anything to add to whatever set of religious exercises she was to perform to gain forgiveness.

Marnissey went home and ate her dinner with a good appetite, not wanting to say too much to her family, knowing that she had much to atone for. Then in the early morning, two scant hours past midnight, the police came.

★★★

"You know this man, then," the Malcontent said, and Marnissey shrank away from the promise in his voice with dread. The

Malcontent—Cousin Jirev, he'd told her to call him—wasn't a priest; religious professionals who were devoted to the Order of Saint Andrej Malcontent could never be elevated to that dignity. They were disgraced and disgusting, the secret service of the Dolgorukij church, and they did the Autocrat's dirty work for the Holy Mother outside the boundaries of decent society.

In the chill of the morgue the stink of the lefrol that Cousin Jirev was smoking was even more nauseating than it would otherwise have been. "Yes, step up close, child, you are required to identify the corpse. I am told you knew him better than anyone else here."

He pulled the simple shroud off of the body as he spoke, holding his lefrol in one hand, uncovering the body with the other. How could that be respectful of the dead? Reluctantly Marnissey came closer, fearful of what she would discover. She'd seen Camm just yesterday, no, just day before yesterday, and he'd been beautiful Camm even if she'd realized that she wasn't going to marry him. The police had to be mistaken.

She raised her eyes reluctantly to look at what was lying there, and for a moment her relief was almost boundless; no, that couldn't be Camm. Nodding with conviction Marnissey started to speak to Cousin Jirev—there'd been a mistake, she was so glad—but even as she opened her mouth she realized she was the one who'd made the mistake; because it was Camm after all, even if he'd been so badly beaten that she wanted more than anything not to recognize him.

Camm. The police forensics team had cleaned up the body and done something to his face to draw down the swelling associated with gross trauma. There were places where the skin had been split to the bone; she'd never seen anything that could approach this horror. She recoiled by instinct, putting her hand out to ward off the terrible image; but Jirev stuck his lefrol between his teeth and put his hand to the small of her back, pushing her forward again. Marnissey had to reach out to the cold-slab to steady herself, to keep her legs from collapsing out from underneath her. Camm.

They'd broken his face, they'd beaten his body, they'd beaten his hands and his feet; why?

Apparently confident that she wouldn't be moving, Jirev left her side and walked around to the other side of the body where he could face her. "Somebody did not like this fellow," Jirev said cheerfully. "Notice especially the way he has been beaten across the loins, that was done before he died so that he would be sure to suffer from it. Characteristic. It explains an otherwise unmotivated killing, though, wouldn't you say? Blood-soil."

"No," Marnissey said, and heard the abject plea in the tone of her voice. "It doesn't make sense. It can't be. We had broken off our engagement. There wasn't any."

Jirev's lefrol was smoked down to a stub that he was apparently not interested in pursuing any longer. He laid it in the blood-gutter of the cold-slab to go out, and shrugged. "You aren't thinking clearly, it is perhaps because you have been doing penitence-exercises, I understand. You had a long discussion with Uncle Danitsch yesterday, by report. It might have been a good idea to have warned this young Sarvaw that you were going to do that, and given him a chance to escape."

Now not even her grip on the edge of the cold-slab could save her. Marnissey sat down suddenly and hard on the cold floor; two of the Malcontent's cohorts were by her side in an instant, to raise her up and support her. She had no strength to lift her head; and there was Camm's body, poor Camm's body, right in front of her.

She had talked with Danitsch. She had. After what she knew about Danitsch and Abythia, she had, but a bucketful of excrement was a completely different thing than beating a man to death for the crime of being Sarvaw. She couldn't comprehend it; she closed her eyes in horror.

"I require you to look upon this evidence," Jirev warned; Marnissey opened her eyes again, startled, and all but overwhelmed by nausea that seized her when she understood what he meant. He wanted her to look, because he blamed her for it. "A man's life has been cruelly taken from him. There will be reparations to be made, the Holy Mother herself demands no less."

Camm. "The Holy Mother is an Aznir bitch," she said. She remembered. Camm had said that once. He had been joking, mostly, but she had been horrified nonetheless. "And this was done according to Her will. She deserves no such reparations."

Now Jirev nodded at Marnissey's escort and they backed away from the cold-slab while Jirev covered up the body with its shroud. A charity-shroud. Camm had family on Sarvaw; would the body be sent home, would Camm's family have to look at this?

"I will be the judge of that, if you please," Jirev said. He was Aznir Dolgorukij, by his accent. "It is quite true that you are not under the criminal code to blame for this. Uncle Birsle will assess your penance for the error of an over-hasty promise. You will not be seeing Danitsch again, or several of your classmates either."

She could not be a murderess just because she'd wanted her life back. She could not. It was too horrible; it was too insane. "What have I done?" Marnissey whispered, and looked to Jirev for an answer. The people who were with her helped her into a chair; Jirev squatted down to crouch on his heels in front of her, and look into her eyes with resigned sympathy.

"You only wished somewhat too passionately to be rid of an association whose demands had overwhelmed you," Jirev said. Marnissey did not hear accusation in Jirev's voice; she listened to him greedily. "Because of that, the man is dead. He did not deserve to be killed, nor so cruelly. Nor do you deserve to be held to account for it, it was an error, but you know that you will be blamed for it. We must decide."

It was too true. She could see her future, and there was nothing in it; she would be blamed—people would rather blame her, howsoever irrationally, than recognize the darkness in themselves that had made such a thing possible. She would be blamed. And she had not yet even won back her family. "What can I do?"

Jirev nodded. "It is not fair, nor is it just," he warned her. "Mourn him, Marnissey, as though you were true lovers, and your attempts to make a distance had been attempts to shelter him from his enemies. You shall have support and protection from the Order of the Malcontent, but you must do your part. Birsle will explain. Now you may go, but I will send the doctor to attend you."

✭★✭

"So we've come to ask your blessing," Nebrunne finished, folding her hands in her lap and lowering her eyes to the carpeted floor in front of her feet, very aware of Cilance's tense figure on the old-fashioned two-sitter beside her. "We intend to be married. There's a clinic in Fibranje with a vacancy for his specialty and mine, so we can be together."

Great-Aunt Marnissey was thin with age, but her slim figure almost resonated still with the fearless will and determination that had defined her life since the day her lover had been murdered. Tirelessly she had worked for the cause of integration; tirelessly she'd struggled to build lines of communication within the schools, to teach that the Holy Mother never asked one of her children to strike another for the crime of being a different sort of Dolgorukij. Never.

And every day without exception she had gone down the hill into the city, to where the old university grounds used to be, and spent her morning hour of prayer in the chapel that had once been attached to the school. She took a mover, now; at more than eighty-seven years old Standard she could no longer walk so far quickly or well. But she had never failed to speak every day in the morning to the Holy Mother and the man she was to have married, never once in more than sixty years.

Now she sighed, and the weariness of the sound made Nebrunne raise her eyes and blink at her great-aunt in moderate surprise. Aunt Marnissey looked pained, in some sense, and Nebrunne had thought her news would be more welcome than it seemed. Unfolding her hands Aunt Marnissey set them to the arms of her straight-backed chair.

"You met in the hospital, you say." She was speaking to Cilance; Nebrunne nudged him nervously with her elbow, to make sure he knew that he was to answer. Cilance cleared his throat.

"Yes, ma'am. I'm in anesthesiology, so Nebrunne and I work together on emergency most shifts."

Aunt Marnissey frowned, to Nebrunne's confusion. "How do your coworkers feel about your plans, niece? Do they know that you and this young man intend to have a family?"

What could Aunt Marnissey be expecting, after her life spent in public education efforts? "Some of our friends know, Aunt Marnissey. And some of them suspect. We haven't made any formal announcements. We want to make sure nobody's surprised when we do."

"Have there been any incidents? What about your mother, does she know?"

This was more serious an examination than Nebrunne had expected. She began to worry; but why would Aunt Marnissey deny her blessing? "Well, there's been teasing, Aunt, because my uniform isn't always perfect." And people affecting to check in linen stores to find her when Cilance was on shift, and making remarks about weddings and gestation periods.

It was only the way they teased all courting couples. "And I've told Mam about Cilance, that I want to bring him home. I wanted to talk to you first of all. Please. Let us know that we can have your blessing, to be married."

She sounded a bit more desperate than she liked, but it was because she didn't understand. "And your people," Aunt Marnissey said, turning again to Cilance. "Have you spoken to your family? What do they say?"

Cilance was bearing up under inquisition with grace and tact and forbearance, and if Nebrunne hadn't loved him when they'd gotten here, she would have loved him now for how gently he handled her great-aunt. Cilance nodded, as though considering her question.

"My mother already knows Nebbie, ma'am, she's in administration at the hospital. I haven't really talked to my father or my brother and sisters, not yet. Nebbie wanted to speak to you first." A person's family knew when something was up, that went without saying. Nebrunne had actually almost-met one of Cilance's sisters before she'd met Cilance; they'd gone to the same intermediate school, as it turned out, but they'd been three years apart.

Aunt Marnissey sighed. "The world has changed," she said. "I only wonder if it's changed enough. The Holy Mother knows it's difficult enough just to be married without any additional complications, but they tell me that Fibranje is a nice station, a developing world."

One outside the Combine, more to the point, where the impact of octaves of prejudice would be diminished by distance and dilution in the company of a majority of souls who weren't any kind of Dolgorukij. Cilance's family had been happy and prosperous in Orachin, but they both knew that there were better places to found a mixed marriage than Orachin: and Fibranje was likely to be one of them.

"Difficult to be married," Cilance agreed, surprising Nebrunne. "Impossible to imagine life without Nebbie in it, ma'am. We mean to make a go of it."

Nebrunne could hear the weight of the long nights of discussion in his voice, hours spent with their heads together arguing the yes against the no of it to see if they were equal to the challenge. What was more to the point it seemed that Aunt Marnissey could hear it, too, because she pushed herself up out of her chair to stand and beckoned them both to her.

"Good answer," she said. "You give me hope for the future. Come here, children." Gathering both Nebrunne and Cilance to her as they knelt, she kissed their foreheads, each in turn. "May the Holy Mother bless this match toward the working of Her will, and send you long life, health, and happiness, and children in due season."

She sat back down. "Now go and speak to your families. Both of you. And I hope to not hear any of that disgusting Metoshan so-called music, at your wedding. Good-greeting, children, go away."

Cilance helped her to her feet. Nebrunne leaned over her aunt and kissed her cheek with heartfelt gratitude; and then they fled the house together, with the housekeeper on their heels to see them out. It was a beautiful evening. She was too happy to want to talk, but Cilance had something on his mind, she could tell.

Once they had walked a suitable distance away from the house, she poked him in the side to get him to talk. Cilance looked sidewise at her and shrugged. "What do people have against Metoshan music, anyway? It's a very cheerful idiom. What's the problem?"

It was a familiar complaint, requiring no answer. Nebrunne smiled happily at him, her heart full of love. "All right, Ipoxlotl music, then," she promised, and went arm-in-arm with Cilance down the street to catch the public-mover, and go home.

✦★✦

End Note

My sister said she'd listened to Janis Ian perform "Society's Child" with my mother, one time. Mom said that the point-of-view character had made the correct choice; my sister was quite naturally provoked with her about that.

I'm pretty sure that my mom wasn't making a racist value judgment so much as a strictly mom-based "I'd want my children to be happy, and it's easier to be happy when you're not struggling for acceptance at every turn" one. I wanted to do something with this song that might communicate the "you're both right" reaction I had, listening to my sister tell the story.

When I first revisited the lyrics I meant to present Marnissey very coldly as a woman who'd made a self-aware choice to have an inconvenient lover beaten, and who would be punished for the rest of her life for arranging the murderous assault.

Listening again to Janis perform this song, however, reminded me powerfully of the difference between the lyrics as text and the more complete story communicated by the words and the way the singer sings them. It became a gentler story—still ugly, but I hope more charitable.

Murdering Stravinsky
or
Two Sit-Downs In Paris

by Barry N. Malzberg

We're bringing down the Beatles
Dylan and his pals
We're working very hard
to be the avant-garde
Murdering Stravinsky
—from Murdering Stravinsky
by Janis Ian & Philip Clark

THEIR brutal faces, clamorous voices, all one voice. In the theater and then out of it. Me, Igor Stravinsky, the force that
through the green fuse drove the flower of the century.

Murdered? Impossible? Believe none of it!

Murdered!

★★★

"You understand that decisions must be made," Diaghilev said
to me in Paris, discussing our various career choices. *Petrouchka* a
success, *Firebird* a success, *Pulcinella* so-so. Then came the War.
This discussion in Paris was many years after the premiere when
the memory of the riots was no longer so painful. The world had

found much larger concerns, much bigger riots, since the Romanovs were so inconveniently upended. ("Come, Alexandra, there
seems to be a little bit of an uprising. I am sure there is nothing
worth our concern, but we should be cautious.")

"This is a risky circumstance; everything has changed since the
War. People have become more serious, more fearful, less interested in sensation. We artists who flourished through sensation, we
must learn to moderate our work, to respect form. The winds of
history blow against us now."

So there we sat, the ballet master and myself, the soon-to-be-
recognized-as-immortal Stravinsky and his attendant and onetime
professional colleague, what is known in Hollywood as the side-
kick, Serge. Stravinsky still deep at that time into his irreligious
period, I am ashamed to admit. Here poised our young, still-defi-
ant codger, sitting calmly if somewhat nervously at that outlandish
café in Paris, masks leering from the walls. Scuffling and incautious
boulevardiers topped tables in their haste to lay passionate hands on
one another, whether from desire or fury. We felt ourselves to be
inconspicuous. A pair of fortunate refugees from the Revolution,
fled from the steppes to take their ease in this decadent, shimmering Paris. Scandalous! But there we were twinned in exile, and all
the better for it.

This was the Twenties. What a lavishly misspent time! What
foolishness! You could get away with almost everything in Paris:
Hemingway and the other louts making plans for bullfights and
whores in Spain, Joyce tippling his way through *Ulysses* and making
a little time with Sylvia Beach whenever he could get away from
Nora. Diaghilev was still obsessed by *pirouettes* and *fouees* and the
attitudes of the altar boys at the *barre*. The War had changed everything, but he refused to notice. It was an offstage thumping
struggle; the stink of cannon smoke affecting the dancers' respira-
tion, that was all. "The sounds you make, the shapes and colors I
have created are unbearable to them. They may tolerate us for a
little while, but soon that will come to an end. The Czar upon his
throne thought that he was safe, too; now consider his condition.
And those Bolsheviks—"

"Must we hear again about the Bolsheviks?" I said. "Haven't they done enough in Russia? Here at least we can sit in the sun and look at the women." Lechery, I am ashamed to admit, in those decades before at last I returned to the faith, was so much a part of Stravinsky in those difficult, changing years. I lived too much for the poetry of the Earth. Expatriation is a problematic business anyway, unleashing the soul in unpleasant and damaging ways. Still, lechery always feels good at the time, which is one of its great lures.

"No," Serge said, "we cannot hide. We can try our old tricks, old burglaries. Ah, lies and the curse of enchantment! They do not want the truth." He motioned in the general direction of Moscow, several thousand miles to the East but close as always, of course, to our hearts. "The Czar in his box did not want the truth either, but he learned after a while and tragically to respect it. The people here, however, they are trivial. They respect nothing."

Were they trivial? If so, what was wrong with that? What terrors from frivolity after the horrors of great seriousness and international debate? This old, this exhausted world had staggered from the abyss of a terrible war, a generation laid to waste and etc., what was wrong with triviality, with burgundy at a café at midday? This was not a question worth arguing with Serge, however. Nothing would change him. There had been plenty of trouble in Moscow once we realized that the Second Revolution was not going to be at all like the First. Everyone but the Romanovs came to see that quickly.

What had Anastasia, the last daughter of the Romanovs, been thinking in the basement of the Palace? Was she making any plans at all or simply praying? Did she think that rescue was coming? Did she think that the Bolsheviks were unarmed peasants who in the presence of the Czar would bow and retreat? Who can judge the thoughts of a little girl so long ago? Yet somehow this is of crucial importance; if I could deduce Anastasia's state of mind, I might somehow have comprehended my own.

Serge had said: stay, stay, your time is coming. We should not go anywhere. This is only a temporary situation. He, no scholar of historical trends, liked his caviar and routine and the thunder of bells in the Square. He thought that it would go on that way. "Do not anger royalty. The pleasures of royalty are our only way toward salvation." He was wrong then as thirty years later he would have been wrong about the House Un-American Activities Committee.

"Nonsense," he said at the worst of it. "This will come to nothing. This rabble will never win." At that moment Anastasia was hiding in the basement, the last of the survivors. The castle shook. She knew that soon they would find her. They would come into the basement, lay enormous hands upon her, spirit her away. Like the rowdies at *The Rite of Spring* they had no respect for the abominable truth of desire, even for the hopeless damaged fabric of a little girl lost in the entrails of the Palace.

✶★✶

Fifty years later, after all of the changes, after the unpleasant business which was the Soviet system itself had broken free and poured into the West, I felt once again that I was done for. I knew that it was only a matter of time before they came for me as well. They had even done away with those young British hoodlums, the Insects, I used to call them. Sam Goldwyn would have appreciated that, and the replacement of the Insects was no great loss. No loss to music, to humanity, to anything with ears. Good riddance, in fact.

But the business with Britten had been a scandal. They shot him—as they had shot Magritte and with a fine sense of justice—in his hat while he was conducting an Altenbergh. Britten had been knighted, he composed a ballet for the Coronation, was a courtier to Elizabeth, the Queen's composer . . . but unlike the Insects, he could tell a hawk from a handsaw and he had managed to escape.

Britten must have been thinking: the world will see yet another *Peter Grimes* before I kick the bucket. I have written the *War Requiem* and in so doing have beaten them. He must have been dismayed when they shot him. How could they do this? He had been knighted. Britten must have also thought that he was exempt from all historical judgment.

Rumors persist that he fled successfully to a remote village in Poland whose name cannot be translated. Pushgorny? Pvgorny? If so, it is there that he sits beside the equally traumatized and furious Peter Pears, sulking at the blasted landscape, the unhappy peasants, the rumble of distant gunfire. A long way from the *Four Sea Interludes* for the Queen's Musician. A goodly distance from Altenburg, yes? Of course, Britten's gifts were always overrated, a feeble and pretentious composer whose work in no way approached the heights of my own distinguished canon. Britten did to English composition what that charlatan Schoenberg had done to the diatonic scale. (It is merciful that Schoenberg has been dead seventeen years now. What they would have done to him is too fierce to contemplate. His small pension from the university and unhealthy arrogance would have ill-prepared him for this cataclysm.)

And old Pablo. They got Pablo all right. They caught him in bed with Francoise and made short work of the old lecher. When they buried him, his own brush slashed the sky, the bloody cubist sky and his sketches, those wild and improbable explosions of his need spinning maniacally before the world's gaped spaces . . . A tornado of fingers and shattered horses and then, after he was planted, the silence, rain on the grave, Francoise weeping, unholy water drowning the past. Another charlatan, old Pablo, but lovable in his folly and as a lecher myself, I could appreciate his predilection. Of course the panels from Diaghilev had been snatched from his paintings. Any fool could see this. Cubism and the twisted limbs of sacrifice merged.

I knew that I would be next. They were implacable, these young Bolsheviks. Daniel Cohn had me measured, had me on the list. There was no reason, no argument possible. I was on the list there with Britten, Picasso, and those puerile Insects. "We're coming for you, Igor," they whispered. I knew their peculiar tilted handwriting, the texture of the notepaper which their messengers would deliver to my premises, those clever troops slipping them under my pillow. "You're the next to be replaced," they advised. "Neoclassicism won't save you. Your return to Russian Orthodoxy certainly will not save you. Did hiding out in those parties with

Goldwyn and Disney and scowling Rachmaninoff give you a day's extra time? You have outlived your usefulness. You are going to be replaced. We have big and certain plans. We may allow you a motet or two or a Russian Orthodox chant."

Ah, their dry, mocking precision! But of course that was the stern decree itself.

For all of this—waiting in the dusk, listening for the footsteps, listening to the gunfire in the streets as piece by piece it was all dismantled—it was a strangely peaceful time, knowing that I was in all senses, beyond salvation, that I would not flee like Britten, that it was better to be snatched from my own place than from some Polish village. Shuffling Vera away, glad to get rid of her at least, packing her away unmoved by her tears and hysterics. Good-bye, Vera, good-bye. Craft had left, of course, at the first warning of trouble, the first indication that I was on the list. At least he had the decency to have dragged Vera away by her delicate wrist. Good-bye, Vera, good-bye, go away, yield. Vera, my dry Dumbarton Oaks of a spouse, creature of happenstance and odd chiaroscuro, all form, the only substance in that form. I wrote *Persephone* to mark her emptiness and no one ever got the joke. That jokester Schoenberg's entire canon was a rib-tickler, but no one believed that. I had other plans, but could not resist a joke now and then.

But let them come, let them take me away. No Pvgornys for Igor. I know instead that the Church will protect me in any afterlife I am given. Christ upon the throne awaits me; that gracious Czar of eternity. The Theotokos in its Mystery and Transcendence. Gloria in Excelsis Dei. Etc. Amen. Etc., etc. The merits of a religious return may be overrated, but it has its satisfaction, reduces the question.

Sitting, waiting. The cries in the distance. The Romanovs must have felt this way in 1917, peering through the windows of the ruined Palace. "Aleksandr, something strange is happening outside and the guards seem to have fled. I would have thought them more loyal than this. Ring the bells, ring the bells!! Surely someone will save us!"

No one to reach the rope, the bells are silent. For the first time it is possible to feel some sympathy for them. Anastasia deep in the basement, hiding under blankets. They came to the Romanovs and they will come to me. Of course, I have no plans. Britten had connections worldwide, a passport; the Insects felt that their wealth would protect them. They were wrong. The Romanovs, of course, knew that their position was unassailable. They were wrong, too. The force that took them took fifty years to get to the others, but as that castle is breached, Serge noted, it is always just a moment of time.

So I give them the patience and serenity which are the only gifts I can give myself. Here I sit most calmly. Let them take me: after that brief explosion, pain, the blood, the slow diminution of light . . . and then the blessed tunnel, a passage toward that exquisite future. My history recorded on its walls like prehistoric painting: the Russia, the Conservatory, France. Moscow. Hollywood! Switzerland! London and Diaghilev, my life a scroll of sound and unreeling light, birds of fire escorting me in excelsis Deo.

They can take me but, Agnus Dei, they cannot take my soul, I pray. My soul inviolate.

But I am wrong. I have learned better. I am learning as did the Romanovs at the end: they can take everything.

✹★✹

So this is what I came to understand. I had seen these faces, this implacability, many times. I had first seen them at the premiere in 1913, sitting amidst the careening, screaming throng, terrified by the waves of noise streaming from the boxes. The terrified dancers leaping nonetheless, colliding. The Consecration of the Earth.

Objects hurled from the balconies. Cursing, screaming. Close the curtain! Stop the madness! There must have been some way that I could have made clear to them that *Sacre* was not the enemy, that they and I sought the same outcome: impalement. The burning spear.

Vera, beside me, replacing Serge if such were possible, muttered disapproval, not only of the rioters but of me.

Well, she disapproved of everything. I do not think I truly realized until this moment in memory, the depth of that disapproval,
the certainty of her disregard. How profoundly she felt, no less
than the Bolsheviks, that this was the truest evocation of evil and
that it must be contained.

And there it is, then, the virgin swept high and carried offstage,
gutted, lifted high above them and set on fire, no screams, the silence of the dance and then the simple, terrible conclusion. The
violation of the Earth. Boos, missiles. "Do you see what you have
done? If the Czar only knew!"

The auditorium dwindles, becomes a cubicle, becomes a stall
which grips me, snatches, takes me away and I hear Diaghilev's
fierce whisper. "Don't you understand? The reason they rioted is
because you have shown them exactly what they want and they
cannot bear it, cannot live with this: revolution, rape, apostasy."

Ah, we seem to have returned to Paris. A decade is obliterated,
now we draw the attention of *boulevardiers* in that café. "You," I
say then. "You created this madness! You made of my pastoral
scene, my ceremony of fertility, a rape!" Perception seizes me and
I grab him by the shoulders, yank him toward me. "You let this
loose upon the world. My ceremony of innocence was drowned!"
I do not know if I accept this fanciful outburst, but it has a certain
logic, and Diaghilev falls away, gasping, stunned by my certainty.

And certainty it is. What purity! What understanding! Surely I
have gripped the attention of everyone on the Champs Elysees; the
café has become a riot of attention, fixation really; I am enveloped
by stares. "It was you with the Czar also!" I say. "The *Sacre*, the
Czar, the assassins!" I am trembling with rage, or perhaps it is
merely the epiphany which has made me tremble. "Repent!" I say,
recalling certain words, chants from the Russian Orthodox service.
"It is not too late!"

Madness! Now I have gone mad. It is almost fifty years past
the café, Diaghilev is long dead, having savaged my career to his
satisfaction, and I must be crazy. Stravinsky himself has gone mad,
neoclassicism will not save him from these Furies. There is no need
to recount the appearance of the *gendarmerie*, the way in which

they seize Diaghilev and rescue him from my distraught self, the shouting and disorder as they seize and carry me from the café. Head wobbling, brain aflame, eyes wobbling in their sockets, I am overwhelmed by what *Sacre* should have led me to understand ten years ago—*this* is what they wanted, to clean out the world: to give us a world in which Britten was in Poland, Picasso's studio was plundered, even the Beatles murdered. The Beatles! I had once taken them for Bolsheviks, but here was the surprise: they had been caught in the general melee. George, Paul, John, and Richard Starkey in the ground. What true reparation!

In this discovered world they murder. They are not creatures of gesture. Britten in exile, Paris in flames, de Gaulle's Fourth Republic under siege fifty-one years after the tumult in the Palace. Is Paris burning?

I am a very old man, older than Ralph Vaughn-Williams when he died. But I am strong enough to absorb the truth. Tell me that truth, then, and help me avoid the stern decree.

No. No, there is not time for that, for here come the barbarians, roaring through the Place de la Concorde, pushing one another in their eagerness to appropriate. There they are, commandeering planes at Orly, whisking overseas as combatants, overtaking the world. Here they come, here and here they go: they have plans. They have been made enormous by their plans; they inflate like the Hindenburg, bump one another, stride in air. Plans for the vanishing Fourth Republic, plans for Britten, plans for Stravinsky.

Stravinsky! That is me! Do not forget this. I returned to the Church. I renounced, no denounced, that reprobate who was my younger self. In the stillness of the Church surrounded by the clamor of bells I pledged my renunciation. But too late, too late for all of that. The forces I released stormed first the theater, then the Palace and now the world. "You have always been a fool," my beloved Vera pointed out a long time ago. "You thought only of yourself. You would sacrifice the world to your lazy ambition, your stupid notes and theories of neoclassicism."

Is this possible? In Moscow, in the provinces, in Hollywood or

Paris, in all of the spaces of exile I held to the pure contest of flame, believed this. But now Paris evanesces; it is no longer Paris in which I huddle but the outskirts of Watts, awaiting their enormous captivity, that most definitive calamity. The impaled virgin. The garroted lover. This sewer of a century.

This disgusting sewer of a century.

Society's Goy

by Mike Resnick

*O*ctember 47, 4227 G.E.
   He's GORGEOUS!

I mean, it's as if Morvich and Casabella and that old guy, Michael something, you know, the one who painted some big ceiling, as if they all got together and said, what's the most beautiful thing we can paint, the most beautiful thing in all the galaxy? I have to stop, Dear Diary. He's got me so . . . so I don't know . . . that I just can't dictate anymore.

October 49

I saw him in the library today—so he's not just beautiful, he's bright, too. I brushed past him, but he didn't notice. Except for sneezing. It must be the cologne. Maybe three ounces was too much. Tomorrow I'll use less. And I'll change from "Ecstasy" to "Ravage Me."

I wonder what his name is.

October 50

He was at the library again today. Maybe he's a student. Whatever he is, he just stands out. I've *got* to find a way to meet him!

Octember 51

He wasn't there today. I came home and cried and counted 51 ways to kill myself, but then I cracked a nail and had to go to the beautician to get the acrylic fixed.

Octember 52

Rabighan! That's his name—or as near as I can come to spelling it. These foreign names are murder. I heard the lib-mech report to him that a disk he wanted had been damaged and he'd have to wait until tomorrow.

Rabighan. Rabighan. Rabighan.

It's gorgeous.

Octember 53

He noticed me!!!!!

He dropped something—I'm not sure exactly what it was; kind of like a little flower he wears on his chest—and I picked it up, and he said, "Thank you."

Plain as day. He just looked at me, and I think he smiled a bit, and he said, "Thank you!"

What a beautiful voice he has!

Octember 54

I was walking past him today, and I just blurted "Hi, Rabighan," and he said "Hi" right back at me.

Isn't life wonderful!!!!!

Naugustus 1

I saw him in the cafeteria today, and I sat right down next to him and said, "Hi."

"Are you sure you're supposed to be here?" he said, like only grad students were allowed.

"I don't mind if you don't," I said. Sometimes I can't believe how *bold* I can be!

"You're a very unusual young lady," he said.

I was about to say he was very unusual, too, but instead I

blurted out that he was very beautiful. Well!!! I could have sunk right through the floor, except that he seemed flattered.

"We haven't been introduced," he said. "My name is Rabighan."

I'd thought about this moment for days. "And mine is Valpariso," I said.

"Valpariso?" he repeated. "Isn't that a city back on old Earth?"

"Valencia!" I said quickly. "I meant Valencia!"

He stared at me for a minute. It was like he was seeing right through all my clothes. I liked it!!!

"I'm pleased to meet you, Valencia," he said. "I've met very few young women since I came to Society III. Perhaps, when you have time, we could talk together. There's so much I'd like to learn about your world."

I screwed up my courage. "How about this afternoon?" I asked him. "I can tell you everything you ever wanted to know about Society."

"This afternoon would be fine."

And so we walked all over the campus, talking about this and that, and thank goodness he didn't ask me who was Governor because I never remember stuff like that. He told me he'd never met anyone who was majoring in aerobics before, and he seemed fascinated by it, so I invited him to come to the game tomorrow night and watch me cheerlead, and he agreed.

I think I'm in love!!!!!!!!

Naugustus 2

He came, and he watched, and he was so polite he never once mentioned how I fell into the crowd when I was doing my backflip or how I was so busy watching him watching me that I forgot to catch Darlene when she jumped down from the top of the Human Pyramid. (They say she'll be out of the hospital in less than a week.)

He waited while I showered and changed, and then we talked some more. I'm afraid to ask him how long he'll be staying on Society III.

Naugustus 4

Rabighan saw me crying today. I tried to hide it, but I couldn't.

"What's wrong, Valencia?" he asked.

"I'm in love with you and you're going to be leaving soon!" I sobbed.

"I have no intention of leaving Society for years," he said. "I like it here." He watched me for a moment, and then added: "You are still crying."

"You've never once said you liked me," I said.

"I like you."

"Very much?" I asked, blowing my nose.

He shrugged. "Very much."

"Then how come you never walk me home, or ask to meet my parents?"

"I grew up on a different world," he said. "I am not aware of your social traditions. Is that what is expected of me—that I should meet your parents?"

I was still crying too hard to speak, so I just nodded.

"Then I shall."

"They're playing bingo tonight," I said. "But you could come for dinner tomorrow."

"If that is what you wish."

I wonder if a grad student can afford a real starstone, or if my engagement ring will have to be something dull and ordinary, like a blue diamond?

Naugustus 5

All day I was too nervous to eat. I put on my half-inch eyelashes and the rouge and the phosphorescent purple lipstick so I'd look more mature, and then I waited in my room for Rabighan to come.

I must have fallen asleep, because then next thing I knew the Spy-Eye was saying that we had a visitor, and even though I ran as fast as I could, Mama beat me to the front door by a good five steps. She opened it, and there he was in all his splendor.

"Yes?" she said, staring at him.

"Rabighan," he replied.

"You've made a mistake," said Mama. "I think the Rabighans live over on the next block."

"I *am* Rabighan."

For a moment Mama looked confused. Then suddenly she nodded. "Ah, you must be here to fix the trash atomizer. It's around the back."

"I am here at Valencia's request," he said.

"We don't have any Valencia here."

It was his turn to look confused. "Valpariso, perhaps?"

"No," said Mama, getting annoyed.

"Do you have a daughter?"

"Yes."

"And her name is not Valencia or Valpariso?"

"Her name is Gertrude."

I wanted to shrink down to insect size, but I knew if I did Mama would slam the door in his face before I could explain, so I walked up and stood where she couldn't shut it without smashing my head.

"Why, Rabighan!" I said. "What a surprise!"

"You know this Rabighan?" said Mama.

"He's an old friend."

"You don't *have* any old friends," she said. "We just moved here from New Brooklyn two months ago."

"Well, we're so close that he *feels* like an old friend," I said.

"*How* close?" demanded Mama, cocking an eyebrow and giving me The Look.

"What a thing to ask!" I said, trying to look offended.

I'm not half as good at looking offended as Mama is. She turned toward the living room and called for Daddy.

"Milton!" she hollered. "Come quick!"

Daddy plodded in a minute later, looking like she'd just woken him up.

"What is it and why is the door open and who is standing in it?" he said.

"This is Rabighan," I said.

Daddy stared at Rabighan, who smiled at him. Daddy ignored it.

"Rabighan is the Moslems' holy month," he said at last. "Who is *this*?"

"His name is Rabighan," I repeated. "He's my friend."

"Her *close* friend," added Mama.

"We're in love!" I blurted out.

Daddy blinked his eyes. "How can you be in love?" he said. "He's a vegetable!"

"But he's the most gorgeous, intelligent vegetable I've ever met!"

"You don't *meet* vegetables," said Daddy. "You buy them at the market and then you eat them with salad dressing."

"I resent that!" said Rabighan.

"You keep out of this!" snapped Daddy. He glared at Rabighan. "And while I'm thinking of it, where's your *yarmulka*?"

"My what?" asked Rabighan.

"Hah!" said Daddy. "I knew it! You're outta here!"

"You can't talk to him like that!" I said fiercely. "I'm going to marry him!"

I thought Mama was going to faint, but Daddy just looked stern.

"The hell you are!" he said.

"You're just biased against vegetables!" I cried.

"I've got nothing against vegetables," he said. "Some of my favorite meals are vegetables."

"Then what have you got against Rabighan? You don't even know him!"

"I know everything I have to know."

"You used to tell me that when I grew up I could marry who-ever I wanted!" I sobbed. "You never said anything about vegetables!"

"I don't care that he's a vegetable!" said Daddy. "I care that he's a *goy*!"

There was a sudden silence.

Finally Rabighan spoke up. "What is a goy?" he asked.

"You are," said Daddy. "A goy is anyone that's not Jewish," he explained, as if that was the worst thing in the universe.

"You mean I could marry a Jewish vegetable?" I asked sarcastically.

"Find one and we'll talk," he said.

Mama finally spoke up. "I'm afraid you'll have to go now, Mr. Rabighan. I'd invite you to stay for supper, but we're probably eating a bunch of your relatives."

She closed the door in his face and then turned to me. "Couldn't you see he wasn't our kind, Gertrude?"

"This isn't over," I promised her as I ran off to my bedroom. "Not by a long shot!"

The last thing I heard before I slammed the door was my father complaining: "What's the world coming to when your own daughter brings one of *them* home for supper?"

★★★

> *"Walk me down to school, baby*
> *Everybody's acting deaf and blind*
> *until they turn and say*
> *'Why don't you stick to your own kind?'"*

★★★

Naugustus 6

I cried myself to sleep last night. Daddy can be so unreasonable.

This morning I cut classes and looked all over the campus until I found Rabighan. Most of the kids just averted their eyes and pretended we weren't together.

"I'm sorry they treated you so bad, baby," I said sympathetically, taking hold of one of his six arms. "I hope you didn't take it too hard."

"A vegetable has no ego," he said.

"No ego?"

"None."

A frightening thought occurred to me. "Does that mean we can't . . . uh . . . well, you know?"

He stared at me curiously but didn't say anything. It's like he had no idea what I was trying to ask him.

"Never mind," I said. "I just want you to know that no matter what Daddy says, nothing's going to keep us apart."

I held his arm tighter, to show how much I loved him.

It broke off in my hands.

"Ohmygod!" I said. "Are you all right? Should I get you to a hospital?"

"I'm fine," said Rabighan.

"But your arm . . ." I said, holding it up for him to see.

"I'll just grow another one."

"You can do that?"

"Of course."

I decided not to mention it to Daddy. He'd just point out that Jewish boys hardly ever grow back body parts.

"Hiya, Trudy," said Benny Yingleman as he walked toward us. "What have you got in your hands there?"

"Oh, nothing," I said, trying to hide Rabighan's arm behind my back.

"That's some boyfriend you've got yourself," he said with a nasty smile. "Most plants just shed leaves."

"Yeah?" I said heatedly. "Well, he can grow anything to any size he wants whenever he wants." I gave him a withering look of contempt mixed with pity. "Can *you* do that?"

"Are you guessing, or is that a firsthand observation?" asked Abe Silverman, who I didn't know was coming up behind us but obviously heard every word I said.

"Why don't you leave us alone!" I screamed.

"Hey, are we asking to come along on one of your dates?" said Abe.

"Where does he take you, Trudy?" asked Benny. "The biology department's greenhouse, or do you just find a cozy swamp some-where?"

I turned to Rabighan. "Are you just going to stand there and let them tease you like that?"

He looked confused. "I thought they were teasing *you*."

"It's the same thing!" I snapped. "We're one flesh and one soul!"

"Actually, she's got the math right," said Benny. "He hasn't got any flesh . . ."

". . . and no vegetable has a soul," concluded Abe.

"He's got more soul than *you* do!" I said furiously.

"You think so?" said Abe. He turned to Rabighan. "Hey, Veggie—where do you guys go when you die?"

"We don't go anywhere when we die," answered Rabighan. "Our limbs no longer function." He looked curious. "Do you continue to ambulate after death?"

Abe shot me a triumphant grin. "See?"

"All I see are a bunch of bigots teasing the most beautiful, most perfect thing in the universe," I said.

They just laughed and kept on walking.

"I hate them!" I muttered.

"I thought they were your friends," said Rabighan.

"I thought so, too," I said. "I was wrong." I turned to him. "Once we're married, let's leave Society and go to a world where people will accept us."

"You keep using that term," he said. "What is married?"

"You're joking, right?" I said.

"I am a vegetable," he said. "Very few vegetables know how to make jokes." He paused. "What is married?" he asked again.

"It's a ceremony that will make us man and wife."

"I will become a wife?"

"No, silly!" I laughed. "*I* will be the wife."

"Then this ceremony—it will make me into a man?" he asked uneasily. "It sounds painful."

"You don't understand," I replied. "It's a beautiful ceremony, and when it's over we will spend the rest of our lives together."

He stopped in his tracks. "But that's horrible!" he said.

Suddenly he didn't look quite so beautiful. "What's so horrible about spending the rest of your life with me?" I demanded.

"You will die in another seventy or eighty years," he answered. "And if I am to share the rest of my life with you, then that's when I will die, too." He paused. "But if I am not married, then I can expect to live at least two millennia, perhaps three if I find some exceptionally favorable soil in which to root."

"What are you talking about?"

"My adolescence will only last another few centuries," he said. "After that, I will find a planet with acceptable rainfall and the proper nutrients in the soil and extend my roots into it. I will then delve silently into the universal and ageless questions of philosophy and examine the eternal verities, and if I should be fortunate enough to gain some new insights, I will pass them along to my seedlings."

And suddenly I realized what a fool I had been, what kind of a future I had almost let myself in for—no dancing, no holo theaters, no pizza, just standing around *thinking*. With each passing second, he was looking less like the most gorgeous lover in the galaxy and more like an animated fern.

"All right, Rabighan," I said. "It's time to admit that we came very close to making a terrible mistake. Let's be mature and shake hands and walk away from each other and not look back." I even forced a tear for dramatic purposes, but it caught in my half-inch eyelash and never rolled down my cheek.

"If that is your wish," he said. "But I would prefer not to shake hands."

"Why not?" I mean, if I could touch a goy, what was his problem?

"I really can't spare any more."

✦★✦

I can't see you any more
No, I don't want to see you any more, baby . . .

✦★✦

Naugustus 39

I think I'm in love—and this time I know it's the Real Thing. My God, he's just *BEAUTIFUL!!!!!*

His name is Krffix, and he can't be away from water for more than an hour at a time, but that's okay—I've always thought it would be neat to live by the seashore.

The problem is that the world is filled with small-minded bigots, but at least I've had some experience with them, thanks to the time I spent with—what was his name now?—Rasputin? Ramses? Oh, well, I know who I mean.

Back to Krffix. We can put a shirt on him, so Daddy won't notice the scales right away, and if we say he's an artist, he can wear an ascot and cover his gills and nobody will think anything of it. As for his nose . . . well, he can always tell people that he lost it in the war.

He never blinks, which can be a little disconcerting at first, but after you get used to it, it just makes him look very intellectual, like he's concentrating on whatever people are saying to him.

Okay, he eats worms—but if I tell Daddy they're kosher worms, how can he object?

Mrs. Krffix. Mrs. Morning Glory Krffix. *I like it!!!*

I wonder if he's willing to convert?

Second Person Unmasked

by JANIS IAN

He said—I've broken stallions
I've broken mares, too
Given time, and the right frame of mind
I swear I'll break you
*   —from "His Hands" by Janis Ian*

SO by the time you get there, you figure you've done pretty much everything a man can do in this life, right?

And you're tired of worrying about consequences and all that—right?

I know. I've been there.

Under the leaded skies of Low Port, anything looks possible. You amble out of the ship like you haven't got a care in the world, when all the time you're feeling just a tiny twinge of discomfort. Like there's something you ought to remember, something from way back when, before you were so God-almighty sure of yourself and everything you do. Only it's just on the tip of your tongue, and you're not talking.

They left a map in the cabin yesterday, when they finished cleaning up your mess and changing the sheets. Something to guide you through the down time, while the ship's in for maintenance. You leaf through it while you eat breakfast in the morning, checking out the ads, looking over the list of local customs. Amateur stuff, really, complete with tips for getting along with the natives. There's a picture of one, and some small print you ignore. They're humanoid, like most of the settled universe. That'll do.

You hadn't thought about natives when you decided to come here, but it's no big deal. You're always a stranger, and strange places are nothing new. You've always landed on your feet. Sometimes, when you're drunk enough to believe in an Almighty, you think He probably has a special place in His heart for you. Nothing else could explain your kind of luck, or the bullets you've dodged. Even on the ship, your luck's been holding, but you only indulged yourself once. You're pretty proud of that, showing some restraint. It isn't easy.

So you walk down the gangway and out into the night.

★★★

There's got to be some action in a port this size, paid action if necessary, though you'd prefer to talk her into it. Always feels better that way, watching their eyes go wide after they find out just how complete a seduction you intend. The lamb that goes willingly to slaughter tastes all the sweeter, or something like that.

You amble down toward what the guidebook identified as the "dangerous zone," smiling as you recall its dire warnings about pickpockets and slave traders. You've been here before. You know the drill.

One hand's in your pocket, and the other's tucked into your belt, but the money's not in either place, right? Anyone knocking into you with the thought of sticking a hand in there is in for a nasty shock. That little spring-loaded double switchblade you picked up at the last stop might come in handy tonight, and you won't need to lift a finger to make blood flow.

The belt, now, that's seen a lot of usage. You'd hate to lose it, so your hand stays where it is, tucked right in between the sharpened buckle and the first loop on the right.

Versatile things, belts.

As you walk down the sidewalk, past the drifters and the grifters who have nowhere better to go, you catch a glimpse of yourself in a tourist shop window. You've put on quite a bit of weight, eating three meals a day on the ship. Not terribly pleasing to look at, but then again, you aren't here to please. You're just here to survive, and have a little fun. Your kind of fun.

Your stride takes you past the tourist section and into the low rent area. You can tell it right away; the buildings are narrow, jammed together as closely as possible to block out any opportunity for light. The streetlamps flicker, casting hallucinatory shadows against the dingy shop windows. Old-fashioned neon flames here and there, injecting a note of false warmth into the gathering dark. Not many people on the street, and those that are, mind their business. It's a quiet night, almost spooky in its intensity, but that's just as well for your purpose.

You've got a high forehead, with *Don't-fuck-with-me* written across it in lines that took decades to accumulate. Filthy beggars reach out to you, whining *I lost my leg on* The Charon, *Mister, help me out, wouldja?*, or pretending they spent time in the slave pits cracking rock. Anything for a handout. Once they see your face, they melt back into the shadows.

You walk a little farther, enjoying the sense of conquest. You'll find what you're looking for, you always do.

About halfway down, when your legs are just about starting to feel tired, you spy the place. It's the same in every port. Same cheap signs, half-eaten by time and negligence. Same run-down decorations in the window, beckoning the weary traveler, promising companionship and good cheer. Same fake atmosphere, same sluggish trade, same flat-line employees, all the same. Nothing new under the sun, as they say.

You pause at the threshold, letting your eyes become accustomed to the darkness. Perfect. There's a jukebox in the corner playing some godawful thrash-band thing, and a sign saying WE RESERVE THE RIGHT TO REFUSE SERVICE THIS MEANS YOU! over the bar. You walk toward the mirrored counter, and the bartender suddenly gets busy mopping out a beer stein. You know you've made an impression with your entrance, because everyone in the place looks away from you.

You'd better have made an impression; the suit cost enough. Let them think you're a rube out for a good time, spending his savings on keeping up appearances. Let them think you're a fool. You've fooled them before.

And the extra weight doesn't hurt here, does it? Just adds to the overall impression of untraveled stupidity, mixed with a shy desire to try something, anything, new, before you go back home for good.

So you sit yourself down at one end of the tattered bar, where you can survey the room in the mirror without appearing too interested. Shadows veil your face like a shroud, keeping it anonymous and forgettable. The bartender takes his time getting to you, suspiciously eyeing the tailored shirt. Don't get many of those in these parts, I can tell you that right now. But you put him at ease with a couple of carefully chosen words, and before too long he's back with a tall one, chilled just the way you like it.

You put everyone at ease. It makes things so much simpler, in the long run.

★★★

After a while you get up to use the facilities, and on the way back you sling a couple of creds into the juke, just for laughs. You have a tin ear, so you ask the nearest table what they'd like to hear. The man bristles, but the two floozies sitting with him light up, pleased at the interruption on a dull weekday night. They think it's cute, you apologizing for intruding. You play on that first impression, explain about the tin ear, ask them diffidently if they'd mind choosing their own favorites instead of leaving you in this awkward position. It would be a real favor to you, an off-planet tourist who just wandered into the area, drifted in by accident one might say, not really familiar with this sort of place, no. You add a little stammer for effect, then you offer to buy the guy a beer.

He relaxes and declines, asks where you're from, why don't you bring your own drink over and sit a while. *The girls'll take forever picking their songs, women are like that. You know.* He winks as he says it. You'd wondered if he was a fag, from that shiny piece of hardware around his neck, but now you guess not.

So you agree, looking serious and man-to-man, then excuse yourself to fetch the half-finished beer from its lonely spot at the bar. When you return, the girls are slow-dancing to a song that sounds vaguely familiar. You recall hearing it a few years ago, when it was a big hit. Now it's just nostalgia, like everything else in your life. Nothing new under the sun, no.

The man finishes his drink and rises to get another, offering to buy you a refill. No, no, you protest, it's not right, after all, I'm intruding on your evening, and you so kind to take in a lonely stranger for a few moments of all-too-rare *camaraderie.* Not at all, he replies, after all, we're a friendly port. Don't believe the rumors you hear out there, my pleasure. You protest again, observing the forms, and before you know it, he's back with two cold ones.

He continues to talk, and you continue to listen as though you're paying attention, but you're really focused on the girls and their movements. You have a fair amount of practice looking like you're paying attention when you're not.

They slow-dance together as though they've had a lot of practice doing it that way. You wonder if they come in a pair, a matched set, *there's* something you haven't done in a while. The girls are strikingly similar, blonde, full-chested, with long lean legs and vacant eyes. Just your type.

You notice they're wearing similar jewelry around their necks, similar to the guy that is, and there's a certain family resemblance. Maybe sisters and brother. That could be a problem. You try to find a delicate way of broaching the subject, not wanting to offend local custom. He might take offense if you hit on a family member, always best to be cautious.

But you don't have to worry, he's already taking care of it. Dragging your thoughts away from the women, you hear him say something about tits and ass, nothing new under the sun, only tits and ass. Just a couple of friends, easy on the eye, that's about the size of it. He's ogling them himself now, so you relax.

The girls come back, flushed and giggling. Pretty, pretty, you say to yourself. Pretty, pretty, and they snuggle up to you like kittens on a rainy night. You buy another round, and he takes off to empty his bladder.

One of the girls asks if you want to go into the back room with her. The other one asks, too. Then they both grin, and giggle into the air around your face. You laugh shyly, nervously twisting the cheap wedding band you picked up at another port last week. You look bashful, stunned at your good fortune. It's all new to you now, isn't it?

I've just, you say, I always wondered, small town back home, everybody knows everybody, never even thought to ask anyone, just wouldn't do, right? And what about me looking silly you add, wouldn't laugh at me or anything would you? No, they say, wouldn't laugh, no. Lots of fun, you should try it, let's go, let's go. You let them urge for a few moments, then you put the worried look on your face, so they'll ask what's the matter.

My wife, you say, my wife will maybe, twenty-eight years and I never, she's always been, and me too you assure them, but the girls promise no one will ever know. Ever. You can trust us, they say, wide-eyed with eyelashes fluttering. Honesty. It's a good trick, you've used it before yourself.

You trade the worried look on your face for slit-eyed deep thought, rube from the country faced with perils of the big city. Clothes don't make the man, they know that already, you wear them like you've never worn anything so good before. Easy mark.

You draw a deep breath, expel your worries in one quick run-on sentence, saying with a sheepish smile—You're not, you know, I mean you seem like nice girls, I couldn't afford, you're not a couple of those—

No no, they both giggle at the thought, no need, plenty of money of our own, but you seem like such a nice guy, let's go, let's go.

What about the man you say, he won't like it, don't want to

offend. Oh, they laugh, our friend won't mind, he's used to us taking off suddenly.

Easy pickings. Just like you figured.

So you follow them out the back door of the bar, and down a small alleyway that's littered with the memory of a thousand other encounters. Your hand's on the belt again, slowly undoing the buckle, just to be ready. The room looks like any other room, just a bed with a nightstand, and a cheap clock that once glowed in the dark. The only light's a small lamp covered by a red scarf. Locally made, cheap looking; no imports here, nothing to distract, but it casts a nice glow. Sexy. You like that, sexy. They'll look better in red. As for you, it doesn't matter what you look like, does it?

They ask you to take off your pants and you demur, saying there's plenty of time for that later. So they take off their blouses, still giggling, and it begins to irritate you, the giggling, and you're pleased about the annoyance because if they'll just keep it up, you can goad that feeling into real anger. Makes it simpler, having something to focus on.

You step through the motions, slack-jawed and admiring, looking slightly star-struck in a country-ass way, and they think you're even cuter. Edge toward the window to lock it, see that it's already been painted shut half a dozen times or more. Good, only one way out. No need for much air at this point anyway. Later, when you go back to the bar, you'll have plenty of time to breathe.

You're just reaching for the belt when the girls grab your hands and pull them behind you, still giggling, and one of them holds your hands there while the other undoes your pants for you. You realize vaguely that with the pants down around your ankles, you can't really move very fast, but they're both laughing now, running their hands up and down your body, and before you know it you're laughing, too, and it's all the better because it will take more time this way. You've got plenty of time, even if they don't.

So you let them pull off the rest of your clothes and fling them in a corner, and you mark where they went with your eyes, because as soon as you're done with the preliminaries, you plan to go retrieve them and really get down to business. Which is what they do once you hit the bed, get down to business that is, one on each side of you for good measure, and you feeling like a hot piece of meat between two slices of toast. It's pretty good this way, you ought to do it more often. You relax, letting them do the work, and pretty soon it's over, and you still laying there between them like an overturned beetle.

They clean you up with a washcloth and start giggling, ready to do it all over again, only they seem a little anxious now, like they're watching the clock. So you glance at it yourself and say, holy cow look at the time, gotta go, gotta go, thanks a lot, be back tomorrow, buy you dinner or something.

Liar.

And they seem to know you're lying, because they stop giggling and press you down even harder into the bed, looking toward the door. You struggle a little, just part of the game, but then you decide you've got to get up *now*, and you begin making your excuses again, trying to leave, explaining you'll be late, asking them to get off. Only they're not listening.

You've done this before, but never with the clothes so far away, and this time you're stuck between them without your belt, and the two girls are a whole lot stronger than they looked.

So they hold you down, giggling, as a form detaches itself from the shadows by the door. He's a lot bigger than you remember, the fellow from the table, and he doesn't seem interested in playing. You offer him the girls, but he doesn't even bother glancing at them; he's only interested in you. They back off a little so he can check you out, and you feel your manhood shrivel into nothingness under his gaze.

You lay there for a while with them all staring at you, feeling like a goldfish in a bowl of brand-new water, and then you decide to make a break for it. You're a man of action, after all, though without the belt or the stuff in your pockets there's not much action to be had. Besides, the girls are doing a pretty good job of holding down your arms, and he's slowly taking off his clothes.

You close your eyes once you've had a glimpse of what's underneath. You never were much good at facing reality.

When they're done playing with you, they let you vomit into the wastebasket, then they load you into a truck and bring you to a cargo freighter. You're pretty out of it by then, it doesn't occur to you that you might make a run for it. They figured on that, they figured on everything well before you walked into the bar. They've already got your ID, it's no problem to 'net your ship and ask it to send your effects over to a rooming house on the better side of town. That's probably where they live, when they're not slumming with strangers like you.

They dump you on a floor that reeks of old wounds, and the captain comes in to negotiate. It's quick, they've all been through the drill. Credits change hands, doors slam, and it's a good thing you're already blissfully unconscious at take off. No frills for the animals here, no separate cabins with real water for the showers and cool clean sheets on the bed. Just a bucket now and then, when they remember. You lose track of the time, and it's always night these days.

The captain dumps you off as part of his regular freight run, to some handler who makes sure you're too malnourished to care, and he sells your ass to the slave pits, where things work a little differently from the mainland. No pretty sheets here, not even cheap red cloth over a lamp by the bed. No lamp. No bed. Just the mines, day in and day out, and the glare of a sun that never fully goes down.

You manage to work your way up to overseer, but that's not going to get you out, so after being stuck in that position for a while you cleverly decide to escape. They catch you, of course. They always do. There's no thought of execution here; in fact, they're looking for a few good men like you. Men who will always believe they have the advantage. Men who always think they know better than anyone else. Men who are willing to do anything.

You spend a few years in the re-education camp, where you brownnose the guards and try to stay out of trouble. Once, just once, you try to escape again, only to discover that there are punishments that beat death hands down. A few more of those for good measure, and you learn to play by the rules. All you really want, at that point, is to get out of there. You're a model prisoner by now. In fact, you're such a model that they take you into the pit hospital one day and make a few adjustments.

Not much of your old self left by the time they get through.

Once you realize what they've done, you try to work up the energy to be angry, really angry, cat-spitting clawing-at-the-walls angry. You're searching for that same anger that used to stand you in such good stead, but it doesn't feel familiar anymore. You have no anger left, just a dull, blind acceptance of wherever and whatever comes. They've done a good job, they always do. You didn't think you were the first, did you?

When they're sure you're too beaten down to have any mind of your own left, they send you out with a monitoring collar around your neck. It's a promotion of sorts, you understand that by now. There are plenty of jobs for someone like you, if you just know where and how to look. Not that anyone trusts you yet; there's the collar, after all, and you realize there's no privacy in this new world you inhabit. You'll be partnered everywhere, by someone more experienced, with the extra brawn to get the job done. You can't do it by yourself anymore, you know that, but maybe someday you can graduate to being the lead partner yourself. Then you'll get to be the one who chooses method and madness.

So you do a pretty good job, knowing it beats sweating it out on the rocks. You always liked to travel, after all. And after a few years you hit a planet that feels familiar, but you're in different circumstances these days, and you sashay down to the assigned meeting place with a different spring to your step. You barely remember being here before, and there's not much to remind you of it now. Not that anything would look familiar at this stage of the game anyway. The buildings change hands, the signs change names, only the tourists stay the same. But there's nothing really new under the sun, not where making a living's concerned.

So you wind up here, in a seedy bar that stirs vague memories of a time when you were still in control, and it worries you, the memory, because the collar around your neck seems to tighten when you think about the old days. You can't breathe very well with it that tight, I know. Stop thinking about who you were, think about who you are instead. Just relax, focus on the present. Think about how pretty you are now, how much fun it is to watch the men's eyes follow you when you dance. Think about the important role you're filling in the economy, how you're taking psychopaths and sociopaths off the street, making the world safe for society. Think of all the little perks, and how much fun this can be, if you just keep the right attitude. Attitude's a valuable thing in this job, a lot more valuable than old memories.

So set the bad thoughts aside and relax. Have a drink, it's okay. I know how it is. Just keep your eye on the important things, and you'll do fine. Don't let yourself be distracted. What's important is that you're here, not there, squeaking out your protests under a blazing sun as you chip away at rocks that seem to grow out of nowhere. What's important is that we've all got a job to do, and you've finally found yours, so don't fuck it up now. What's important is meeting me on time, and doing what I say, and maybe you'll get to have a little fun later, when I'm done with him myself. Yeah, that fellow sitting over there in a corner, nursing his drink, looking at you in the mirror. The one with the bulge in his pocket, trying to act nonchalant. Don't look, just sit here and be cute. Your hair looks good, by the way.

And if you play your cards right, maybe someday they'll take you into that medical ward again and change you back. Then you can be on the giving end, instead of just sitting here in the receiving line. You can always hope.

I know. I've been there.

Play like a Girl

by KRISTINE KATHRYN RUSCH

I just want to make some music
Have a good time while I do it
—from "Play Like A Girl" by Janis Ian

SHE haunts me—a little slip of a woman, barely five two, not even one hundred pounds. The features that mark my face are from her family: the high cheekbones, the narrow chin and delicate mouth. The body beneath them comes from my father's family: solid, Germanic, thickening with age. Someday people will call me a sturdy woman, square and matronly. But my face will always have a touch of the exotic—the silver hair that first appears in the photographs of her father, the dark brows over grayish blue long-lashed eyes.

It is her voice that comes to me most often, simple sentences usually starting with I can'ts, I wishes, and I don'ts. It is her heartaches I carry, her wounds I bear.

As I get older, I understand her more, and I wonder, with each incident explained, if I'll ever be able to forgive her.

✦★✦

I am the youngest, although not by design. My sister holds that honor. Sixteen years older than I am and planned, her conception a happily remembered occasion that apparently started with my father's impish grin and the statement, "C'mon, let's go make a baby."

I come from a drunken night in New Hampshire, after my parents dropped my brother at Dartmouth. I was my father's New York dividend, my mother's accident.

I was the child she never wanted, the reason for her imprisonment, the death of her hope. At forty-two, she was saddled with diapers and bottles, forced to spend endless days with a baby whose sunny disposition hid one of the most relentless stubborn streaks people have ever encountered.

It wasn't pleasant for either of us, but when I turned forty-two, I realized it was probably least pleasant for her.

★★★

My mother has been dead for five years, but she visits me every day. Usually she passes through, making a snide remark about the cleanliness of my kitchen or handing me a utensil, reminding me silently of the way she had actually taught me how to do a particular chore.

But sometimes she stands in front of me, giving me a look she rarely gave me in life—an aware, startled look as if she can't believe I have accomplished something she thought impossible, something she believed no one could ever do.

★★★

Once a therapist confided in me that her most difficult patients were the women who came of age just before World War II.

"They discard their pasts," she said. "They move forward and never look back. They demean themselves, their accomplishments, and the accomplishments of others. And, as I try to work with them, they resist me, until eventually they leave, as unhappy and frustrated as they were when they arrived."

I was so young when the therapist and I had this conversation—in my twenties—so certain that everything had an answer, if we only knew where to look.

"Maybe it's disappointment," I said. "Rosie the Riveter forced to leave her job and become Mommy."

The therapist shook her head. "It's more than that. It's as if there's a gaping hole in their lives, and returning to it will destroy them, this time maybe forever."

Fear, I remember thinking. It was only fear. And fear can always, always be conquered.

★★★

Fifteen years later, I stand on a makeshift stage in the Elks Club basement, wearing makeup someone else has applied and a long gown that would make a frilly bridesmaid's dress seem beautiful. My chorus is doing a benefit for a local charity, performing in front of an enthusiastic crowd of fifty people, all friends and family. The "friendly" crowd, our director calls it, because next week, we compete; next week, we stand on the stage in the Arlene Schnitzer Concert Hall in Portland and sing before judges who will evaluate our every sound.

I stand second row back with the altos, although I am technically a first soprano, with a voice so high that, with the proper refresher training, it can break glass.

But my range runs more than three octaves and, since I am one of the few women in this small town who can read music and sing harmony, I spend my nights at the bottom of my register, harmonizing as softly as I can so that my powerful voice doesn't overwhelm the melody.

I am the best singer in the group. I have been the best singer in every group I have ever joined, from grade school through high school, from music camp to regional festivals, from college to adulthood. Choir directors seek me out, make me lead, have me sing each part except contralto so that the others can hear how the music should sound.

And yet, when I step on stage, my throat seizes up, I swallow too much air, I miss easy cues. I listen with an acuity that's preter-natural, hearing the mispronunciation, the slightly missed note, the harmony one-sixteenth of a tone off. My hands sweat, my shoulders tense. I stand alone in a chorus of thirty, as if a spotlight shines on me, only me.

My mother, five years dead, sits on a folding chair in the front row, her hands folded in her lap, her legs crossed at the ankle and tucked to the side. She is forty pounds heavier than she was when she died, and her spectacular silver hair still has threads of black.

She listens with a concentration that's fierce, staring straight ahead as if each note were written before her.

And when the chorus finishes with our signature song—a World War I ballad so barbershop that it makes all the poles in town spin—the friendly crowd rises enthusiastically to its feet, screaming and shouting and clapping as if we are the best performers they have ever heard.

The crowd rises—all except my mother, who remains in her chair, hands clasped, legs tucked to the side. She smiles, just a little upturn of the lips, barely noticeable to anyone but me, as if to say, *What fools these people are. They actually believed this was good.*

By the time we troop offstage, she is gone. But her critique lingers as if she gave it to me personally. One missed cue, five flat notes, and one gulp of air. Not to mention, honey, that the dress does nothing to flatter you, and your hair covered your tiny face.

I sit down in the chair she has vacated, still warm from the heat of her body, and shake. Now that the performance is done, I am so exhausted, I can hardly move. It's hard to listen to every nuance, to be alert to the smallest mistake.

But I am, and I do, and the performances drain me, as if they suck the essence of my being out with each note.

★★★

My sisters and I have the same voice. We use it differently. My oldest sister pitches hers low and adds a twang, acquired after nearly a decade in Texas. My other sister, the former baby of the family, uses hers stridently, banishing the music from it as if music never existed.

My voice varies depending on what I need it for. It is, perhaps, the most trained part of me—trained, at one point, to be a singer, an actor, and a broadcaster. My face gives away my emotions, but my voice hides my secrets. Put me behind a microphone, obscure my face, and I can lie better than anyone else in the world.

I also do impressions, and the ones I do best are the ones I learned to do first: my sisters. It is amazing what a person can learn by phone, calling her parents and pretending to be her siblings. It soon becomes clear who is loved the most.

The one impression I have never done is my mother—which is odd, when you consider that our voices, my sisters and mine, come from her, just like our features do, like my hair does. Our voices are her voice, so much alike that when she was alive and we all gathered in one room, people in the next room could not tell us apart.

In 1930-something, my mother, then a girl in her teens, met a famous opera singer, a woman whose name I now forget. The choir director at my mother's church introduced the woman to my mother because my mother, like me, was the person directors sought out, making her lead, having her sing each part except contralto so that the others could hear how the music should sound.

The opera star offered my mother private lessons, said she should be auditioning for the major opera companies. *You have the talent to become one of the most famous singers in the land*, the opera star told her.

The story always ended there, with the validation of my mother's skill, not with the explanation of why she chose to remain home. We were left to guess: did a lack of money hold her back? Or fear that she wasn't good enough? Did my aunt—younger then, her flapper's marcel appropriate and stylish—convince my mother that the sinful city was not a good place for an orphan girl still stuck in her teens?

It is a fleeting glimpse of a well-worn dream, a story told more and more rarely as time went on. I would think I imagined it, except my sisters know it too.

We discuss it in our matching voices, forming a trio of doubt. For we have learned over the years that we cannot trust our mother's stories. She altered them almost by whim.

But there is always a kernel of truth. And we know this: there was an opera singer—although she may not have been a star. And we also know our mother was talented because, at one point or another, we have heard her sing.

★★★

She sings to me every Christmas, her voice growing strong as her death recedes into the past. Somehow, on Christmas Eve, I find myself standing beside her in the church of my youth.

The pews are made of polished wood, the air smells of pine boughs, and the sanctuary is dark except for hundreds of candles, held by each member of the congregation. The midnight service always ends with "Silent Night," which the congregation sings in unison.

All except my mother. She sings a descant, her beautiful voice soaring above the others. She is not singing the song as a lullaby—for there is no gentleness in this woman; there never has been—but she is performing, and the performance is breathtaking.

Her eyes are closed, her head tilted upward, her striking features accented by the candlelight. She is, for this moment and this moment only, somewhere else—a place where she is loved, where music is more than notes on a page.

Try as I might, I cannot replicate that moment, even with the voice she has given me. The descant does not exist in any hymnal or book of carols, and the words—the words aren't even English. For when she tilts her head back and sings like one of the heavenly host, my mother reverts to the language of her childhood.

Every year, alive or dead, my mother sings "Silent Night" in German.

✯✯✯

She also spoke German as she gave birth to me—and this story I know to be true because my father told it to me first.

My mother went into labor, forty-two years old and unhappy, terrified that my birth would kill her. The doctor could not calm her and finally put her under—a full anesthetic so that her body could expel me without interference from her all-powerful mind.

But her mind protected her all the same. Tears ran down her cheeks, and she repeated something, singsong in that beautiful voice, so many times that a nurse finally wrote a phonetic version of my mother's utterances.

The nurses brought the paper to my father in the waiting room at the same time they brought me, and recited, as best they could, my mother's words. My father laughed, as he was wont to do where my mother was concerned, and shrugged off the significance.

But the nurses did not. They remembered, and later told my mother.

She had done something she could not do while conscious.

Throughout my birth, she had recited the Lord's Prayer.

In German.

✯✯✯

My mother learned to sing in German. Every Christmas, her father would line up his children in the front parlor, near the piano. Each child, from the oldest to the youngest, would sing to my grandmother—and, if possible, that child accompanied herself on the piano.

Everyone in my mother's family learned to play the piano. It was required, like singing was required, like German was required, like God was required.

My mother's father was a minister, who came from a family of ministers. He emigrated to the United States from Germany in the first decade of the twentieth century, brought over by his elder brother, also a minister.

My grandfather married into a family of women, all of whom worked as maids at a seminary, and all of whom married ministers.

At home, my mother's family spoke German. My mother, also the baby, did not have as many years of indoctrination in that language as her siblings had: her father died when she was eight—or was it ten? These stories are never clear—and her mother, destitute, opened a boarding house where English became the primary tongue.

But German was locked inside my mother, locked as so many other things were, locked and kept close, never to be released.

Not even now, when she haunts me all these years after her death.

★★★

I no longer sing with the chorus. I adored rehearsal, but performances destroyed me. For the two days before we sang, my stomach churned, and for the two days after, my head ached so badly I could hardly think.

I am an adult now. I realized I did not have to do something I did not enjoy. And much as I loved to sing, I could not exorcise the ghost of my mother from her seat in the front row.

★★★

When I first became a writer, I wrote stories about music. My first professional fiction sale featured aliens whose souls were songs, played with variations each and every day.

Music is my life, my heart, and my dreams. I cannot live without it. A sound track runs through my mind, always cuing me to the feelings I bury within me.

Over time, music left my fiction. I no longer sang at home, and I rarely listened to the radio. I locked music deep inside me, sealing it up along with its five-foot-two-inch ghost.

Yet I dreamed of it, like a drowning man dreams of air.

And when my husband, good kind gentle man that he is, asked

me what I wanted for my fortieth birthday, a voice from deep inside me escaped the lock and answered him:

I would like, the voice said with a child's breathiness, a child's hope, *I would like . . . a piano.*

✦✦✦

A piano. Sacred totem of my childhood, as forbidden as the name of God.

One of my earliest memories: sitting on the piano bench in the church basement—that same church where my mother still sings every Christmas Eve—my fingers finding scales on ivory keys. I play with the door closed, one ear trained on the slightest sound outside, so that I cannot be overheard.

I am happy there, in that little room, where a woman named Miss Mlsna teaches me how to sing, and asks me to direct the other children whenever she must leave the room.

My mother never touched that piano. In fact, I never saw her touch a musical instrument in her life. When I was seven, and the school I attended mandated that we all learn a musical instrument, my mother made me learn the flute.

Beginning woodwind players squeak and squeal, but they do not torture the ear the way beginning string players do. Nor do they offend the neighbors the way beginning percussionists do.

But the only instrument which sounds passable even under a beginner's hands is the piano.

My mother would not allow a piano in her house.

✦✦✦

There is a piano in mine. It is a Baldwin baby grand, black and shiny, with tone so pure and wondrous it should grace a stage instead of my living room.

I adore that piano.

It is the only place in the world where I do not see my mother's ghost.

Oh, she tried to haunt it with her disapproving looks and her sideways comments—*music is about perfection*, she would say, and my flute teacher, a strict Greek Orthodox woman who never smiled, would chime in, reminding me that I am the laziest musician she has ever met.

I am lazy. I slid by on talent and on the ear I inherited from my father's mother. That grandmother—the best dancer in Fond du Lac County in the decade before World War I—also played the piano, but she never learned to read music, preferring instead to play the popular songs of the day after listening to someone else perform them.

In the last two years, the years the piano has decorated my living room, I have learned that my laziness no longer matters. I do not practice for performance. I practice because I want to. I am amusing myself. Perfection is irrelevant, since the only people who will grade me on my abilities are my mother—and myself.

But my mother refuses to come into the living room. She will not sit near the piano—has not even looked at it since it arrived two years before.

She doesn't even hover near the archway, peering into the room like she used to do when I sang or listened to music on the radio. Instead, she hides in my kitchen, paging through my cookbooks as if they hold the secrets to the universe.

Her absence is liberating. I pound the keys, playing loud, playing soft, playing discordant notes, playing random chords. Sometimes I sing as I play, and I remain alone in the room, no silverhaired, five-foot-two-inch, sharp-faced woman sitting with her hands clasped, peering at me, waiting for me to make a mistake.

Oddly, the songs that I play, the ones that I learn all the way through, come from my mother's youth. Big bands, sentimental journeys, smoke getting in your eyes.

Once my mother said to me, her voice breathy, childlike, and full of hope, that while she thought the music of my generation had beauty, no one knew how to write love songs like the people from hers.

The generation my therapist friend called lost, the generation with the gaping hole in their collective psyche, the generation forever embittered, forever lost.

When my mother made her statement—the only one, I recollect, she ever made about the music she grew up with—I poohpoohed it. I was sixteen, full of myself, and convinced no one else could be right.

Yet as I climb inside these songs, learn their chords, their lyrics, their intricacies, I realize she *was* right. For these love songs have depth, a depth that comes from history. And only if you know the history do you understand them, do you realize that beneath the words of love are discordant hymns to unspeakable loss.

★★★

My generation sings of empowerment. I went through puberty listening to "I am Woman," and followed the singer-songwriters who rejected the woman-needs-man-to-thrive thread that coexisted with the Take Back the Night marches of my college years.

First we sang of our right to a place in the world, and now we sing of our victories. Like this from Janis Ian:

> *"I don't need permission*
> *to change this tradition*
> *When they tell me 'You can't play'*
> *Well, I just turn my back and say . . .*
> *'Now all over this big wide world*
> *I play like a girl'"*

The insult of our youth turned back on all of those who slung it.

I play like a girl.
But that isn't the victory.
The victory is that I play at all.

★★★

By the time she died, my mother had stopped singing. She listened to news on the radio, soap operas on TV. Her house, once filled with the classical sounds of public radio, more often than not held silence, like someone was holding a breath they would never, ever let go.

The day after her funeral, my sisters and I began to clean that barren place. We did not turn on a radio to cover the silence. We barely spoke, and when we did, it was of sadness and disappointments, in simple sentences usually starting with I can'ts, I wishes, and I don'ts.

We found no hidden treasures, no caches of memories, no marvelous and unknown things. But we did find a stack of CDs hidden behind my father's albums in the hallway—all big bands: Tommy Dorsey, Benny Goodman, Collected Songs from World War II.

Sentimental journeys. Songs ostensibly about love, but really about loss so deep it leaves a gaping, unimaginable wound.

I have the CDs now. I listen to them, late at night, in the piano room, alone—always alone—and feel echoes of that wound. It is not mine; it is hers. And I do not understand it.

But for years it stopped me, forced me to trap my music and lock it up inside my soul.

The piano has set my music free. Sometimes I leave my practice sessions, my playing sessions, and wander into the kitchen, to find my mother standing there, a cookbook held like a shield in her left hand.

She watches me with that look she never had in life, that aware, startled look as if she can't believe I have accomplished something she thought impossible, something she believed no one could ever do.

Then she turns away, and I can see through her—a five-foot-two-inch ghost with more substance than she ever held in life.

I want to ask her what happened; why she locked the music away along with her hopes, her dreams; what caused the hole in her life—the hole that haunts her, even in her death.

But as I frame the question, she vanishes like she's never been—not exorcised, for she shall never be fully exorcised. She lives in my face, in my voice, in everything I touch and everything I do—but vanquished by a piano and the threat of sound.

We are each a product of our own history, our own generation.

I play like a girl.

And sadly, she did, too.

All In a Blaze

by
STEPHEN BAXTER

Stars, they come and go
They come fast or slow
They go like the last light of the sun
all in a blaze
and all you see is glory
        —from "Stars" by Janis Ian

IT all came to a head on the day of the Halo Dance.

On some level Faya Parz had known the truth about herself. In the background of her life there had always been the bits of family gossip. And then as she grew older, and her friends began to gray, she stayed supple—as if she was charmed, time sliding by her, barely touching her.

But these were subtle things. She had never articulated it to herself, never framed the thought. On some deeper level she hadn't wanted to know.

She had to meet Luru Parz before she faced it.

The amphitheater was a great bowl gouged out of the icy surface of Port Sol. Over Faya's head the sun, seen here at the edge of the solar system, was just a pinprick in a tapestry of stars, its sharpness softened a little by the immense dome that spanned the theater. Of course the amphitheater was crowded, as it was every four years for this famous event; there was a great sea of upturned faces, all around Faya. She gazed up at the platforms hovering high above, just under the envelope of the dome itself, where her sister and the other Dancers were preparing for their performance.

". . . Excuse me."

Faya glanced down. A small woman faced her, stocky, broad-faced, dressed in a nondescript coverall. Faya couldn't tell her age, but there was something solid about her, something heavy, despite the micro-gravity of Port Sol. And she looked oddly familiar.

The woman smiled at her.

Faya was staring. "I'm sorry."

"The seat next to you—"

"It's free."

"I know." With slow care, the woman climbed the couple of steps up to Faya's row and sat down on the carved and insulated ice. "You're Faya Parz, aren't you? I've seen your Virtuals. You were one of the best Dancers of all."

"Thank you."

"You wish you were up there now."

Faya was used to fans, but this woman was a little unsettling. "I'm past forty. In the Dance, when you've had your day, you must make way."

"But you are aging well."

It was an odd remark from a stranger. "My sister's up there."

"Lieta, yes. Ten years younger. But you could still challenge her."

Faya turned to study the woman. "I don't want to be rude, but—"

"But I seem to know a lot about you. I don't mean to put you at a disadvantage. My name is Luru Parz."

Faya did a double take. "I thought I knew all of us Parz on Port Sol."

"We're relatives. I'm—a great-aunt, dear. Think of me that way."

"Do you live here?"

"No, no. Just a transient, as we all are. Everything passes, you know; everything changes." She waved her hand, indicating the amphitheater. Her gestures were small, economical in their use of time and space. "Take this place. Do you know its history?"

Faya shrugged. "I never thought about it. Is it natural, a crater?"

Luru shook her head. "No. A starship was born here, right where we're sitting, its fuel dug out of the ice. It was the greatest of them all, called *The Great Northern*—we think. We'll never know its fate; the Extirpation saw to that."

"You know a lot of history," said Faya, a little edgy. The great Extirpation of the Qax, once alien overlords of Earth, had succeeded in erasing much of the human past. And now the ruling Coalition of Interim Governance, focusing on mankind's future, frowned on any obsession with lost, heroic days.

Luru would only shrug. "Some of us have long memories."

A crackling, ripping sound washed down over the audience, and a pale blue mist erupted over the domed sky.

"What a beautiful effect," said Luru.

"But it's just water," Faya said. So it was. The dome's upper layers of air were allowed to become extremely cold, far below freezing. At such temperatures you could just throw water into the air and it would spontaneously freeze. A water droplet froze quickly from the outside in—but ice was less dense than water, and when the central region froze it would expand and shatter the outer shell like a tiny bomb.

And now the first halos formed, glowing arcs and rings around the brighter stars and especially around the sun itself, light scattered by air full of tiny ice prisms. There were more gasps from the crowd.

On this ice moon, cold was art's raw material.

And now it began. One by one the Dancers leaped from their platforms. They were allowed no aids; they followed simple low-gravity parabolas that arched between one floating platform and the next. But the art was in the selection of that parabola among the shifting, shivering ice halos—which were, of course, invisible to the Dancers—and in the way you spun, turned, starfished and swam against that background.

As one Dancer after another passed over the dome, ripples of applause broke out around the amphitheater. Glowing numerals and Virtual bar graphs littered the air in the central arena; the voting had already begun. But the sheer beauty of the spectacle silenced many, as the tiny human figures, naked and lithe, danced defiantly against the stars.

Luru, though, was watching Faya.

"Tell me why you gave up the Dance. Your performances weren't declining, were they? You felt you could have kept going forever. Isn't that true? But something worried you."

Faya wasn't sure how to respond. She looked away, disturbed.

Here, at last, was Lieta herself, ready for the few seconds of flight for which she had rehearsed for four years. Faya remembered how it used to feel, the nervousness as her body tried to soar—and then the exhilaration when she succeeded, one more time.

Lieta's launch was good, Faya saw, her track well chosen. But her movements were . . . stiff. They lacked the liquid grace of her competitors. Lieta, her little sister, was already thirty years old, and one of the oldest in the field.

At the center of the arena a display of Lieta's marks coalesced. A perfect score would have showed as bright green, but Lieta's bars were flecked with yellow. A Virtual of Lieta's upper body and head appeared; she was smiling bravely.

"There is gray in her hair," murmured Luru. "Look at the lines around her eyes, her mouth. You have aged better than your ten-years-younger sister. You have aged less, in fact. There is no gray in your hair."

Faya turned on her in irritation. "Look, I don't know what you want—"

"It's a shock when you see them grow old around you. I remember it happening to me, the first time—long ago, of course." She grinned coldly.

"You're frightening me." Faya said it loud enough to make people stare.

Luru stood. "I'm like you, Faya Parz. The same blood. You

know what I'm talking about. When you want to see me, I'll find you."

Faya waited in her seat until the Dance was over, and the audience had filed away. She didn't even try to find Lieta, as they'd arranged.

Instead she made her own way up into the dome.

She stood on the lip of the highest platform. The amphitheater was a pit, far below, but she had no fear of heights. The star-filled sky beyond the dome was huge, inhuman. And, through the subtle glimmer of the dome walls, she could see the tightly curving horizon of this little world of ice.

She closed her eyes, visualising the pattern of halos, just as it had been when Lieta had launched herself into space. And then she jumped.

She had the automated systems assess her. She found the bars glowing an unbroken green. She had recorded a perfect mark. If she had taken part in the competition, against these kids half her age, she would have won.

She had known what Luru had been talking about. Of course she had. Where others aged, even her own sister, she stayed young. It was as simple as that. The trouble was, it was starting to show.

And it was illegal.

★ ★

Home was a palace of metal and ice she shared with her extended family. This place, one of the most select on Port Sol, had been purchased with the riches Faya had made from her Dancing.

Her mother was here. Spina Parz was over sixty; her gray, straying hair was tied back in a stern bun.

And, waiting for Faya, there was a Commissary, a representative of the Commission for Historical Truth, the police force of the Coalition. He wore his head shaved, and a simple ground-length robe. Somehow she wasn't surprised to see him; evidently today was the day everything unraveled.

The Commissary stood up and faced her. "My name is Ank Sool."

"I'm not aging, am I?"

"I can cure you. Don't be afraid."

Spina said wistfully, "I knew you were special even when you were very small. You were an immortal baby, born among mortals. You were wonderful."

"Why didn't you tell me?"

Spina looked tired. "Because I wanted you to figure it out for yourself. On the other hand, I never thought it would take you until you were forty." She smiled. "You never were the brightest crystal in the snowflake, were you, dear?"

Faya's anger melted. She hugged her mother. "The great family secret . . ."

"I saw the truth, working its way through you. You always had trouble with relationships, with men. They kept becoming too old for you, didn't they? When you're young, even a subtle change is enough to spoil things. And—"

"And I haven't had children."

"You kept putting it off. Your body knew, love. And now your head knows, too."

Sool said earnestly, "You must understand the situation."

"I understand I'm in trouble. Immortality is illegal."

He shook his head. "You are the victim of a crime—a crime committed centuries ago."

It was all the fault of the Qax, as so many things were. During their Occupation of Earth the Qax had rewarded those who had collaborated with them with an anti-aging treatment. The Qax, masters of nanotechnological transformations, had rewired human genomes.

"After the fall of the Qax, the surviving collaborators and their children were treated, given the gift of mortality, permitted to re-join the great adventure of mankind."

"But you evidently didn't get us all," Faya said.

Sool said, "The genome cleansing was not perfect. After centu-

ries of Occupation we didn't have the technology. In every generation there are throwbacks."

Faya felt numb. It was as if he were talking about somebody
else. "My sister—"

Her mother said, "Lieta is as mortal as I am, as your poor father
was."

"I could stay young," Faya said slowly. She turned to Sool.
"Once I was famous for my Dancing. They even knew my name
on Earth." She waved a hand. "Look around. I made a fortune. I
was the best. Grown men of twenty-five—your age, yes?—would
follow me. You can't know what that was like; you never saw their
eyes." She stood straight. "I could have it all again. I could have it
forever, couldn't I?"

Sool said stiffly, "The Coalition frowns on celebrity. The species, not the individual, should be at the center of our thoughts."

Her mother was shaking her head. "Faya, it can't be like that.
You're still young; you haven't thought it through. Once I hoped
you would be able to—hide. To survive. But it would be impossible."

"Your mother is right. You would spend your life tinting your
hair, masking your face. Abandoning your home every few years.
Otherwise they would kill you." He said this with a flat certainty,
and she realized that he was speaking from experience.

"I need time," she said abruptly, and forced a smile. "Ironic,
yes? As I've just been given all the time anybody could ask for."

Spina sighed. "Time for what?"

"To talk to Luru Parz." And she left before they had time to
react.

***

"I am nearly two hundred years old. I was born in the era of
the Occupation. I grew up knowing nothing else. And I took the
gift of immortality from the Qax. I have already lived to see the
liberation of mankind."

They were in a two-person flitter. Faya had briskly piloted

them into a slow orbit around Port Sol; beneath them the landscape stretched to its close-crowding horizon. Here, in this
cramped cabin, they were safely alone.

Port Sol was a Kuiper object: like a huge comet nucleus, circling the sun beyond the orbit of Pluto. The little ice moon was
gouged by hundreds of artificial craters. Faya could see the rem-
nants of domes, pylons, and arches, spectacular microgravity archi-
tecture which must have been absurdly expensive to maintain. But
even after decades of reoccupation, most of the buildings were
closed, darkened, and thin frost coated their surfaces; the pylons
and graceful domes were collapsed, with bits of glass and metal
jutting like snapped bones.

Luru said, "Do you know what I see, when I look down at this
landscape? I see layers of history. The great engineer My-kal Puhl
himself founded this place. He built a great system of wormholes,
rapid-transit pathways from the worlds of the inner system. Here,
at the outermost terminus, Puhl's disciples used great mountains
of ice to fuel interstellar vessels. It was the start of mankind's First
Expansion. But then humans acquired a hyperdrive." She smiled
wistfully. "Economic logic. The hyper-ships could fly right out of
the crowded heart of the solar system, straight to the stars. Nobody
needed Puhl's huge wormhole tunnels, or his mighty ice mine."

"But now Port Sol has revived."

"Long before you were born, yes. Because now we have a new
generation of starships, great living ships thirsty for Port Sol's
water. Layers of history."

"I don't know what to do."

"There is an evolutionary logic here." Luru clutched a fist over
her heart. "Listen to me. Once we were animals, less than human.
And we died after the end of our fertile years, like animals. But
then, as we evolved, we changed. We lived on, long after fertility
ended. Do you know why? So that grandmothers could help their
daughters raise the next generation. And that is how we overcame
the other animals, and came to own the Earth—through longevity.
Immortality is good for the species."

"I don't want to hide."

"You don't have a choice. The Coalition are planning a new future for mankind, a final Expansion that will sweep on, forever. There will be no place for the old. But of course, that's just the latest rationalization. People have always burned witches."

Faya didn't know what a witch was.

And then a Virtual of Faya's mother's face congealed in the air before her, the bearer of bad news.

★★★

Faya and Spina held each other, sitting side by side. For now they were done with weeping, and they had readmitted Ank Sool.

"I don't understand," Faya said. "Why Lieta? Why now?" It was the brevity that was impossible to bear—a handful of Dances, a flash of beauty and joy, and then dust.

Sool said, "Blame the Qax. The collaborators never bred true. Many of their offspring died young, or their development stopped at an unsuitable age, so that immortality remained in the gift of the Qax. The Qax were always in control, you see."

But, Faya thought, why should my sister die so suddenly now, why is her life cut short just as the prospect of eternity is opened up for me?

She said carefully, "Commissary, I think I will always suspect, in a corner of my heart, that you allowed this death to happen, in order to bring me under control."

His eyes were blank. "I have no need of such devices."

Spina grasped her daughter's hands. "Take the treatment, dear. It's painless. Get it over, and you will be safe."

"You could have sent me to the Commission as a child. I could have been cured then. I need never have even known."

Sool said dryly, "You would blame your mother rather than the Qax. How—human."

Spina's face crumpled. "Oh, love, how could I take such a gift away from you—even to protect you?"

"It's your decision," said Sool.

★★★

Again they swept into orbit, seeking privacy.

This is how it will be for me from now on, she thought: I will be one of a handful of immortal companions, like crabbed, folded-over Luru here, standing like unchanging rocks in a landscape of evanescent flowers.

"I can't stand the thought of seeing them all growing old and dying around me. Forever."

Luru nodded. "I know. But you aren't thinking big enough, child. On a long enough timescale, everything is as transient as one of your Halo Dances. Why, perhaps we will even live to see the stars themselves sputter to life, fade and die." She smiled. "Stars are like people. Even stars come and go, you see. They die all in a blaze, or fade like the last light of the sun—but you've never seen a sunset, have you? The glory is always brief—but it is worth having, even so. And you will remember the glory, and make it live on. It's your purpose, Faya."

"My burden," she said bleakly.

"We have great projects, long ambitions, beyond the imagination of these others. Come with me."

Tentatively Faya reached out her hand. Luru took it. Her flesh was cold.

"I will have to say farewell—"

"Not farewell. Good-bye. Get used to it."

Before they left, she visited the amphitheater, one last time. And—though she knew she could never let anybody watch her, ever again—she Danced and Danced, as the waiting stars blazed.

Cartoons

by ALEXIS GILLILAND

*In books and magazines
of how to be and what to see
while you are being*
—*"Between the Lines" by Janis Ian*

This gift is flawless
This gift is cordless
so enjoy it to the hilt . . .
—*"Cosmopolitan Girl" by Janis Ian*

Rate my music, one to three
Keep your children safe from me
—*"Rate My Music" by Janis Ian*

*Applause, applause
She'll stand upon her head*
—*"Applause" by Janis Ian*

Old Photographs

by Susan Casper

Close the light, still the flame
Candles light the empty frame
A photograph will never be
the song you are to me
—from "Photographs" by Janis Ian

IT was usually pretty cold right after Thanksgiving, when the Christmas windows were unveiled in the local department stores and the lights and wreaths went up on Market Street. Every year my mother would dress me up in my holiday best and take me downtown to look in those windows and get my picture taken with Santa Claus.

Being Jewish, we didn't celebrate the birth of Christ, about which I knew only what I learned from TV and the annual Bible reading in school, but Christmas was everywhere, enchanting and unavoidable. For us it was a secular holiday full of colored lights and bright, shiny ornaments, eggnog, candy canes, and, of course, presents. I suppose it was with great reluctance that my mother gave in to the pressure of television and our Christian friends and took my sister and me to see the great bearded one every year. We would sit on his lap and tell him what gifts we wanted, posing nicely, or sometimes not so nicely, for a photograph, and in exchange we'd get a mesh stocking of toys and candy that probably wasn't even worth the cost of the subway ride downtown.

Santa was her one concession to the holiday. We weren't allowed a tree. Nor was there a chimney. We never had a formal discussion about how the Christmas Elf obtained admission to the house, but I always assumed him to be an excellent second-story man, capable of slipping in the windows without making a sound. However he entered, once inside he arranged to leave the presents under a large, stand-up radio that sat in our living room. More decoration than sound system, it was a blond wood item, taller than I was, with beige fabric splitting the front in two and a wide yellow dial underlined by buttons, much like the ones in our ancient black Chevy. When it wasn't doing double duty as a Christmas tree, it would be turned on, sometimes, for ball games and boxing matches that weren't carried on our brand-new ten-inch television.

This was the last year we celebrated Christmas. Once I was old enough to know the truth about Santa, the holiday went away completely and we were back to dreidels and menorahs and occasional sips of very bad wine. But I remember this last Christmas in Mom and Dad's row home very well. It was the year I got my posable ballerina doll with the long, beautiful auburn hair. She had articulated ankles so that she could even point her toes. For weeks I lusted after her in the store window, but I didn't know I had gotten her until I saw the long green box with "For Sandy, From Santa" written across the top. Oh, and how beautiful she was! I immediately named her Sharon Elizabeth, my two favorite names of the period. There's a picture of her somewhere, being held in my arms. I was neither a beautiful nor a graceful child, but this was the first picture Mom took with her brand new Instaluxe 500 Camera. Surely you remember them, since they were all the rage for about a year until someone discovered that's about how long it took for the photos to fade. But for that one year the ads for them were all over the TV, with that stupid little cartoon elf hopping around and tapping everything with his wand, turning them all into photos, and that bouncy little "Snap, snap, snap, it's magic" theme song. They advertised on several of the big shows, *Sid Caesar*, maybe, or it could have been *Ed Sullivan* or *Lucy*. We could see the way Mom's eyes lit up whenever the ads came on, had heard her grumble enough at having to borrow her brother's Polaroid. It certainly wasn't the kind of thing Dad would buy. Besides, Chanukah was over and my parents didn't exchange presents at Christmas, so Linda and I bought it for her with our very own money. We saved from long months of allowance and chores. It took instant pictures, but claimed they were nothing like the curled and streaky images you got from a Polaroid. And the best part of all, at least so the package claimed, was that it came with a "lifetime" supply of film. Even at the age of six or so, I wasn't sure exactly what that meant, but it certainly did come with a huge box full of the paper strips used in the camera. Each one was individually wrapped in a waxed paper wrapper, silver for black and white and bright red for color shots. There was even a small supply of gold wrappers marked only, "For those specials photographs that you want to live on in your memory."

We watched with excitement as Mom took a waxed paper packet from the box and slid one silvery end into the machine. With a soft *whhhhr* the tip was snipped off and ejected out the side. Slowly, the paper shrank and bunched into a ball as the inner card flowed into the slot. A light on the back blinked green and Mom carefully fitted a large, blue bulb into the flash attachment. *Click*, the light went off, blinding us momentarily. Before we could even regain our sight another *whhhhr* alerted us that the process was done. A stiff and shiny photograph slid out of the bottom of the device. She took another one, Linda, Dad and me, in glorious black and white, standing in front of our Christmas radio.

I don't remember spending much time looking at the pictures again for many years, until after Dad and Mom had to be moved to the assisted living facility. I'm sure that, just as I did, Linda felt very guilty about this. Weren't they supposed to come live with us? Somehow I felt that it was our job to look after them, but nobody seemed to do that anymore. And where would we put them? My husband and I both had full-time jobs, and Linda had been a single mother ever since the divorce. Now she watched her grandchildren during the day. We simply couldn't take care of them. Neither of us had the room, and besides, we were just too busy—"busy" was the word I said, but "selfish" was the one that always came to mind when I thought about it—to give them the special care they were beginning to need. There was something else they needed that I no longer had, though I hated admitting this even more. It was patience. So, while Linny took care of the finances, the medications, and the doctor visits, it became my job to prepare their house for sale. This wasn't as easy as boxing everything up and removing it for garage sales and the Salvation Army. Mom, who hadn't really wanted to go, made us promise, even though we both knew that neither of them was coming back, that we would keep all their stuff for them until they were ready. That meant, most likely, storing everything in our garage. Someday, Linny and I would go through it and decide what we would want to keep when the time came to get rid of it all. For me, that mostly meant the box.

The "box" was a large cardboard carton that had once contained the "lifetime" supply of film for Mom's camera. I suppose it was, in a way, the ideal place to store old pictures, though few of them were from the Instaluxe, which didn't last all that long. As far as I knew, the camera itself was long gone. The sides of the box were broken and torn, and inside were kept the treasures of a lifetime. My parents' wedding certificate, and several of the Mother's Day and birthday cards my sister and I had painstakingly crafted over the years of school and summer camp out of blotting paper and construction paper, leaves, seeds, and tracings of feet and hands. They were all slowly crumbling to dust inside the box. There were other things in there, too—old wedding invitations, thank-you cards, Hebrew school diplomas, a Popsicle stick bird feeder and a glued-together jigsaw puzzle of "Starry Night" with several pieces missing. And piled loosely in a small hill, slowly metamorphing into confetti, a lifetime of photographs. No, more than a lifetime. Heavy cardboard pieces opened up to reveal my grandmother's wedding, my great aunt's first birthday, and a hundred friends and relatives who no longer had names, let alone relationships.

I noticed off to one side a Kodachrome picture of my father. Probably taken not too long after I was born, he was holding a very young Linda's hand and gazing down lovingly into a carriage that most likely had yours truly inside. Like most old Kodachrome photographs, the colors were odd and tinged toward the yellow. I looked through the stack quickly to see if there was a better one, perhaps a more recent one, but the photos seemed to be crumbling in my fingers. Something had to be done. There had to be some way to fix them, to preserve them, to hang onto them, as if they were the past itself and not just the memories. From somewhere in the back of my mind came an image of my mother, going through the box just after Grammy died. She pulled out a picture of me from one Halloween long past. I was wearing a drugstore Cinderella costume of cheap plastic with a gauze mask, the kind that would not only smell just awful when it got wet, but which would lose its shape as well, which it somehow always did around the mouth area before the night was over. Being only sixteen or so, I saw all reminders of my baby years as proof that I was still the skinny, ugly thing I had been at five. I didn't think anyone should ever be allowed to look at them, and sneering at my mother I told her I was going to destroy the evidence. She lifted the picture out of my reach and laughed at me.

"You mustn't do that," she told me. "Our memories aren't just reminders of the past, Sandy. They're who we are."

I wondered if that picture was still there among the other memory debris, as I gazed down into the face of a woman I did not recognize. Was she family or family friend? I thought about how much closer I felt to some of my friends than I did to my own sister and wondered if there was a difference. My parents could no longer tell me who anyone was. My father was an only child and my mother the baby of her family by so many years that her siblings had long gone to their reward. There was no one left to turn to. I pulled out a photo at random and looked into the face of a stranger. Whether he was my father's best friend, the last serious date Mother had before Daddy, or my Uncle Horsham from Connecticut, a stranger he would remain forever. I placed the box carefully into a small white trash bag and carried it home.

The next day I bought a scanner. My husband, Ray, complained about the money, but money didn't enter into it for me. I knew nothing about computer graphics, but, by God, I was going to learn. These pictures were my history and they had to be preserved. I bought a book and a photo program and carefully practiced restoring their example until I knew just what to do. For several days I practiced sampling from various parts of the image to repair a tear or cover a dull red drop of strawberry juice. Then I opened the box, wanting to find a good head shot of my father. He had taken the position of photographer and managed to appear in only a few of the photos. There were several of my mother at various ages, but like the woman herself, these were heavily decayed. Corners, if not whole chunks, were missing. The colors were faded and all were cracked and lined. Those that had names, places and dates written on the back sometimes had spots where the ink had seeped through, or perhaps smeared on from another photo, and several had stuck together and were now impossible to pull apart without damage. The ancient Kodachrome squares had taken on a yellow, metallic tinge, the old Polaroids had curled and cracked and paled into uselessness. I did find a picture of Dad, old enough that it might have been from before their marriage. I remember as a child, laughing to see him young, his head covered with hair, a mustache on his face. He looked almost nothing like the chubby, bald man on whose shoulders I sat, searching for a handhold on that naked scalp during the chilly Mummers' Parades past. I could remember the man with his large tummy, emphasized by skinny chicken legs sticking out of the massive leg holes of his bathing suit when we went to Atlantic City. And all these years I thought that all my mother had seen in him was his warm pliant character with occasional bursts of humor. Now he was just an old man, quietly waiting to die, but hanging on to allow my mother the courtesy of going before him. I knew that, uncomfortable as he was, his biggest fear was going before her, leaving her alone. If he could have his way, he would take her hand and the two of them would pass quietly out of this world together.

For her part, he seemed, almost, to no longer exist. Half the time she didn't recognize him, and once, for a moment, scared me deeply by announcing to me, "Sandy, that's not your father." I thought perhaps I was in the midst of a family revelation for which I was just not ready, but realized after a bit that she simply didn't recognize him. Worst of all, she seemed to find his touch repellent. When he reached for her hand, she pulled away. If he minded, he never showed it, but it made me sad.

Now, as I went through the box I began to realize that some of these many versions of my parents, my sister, myself, cousins, aunts, and even the occasional old friend, were more real to me than others. Certainly this father of the five-year-old me, standing proudly in front of our brand new ten-inch television set, while Ozzie and Harriet faded into the background, was my father, not this suave, mustachioed creature who wouldn't sire a child for years yet. I sorted the photos into two piles, leaving the other memorabilia alone for the moment. Into a shoebox went all the photos that I wanted to save. A large manila envelope received all the ones I no longer had any means of identifying, though some of them were interesting. For now, I would scan the former and fix what I could. The rest would have to wait.

It was easy fixing tears and cracks, lighting photos that had darkened to obscurity and darkening those that had faded to almost nothing. Even correcting color distortion got to be fairly easy. I had taken the photo of my father and colorized it so that it now looked like one of those oil photographs that were so popular when I was a kid. Linny found this all to be a crashing bore, but the rest of us enjoyed looking at them. Still, I knew our time was limited. Mom was getting worse. She had been sent back to the hospital for the fourth time, and though she was home now, it didn't bode well for the future. I wanted to make a compilation photo of her and Daddy to hang in their room. I suppose I hoped it would help her to focus, to remember, to get better. I knew it was nonsense, but I had to try. The pictures came up on the screen and I lifted out the head and shoulders from one each of Mom and Dad, fitted them together on the same canvas and added color. The mouse fit my hand as if it grew there, and each stroke formed on the screen as if I had drawn it on paper. As if the machine itself was alive and attuned to my will.

The one thing I had forgotten was photo paper. I had regular paper and stiff card stock for making greeting cards, but no photograph paper. I tried printing the damn thing out on the card stock, but it didn't look right. Lacking the smooth skin of a glossy stock, or even the creamy texture of a matte finish, it merely looked lumpy. I looked around for something that would do. The inside of a book dust jacket might work. I wasn't sure if I cut a file folder in half if it would fit through the complex contortions of the printer, but I was fairly sure that even if it did, the manila color would have an effect on the photograph. I had worked long and hard putting this together, smoothing out the wrinkles and scars, coloring in the old black and white. I wanted it to be perfect. There was one possibility. I didn't yet know if it would work, but it couldn't hurt anything—at least I didn't think it could.

In the back of the box I had spotted them when I was sorting the pictures. Since I didn't really want them, I hadn't paid much attention at the time, but there they were, the individual cards from the Instaluxe camera. Judging by eye, the entire "lifetime" supply of special cards was still there, untouched. I doubted that Mom had ever used them. Of course I had no idea what they were coated with, or if they were too old to use, but one thing I was sure of was that they were just the right thickness of paper to slide through the threads of the inkjet printer. Whether or not it would accept the ink once it was applied, I could only guess at. I shrugged as I peeled the waxed paper away, half expecting the card to be dry and worthless after all this time, but it was as soft and pliant as if it were brand new. I slid it into the photo-paper slot and printed my picture. It came out so well I couldn't wait to take it to show them. I wasn't sure my mother would recognize it, but Dad would be delighted. At least, I hoped he would.

"Look," I said to my mother as I entered her room. She sat on the sofa all crumpled into herself, her skin like parchment. Her reaction surprised me. Almost as if the photo itself revived her, she took a renewed interest in the picture. I could almost see it bringing the memories back. Though she looked about the same as always, there was, somehow, something different about her. Perhaps it was just that her eyes, which rarely seemed to focus on much of anything lately, took in the picture with a new light of intelligence for the first time in ages. Dad, too, looked somehow more alert. He was seated in his favorite lounge chair, unable, for the past year, to get up without assistance, but his eyes were focused on the ball game that constantly ran on their little television, and he seemed to care when a ball was hit out of the park. At least, I heard him say "Damn!" softly and knew it was the other team that hit it. Strange, but they were always having good days and bad days. I laughed at my silly notion that bringing the picture had done anything for them, except, perhaps, to revive old memories.

"Oh, look at that!" she said, taking the photograph and showing it to my dad. "I remember that picture. But I could have sworn your aunt Margie was in that one with me. I don't remember being with your father when that was taken."

"Wow, you remember that?" I said. I'm not sure I'd have recognized it if I hadn't been the one who'd spent several days extracting Aunt Margie and putting Dad in instead.

Mom puzzled over the photo for a moment more. "No, I'm sure it wasn't you, Dave," she said, "because that one of you was taken just before our wedding and I know we were already married when I got that dress." For just a moment that confused look was back on her face but it didn't last long. "I'm sure that dress wasn't red," she said.

"It was blue," my father said softly. "I remember how it made your eyes shine." He reached for her hand and she smiled at him, took his hand and squeezed it gently. Then she looked at me.

"Did you do this?" she asked. "Dave, I think Sandy did this," she told Dad without waiting for an answer. She said it in the exact same tone of voice with which she greeted my macaroni art when I was seven. "We'll have to hang it right up here." She placed it on the wall right next to the window.

It was good seeing them like this. I wished we might always have such good visits. I stayed as long as I could, promising to bring the kids as soon as possible, and maybe some of the photos for her to identify on my next visit. She seemed happy about that, but as she leaned over to kiss me good-bye, I could see that her hands hurt her badly and she still had trouble walking.

It was gratifying to see her so much better, but in a way, worse as well. Now that she was more aware of her crumbling body it had to be much more painful to her. At least, I thought it had to be. I wanted to do something to cheer her up, but I didn't have much time. My workload was heavy and my daughter had a new job and no sitter yet, so that work fell to me. I would be both a fool and a liar to say that I didn't adore my grandchildren, but they were a lot of work and required much more energy than I had. I did manage, with the aid of a few cartoons and much help from Ray, to work on a photo that I thought would cheer my mother up. It was a picture of my dad, the one with Linny and the baby carriage. Taking both out of the picture it became a picture of my father, leaning slightly and looking down. He looked reflective and happy, much more poetic than was usual for him. I added grass and flowers to cover the spots where Linda and the carriage had been, and replaced the houses of the street with trees and sky. Now it was a picture of a man admiring flowers, and though my dad, who had hay fever, never spent much time around flowers, somehow it still looked natural. I found a great one of my mother I wanted to work on, but my job kept me much too busy to get around to photo work. Linda kept me busy as well. I knew that Mom wasn't doing well. She had slipped into a bad period after I left the last time. The constant back and forth of worried phone calls from my sister made me aware of that. She had been sent to the hospital twice in the last week, given fluids overnight and sent home early the next day before I could even get out for a visit. When I did finally get there the following weekend, I was shocked by what I saw. This couldn't be the same woman who had sat there on the sofa talking to me the weekend past. This woman barely resembled the Marion Zifkin Brodsky I'd known all my life. She looked like a crumpled tissue, curled up in the very back of the chair, barely willing to speak to me.

"I brought you a present," I said brightly. She ignored me. I took out the picture and waved it at her. "Look, it's Daddy!" I said.

I went to hang it up on the same wall where the last one I had brought was hanging, only it wasn't there. No, that's not quite correct, it was still hanging there, but somehow, the half with my mother's face was missing, torn right out of the photograph. Dad seemed about the same as he had the week before. Aware of me, and still alert, but now also very anxious for my mother. He noticed where I was looking.

"The kid tore it," he said. "He was fixing the window and he accidentally ripped it. He didn't mean to hurt her," he added. How odd that he would refer to a torn photo as if it was actually my mother.

"Hurt her, Daddy?" I asked.

"Look at her. She's been like that ever since he ripped the picture." I shook my head. One thing Dad had always been was clearheaded. This was very sad. "What's that?" he asked me. He got up out of his seat and came over to look. I could feel my jaw dropping open. Dad walking? This was something I hadn't seen him do for months. I asked him about it.

"Yeah, I do, from time to time, but usually it hurts too much. Just this week, though, it's been a little better." Then he looked at me and shook his head. "Why do me? Do pictures of *her*. She's dying," he said, his eyes filled with deep pain. I had to admit that she didn't sound good. She had fallen asleep in the chair and her breathing was deep and rattling. He walked over and put his hand on her head, but she didn't wake. I tried shaking her, but that didn't wake her either.

"Let me get someone," I said. I ran to the main desk asking help from anyone I passed. I called Linda, who arrived while we waited for the ambulance. They took Dad down to the TV room and kept him there while we waited for the EMTs to show up. I had mixed feelings about that. The two of them had been together so long, why not let them be together now? But nobody asked my opinion. My sister and I were allowed to stay, and we held Mom's hands and talked to her as she slowly slipped out of this life before help could come.

Linda and I stayed to keep Dad from being alone, but he didn't want any company. He didn't sob either, but quiet tears rolled down his cheeks. While my sister and I made the occasional lame joke to ease the pain and tension of death, he stared straight ahead, occasionally looking up to say, "She was so beautiful."

When it was time for us to leave, I kissed him good-bye. "You want the limo to come get you for the funeral?" I asked, and was surprised to see him shake his head.

"You won't need to, but don't worry, I'll be there," he answered. "Good-bye, Sandy," he said, with an air of finality as if he was about to walk out the door. "Good-bye, Linda. You girls take care of those kids of yours. Tell them Grampy loves them."

"Dad, don't be silly. I know you miss her, but you're fine. You're better than you've been for months," I told him.

"But that's not me anymore," he said, pointing at the photograph I'd hung on his wall. "I'm tired. It's time," he said, and oddly enough he gave me a smile.

On the way out I stopped to talk to Sarah Goldstein, the woman in charge of the desk. "Please keep an eye on him tonight," I asked her. "He won't want to go to the TV room or anything, but if someone could just keep him company . . ."

"Of course we will. Are you sure you're okay to drive home?" she asked, to which I could only shrug.

"Do I have a choice?"

I told Linda what Dad had said as we walked through the parking lot to our respective cars.

"He looked good," she said absently, almost as if she'd forgotten why we were there. "I mean, under the circumstances he looked better than he has in a while," she continued. "I don't think he'd do anything, suicide or anything. You really don't have to worry."

"I don't know. He hasn't really wanted to live for a long time now. Sometimes I think he was only waiting for her," I paused, waiting for the tears that felt like they were going to flood my eyes, but none came and I went on talking. "Now I don't know. I don't think we'll have him much longer. Do you think a person can will himself to die?"

"Well," she said, thoughtfully, "he's so unhappy I almost hope for his sake that it's not long." Suddenly she realized what she said and looked guilty, but I patted her shoulder in support. It might sound awful, but she was right. He wasn't happy, not even comfortable. What kind of life was that? Now, without even her to live for. I thought of Ray. We weren't together for sixty-five years yet, but even so I could understand a little bit. Certainly, if he were to leave, I'd be lost.

"Why don't you come back to my place tonight?" I said. "You can stay in Joey's room."

She kissed me and declined. "I just want to be alone for a while. I probably won't get to be alone for a long time after tonight. Not once the kids come in for the funeral, and Liza and the rest of the cousins. God, there's so much to do!"

I promised to pick her up in the morning to go to the funeral home. The arrangements had been made years ago, but we had to make sure they were carried out as instructed.

The drive home was tedious. I felt too guilty to turn on the radio and my mind was a jumble of thoughts, razor cut like an MTV video, jumping from one thing to the next, barely aware of road or traffic, like an automaton going through its paces. I pulled up in front of the house, not even seeing Ray outside, sitting on the steps and obviously waiting for me. When I noticed him, I felt my stomach lurch. Something was wrong. He stood before I could back into the space and waved for me to stop. When I did, he opened the driver's side door and waited for me to get out.

"We've got to go back," he said. I looked at him, puzzled, but I don't remember saying anything. I think I knew before he even said it. After all, I'd been expecting it. "It's your dad."

I don't remember much about the drive back. The only thing that stands out in my mind was Sarah Goldstein standing outside the door to his room. "What happened?" I asked her.

"It was strange. Mary came in to sit with him. She said he had asked her for a scissors, and at first she though he stabbed himself with them, but he just suddenly keeled over," she said.

"Can I see him?" I asked her, not even waiting for an answer before starting for his room. They had moved him to the bed and he looked more peaceful than I'd seen him in years. It had certainly been that long since the last time I'd seen him smile. I walked over to see if I could figure out what he'd been doing. I didn't notice anything at first, and then I saw the cut up pieces of his photograph lying on the floor, and on the wall where the photos had been, merely a rip in the wallpaper where the tape had attached them.

Was it suicide? I suppose I will wonder for the rest of my days. And what would happen if I took those tiny jigsaw pieces of picture and taped them back together? I looked at the smile on my father's lips and kissed his forhead gently. They had lain together for sixty-five years and now they would lie side by side for all eternity.

"Sleep well," I said and walked out of the room.

EJ-ES

by Nancy Kress

Jesse, come home
There's a hole in the bed
where we slept
Now it's growing cold
Hey Jesse, your face
in the place where we lay
by the hearth, all apart
It hangs on my heart. . . .
Jesse, I'm lonely
Come home
—from "Jesse," by Janis Ian, 1972

"WHY did you first enter the Corps?" Lolimel asked her as they sat at the back of the shuttle, just before landing. Mia looked at the young man helplessly, because how could you answer a question like that? Especially when it was asked by the idealistic and worshipful new recruits, too ignorant to know what a waste of time worship was, let alone simplistic questions.

"Many reasons," Mia said gravely, vaguely. He looked like so many medicians she had worked with, for so many decades on so many planets . . . intense, thick-haired, genemod beautiful, a little insane. You had to be a little insane to leave Earth for the Corps, knowing that when (if) you ever returned, all you had known would have been dust for centuries.

He was more persistent than most. "What reasons?"

"The same as yours, Lolimel," she said, trying to keep her voice gentle. "Now be quiet, please, we're entering the atmosphere."

"Yes, but—"

"Be quiet." Entry was so much easier on him than on her; he had not got bones weakened from decades in space. They *did* weaken, no matter what exercise one took or what supplements or what gene therapy. Mia leaned back in her shuttle chair and closed her eyes. Ten minutes, maybe, of aerobraking and descent; surely she could stand ten minutes. Or not.

The heaviness began, abruptly increased. Worse on her eyeballs, as always; she didn't have good eye socket muscles, had never had them. Such an odd weakness. Well, not for long; this was her last flight. At the next station, she'd retire. She was already well over age, and her body felt it. Only her body? No, her mind, too. At the moment, for instance, she couldn't remember the name of the planet they were hurtling toward. She recalled its catalog number, but not whatever its colonists, who were not answering hails from ship, had called it.

"Why did you join the Corps?"

"Many reasons."

And so few of them fulfilled. But that was not a thing you told the young.

✦★✦

The colony sat at the edge of a river, under an evening sky of breathable air set with three brilliant, fast-moving moons. Beds of glorious flowers dotted the settlement, somewhere in size between a large town and a small city. The buildings of foamcast embedded with glittering native stone were graceful, well-proportioned rooms set around open atria. Minimal furniture, as graceful as the buildings; even the machines blended unobtrusively into the lovely landscape. The colonists had taste and restraint and a sense of beauty. They were all dead.

"A long time ago," said Kenin. Officially she was Expedition Head, although titles and chains of command tended to erode near the galactic edge, and Kenin led more by consensus and natural calm than by rank. More than once the team had been grateful for

Kenin's calm. Lolimel looked shaken, although he was trying to hide it.

Kenin studied the skeleton before them. "Look at those bones—completely clean."

Lolimel managed, "It might have been picked clean quickly by predators, or carnivorous insects, or . . ." His voice trailed off.

"I already scanned it, Lolimel. No microscopic bone nicks. She decayed right there in bed, along with clothing and bedding."

The three of them looked at the bones lying on the indestructible mattress coils of some alloy Mia had once known the name of. Long clean bones, as neatly arranged as if for a first-year anatomy lesson. The bedroom door had been closed; the dehumidifying system had, astonishingly, not failed; the windows were intact. Nothing had disturbed the woman's long rot in the dry air until nothing remained, not even the bacteria that had fed on her, not even the smell of decay.

Kenin finished speaking to the other team. She turned to Mia and Lolimel, her beautiful brown eyes serene. "There are skeletons throughout the city, some in homes and some collapsed in what seem to be public spaces. Whatever the disease was, it struck fast. Jamal says their computer network is gone, but individual rec cubes might still work. Those things last forever."

Nothing lasts forever, Mia thought, but she started searching the cabinets for a cube. She said to Lolimel, to give him something to focus on, "How long ago was this colony founded, again?"

"Three hundred sixty E-years," Lolimel said. He joined the search.

Three hundred sixty years since a colony ship left an established world with its hopeful burden, arrived at this deadly Eden, established a city, flourished, and died. How much of Mia's lifetime, much of it spent traveling at just under c, did that represent? Once she had delighted in figuring out such equations, in wondering if she'd been born when a given worldful of colonists made planetfall. But by now there were too many expeditions, too many colonies, too many accelerations and decelerations, and she'd lost track.

Lolimel said abruptly, "Here's a rec cube."

"Play it," Kenin said, and when he just went on staring at it in the palm of his smooth hand, she took the cube from him and played it herself.

It was what she expected. A native plague of some kind, jumping DNA-based species (which included all species in the galaxy, thanks to panspermia). The plague had struck after the colonists thought they had vaccinated against all dangerous micros. Of course, they couldn't really have thought that; even three hundred sixty years ago doctors had been familiar with alien species-crossers. Some were mildly irritating, some dangerous, some epidemically fatal. Colonies had been lost before, and would be again.

"Complete medical data resides on green rec cubes," the recorder had said in the curiously accented International of three centuries ago. Clearly dying, he gazed out from the cube with calm, sad eyes. A brave man. "Any future visitors to Good Fortune should be warned."

Good Fortune. That was the planet's name.

"All right," Kenin said, "tell the guard to search for green cubes. Mia, get the emergency analysis lab set up and direct Jamal to look for burial sites. If they had time to inter some victims—if they interred at all, of course—we might be able to recover some micros to create vacs or cures. Lolimel, you assist me in—"

One of the guards, carrying weapons that Mia could not have named, blurted, "Ma'am, how do we know we won't get the same thing that killed the colonists?"

Mia looked at her. Like Lolimel, she was very young. Like all of them, she would have her story about why she volunteered for the Corps.

Now the young guard was blushing. "I mean, ma'am, before you can make a vaccination? How do we know we won't get the disease, too?"

Mia said gently, "We don't."

✴★✴

No one, however, got sick. The colonists had had interment practices, they had had time to bury some of their dead in strong, water-tight coffins before everyone else died, and their customs didn't include embalming. Much more than Mia had dared hope for. Good Fortune, indeed.

In five days of tireless work they had the micro isolated, sequenced, and analyzed. It was a virus, or a virus analogue, that had somehow gained access to the brain and lodged near the limbic system, creating destruction and death. Like rabies, Mia thought, and hoped this virus hadn't caused the terror and madness of that stubborn disease. Not even Earth had been able to eradicate rabies.

Two more days yielded the vaccine. Kenin dispensed it outside the large building on the edge of the city, function unknown, which had become Corps headquarters. Mia applied her patch, noticing with the usual distaste the leathery, wrinkled skin of her forearm. Once she had had such beautiful skin, what was it that a long-ago lover had said to her, what had been his name . . . Ah, growing old was not for the gutless.

Something moved at the edge of her vision.

"Lolimel . . . did you see that?"

"See what?"

"Nothing." Sometimes her aging eyes played tricks on her; she didn't want Lolimel's pity.

The thing moved again.

Casually Mia rose, brushing imaginary dirt from the seat of her uniform, strolling toward the bushes where she'd seen motion. From her pocket she pulled her gun. There were animals on this planet, of course, although the Corps had only glimpsed them from a distance, and rabies was transmitted by animal bite. . . .

It wasn't an animal. It was a human child.

No, not a child, Mia realized as she rounded the clump of bushes and, amazingly, the girl didn't run. An adolescent, or perhaps older, but so short and thin that Mia's mind had filled in "child." A scrawny young woman with light brown skin and long, matted black hair, dressed carelessly in some sort of sarong-like wrap. Staring at Mia with a total lack of fear.

"Hello," Mia said gently.

"Ej-es?" the girl said.

Mia said into her wrister, "Kenin . . . we've got natives. Survivors."

The girl smiled. Her hair was patchy on one side, marked with small white rings. *Fungus*, Mia thought professionally, absurdly. The girl walked right toward Mia, not slowing, as if intending to walk through her. Instinctively Mia put out an arm. The girl walked into it, bonked herself on the forehead, and crumpled to the ground.

✦✦✦

"You're not supposed to beat up the natives, Mia," Kenin said. "God, she's not afraid of us at all. How can that be? You nearly gave her a concussion."

Mia was as bewildered as Kenin, as all of them. She'd picked up the girl, who'd looked bewildered but not angry, and then Mia had backed off, expecting the girl to run. Instead she'd stood there rubbing her forehead and jabbering, and Mia had seen that her sarong was made of an uncut sheet of plastic, its colors faded to a mottled gray.

Kenin, Lolimel, and two guards had come running. And *still* the girl wasn't afraid. She chattered at them, occasionally pausing as if expecting them to answer. When no one did, she eventually turned and moved leisurely off.

Mia said, "I'm going with her."

Instantly a guard said, "It's not safe, ma'am," and Kenin said, "Mia, you can't just—"

"You don't need me here," she said, too brusquely; suddenly there seemed nothing more important in the world than going with this girl. Where did that irrational impulse come from? "And I'll be perfectly safe with a gun."

This was such a stunningly stupid remark that no one answered her. But Kenin didn't order her to stay. Mia accepted the guard's tanglefoam and Kenin's vidcam and followed the girl.

It was hard to keep up with her. "Wait!" Mia called, which

produced no response. So she tried what the girl had said to her:
"Ej-es!"

Immediately the girl stopped and turned to her with glowing
eyes and a smile that could have melted glaciers, had Good Fortune
had such a thing. Gentle planet, gentle person, who was almost
certainly a descendant of the original dead settlers. Or was she?
InterGalactic had no record of any other registered ship leaving
for this star system, but that didn't mean anything. InterGalactic
didn't know everything. Sometimes, given the time dilation of
space travel, Mia thought they knew nothing.

"Ej-es," the girl agreed, sprinted back to Mia, and took her
hand. Slowing her youthful pace to match the older woman's, she
led Mia home.

★★★

The houses were scattered, as though they couldn't make up
their mind whether or not to be a village. A hundred yards away,
another native walked toward a distant house. The two ignored
each other.

Mia couldn't stand the silence. She said, "I am Mia."

The girl stopped outside her hut and looked at her.

Mia pointed to her chest. "Mia."

"Es-ef-eb," the girl said, pointing to herself and giving that
glorious smile.

Not "ej-es," which must mean something else. Mia pointed to
the hut, a primitive affair of untrimmed logs, pieces of foamcast
carried from the city, and sheets of faded plastic, all tacked crazily
together.

"Ef-ef," said Esefeb, which evidently meant "home." This language was going to be a bitch: degraded *and* confusing.

Esefeb suddenly hopped to one side of the dirt path, laughed,
and pointed at blank air. Then she took Mia's hand and led her
inside.

More confusion, more degradation. The single room had an
open fire with the simple venting system of a hole in the roof. The

bed was high on stilts (why?) with a set of rickety steps made of rotting, untrimmed logs. One corner held a collection of huge pots in which grew greenery; Mia saw three unfired clay pots, one of them sagging sideways so far the soil had spilled onto the packed-dirt floor. Also a beautiful titanium vase and a cracked hydroponic vat. On one plant, almost the size of a small tree, hung a second sheet of plastic sarong, this one an unfaded blue-green. Dishes and tools littered the floor, the same mix as the pots of scavenged items and crude homemade ones. The hut smelled of decaying food and unwashed bedding. There was no light source and no machinery.

Kenin's voice sounded softly from her wrister. "Your vid is coming through fine. Even the most primitive human societies have some type of artwork."

Mia didn't reply. Her attention was riveted to Esefeb. The girl flung herself up the "stairs" and sat up in bed, facing the wall. What Mia had seen before could hardly be called a smile compared to the light, the sheer joy, that illuminated Esefeb's face now. Esefeb shuddered in ecstasy, crooning to the empty wall.

"Ej-es. Ej-es. Aaahhhh, *Ej-es!*"

Mia turned away. She was a medician, but Esefeb's emotion seemed too private to witness. It was the ecstasy of orgasm, or religious transfiguration, or madness.

"Mia," her wrister said, "I need an image of that girl's brain."

★★★

It was easy—too easy, Lolimel said later, and he was right. Creatures, sentient or not, did not behave this way.

"We could haul all the neuro equipment out to the village," Kenin said doubtfully, from base.

"It's not a village, and I don't think that's a good idea," Mia said softly. The softness was unnecessary. Esefeb slept like stone in her high bunk, and the hut was so dark, illuminated only by faint starlight through the hole in the roof, that Mia could barely see her wrister to talk into it. "I think Esefeb might come voluntarily. I'll try in the morning, when it's light."

Kenin, not old but old enough to feel stiff sleeping on the ground, said, "Will you be comfortable there until morning?"

"No, but I'll manage. What does the computer say about the recs?"

Lolimel answered—evidently they were having a regular all-hands conference. "The language is badly degraded International, you probably guessed that. The translator's preparing a lexicon and grammar. The artifacts, food supply, dwelling, everything visual, doesn't add up. They shouldn't have lost so much in two hundred fifty years, unless mental deficiency was a side effect of having survived the virus. But Kenin thinks—" He stopped abruptly.

"You may speak for me," Kenin's voice said, amused. "I think you'll find that military protocol degrades, too, over time. At least, way out here."

"Well, I . . . Kenin thinks it's possible that what the girl has is a mutated version of the virus. Maybe infectious, maybe inheritable, maybe transmitted through fetal infection."

His statement dropped into Mia's darkness, as heavy as Esefeb's sleep.

Mia said, "So the mutated virus could still be extant and active."

"Yes," Kenin said. "We need not only neuro-images but a sample of cerebrospinal fluid. Her behavior suggests—"

"I know what her behavior suggests," Mia said curtly. That sheer joy, shuddering in ecstasy . . . It was seizures in the limbic system, the brain's deep center for primitive emotion, which produced such transcendent, rapturous trances. Religious mystics, Saul on the road to Damascus, visions of Our Lady or of nirvana. And the virus might still be extant, and not a part of the vaccine they had all received. Although if transmission was fetal, the medicians were safe. If not . . .

Mia said, "The rest of Esefeb's behavior doesn't fit with limbic seizures. She seems to see things that aren't there, even talk to her hallucinations, when she's not having an actual seizure."

"I don't know," Kenin said. "There might be multiple infection sites in the brain. I need her, Mia."

"We'll be there," Mia said, and wondered if that were going to be true.

But it was, mostly. Mia, after a brief uncomfortable sleep wrapped in the sheet of blue-green plastic, sat waiting for Esefeb to descend her rickety stairs. The girl bounced down, chattering at something to Mia's right. She smelled worse than yesterday. Mia breathed through her mouth and went firmly up to her.

"Esefeb!" Mia pointed dramatically, feeling like a fool. The girl pointed back.

"Mia."

"Yes, good." Now Mia made a sweep of the sorry hut. "Efef."

"Efef," Esefeb agreed, smiling radiantly.

"Esefeb efef."

The girl agreed that this was her home.

Mia pointed theatrically toward the city. "Mia efef! Mia eb Esefeb etej Mia efef!" *Mia and Esefeb come to Mia's home.* Mia had already raided the computer's tentative lexicon of Good Fortunese.

Esefeb cocked her head and looked quizzical. A worm crawled out of her hair.

Mia repeated, "Mia eb Esefeb etej Mia efef."

Esefeb responded with a torrent of repetitious syllables, none of which meant anything to Mia except "Ej-es." The girl spoke the word with such delight that it had to be a name. A lover? Maybe these people didn't live as solitary as she'd assumed.

Mia took Esefeb's hand and gently tugged her toward the door. Esefeb broke free and sat in the middle of the room, facing a blank wall of crumbling logs, and jabbered away to nothing at all, occasionally laughing and even reaching out to touch empty air. "Ej-es, Ej-es!" Mia watched, bemused, recording everything, making medical assessments. Esefeb wasn't malnourished, for which the natural abundance of the planet was undoubtedly responsible. But she was crawling with parasites, filthy (with water easily available), and isolated. Maybe isolated.

"Lolimel," Mia said softly into the wrister, "what's the best dictionary guess for 'alone'?"

Lolimel said, "The closest we've got is 'one.' There doesn't seem to be a concept for 'unaccompanied,' or at least we haven't found it yet. The word for 'one' is 'eket.'"

When Esefeb finally sprang up happily, Mia said, "Esefeb eket?"

The girl look startled. "Ek, ek," she said: *no, no.* Esefcb ek eket! Esefeb eb Ej-es!"

Esefeb and Ej-es. She was not alone. She had the hallucinatory Ej-es.

Again Mia took Esefeb's hand and pulled her toward the door. This time Esefeb went with her. As they set off toward the city, the girl's legs wobbled. Some parasite that had become active overnight in the leg muscles? Whatever the trouble was, Esefeb blithely ignored it as they traveled, much more slowly than yesterday, to Kenin's makeshift lab in the ruined city. Along the way, Esefeb stopped to watch, laugh at, or talk to three different things that weren't there.

★★★

"She's beautiful, under all that neglect," Lolimel said, staring down at the anesthetized girl on Kenin's neuroimaging slab.

Kenin said mildly, "If the mutated virus is transmitted to a fetus, it could also be transmitted sexually."

The young man said hotly, "I wasn't implying—"

Mia said, "Oh, calm down. Lolimel. We've all done it, on numerous worlds."

"Regs say—"

"Regs don't always matter three hundred light-years from anywhere else," Kenin said, exchanging an amused glance with Mia. "Mia, let's start."

The girl's limp body slid into the neuro-imager. Esefeb hadn't objected to meeting the other medicians, to a minimal washing, to the sedative patch Mia had put on her arm. Thirty seconds later she slumped to the floor. By the time she came to, an incision ten cells thick would have been made into her brain and a sample removed. She would have been harvested, imaged, electroscanned, and mapped. She would never know it; there wouldn't even be a headache.

Three hours later Esefeb sat on the ground with two of the guards, eating soysynth as if it were ambrosia. Mia, Kenin, Lolimel, and the three other medicians sat in a circle twenty yards away, staring at handhelds and analyzing results. It was late afternoon. Long shadows slanted across the gold-green grass, and a small breeze brought the sweet, heavy scent of some native flower. *Paradise*, Mia thought. And then: *Bonnet Syndrome*.

She said it aloud, "Charles Bonnet Syndrome," and five people raised their heads to stare at her, returned to their handhelds, and called up medical deebees.

"I think you're right," Kenin said slowly. "I never even heard of it before. Or if I did, I don't remember."

"That's because nobody gets it anymore," Mia said. "It was usually old people whose eye problems weren't corrected. Now we routinely correct eye problems."

Kenin frowned. "But that's not all that's going on with Esefeb."

No, but it was one thing, and why couldn't Kenin give her credit for thinking of it? The next moment she was ashamed of her petty pique. It was just fatigue, sleeping on that hard cold floor in Esefeb's home. *Esefeb efef.* Mia concentrated on Charles Bonnet Syndrome.

Patients with the syndrome, which was discovered in the eighteenth century, had damage somewhere in their optic pathway or brain. It could be lesions, macular degeneration, glaucoma, diabetic retinopathy, or even cataracts. Partially blind, people saw and sometimes heard instead things that weren't there, often with startling clarity and realism. Feedback pathways in the brain were two-way information avenues. Visual data, memory, and imagination constantly flowed to and from each other, interacting so vividly that, for example, even a small child could visualize a cat in the absence of any actual cats. But in Bonnet Syndrome, there was interruption of the baseline visual data about what was and was not real. So all imaginings and hallucinations were just as real as the ground beneath one's feet.

"Look at the amygdala," medician Berutha said. "Oh, merciful gods!"

Both of Esefeb's amygdalae were enlarged and deformed. The amygdalae, two almond-shaped structures behind the ears, specialized in recognizing the emotional significance of events in the external world. They weren't involved in Charles Bonnet Syndrome. Clearly, they were here.

Kenin said, "I think what's happening here is a strengthening or alteration of some neural pathways at the extreme expense of others. Esefeb 'sees' her hallucinations, and she experiences them as just as 'real'—maybe more real—than anything else in her world. And the pathways go down to the limbic, where seizures give some of them an intense emotional significance. Like . . . like orgasm, maybe."

Ej-es.

"Phantoms in the brain," Berutha said.

"A viral god," Lolimel said, surprising Mia. His tone, almost reverential, suddenly irritated her.

"A god responsible for this people's degradation, Lolimel. They're so absorbed in their 'phantoms' that they don't concentrate on the most basic care of themselves. Nor on building, farming, art, innovation . . . *nothing.* They're prisoners of their pretty fantasies."

Lolimel nodded reluctantly. "Yes, I see that."

Berutha said to Kenin, "We need to find the secondary virus. Because if it is infectious through any other vector besides fetal or sexual . . ." He didn't finish the thought.

"I know," Kenin said, "but it isn't going to be easy. We don't have cadavers for the secondary. The analyzer is still working on the cerebral-spinal fluid. Meanwhile—" She began organizing assignments, efficient and clear. Mia stopped listening.

Esefeb had finished her meal and walked up to the circle of scientists. She tugged at Mia's tunic. "Mia . . . Esefeb etej efef." *Esefeb come home.*

"Mia eb Esefeb etej Esefeb efef," Mia said, and the girl gave her joyous smile.

"Mia—" Kenin said.

"I'm going with her, Kenin. We need more behavioral data. And maybe I can persuade another native or two to submit to examination," Mia argued, feebly. She knew that scientific information was not really her motive. She wasn't sure, however, what was. She just wanted to go with Esefeb.

✦✦✦

"Why did you first enter the Corps?" Lolimel's question stuck in Mia's mind, a rhetorical fishbone in the throat, over the next few days. Mia had brought her medkit, and she administered broad-spectrum microbials to Esefeb, hoping something would hit. The parasites were trickier, needing life-cycle analysis or at least some structural knowledge, but she made a start on that, too. *I entered the Corps to relieve suffering, Lolimel.* Odd how naive the truest statements could sound. But that didn't make them any less true.

Esefeb went along with all Mia's pokings, patches, and procedures. She also carried out minimal food-gathering activities, with a haphazard disregard for safety or sanitation that appalled Mia. Mia had carried her own food from the ship. Esefeb ate it just as happily as her own.

But mostly Esefeb talked to Ej-es.

It made Mia feel like a voyeur. Esefeb was so unselfconscious—did she even know she had a "self" apart from Ej-es? She spoke to, laughed at (with?), played beside, and slept with her phantom in the brain, and around her the hut disintegrated even more. Esefeb got diarrhea from something in her water and then the place smelled even more foul. Grimly, Mia cleaned it up. Esefeb didn't seem to notice. Mia was *eket*. Alone in her futile endeavors at sanitation, at health, at civilization.

"Esefeb eb Mia etej efef—" How did you say "neighbors?" Mia consulted the computer's lexicon, steadily growing as the translator program deciphered words from context. It had discovered no word for "neighbor." Nor for "friend" nor "mate" nor any kinship relationships at all except "baby."

Mia was reduced to pointing at the nearest hut. "Esefeb eb Mia etej efef" *over there.*

The neighboring hut had a baby. Both hut and child, a toddler who lay listlessly in one corner, were just as filthy and diseased as Esefeb's house. At first the older woman didn't seem to recognize Esefeb, but when Esefeb said her name, the two women spoke animatedly. The neighbor smiled at Mia. Mia reached for the child, was not prevented from picking him up, and settled the baby on her lap. Discreetly, she examined him.

Sudden rage boiled through her, as unexpected as it was frightening. This child was dying. Of parasites, of infection, of something. A preventable something? Maybe yes, maybe no. The child didn't look neglected, but neither did the mother look concerned.

All at once, the child in her arms stiffened, shuddered, and began to babble. His listlessness vanished. His little dirty face lit up like sunrise and he laughed and reached out his arms toward something not there. His mother and Esefeb turned to watch, also smiling, as the toddler had an unknowable limbic seizure in his dying, ecstatic brain.

Mia set him down on the floor. She called up the dictionary, but before she could say anything, the mother, too, had a seizure and sat on the dirt floor, shuddering with joy. Esefeb watched her a moment before chattering to something Mia couldn't see.

Mia couldn't stand it anymore. She left, walking as fast as she could back to Esefeb's house, disgusted and frightened and . . . what?

Envious?

"Why did you first enter the Corps?" To serve humanity, to live purposefully, to find, as all men and women hope, happiness. And she had, sometimes, been happy.

But she had never known such joy as that.

Nonetheless, she argued with herself, the price was too high. These people were dying off because of their absorption in their rapturous phantoms. They lived isolated, degraded, sickly lives, which were undoubtedly shorter than necessary. It was obscene.

In her clenched hand was a greasy hair sample she'd unobtrusively cut from the toddler's head as he sat on her lap. Hair, that dead tissue, was a person's fossilized past. Mia intended a DNA scan.

✶★✶

Esefeb strolled in an hour later. She didn't seem upset at Mia's abrupt departure. With her was Lolimel.

"I met her on the path," Lolimel said, although nothing as well-used as a path connected the huts. "She doesn't seem to mind my coming here."

"Or anything else," Mia said. "What did you bring?" He had to have brought something tangible; Kenin would have used the wrister to convey information.

"Tentative prophylactic. We haven't got a vaccine yet, and Kenin says it may be too difficult, better to go directly to a cure to hold in reserve in case any of us comes down with this."

Mia caught the omission. "Any of *us?* What about them?"

Lolimel looked down at his feet. "It's, um, a borderline case, Mia. The decision hasn't been made yet."

"'Borderline' how, Lolimel? It's a virus infecting the brains of humans and degrading their functioning."

He was embarrassed. "Section Six says that, um, some biological conditions, especially persistent ones, create cultural differences for which Corps policy is noninterference. Section Six mentions the religious dietary laws that grew out of inherited food intolerances on—"

"I know what Section Six says, Lolimel! But you don't measure a culture's degree of success by its degree of happiness!"

"I don't think . . . that is, I don't know . . . maybe 'degree of success' isn't what Section Six means." He looked away from her. The tips of his ears grew red.

Poor Lolimel. She and Kenin had as much as told him that out here regs didn't matter. Except when they did. Mia stood. "You say the decision hasn't been made yet?"

He looked surprised. "How could it be? You're on the senior Corps board to make the decision."

Of course she was. How could she forget . . . she forgot more things these days, momentary lapses symbolic of the greater lapses to come. No brain functioned forever.

"Mia, are you all—"

"I'm fine. And I'm glad you're here. I want to go back to the city for a few days. You can stay with Esefeb and continue the surveillance. You can also extend to her neighbors the antibiotic, antiviral, and antiparasite protocols I've worked through with Esefeb. Here, I'll show you."

"But I—"

"That's an order."

✸★✸

She felt bad about it later, of course. But Lolimel would get over it.

At base, everything had the controlled frenzy of steady, unremitting work. Meek now, not a part of the working team, Mia ran a DNA scan on the baby's hair. It showed what she expected. The child shared fifty percent DNA with Esefeb. He was her brother; the neighbor whom Esefeb clearly never saw, who had at first not recognized Esefeb, was her mother. For which there was still no word in the translator deebee.

"I think we've got it," Kenin said, coming into Mia's room. She collapsed on a stone bench, still beautiful after two and a half centuries. Kenin had the beatific serenity of a hard job well done.

"A cure?"

"Tentative. Radical. I wouldn't want to use it on one of us unless we absolutely have to, but we can refine it more. At least it's in reserve, so a part of the team can begin creating and disseminating medical help these people can actually use. Targeted microbials, an antiparasite protocol."

"I've already started on that," Mia said, her stomach tightening. "Kenin, the board needs to meet."

"Not tonight. I'm soooo sleepy." Theatrically she stretched both arms; words and gesture were unlike her.

"Tonight," Mia said. While Kenin was feeling so accomplished. Let Kenin feel the full contrast to what she could do with what Esefeb could.

Kenin dropped her arms and looked at Mia. Her whole demeanor changed, relaxation into fortress. "Mia . . . I've already polled everyone privately. And run the computer sims. We'll meet, but the decision is going to be to extend no cure. The phantoms are a biologically based cultural difference."

"The hell they are! These people are dying out!"

"No, they're not. If they were heading for extinction, it'd be a different situation. But the satellite imagery and population equations, based on data left by the generation that had the plague, show they're increasing. Slowly, but a definite population gain significant to the point-oh-one level of confidence."

"Kenin—"

"I'm exhausted, Mia. Can we talk about it tomorrow?"

Plan on it, Mia thought grimly. She stored the data on the dying toddler's matrilineage in her handheld.

✦★✦

A week in base, and Mia could convince no one, not separately nor in a group. Medicians typically had tolerant psychological profiles, with higher-than-average acceptance of the unusual, divergent, and eccentric. Otherwise, they wouldn't have joined the Corps.

On the third day, to keep herself busy, Mia joined the junior medicians working on refining the cure for what was now verified as "limbic seizures with impaired sensory input causing Charles Bonnet Syndrome." Over the next few weeks it became clear to Mia what Kenin had meant; this treatment, if they had to use it, would be brutally hard on the brain. What was that old ditty? *"Cured last night of my disease, I died today of my physician."* Well, it

still happened enough in the Corps. Another reason behind the
board's decision.

She felt a curious reluctance to go back to Esefeb. Or, as the
words kept running through her mind, *Mia ek etej Esefeb efef.* God,
it was a tongue twister. These people didn't just need help with
parasites, they needed an infusion of new consonants. It was a relief
to be back at base, to be working with her mind, solving technical
problems alongside rational scientists. Still, she couldn't shake a
feeling of being alone, being lonely: *Mia eket.*

Or maybe the feeling was more like futility.

"Lolimel's back," Jamal said. He'd come up behind her as she
sat at dusk on her favorite stone bench, facing the city. At this time
of day the ruins looked romantic, infused with history. The sweet
scents of that night-blooming flower, which Mia still hadn't identified, wafted around her.

"I think you should come now," Jamal said, and this time Mia
heard his tone. She spun around. In the alien shadows Jamal's face
was as set as ice.

"He's contracted it," Mia said, knowing beyond doubt that it
was true. The virus wasn't just fetally transmitted, it wasn't a slow-
acting retrovirus, and if Lolimel had slept with Esefeb . . . But he
wouldn't be that stupid. He was a medician, he'd been warned . . .

"We don't really know anything solid about the goddamn
thing!" Jamal burst out.

"We never do," Mia said, and the words cracked her dry lips
like salt.

✦✦✦

Lolimel stood in the center of the ruined atrium, giggling at
something only he could see. Kenin, who could have proceeded
without Mia, nodded at her. Mia understood; Kenin acknowledged
the special bond Mia had with the young medician. The cure was
untested, probably brutal, no more really than dumping a selection
of poisons in the right areas of the brain, in itself problematical
with the blood-brain barrier.

Mia made herself walk calmly up to Lolimel. "What's so funny, Lolimel?"

"All those sandwigs crawling in straight lines over the floor. I never saw blue ones before."

Sandwigs. Lolimel, she remembered, had been born on New Carthage. Sandwigs were always red.

Lolimel said, "But why is there a tree growing out of your head, Mia?"

"Strong fertilizer," she said. "Lolimel, did you have sex with Esefeb?"

He looked genuinely shocked. "No!"

"All right." He might or might not be lying.

Jamal whispered, "A chance to study the hallucinations in someone who can fully articulate—"

"No," Kenin said. "Time matters with this . . ." Mia saw that she couldn't bring herself to say "cure."

Realization dawned on Lolimel's face. "Me? You're going to . . . *me?* There's nothing wrong with me!"

"Lolimel, dear heart . . ." Mia said.

"I don't have it!"

"And the floor doesn't have sandwigs. Lolimel—"

"No!"

The guards had been alerted. Lolimel didn't make it out of the atrium. They held him, flailing and yelling, while Kenin deftly slapped on a tranq patch. In ten seconds he was out.

"Tie him down securely," Kenin said, breathing hard. "Daniel, get the brain bore started as soon as he's prepped. Everyone else, start packing up, and impose quarantine. We can't risk this for anyone else here. I'm calling a Section Eleven."

Section Eleven: *If the MedCorps officer in charge deems the risk to Corps members to exceed the gain to colonists by a factor of three or more, the officer may pull the Corps off-planet.*

It was the first time Mia had ever seen Kenin make a unilateral decision.

★★★

Twenty-four hours later, Mia sat beside Lolimel as dusk crept over the city. The shuttle had already carried up most personnel and equipment. Lolimel was in the last shift because, as Kenin did not need to say aloud, if he died, his body would be left behind. But Lolimel had not died. He had thrashed in unconscious seizures, had distorted his features in silent grimaces of pain until Mia would not have recognized him, had suffered malfunctions in alimentary, lymphatic, endocrine, and parasympathetic nervous systems, all recorded on the monitors. But he would live. The others didn't know it, but Mia did.

"We're ready for him, Mia," the young tech said. "Are you on this shuttle, too?"

"No, the last one. Move him carefully. We don't know how much pain he's actually feeling through the meds."

She watched the gurney slide out of the room, its monitors looming over Lolimel like cliffs over a raging river. When he'd gone, Mia slipped into the next building, and then the next. Such beautiful buildings: spacious atria, beautifully proportioned rooms, one structure flowing into another.

Eight buildings away, she picked up the pack she'd left there. It was heavy, even though it didn't contain everything she had cached around the city. It was so easy to take things when a base was being hastily withdrawn. Everyone was preoccupied, everyone assumed anything not readily visible was already packed, inventories were neglected and the deebees not cross-checked. No time. Historically, war had always provided great opportunities for profiteers.

Was that what she was? Yes, but not a profit measured in money. Measure it, rather, in lives saved, or restored to dignity, or enhanced. *"Why did you first enter the Corps?"* Because I'm a medician, Lolimel. Not an anthropologist.

They would notice, of course, that Mia herself wasn't aboard the last shuttle. But Kenin, at least, would realize that searching for her would be a waste of valuable resources when Mia didn't want to be found. And Mia was so old. Surely the old should be allowed to make their own decisions.

Although she would miss them, these Corps members who had

been her family since the last assignment shuffle, eighteen months ago and decades ago, depending on whose time you counted by. Especially she would miss Lolimel. But this was the right way to end her life, in service to these colonists' health. She was a medician.

✭✭✭

It went better than Mia could have hoped. When the ship had gone—she'd seen it leave orbit, a fleeting stream of light—Mia went to Esefeb.

"Mia etej efef," Esefeb said with her rosy smile. *Mia come home.* Mia walked toward her, hugged the girl, and slapped the tranq patch on her neck.

For the next week, Mia barely slept. After the makeshift surgery, she tended Esefeb through the seizures, vomiting, diarrhea, pain. On the morning the girl woke up, herself again, Mia was there to bathe the feeble body, feed it, nurse Esefeb. She recovered very fast; the cure was violent on the body but not as debilitating as everyone had feared. And afterward Esefeb was quieter, meeker, and surprisingly intelligent as Mia taught her the rudiments of water purification, sanitation, safe food storage, health care. By the time Mia moved on to Esefeb's mother's house, Esefeb was free of most parasites, and Mia was working on the rest. Esefeb never mentioned her former hallucinations. It was possible she didn't remember them.

"Esefeb ekebet," Mia said as she hefted her pack to leave. *Esefeb be well.*

Esefeb nodded. She stood quietly as Mia trudged away, and when Mia turned to wave at her, Esefeb waved back.

Mia shifted the pack on her shoulders. It seemed heavier than before. Or maybe Mia was just older. Two weeks older, merely, but two weeks could make a big difference. An enormous difference.

Two weeks could start to save a civilization.

✭✭✭

Night fell. Esefeb sat on the stairs to her bed, clutching the blue-green sheet of plastic in both hands. She sobbed and shivered, her clean face contorted. Around her, the unpopulated shadows grew thicker and darker. Eventually, she wailed aloud to the empty night.

"Ej-es! O, Ej-es! Ej-es, Esefeb eket! Ej-es . . . etej efef! O, etej efef!"

You Don't Know My Heart

by SPIDER ROBINSON

Tried to fit, I tried to blend
I learned young to pretend
'cause if they knew, the world would end
—"You Don't Know My Heart" by Janis Ian

I WAS onstage at Slim's, halfway through my last set, when I saw the two hitters come in.

It wasn't hard to spot them, even in the poor light. They were both *way* too straight for Slim's Elite Cafe. They were pretending to be a leather couple, even holding hands, but I didn't buy it and doubted many others would. No gunfighter mustaches, no visible piercings, no jewelry, the leather was brand new, the tats were fake, and the stubble on their skulls and faces was two days old, tops. Either of them alone might have been exploring the darker corners of his sexuality on vacation, a Key West cliché; together, though, the only use they'd have for a queer was as a punching bag. They were not at all uneasy in a place where their kind was doubly outnumbered—about two dykes like me to every fag, a normal night—so I assumed they were armed. I didn't panic. I know a way to get from the stage of Slim's to *elsewhere* faster than most people can react, and since I've never had to use it I'm pretty sure it will work. I kept playing without missing a beat—okay, I fluffed a guitar fill, but it wasn't a train wreck. An old Janis Ian song, "Arms

Around My Life"; she goes over well at Slim's and I can sing in her key.

All the broken promises
all the shattered dreams
all this aching loneliness
will finally be set free
I have waited for so long
to remember what it's like
to feel somebody's arms around my life

After a minute or so, my adrenaline level dropped back to about performance-normal. I couldn't decide whether they were Good Guys or Bad Guys, but either way they didn't seem to be looking for me, so the question held little urgency. It was hard to tell who they *were* after. The whole room was basically a big poorly-lit box of suspicious characters, flight risks, and hopeful victims—disasters looking for the spot marked X. Or, of course, I could be mistaken: the pair could be off-duty, their real assignment elsewhere. Or, just possibly, they might be two men in their early thirties who'd suddenly realized they were leatherboys, and by great fortune had met out on the street five minutes ago.

They had been chatting quietly together since they'd come in, ignoring those around them and, far more unforgivably, my music. But when I finished the song, the applause caused one of them, the uglier of the two, to glance up at the stage and see me. One look was all he felt he needed. *Dyke*, said his face, and he looked away, subtracting me from his landscape. No, they weren't novice leatherboys—or even postulants.

Well, when someone insults my sexuality while I'm on stage, out loud or silently, I have a stock response: I sing "You Don't Know My Heart." It's another Janis Ian song, actually—one of the best songs I know about being gay, because there isn't a drop of anger in it anywhere that I can see. Just sadness. It sums up everything I've always wanted to say to dyke-hasslers and queer-bashers and minority-abusers of all stripes, all they really deserve to know, and all they should need to know, without the rage that always makes me choke if I do try and talk to them, and keeps them from listening if I succeed.

> *We learn to stand in the shadows*
> *watch the way the wind blows*
> *thinking no one knows*
> *we're one of a kind*
> *Shy glances at the neighboring team*
> *Romance is a dangerous dream*
> *never knowing if they'll laugh or scream*
> *Living on a fault line*
> *Will you/won't you be mine?*
> *Hoping it will change in time*

One of the two hitters got up to go to the can, leaving his friend at the table. To get there, he had to pass in front of the stage. I caught his eye and pointedly aimed the chorus of the song at him as he approached, not quite pointing to him and singing straight at him, but almost.

> *And if people say we chose this way*
> *to set ourselves apart—I say*
> *you don't know my heart*
> *You don't know my heart*

He got the message—as much of it as would penetrate—grimaced at me and glanced away.

> *You don't know my heart*
> *You don't know my heart*

It was when he glanced away that he suddenly acquired his target. I saw his face change, followed his gaze, and realized they were after Dora Something-or-Other.

It seemed ridiculous. Who sends a pair of pros after a drag queen?

✦✦✦

There are people in Key West who were born in Key West, but statistically you're unlikely to meet one unless you make an effort.

It's a place most people pass through, and others end up. The lucky ones take a moment to recover, then regroup, make a plan, and go somewhere else. Others sit for a long or a short time on the bottom, half-concealed in the ooze, until one vagrant current or another stirs them up and carries them back north into the stream of life. And some sink into the mud for keeps and begin growing barnacles and coral deposits of their own. Key West is Endsville. There's just no farther to run; you have to stop, steal a boat or start swimming.

You might think a town full of losers, runaways, fugitives, and failures would have a high crime rate, but in fact there's almost none. Everyone seems to want to keep their heads down and chill; in many cases an overgaudy lifestyle was why they had to leave America and come here in the first place. There is zero organized crime, except for municipal government. Oh, I'm sure all the big chain hotels have their liquor, linen, and garbage needs dealt with by the right firms out of Miami. Beyond that, there simply isn't anything on The Rock to interest the mob. It's a beehive of small-time tourist hustles, hard to keep track of and beneath their dignity to tax. Circuit hookers can't compete with the constantly changing parade of semipros, beginners, stupified coeds, and reckless secretaries on vacation. Consequently, the gangsters have always treated the place as a neutral zone. No family claims it, and if you see somebody with bodyguards, you know he must be a civilian. In a town full of illegal immigrants and bail jumpers, KWPD has fired more cops than it has shots.

It's a wonderful place to hide. That's why most of us are there. Including, apparently, Dora Whatsername.

✦✦✦

What I wanted to do was catch Dora's eye, hold it long enough to engage his attention, then gesture with my eyes and eyebrows toward the hitters. It would, of course, be good to do this *without* letting the hitters catch me at it. Now was the time, then, with one of them in the can. But the remaining one happened to be the last folk music fan left outside Key West, and was watching me perform.

I had a rush of brains to the head, and began singing "You Don't Know My Heart" directly to him, just as I had to his partner a moment ago.

> *Tried to fit, I tried to blend*
> *I learned young to pretend*
> *'cause if they knew, the world would end*
> *Frightened of my family*
> *Where is anyone like me?*
> *When will I be free?*

Sure enough, the penny dropped. He started hearing the words. He, too, grimaced in disgust—*a tragic waste of pussy*—and looked away.

Moments later I had eye contact with Dora. We didn't know each other very well, and had never shared so much as a conversation—we played in different leagues—so he wasted several long seconds being surprised and puzzled. Fortunately, disgust outlasts confusion. By the time hitter number two got over being grossed out and looked back my way, Dora was discreetly clocking the guy out of the corner of his eye.

Unless specifically asked otherwise, I usually refer to drag queens as "she." I like to think it's more from politeness than political correctness. But every so often you meet one like Dora, who's so hopeless at it that "he" is the only pronoun you can bring yourself to use. I'd never quite been able to pin down what it was he got wrong. He didn't have broad shoulders, muscular arms, thick wrists, deep voice, heavy beard or prominent Adam's apple. He didn't totter on heels or sit with his legs open. His face was kind of cute, in the right light, and he didn't overdo the makeup or the camp more than a drag queen is supposed to. Yet somehow the overall effect was of a female impersonator impersonator.

Which was fine with me. I have no business criticizing anybody else's act: I sing folk. We moved in different circles, was all.

At first, I think Dora thought I was pointing out the leatherboy as someone he might want to fan with his false eyelashes and, if so, he must have thought I was nuts. Nearly at once, though, I saw him pick up on the fact that the guy was a phony—one with hard muscles and empty eyes. He glanced my way with one eyebrow raised, nodded his thanks, and went back to discreetly studying his watcher.

Hitter number one got back to the table and rejoined his partner just as I was finishing the song. Because I was looking for it, I noticed that beneath his leather pants, his right ankle was thicker on the outside than his left. That's where a right-handed man will hide a gun. So: not hitters, but shooters.

There followed an amusing charade in which the shooters tried to discuss Dora without being caught at it, and Dora pretended not to clock the whole thing. It was a lot like the mating dances going on all around the room, except that this one, I was pretty sure, was intended to end with a *literal* bang. Dora looked unconcerned, but I didn't see how he was going to get out of it. His pursuers looked fit enough to run up the side of Martello Tower; no way was he going to unrun them, not in those heels.

So I flanged up my guitar a couple of notches, called out, "Anybody feel like *dancing?*" and launched into Jimmy Buffett's "Fins."

Everybody in Key West knows every song Jimmy Buffett ever wrote; it's one of the few requirements of residence. There are at least a dozen guaranteed to make everyone in the joint pause in their seductions long enough to sing along—but "Fins" is certain to get them on their feet, the way I play it anyway. It's about being hit on in bars—fins to the left, fins to the right, and you're the only bait in town—so the lyrics tend to strike a certain chord, in predator and prey alike.

And the guitar lick would make a preacher dance the dirty boogie: halfway into it there was a roar of recognition and approval, and by the time I started the first verse, half the place was dancing, and the other half was trying to find room to.

I lost track of Dora in the crowd at once. But I could make out the two shooters, trying to force their way across the room to him.

They were better than average at it, spreading out just enough to block his escape path as they came.

I'd just finished the first verse; as I went into my guitar solo, I stepped away from the mike and began doing a Chuck Berry Strut back and forth across the stage. Bingo: an instant line dance organized itself out there on the floor and started to conga back and forth. By the time Frick and Frack managed to work their way through *that*, Dora was long gone. They stood where they'd last seen her, blank-faced as mannequins, and each turned in place five times before they gave up.

I finished the song, got a big round of applause, and, since I had everyone on their feet, went into a slow-dance song, a ballad by Woody Smith called "Afterglow."

> *Tending to tension by conscious intent,*
> *declining declension, disdaining dissent,*
> *into the dementia dimension we're sent:*
> *we are our content,*
> *and we are content.*

The half of the crowd that wasn't doing that well tonight sat down, and the rest went into their clinches. I saw the shooters' eyes meet, saw them both consider and reject the idea of slow-dancing together for the sake of their cover. They left together, and I finished my set feeling the warm glow of the Samaritan who has managed to get away with it.

I glowed too soon. As I stepped out the back door of Slim's Elite to walk home a little after two, I heard someone nearby drive a nail deep into hardwood with a single blow. I was turning to yank the sticky door shut behind me at the time, so I even saw the nail appear, a shiny circle in the doorjamb beside me, where no nail belonged, and no nail had been a moment before. By the time my forebrain had worked out that the nail was the ass end of a silenced bullet, I was already back inside the club, running like hell.

★★★

Ever try and run carrying a guitar case? Fortunately, I gig with one of those indestructible Yamahas; I tossed it, case and all, behind the bar as I went past, and kept on running.

As I burst out the front door onto the deserted poorly-lit street, Dora pulled up in front of me on a Moped. I skidded to a halt. The sight was surreal and silly enough to start me wondering if all of this might not be a bad dream I was having. "Get on," he said, gesturing urgently. "Get *on*." I stood there trying to get my breath, and wondering how Dora knew I needed a ride just then. "Pat, *come o-o-o-on*—"

An angry mosquito parted my hair. Behind me someone snapped a piece of wood with a sound like a muffled gunshot—

—no. Just backward. That had been a muffled gunshot, no louder than a snapping yardstick. That explained why I was in midair, in forward motion, falling toward the back of Dora's Moped—

If a man had landed there, that hard, he'd have gelded himself. It wasn't much more fun for me, and as I drew breath to yell, Dora peeled out. *Fast.* Somehow his Moped had the power of a real motorcycle—without the thunder. I ended up hanging onto his fake boobs for dear life. There was one last ruler-snap behind us, without mosquito this time, and then we were too far away to sweat small arms fire. I shifted my grip down to Dora's waist and began to relax slightly.

Someone ripped my left earring out, and behind us someone snapped a two by four.

"Jesus Christ," I screamed, "rifle fire!"

Dora began to deke sharply from side to side. Since he did it randomly to surprise the shooter, he kept surprising me too, but I managed to hang on. The sniper must have realized his chance for a head shot was gone, and went for a tire. Thanks to the weaving he blew the heel off my left shoe instead, and for the next ten or twenty busy seconds I thought he'd shot me in the foot. I clutched Dora hard enough for a Heimlich, and preposterously he yelled, "*Hang on*," and hung a most unexpected *sharp* right into a narrow driveway. We passed between two sparsely-lit houses in a controlled skid—I told myself it was controlled—heeled so far over to our right that visually it was remarkably like part of the famous scene at the end of *2001: a Space Odyssey*, lights streaking past us above and below. Nearly at once it gave way to the end of the original *Star Wars*, a smashcut montage of *pitch-dark backyard/obstacle course of crap/oncoming stone wall/broken bench reconsidered as ramp/midair, like Elliot and E.T./narrowly missed pool/asskicker landing/many naked people in great dismay/demolished flower bed/long narrow walkway between houses like Luke's final run at the Deathstar/chain-link fence/providentially open gate/sharp left onto a deserted street where no one seemed to be firing any rifles, with or without hellish accuracy/fade to black.*

Roll credits.

★★★

Dora pulled a pair of my pants up over his own red silk g-string and said, "To be honest, I'm kind of surprised."

I snorted. *To be understated, I'm kind of mindfucked.* "What exactly was it that surprised you? The gunfire? Our surviving it? How many of the people at that orgy looked good naked?" I tossed him a balled-up pair of socks.

We were at my place. He'd wrecked his frock driving a Moped like Jackie Chan. He was way too tall—and too slim-waisted, damn him—to fit into any of my jeans, but I'd found a baggy pair of painter pants around that didn't look *too* ridiculous on him, and a maroon sweatshirt, and some one-size-fits-none sandals. Half the people in Key West were dressed worse.

He unrolled the socks and stared down at them. "I'm kind of surprised you stuck your neck out for me in the first place. That's what I meant."

I said nothing. I sat on the edge of my bed, put my left foot up on my knee and checked the heel for signs of damage. The tingling had gone away by now. It looked okay. I put on my good sandals, dropped the ruined shoes in the trash, and tried a few careful steps. The heel felt a little tender, but not enough to make me limp.

"We barely know each other, Pat. We move in different circles. We play on different teams. But you took a risk for me."

"You returned the favor," I said and, even to me, my voice sounded brusque.

He nodded. "Okay. I guess it's none of my business. It's just that . . . well, I know a lot of dykes don't have much use for drag queens. We must make you feel a little like black people watching some clueless, happy white guy do a Step'n'Fetchit routine in blackface. We revel in the very mannerisms and attitudes you're trying to get away from."

I said some more nothing. Partly that was because he was right. I try to be polite to just about anybody, on principle, but drag queens test my principles even more than skinheads. They exaggerate the aspects of stereotypical femaleness I find most infuriatingly embarrassing—and think it's screamingly funny.

"And of course the lipstick Lezzies hate us because we're so much better than they are at makeup—"

He was simply trying to be friendly, but even if he had just saved my life, I didn't want to be his friend. "You don't know my heart," I said harshly, and heard myself sounding just like the kind of uptight judgmental dyke I've always hated.

His face went blank. It was several seconds before he spoke. "You're absolutely right," he conceded then. "I have no business making presumptions. All I know about you in the world is that you sing and play guitar very well, you hate the sight of car engines for some reason, and tonight you—"

"What did you say?"

Somehow he knew which clause I meant. "Don't sweat it: as phobias go it's pretty tame. Once I happened to see you jump a foot in the air and then cross the street when someone popped the hood of his car as you were walking past. And then another time my friend Delilah was working on her old bomber, trying to get the timing right, and she said she asked you to just sit behind the wheel and rev it when she told you, and instead you turned white as a ghost and turned around and ran away. If I had to guess, I'd guess one of your parents was a mechanic—but I *don't* have to guess. Like you said, I don't know your heart. And nothing says I have to."

"That's right." God, would I ever say anything again that wasn't churlish?

"I just wondered why it made you stick your neck out for a stranger. That's all."

"Look, Dora, maybe sometime my heart'll make me feel like telling you why," I said. "Okay?"

He held up his hands. "Understood." His nails clashed with his—with my—sweatshirt. "You haven't asked me why those two are after me. I appreciate that."

"I don't *care* why they're after you," I said. "They're after me, too, now, that's all I care about at the moment. They're crazy enough to fire guns in Key West—big guns, right out in the street—and I've pissed them off. How *you* pissed them off doesn't interest me: I have to know who they are." She was frowning. "I need to know *right now*, Dora."

She looked stubborn. "Why?"

I restrained the impulse to smack her one. "Think a minute! Dangerous men are pissed at me. Pros. If they work for Charlie Pontevecchio up in Miami—or for any other private citizen, whether or not his last name happens to end in a vowel—then there probably isn't a lot they can do to locate me until Slim's reopens at nine, giving me a whole, Jesus, six hours to disappear into thin air somehow. But if those two clowns are cops, any kind of cops at all, they're probably rousting Big Chazz out of bed right now, and tough as she is, she's got her license to think of: they could be here in half an hour. So which—?"

I didn't have to finish the question. His expression answered for him.

"Shit. What *kind* of cops?"

Very expressive face.

"Oh, my god. *Federal?*"

He nodded. "Yes, but—wait!"

I'd be hard pressed to say which was moving faster, me or my brain. I'm pretty sure it took less than a single minute before the carry-on bag I always keep half full under the bed was topped off with the few bits of this life I wasn't ready to abandon, and another fifteen seconds was plenty to reach the pantry, kick aside the small rug on the floor, and pull up the concealed trapdoor. I felt around under the near edge for the little mag lite, found it, and damn near dropped it when I popped it out of its holder.

"What the hell are you doing?" asked Dora.

"In the military they call it retiring to a previously prepared position." I hesitated. "You can follow if you want. There's room enough for someone your size."

She looked appalled. "Under the house? Down there with the roaches and snakes and spiders and . . . not on your life, girl. Forget it."

I didn't have time to argue. I sat at the edge of the hole and let my feet and legs dangle down into the damp dank darkness. "Fine. Walk right out my front door, whenever you feel ready to be shot. Don't bother closing it behind you. Of course, you may not make the door. Every room in this dump has a window."

He shook his head. "I'm not worried about them. And listen, you don't have to be either."

"Right," I said, and let myself down into the crawl space under the house.

Damn, I thought, *I'm going to miss that Yamaha. I just got the action right—*

❄★❄

Only a moron would attempt to flee Key West alone by car. There's exactly one road out of town, and a dozen spots from which it can be conveniently and discreetly monitored with binoculars or longlens camera. Or sniper scope. A clay pigeon would have a much better chance: they move way faster than traffic heading up the Keys.

So my plan was to head for The Schooner, an open-air thatched-roof blues bar right next to the Land's End Marina. Its only neighbors are boat people, and its clientele aren't all fags and dykes, so it gets to stay open a little later than Slim's Elite. I knew a Rasta pot dealer named Bad Death Johnson who would probably still be there, and would certainly be able to put me on a fast boat to West Elsewhere without troubling the harbor master.

But before I'd gotten two blocks I became aware I was being followed, so clumsily that I knew who it was. I could have outrun him. I sighed, found a dark place, and waited for Dora to catch up. When he did, I started to step out of the shadows and call to him, but I got distracted watching him. His walk was so distinctive that even dressed in gender-neutral clothes, wearing sandals, I'd have recognized him by it, even in the poor light. You'd think a drag queen would be better at disguise, but apparently he just knew the one. He was past me by the time I finished that thought train, and I was going to step out behind him and call his name softly—but then I decided the hell with it and stayed where I was. He was just going to tell me again that I didn't have to be afraid of federal agents with clearance to kill. And tell me why he wasn't, which couldn't possibly be anything but moronic.

But since Dora was heading toward the marina, now I couldn't anymore. It took me ten aggravated seconds to come up with a Plan B, and another ten to persuade myself it had a chance of success. That was good: even a few seconds less, and I'd have strolled blithely out there and collided with the two feds as they hurried by on cat feet.

For yet another ten seconds I *couldn't* move; then I managed to take a deep breath, and that rebooted my system. Then there was *another* ten second interlude, of hard thought, at the end of which I went with Plan C. I slipped from my place of concealment and began tailing the two fake leatherboys as they tailed Dora.

Why? Don't ask me. I don't know my *own* heart, I guess. God knows I was scared of those two. I'd been scared of people like them forever. The kind of scared where you don't have a roommate because then you won't have to explain why you wake up sobbing with terror a few nights a week. These two weren't my particular personal nightmare, but they were, as the saying goes, close enough for folk music. Dylan once wrote, "I'll let you be in my dream if I can be in yours." They wanted to kill me for stumbling into theirs. They didn't seem to have their long guns with them this time, but I could make out two lumpy right ankles. Big sticks would have been more than I could cope with.

And there was the question of why they were after Dora. While I've never been a big fan of the government, I had to concede that it probably did not covertly pop caps on American soil without a pretty good reason. On the other hand, a "good reason" in their estimation might be something like Dora having recognized some fellow drag queen as a senator. He wasn't swarthy enough or Irish enough to be a terrorist. What would his cause be, *Free Tammy Fae Baker?*

In between these speculations I kept doing the math. I'd helped Dora, then Dora had helped me. The books balanced. I owed him nothing; if anything, he owed me for clothes and sandals. I didn't have to do this—

After a while they took the last turn. From there it was a straight one-block shot to the Schooner, with almost no cover along the way. If one of them even glanced over his shoulder, he could hardly miss me. So I hung back, waiting to make the turn until they'd had time to at least build up a little more of a lead. Finally, I judged there was enough distance between us that if they did glance back, they might not necessarily recognize me. I was dressed differently than I had been at our last encounter. At the last moment I had a rush of brains to the head and adjusted my walk to be almost as exaggeratedly feminine as Dora's. They'd never suspect it was me. I was congratulating myself on my sagacity when I turned the corner and crashed head-on into Dora, coming the other way.

★★★

It took several confused seconds for Dora to convince me she hadn't seen the feds, and for me to convince her that one minute ago they'd been no more than a block behind her. Then we stood there together and looked up and down that street for anywhere they could reasonably have gone.

After a while Dora shrugged and gave up. "They beamed up," he said, and dismissed the matter.

Some people can do that. I sometimes wish I were one of them. When I don't understand something, I *can't* dismiss it, any more than I can ignore a stone in my shoe. I was convinced the two shooters were concealed in some cunning blind, and any second they were going to get good and ready, and drop us both—

But what could I do about it?

The Schooner was nearly deserted, down to a couple of hard-core regulars nursing the night's last cup of cheer. No sign of Bad Death anywhere. Inside the big old mahogany racetrack of a bar, two tired young bartenders dressed like refugees had stopped serving and were into their close up routines when we arrived, but Dora and I were both known there. The bandshell stage was dark and empty; so was the kitchen-and-washrooms shack adjacent to the bar. We took our beers to a table between them, and thus were mostly concealed from both the street and the marina.

"You're right," Dora said. "I don't know your heart. So I have to ask again: why did you take a chance and follow those two?"

I'd been asking myself that same question all night, and I had a pretty fair answer, but there was no way I was going to share it with him, no way in the world. I tried to think of anyone on the planet with whom I *would* share it, and failed. I thought of a great lie and decided I didn't much want to tell it. "Look—"

"Please," he said softly.

To my astonishment, I heard myself tell him the truth.

★★★

"The only thing I hate worse than winter is cars," I told him. "And the only thing I hate worse than cars is cars in winter. I hate them all the time, but especially on cold mornings. The goddamn things just never want to start when it's really cold, you know?"

He said nothing.

"So I had this old beater, a Dodge. For Detroit iron it wasn't bad. Slant six, not a lot of pickup but hard to kill, easy to work on. Only in the winter, it needed working on a *lot*. On really cold mornings, getting it to start could be a major pain in the ass, that left you with grease and smelly starter fluid all over your frostbitten barked knuckles. Sometimes it *wouldn't* start. Once in a while, you'd get desperate or clumsy from the cold and use a little too much fluid, and then there'd be a carburetor blow back that could perm your bangs and fry your eyebrows right off."

He nodded.

"This was in Boston," I went on, "where the mornings are only cold on days that end in 'y.' It was February, so by now I was thoroughly sick of coaxing that beast into life every morning. So this one morning, the goddamn thing wouldn't wouldn't *wouldn't* wake up, and as I got out to wrestle with it, a big guy came walking by and asked if I needed help. It was so cold, you know? Anyway, I didn't even hesitate." I took a deep breath and a deep gulp of beer. "I stuck out my tits and batted my eyelashes and showed him all my teeth and lied. Yes, I said, I sure did need help."

"And really you just wanted it."

"I never do that kind of shit, you know?" I looked up from my hands to meet his eyes pleadingly. "Not since high school, anyway. But it was so fucking cold."

"Sure."

"I mean, I wasn't proud of doing it . . . but there was at least a little bit of pride in how well I was doing it, after all that time out of practice. By sheer body language I pretty much *forced* him to say, why don't you go back inside and stay warm and I'll take care of everything, little lady. So the only actual injury I sustained, except for the temporary blindness from the flash, was one of his teeth that came through the living room window and buried itself half an inch deep in the meat of my shoulder. It got infected real bad."

"My God," Dora said, wide-eyed.

"It was one of the bigger pieces of him they recovered, actually. Half a scapula, two lawns down, that was another one."

I went to reach for my beer but found my hands were full of Dora's.

"He was a sweet guy, who just wanted to fantasize about fucking me and was willing to pay for the privilege, and I got him turned into aerosol tomato paste."

"How?"

"I had ignored one of the basic rules of Lesbianism: never seduce a capo's daughter."

He raised one exquisite eyebrow. "Oh, dear."

"For fairly obvious reasons Adriana hadn't gotten around to mentioning what her father did for a living, but somebody else had discreetly tipped me off—after it was too late. It excited me. I had the charming idea that as long as nobody knew about me and Adriana but Adriana, I was safe." I realized how hard I was gripping his hands and eased off, marveling that he had betrayed no sign of pain. "So after my car was blown up, I handed Adriana in, and in exchange I got a new name, new street, city, and state address, new appearance, new history, and new occupation. I used to paint, but you can't be a fugitive painter. Thank God for folk music: a chimp could learn it, and there are customers in every hamlet."

He put my right hand on my beer bottle and let go. I took a long sip.

"Now I don't own a car. And I live in a place where nobody but tourists and fools own a car, and the bicycle is king. A place where there are never ever any cold mornings. A place with no local mob, so cheesy and sleazy no self-respecting made guy would bring his *gumar* here on vacation. Endsville. I haven't been as far north as Key Largo in ten years, haven't left the rock in five. I'm a human black hole: so far up my own ass, daylight can't reach me. An ingrown toenail of a person."

Damn. One more sip and that beer would be gone. And the two youngsters behind the bar had just put out the last of the fake hurricane lamps and gone off home.

"So your question was, why did I hang my ass out in the breeze, to help a stranger wearing false tits? And the answer is, I guess because I know a little something about being hunted. Every once in a while, just on general principles, those cocky, remorseless sons of bitches ought to get a big unpleasant surprise." I belched and frowned. "And maybe I've been safe a little too long."

"And don't feel like you deserve to be."

"To this day, I don't know *anything* about him—not his name or address, or where he was headed that morning, or whether or not he left behind a family—zilch. Once I stopped being too terrified to give a shit, stopped running long enough to wonder, I could have found out, without drawing attention. I've never even tried. What the *hell* do you suppose could have happened to those two fetishware feds?"

"Forget it," said Dora.

I nearly did as he said. But then for no reason I can explain, an odd little thought-train went through my head—one of those brain-fission deals, where several seconds worth of thought somehow take place in a split second.

Neither of those feds could possibly have concealed a long gun under that tight leather/so?/so where did they have their rifles stashed?/in a car, obviously, parked in back where the light is poorest: the first shot came as you went out the back door/okay—so if they had wheels, how come they were both tailing Dora on foot just now?/hell, you can't tail a pedestrian in a car without being spotted/fine, but wouldn't one of them at least follow in the car, staying well back? Say they bagged Dora: were they going to carry him back through the streets to their ride? In Key West, that'd be taking a big chance, even at this hour/what's your point?/I don't think they have wheels/so what?/I don't think they have rifles either—or else why leave them behind now?/one last time: so what?/so who did *shoot at us with a rifle?/oh, shit/and where—*

That's as far as I'd gotten when I heard the floorboard creak up on the stage. I've played on that stage, I know exactly where that goddam creaky board is, and I realized instantly that a man standing there would have a clear shot at both of us. "Dora, *run!*" I cried, and kicked my chair over backward trying to move away from him.

The shooter came into view out of the darkness, and apparently let his instincts tell him to choose the larger target first; the rifle barrel settled on Dora. Now I wanted to be going in *that* direction, to take the bullet, and it was like one of those nightmares where you're trying to do a 180 but can't seem to overcome inertia and get moving the right way. Time slowed drastically.

The shooter was definitely not one of the feds: way shorter than either, with hair longer than Dora's wig. A gentle breeze brought scents of lime and coral. Somewhere far above there was a small plane. Like a million gunshot victims before him, Dora flung his hand up in front of his face in a useless instinctive attempt to catch the bullet. A distant dog barked. The shooter fired. Sound no louder than a nail gun. Dora caught the bullet. "Don't do that again," he said to the shooter.

Then nobody said or did anything for several long seconds.

The shooter shook his head once, moved the barrel in a small circle, took careful aim and fired again. Dora caught that slug, too. "I warned you," he said sadly.

The shooter apparently decided that if Dora declined to die, maybe I'd be more cooperative. He was right, I would. I was too terrified even to put my hand up in front of my face. I saw the barrel lock on me, saw the shooter's face past it, I could even see him let out his breath and hold it. Then he squealed, because the rifle was somehow molten, dripping like so much glowing lava from his hands. They burst into flame, and the one near his cheek set his hair on fire. He drew in a deep breath to scream, but before he could he began to vibrate. Ever see one of those machines in a hardware store shake up a can of paint? Like that. In less than a second he began to blur; in three he was gone. Just . . . gone. So were the hot coals on the stage. Not even a bad smell left behind.

Myself and I conferred, and decided that this would be a good time for me to fall down. To help, I became unconscious.

★★★

When I opened my eyes I was at Mallory Square, sitting up against a trash can, staring out across a few hundred yards of dark slow water at Tank Island. I have absolutely no idea how I got there, or why. The breeze was from the south, salty and sultry. Clouds hid the moon.

"I called my equivalent of the Triple A a couple of years ago," Dora said softly from behind me and to my right. "My tow truck should be here in only another day or two, and then I'll be leaving this charming star system behind forever. So I feel kind of bad about the two FBI agents. Hunting me was just their job. And from your point of view, hunting me is the sensible thing to do."

Somehow I was past being astonished. I'd worked it out while I was unconscious, watched all the inexplicable little pieces assemble themselves into an inescapable pattern, and accepted it. "I've never had much success identifying with any kind of hunter at all," I said.

"And you need to identify with someone before you can empathize with them."

"Well . . . yeah. At least a little," I said defensively. "I mean, I can identify with *you* . . . and for all I know, you're not even carbon-based. Hell, you're my imaginary role model. The stranger in a strange land. Brilliant, being a drag queen, by the way. If anybody spots a flaw in your disguise, it just makes them condescending."

"You should do what I'm doing."

"What do you mean? Pretend to be human? Go femme? Kill hit men? Catch b—"

"Go home."

Now I was astonished. I sat up and swiveled to face him. "What the hell are you talking about? You know I—"

He sat cross-legged, staring up at the night sky. At the stars. "Okay, maybe not *home*—but get out of Key West."

I looked away. "Dora, I *can't.*"

"Listen to me," he said. "Pat, will you listen?"

"I'll listen."

"I've been in America a lot more recently than you have. A lot of things have changed, the last ten or fifteen years."

"Nothing really important."

"Cars have changed since you lived there. *They all start on cold mornings, now.*"

"Bullshit!"

"I swear, it's true. Nobody recognizes anything under the hood anymore—but nobody cares, because they don't *need* to."

I searched his face. "Are you serious?"

"Nobody carries *jumper cables* anymore. And the capo is not going to send a second mechanic after you—not after this one just vanishes without a trace, not for a purely personal beef. You can go home any time you want to, Pat. Away from here, anyway."

My head was spinning. The concept of being able to be once again what Larry McMurtry calls "a live human being, free on the Earth," was way more mind-boggling than dodging certain death, or meeting a spaceman. My mother was still alive, last I'd heard. Maybe I could find out the name of the man I'd gotten killed. Maybe he'd left family behind. Maybe there was something I could do for them. Suddenly the universe was nothing but questions.

I grabbed one out of the air. "I'm throwing your own question back at you," I said. "Why did you do this? Why did you kill two men to keep them from blowing your cover . . . and then five minutes later kill another one in front of me and blow your cover?" Absurdly I felt myself getting angry. "Why did I wake up just now? Now you've got to walk around your last few days here wondering how badly I want to be on *Geraldo*. What would you take such a risk for? How the hell can you identify with *any* human well enough to empathize . . . much less a dyke?"

The clouds picked that moment to let the moonlight through. I'd seen him grimace and I'd seen him grin. This was the first time I'd seen him smile, and it was so beautiful my breath caught in my throat. I've painted it several times without ever really capturing it.

"You *really* don't know my heart," he said. "It has five chambers, for one thing."

Then he was gone like the Cheshire Cat.

I never saw him again, and now every night after I get my mother to sleep, and climb into my own bed to snuggle under the covers with my dear partner, I pray to God that Dora got home safely to his own home and loved ones.

I empathize. Like the song says: he waited so long, to remember what it's like to feel somebody's arms around his life.

Riding Janis

by DAVID GERROLD

If we had wings
where would we fly?
Would you choose the safety of the ground
or touch the sky
if we had wings?
—from "If We Had Wings" by Janis Ian & Bill Lloyd

THE thing about puberty is that once you've done it, you're stuck. You can't go back.

It's like what Voltaire said about learning Russian. He didn't know if learning Russian would be a good thing or not unless he actually learned the language—except that after you learn it, would the process of learning have turned you into a person who believes it's a good thing? So how could you know? Puberty is like that—I think. It changes you, the way you think, and what you think about. And from what I can tell, it's a lot harder than Russian. Especially the conjugations.

You can only delay puberty for so long. After that, you start to get some permanent physiological effects. But there's no point in going through puberty when the closest eligible breeding partners are on the other side of the solar system. I didn't mind being nineteen and unfinished. It was the only life I knew. What I minded was not having a choice. Sometimes I felt like just another asteroid in the belt, tumbling forever around the solar furnace, too far away to be warmed, but still too close to be truly alone. Waiting for someone to grab me and hurl me toward Luna.

See, that's what Mom and Jill do. They toss comets. Mostly small ones, wrapped so they don't burn off. There's not a lot of ice in the belt, only a couple of percentage points, if that; but when you figure there are a couple billion rocks out here, that's still a few million that are locally useful. Our job is finding them. There's no shortage of customers for big fat oxygen atoms with a couple of smaller hydrogens attached. Luna and Mercury, in particular, and eventually Venus, when they start cooling her down.

But this was the biggest job we'd ever contracted, and it wasn't about ice as much as it was about ice-burning. Hundreds of tons per hour. Six hundred and fifty million kilometers of tail, streaming outward from the sun, driven by the ferocious solar wind. Comet Janis. In fifty-two months, the spray of ice and dye would appear as a bright red, white, and blue streak across the Earth's summer sky—the Summer Olympics Comet.

Mom and Jill were hammering every number out to the ump-teenth decimal place. This was a zero-tolerance nightmare. We had to install triple-triple safeguards on the safeguards. They only wanted a flyby, not a direct hit. That would void the contract, as well as the planet.

The bigger the rock, the farther out you could aim and still make a streak that covers half the sky. The problem with aiming is that comets have minds of their own—all that volatile outgassing pushes them this way and that, and even if you've wrapped the rock with reflectors, you still don't get any kind of precision. But the bigger the rock, the harder it is to wrap it and toss it. And we didn't have a lot of wiggle room on the time line.

Janis was big and dark until we lit it up. We unfolded three arrays of LEDs, hit it with a dozen megawatts from ten klicks, and the whole thing sparkled like the star on top of a Christmas tree. All that dirty ice, thirty kilometers of it, reflecting light every which way—depending on your orientation when you looked out the port, it was a fairy landscape, a shimmering wall, or a glimmering ceiling. A trillion tons of sparkly mud, all packed up in nice dense sheets, so it wouldn't come apart.

It was beautiful. And not just because it was pretty to look at, and not just because it meant a couple gazillion serious dollars in the bank either. It was beautiful for another reason.

See, here's the thing about living in space. Everything is Newtonian. It moves until you stop it or change its direction. So every time you move something, you have to think about where it's going to go, how fast it's going to get there, and where it will eventually end up. And we're not just talking about large sparkly rocks, we're talking about bottles of soda, dirty underwear, big green boogers, or even the ship's cat. Everything moves, bounces, and moves some more. And that includes people, too. So you learn to think in vectors and trajectories and consequences. Jill calls it "extrapolatory thinking."

And that's why the rock was beautiful, because it wasn't just a rock here and now. It was a rock with a future. Neither Mom nor Jill had said anything yet, they were too busy studying the gravitational ripple charts, but they didn't have to say anything. It was obvious. We were going to have to ride it in, because if that thing started outgassing, it would push itself off course. Somebody had to be there to create a compensating thrust. Folks on the Big Blue Marble were touchy about extinction-level events.

Finding the right rock is only the second-hardest part of comet-tossing. Dirtsiders think the belt is full of rocks, you just go and get one; but most of the rocks are the wrong kind; too much rock, not enough ice—and the average distance between them is fifteen million klicks. And most of them are just dumb rock. Once in a while, you find one that's rich with nickel or iron, and as useful as that might be, if you're not looking for nickel or iron right then, it might as well be more dumb rock. But if somebody else is looking for it, you can lease or sell it to them.

So Mom is continually dropping bots. We fab them up in batches. Every time we change our trajectory, Mom opens a window and tosses out a dozen paper planes.

A paper plane doesn't need speed or sophistication, just brute functionality, so we print the necessary circuitry on sheets of stiff polymer. (We fab that, too.) It's a simple configuration of multi-sensors, dumb-processors, lotsa-memory, soft-transmitters, long-batteries, carbon-nanotube solar cells, ion-reservoirs, and even a few micro-rockets. The printer rolls out the circuitry on a long sheet of polymer, laying down thirty-six to forty-eight layers of material in a single pass. Each side. At a resolution of 36002 dpi, that's tight enough to make a fairly respectable, self-powered, paper robot. Not smart enough to play with its own tautology, but certainly good enough to sniff a passing asteroid.

We print out as much and as many as we want, we break the polymer at the perforations; three quick folds to give it a wing shape, and it's done. Toss a dozen of these things overboard, they sail along on the solar wind, steering themselves by changing colors and occasional micro-bursts. Make one wing black and the other white and the plane eventually turns itself; there's no hurry, there's no shortage of either time or space in the belt. Every few days, the bot wakes up and looks around. Whenever it detects a mass of any kind, it scans the lump, scans it again, scans it a dozen times until it's sure, notes the orbit, takes a picture, analyzes the composition, prepares a report, files a claim, and sends a message home. Bots relay messages for each other until the message finally gets inserted into the real network. After that, it's just a matter of finding the publisher and forwarding the mail. Average time is fourteen hours.

Any rock one of your paper planes sniffs and tags, if you're the first, then you've got first dibsies on it. Most rocks are dumb and worthless—and usually when your bots turn up a rock that's useful, by then you're almost always too far away to use it. Anything farther than five or ten degrees of arc isn't usually worth the time or fuel to go back after. Figure fifty million kilometers per degree of arc. It's easier to auction off the rock, let whoever is closest do the actual work, and you collect a percentage. If you've tagged enough useful rocks, theoretically you could retire on the royalties. Theoretically. Jill hates that word.

But if finding the right rock is the second-hardest part of the job, then the first-hardest part is finding the other rock, the one you use at the other end of the whip. If you want to throw something at Earth (and lots of people do), you have to throw something the same size in the opposite direction. Finding and delivering the right ballast rock to the site was always a logistic nightmare. Most of the time it was just difficult, sometimes it was impossible, and once in a while it was even worse than that.

We got lucky. We had found the right ballast rock, and it was in just the right place for us. In fact, it was uncommonly close— only a few hundred thousand kilometers behind Janis. Most asteroids are at several million klicks from each other. FBK-9047 was small, but it was heavy. It was a nickel-rich lump about ten klicks across. While not immediately useful, it would someday be worth a helluva lot more than the comet we were tossing—five to ten billion, depending on how it assayed out.

Our problem was that it belonged to someone else. The FlyBy Knights. And they weren't too particularly keen on having us throw it out of the system so we could launch Comet Janis. Their problem was that this particular ten billion dollar payday wasn't on anyone's calendar. Most of the contractors had their next twenty-five years of mining already planned out—you have to plan that far in advance when the mountains you want to mine are constantly in motion. And it wasn't likely anyone was going to put it on their menu for at least a century; there were just too many other asteroids worth twenty or fifty or a hundred billion floating around the belt. So while this rock wasn't exactly worthless in principle, it was worthless in actuality—until someone actually needed it.

Mom says that comet tossing is an art. What you do is you lasso two rocks, put each in a sling, and run a long tether between them, fifty kilometers or more. Then you apply some force to each one and start them whirling around each other. With comet ice, you have to do it slowly to give the snowball a chance to compact. When you've got them up to speed, you cut the tether. One rock goes the way you want, the other goes in the opposite direction. If you've done your math right, the ballast rock flies off into the outbeyond, and the other—the money rock, goes arcing around the solar system and comes in for a close approach to the target body—Luna, Earth, L4, wherever. This is a lot more cost-effective than installing engines on an asteroid and driving it home. A lot more.

Most of the time, the flying mountain takes up station as a temporary moon orbiting whatever planet we threw it at, and it's up to the locals to mine it at their leisure. But this time, we were only arranging a flyby—a close approach for the Summer Olympics, so the folks in the Republic of Texas could have a sixty-degree swath of light across the sky for twelve days. And that was a whole other set of problems—because the comet's appearance had to be timed for perfect synchronicity with the event. There wasn't any wiggle room in the schedule. And everybody knew it.

All of which meant that we really needed this rock, or we weren't going to be able to toss the comet. And everybody knew that, too, so we weren't in the best bargaining position. If we wanted to use 9047, we were going to have to cut the FlyBy Knights in for a percentage of Janis, which Jill didn't really want to do because what they called "suitable recompense for the loss of projected earnings" (if we threw their rock away) was so high that we would end up losing money on the whole deal.

We knew we'd make a deal eventually—but the advantage was on their side because the longer they could stall us, the more desperate we'd become and more willing to accept their terms. And meanwhile, Mom was scanning for any useful rock or combination of rocks in the local neighborhood which was approximately five million klicks in any direction. So we were juggling time, money, and fuel against our ability to go without sleep. Mom and Jill had to sort out a nightmare of orbital mechanics, economic concerns, and assorted political domains that stretched from here to Mercury.

Mom says that in space, the normal condition of life is patience; Jill says it's frustration. Myself . . . I had nothing to compare it with. What good is puberty if there's no one around to have puberty with? Like kissing, for instance. And holding hands. What's all that stuff about?

I was up early, because I wanted to make fresh bread. In free fall, bread doesn't rise, it expands in a sphere—which is pretty enough, and fun for tourists, but not really practical because you end up with some slices too large and others too small. Better to roll it into a cigar and let it expand in a cylindrical baking frame. We had stopped the centrifuge because the torque was interfering with our navigation around Janis; it complicated turning the ship. We'd probably be ten or twelve days without. We could handle that with vitamins and exercise, but if we went too much longer, we'd start to pay for it with muscle and bone and heart atrophy, and it takes three times as long to rebuild as it does to lose. Once the bread was safely rising—well, expanding—I drifted forward.

"Jill?"

She looked up. Well, over. We were at right angles to each other.

"What?" A polite what. She kept her fingers on the keyboard.

"I've been thinking—"

"That's nice."

"—we're going to have to ride this one in, aren't we?"

She stopped what she was doing, lifted her hands away from the keys, turned her music down, and swiveled her couch to face me. "How do you figure that?"

"Any comet heading that close to Earth, they'll want the contractor to ride it. Just in case course corrections have to be made. It's obvious."

"It'll be a long trip—"

"I read the contract. Our expenses are covered, both inbound and out. Plus ancillary coverage."

"That's standard boilerplate. Our presence isn't mandatory. We'll have lots of bots on the rock. They can manage any necessary corrections."

"It's not the same as having a ship onsite," I said. "Besides, Mom says we're overdue for a trip to the marble. Everyone should visit the home world at least once."

"I've been there. It's no big thing."

"But I haven't—"

"It's not cost-effective," Jill said. That was her answer to everything she didn't want to do.

"Oh, come on, Jill. With the money we'll make off of Comet Janis, we could add three new pods to this ship. And bigger engines. And larger fabricators. We could make ourselves a lot more competitive. We could—"

Her face did that thing it does when she doesn't want you to know what she really feels. She was still smiling, but the smile was now a mask. "Yes, we could do a lot of things. But that decision has to be made by the senior officers of the Lemrel Corporation, kidlet." Translation: your opinion is irrelevant. Your mother and I will argue about this. And I'm against it.

One thing about living in a ship, you learn real fast when to shut up and go away. There isn't any real privacy. If you hold perfectly still, close your eyes, and just listen, eventually—just from the ship noises—you can tell where everyone is and what they're doing, sleeping, eating, in the fresher, masturbating, whatever. In space, everyone can hear you scream. So you learn to speak softly. Even in an argument. Especially in an argument. The only real privacy is inside your head, and you learn to recognize when others are going there, and you go somewhere else. With Jill . . . well, you learned faster than real fast.

She turned back to her screens. A dismissal. She plucked her mug off the bulkhead and sipped at the built-in straw. "I think you should talk this over with your mom." A further dismissal.

"But Mom's asleep, and you're not. You're here." For some reason, I wasn't willing to let it go this time.

"You already have my opinion. And I don't want to talk about it anymore." She turned her music up to underline the point.

I went back to the galley to check on my bread. I opened the plastic bag and sniffed. It was warm and yeasty and puffy, just right for kneading, so I sealed it up again, put it up against a blank bulkhead and began pummeling it. You have to knead bread in a nonstick bag because you don't want microparticles in the air filtration system. It's like punching a pillow. It's good exercise, and an even better way to work out a shiftload of frustration.

As near as I could tell, puberty was mostly an overrated experience of hormonal storms, unexplainable rebellion, uncontrollable insecurity, and serious self-esteem issues, all resulting in a near-terminal state of wild paranoid anguish that caused the sufferer to behave bizarrely, taking on strange affectations of speech and appearance. Oh, yeah, and weird body stuff where you spend a lot of time rubbing yourself for no apparent reason. Lotsa kids in the belt postponed puberty. And for good reason. It doesn't make sense to have your body readying itself for breeding when there are no appropriate mates to pick from. And there's more than enough history to demonstrate that human intelligence goes into remission until at least five years after puberty issues resolve. A person should finish her basic education without interruption, get a little life experience, before letting her juices start to flow. At least, that was the theory.

But if I didn't start puberty soon, I'd never be able to and I'd end up sexless. You can only postpone it for so long before the postponement becomes permanent. Which might not be a bad idea, considering how crazy all that sex stuff makes people. And besides, yes, I was curious about all that sex stuff—masturbation and orgasms and nipples and thighs, stuff like that—but not morbidly so. I wanted to finish my real education first. Intercourse is supposed to be something marvelous and desirable, but all the pictures I'd ever seen made it look like an icky imposition for both partners. Why did anyone want to do that?

Either there was something wrong with the videos. Or maybe there was something wrong with me that I just didn't get it.

So it only made sense that I should start puberty now, so I'd be ready for mating when we got to Earth. And it made sense that we should go to Earth with Comet Janis. And why didn't Jill see that?

Mom stuck her head into the galley then. "I think that bread surrendered twenty minutes ago, sweetheart. You can stop beating it up now."

"Huh? What? Oh, I'm sorry. I was thinking about some stuff. I guess I lost track. Did I wake you?"

"Whatever you were thinking about, it must have been pretty exciting. The whole ship was thumping like a subwoofer. This boat is noisy enough without fresh-baked bread, honey. You should have used the bread machine." She reached past me and rescued the bag of dough; she began stuffing it into a baking cylinder.

"It's not the same," I said.

"You're right. It's quieter."

The arguments about the differences between free fall bread and gravity bread had been going on since Commander Jarles Ferris had announced that bread doesn't fall butter-side down in space. I decided not to pursue that argument. But I was still in an arguing mood.

"Mom?"

"What, honey?"

"Jill doesn't want to go to Earth."

"I know."

"Well, you're the Captain. It's your decision."

"Honey, Jill is my partner."

"Mom, I have to start puberty soon!"

"There'll be other chances."

"For puberty?"

"For Earth."

"When? How? If this isn't my best chance, there'll never be a better one." I grabbed her by the arms and turned her so we were both oriented the same way and looked her straight in the eyes.

"Mom, you know the drill. They're not going to allow you to throw anything that big across Earth's orbit unless you're riding it. We have to ride that comet in. You've known that from the beginning."

Mom started to answer, then stopped herself. That's another thing about spaceships. After a while, everybody knows all the sides of every argument. You don't have to recycle the exposition. Janis was big money. Four-plus years of extra-hazardous duty allotment, fuel and delta-vee recovery costs, plus bonuses for successful delivery. So, Jill's argument about cost-effectiveness wasn't valid. Mom knew it. And so did I. And so did Jill. So why were we arguing?

Mom leaped ahead to the punch line. "So what's this really about?" she asked.

I hesitated. It was hard to say. "I—I think I want to be a boy. And if we don't go to Earth, I won't be able to."

"Sweetheart, you know how Jill feels about males."

"Mom, that's her problem. It doesn't have to be mine. I like boys. Some of my best on-line friends are boys. Boys have a lot of fun together—at least, it always looks that way from here. I want to try it. If I don't like it, I don't have to stay that way." Even as I said it, I was abruptly aware that what had only been mild curiosity a few moments ago was now becoming a genuine resolve. The more Mom and Jill made it an issue, the more it was an issue of control, and the more important it was for me to win. So I argued for it, not because I wanted it as much as I needed to win. Because it wasn't about winning, it was about who was in charge of my life.

Mom stopped the argument abruptly. She pulled me around to orient us face-to-face, and she lowered her voice to a whisper, her way of saying this is serious. "All right, dear, if that's what you really want. It has to be your choice. You'll have a lot of time to think about it before you have to commit. But I don't want you talking about it in front of Jill anymore."

Oh. Of course. Mom hadn't just wandered into the galley because of the bread. Jill must have buzzed her awake. The argument wasn't over. It was just beginning.

"Mom, she's going to fight this."

"I know." Mom realized she was still holding the baking cylinder. She turned and put the bread back into the oven. She set it to warm for two hours, then bake. Finally she floated back to me. She put her hands on my shoulders. "Let me handle Jill."

"When?"

"First let's see if we can get the rock we need." She swam forward.

I followed.

Jill was glowering at her display and muttering epithets under her breath.

"The Flyby Knights?" Mom asked.

Jill grunted. "They're still saying, 'Take it or leave it.' "

Mom thought for a moment. "Okay. Send them a message. Tell them we found another rock."

"We have?"

"No, we haven't. But they don't know that. Tell them thanks a lot, but we won't need their asteroid after all. We don't have time to negotiate anymore. Instead, we'll cut Janis in half."

"And what if they say that's fine with them? Then what?"

"Then we'll cut Janis in half."

Jill made that noise she makes, deep in her throat. "It's all slush, you can't cut it in half. If we have to go crawling back, what's to keep them from raising their price? This is a lie. They're not stupid. They'll figure it out. We can't do it. We have a reputation."

"That's what I'm counting on—that they'll believe our reputation—that you'd rather cut your money rock in half than make a deal with a man."

Jill gave Mom one of those sideways looks that always meant a lot more than anything she could put into words, and certainly not when I was around.

"Send the signal," Mom said. "You'll see. It doesn't matter how much nickel is in that lump; it just isn't cost-effective for them to mine it. So it's effectively worthless. The only way they're going to get any value out of it in their lifetimes is to let us throw it away. From their point of view, it's free money, whatever they get. They'll be happy to take half a percent if they can get it."

Jill straightened her arms against the console and stretched herself out while she thought it out. "If it doesn't work, they won't give us any bargaining room."

"They're not giving us any bargaining room now."

Jill sighed and shrugged, as much agreement as she ever gave. She turned it over in her head a couple of times, then pressed for record. After the signal was sent, she glanced over at Mom and said, "I hope you know what you're doing."

"Half the rock is still more than enough. We can print up some reflectors and burn it in half in four months. That'll put us two months ahead of schedule, and we'll have the slings and tether already in place."

Jill considered it. "You won't get as big a burn-off. The tail won't be as long or as bright."

Mom wasn't worried. "We can compensate for that. We'll drill light pipes into the ice, fractioning the rock and increasing the effective surface area. We'll burn out the center. As long as we burn off fifty tons of ice per hour, it doesn't matter how big the comet's head is. We'll still get an impressive tail."

"So why didn't we plan that from the beginning?"

"Because I was hoping to deliver the head of the comet to Luna and sell the remaining ice. We still might be able to do that. It just won't be as big a payday." Mom turned to me.

"The braking problem on that will be horrendous." Jill closed her eyes and did some math in her head. "Not really cost-effective. We'll be throwing away more than two-thirds of the remaining mass. And if you've already cut it in half—"

"It's not the profit. It's the publicity. We'd generate a lot of new business. We could even go public."

Jill frowned. "You've already made up your mind, haven't you?"

Mom swam around to face Jill. "Sweetheart, our child is ready to be a grown-up."

"She wants to be a boy."

"So what? Are you going to stop loving her?"

Jill didn't answer. Her face tightened.

In that moment, something crystallized—all the vague unformed feelings of a lifetime suddenly snapped into focus with an enhanced clarity. Everything is tethered to everything else. With people, it isn't gravity or cables—it's money, promises, blood, and feelings. The tethers are all the words we use to tie each other down. Or up. And we whirl around and around, just like asteroids cabled together.

We think the tethers mean something. They have to. Because if we cut them, we go flying off into the deep dark unknown. But if we don't cut them . . . we just stay in one place, whirling around forever. We don't go anywhere.

I could see how Mom and Jill were tethered by an ancient promise.

And Mom and I were tethered by blood. And Jill and I—were tethered by jealousy. We resented each other's claim on Mom. She had something I couldn't understand. And I had something she couldn't share.

I wondered how much Mom understood. Probably everything. She was caught in the middle between two whirling bodies. Someone was going to have to cut the tether. That's why she accepted this contract—so we could go to the marble. She'd known it from the beginning. We were going to ride Janis all the way to Earth.

And somewhere west of the terminator, as we entered our braking arc, I'd cash out my shares and cut the tethers. I'd be off on my own course then—and Mom and Jill would fly apart. No longer bound together, they'd whirl out and away on their own inevitable trajectories. I wondered which of them would be a comet streaked across Earth's black sky.

> *Take me to the light*
> *Take me to the mystery of life*
> *Take me to the light*
> *Let me see the edges of the night*
> *—from "Body Slave" by Janis Ian*

East of the Sun, West of Acousticville

by JUDITH TARR

Welcome to the place where time stands still
You can drink your blues neat or on ice
You can pay your dues any way you like
Welcome to Acousticville
—from "Welcome to Acousticville" by Janis Ian

THE music had stopped.

The sun came up over the bluffs and shot long rays across the dry land. In the worn and grimy buildings below the red cliffs, where the plaint of strings had never paused, there was silence. The wind blew without a sound. It sent weeds tumbling down the long, long road, but they tumbled mutely, with no hiss or skitter of thorns on the cracked asphalt.

It wasn't much of an afterlife to look at, unless your dream of heaven is a Motel Six. The inmates were so drunk on music that they could be in the Garden of Allah and never notice, except for an occasional grab at a houri. The music poured through them out of the empty sky and the barren desert. It soaked into the paper-thin walls and lapped over the grubby carpets, and the pool overflowed with the pure article. The dead swam in it for inspiration, and for the high.

The whole world was music. This morning it had stopped. The silence was as deep as eternity.

One by one the dead came out of their rooms. Their eyes were blinking and their steps were slow. The visitors in the annex, the little brown men and women who had come up the road at about the time I came down it, tried to speak but found that their voices were gone.

I'd been sitting on the bare hillside, watching the sun come up. I was still new to death, and still surprised that there were sunrises here, and nights with stars.

This was not supposed to be my afterlife. Mine was a green isle and a cold ocean. But I died in the desert between sea and sea, and woke in the dry land. The long road had brought me here. The music snared me, and I stayed until my feet got around to breaking me loose and carrying me on again. It wasn't a music I'd ever known or thought I cared to know, but I'd been high on it ever since I saw that ugly little place under the red cliffs and heard the beauty that came out of it.

There had always been a lull just at dawn. New songs were born then, and came up with the light. This morning the sun brought only stillness.

I came down from the hill as quickly as I could. My feet made no noise, no matter how hard I scuffed or stamped. Sound had been sucked out of the world.

All the dead were out by the pool. The water was flat and still. They were dead, but they lived by sound. Once it was taken away from them, they were only mute shades. Some of them had already begun to fade. I could see the cracked wall through old Willie's shirt.

I looked around for the Lady, but there was no sign of her. Sometimes she coiled like a cobra by the pool, and the little brown people worshiped her. Other times she sat behind the counter in the lobby, looking as ordinary and faintly seedy as anybody else, except for the suggestion of scales on her arms and cheeks, and her long, sharp teeth when she smiled. When I first met her, she was naked except for her long iron-gray hair, and she spoke in a slow Southwestern drawl with a hint of a hiss. She checked me in and gave me my key and finished her transformation, slithering away toward the pool and her congregation.

Snakes are deaf, they say. I'd thought it strange to find one as the keeper of this place. Now I wondered what she had to do with this plague of silence.

She wasn't there to ask. Someone had had the bright idea to raid the office for paper and pencils. I was surprised that he'd found any. He brought back an armful and passed them out to whoever would take them.

Not everybody would, or could. Some of them refused. Others were already too faded. If they tried to take a pad or a pencil, their hands passed helplessly through.

Wild-haired Jimi had got hold of an artist's sketchpad. Maybe he'd conjured it out of the air; I wouldn't put it past him. On it he'd written in purple crayon, MUST ACT FAST. LOOK WHO'S FADING.

I'd seen. All the old ones, the great ones, were losing substance. It wasn't just Willie. Furry's edges were fraying. Libba and Sippie were hanging on, but I could see they did it by pure willpower.

One of the young ones, whose name I hadn't learned, drew the question in the dust for all of us: WHY?

No one knew. From the oldest to the newest, which would be me, we had no faintest idea. We didn't even know what was happening, let alone how to undo it.

I scanned faces. Others were doing the same. I looked to the youngest ones, wondering if one of them had brought in a curse. There was a wild red-haired vixen who could sing the vultures down out of the sky, and a thin and quiet man with silver dollars on his eyelids, and a crowd of forgettable faces that, I'd been assured while their voices could still be heard, were determinedly mediocre. They were happy just to be here. I couldn't imagine them cursing the music out of this place.

The guests from the annex had supplied themselves with brushes and inks and stone palettes. They were painting on the deck by the pool. I drifted with some of the others to see what they were doing.

A procession of birds and animals and human figures, or parts of them, marched up and down the deck. The guest who looked oldest painted fastest, and his paintings twitched and wriggled into life while I stared at them. They shaped themselves into words.

This is a curse. We know the smell of it. Rahotep felt it in the night, creeping like a snake through the dark. We were unable to stop it. It is very strong.

I spread my hands and widened my eyes, inviting him to explain. His brush flew over the tile. *We know curses. We invented them. You must track this one to its source and break it, or this afterlife will dissolve into silence.*

Jimi was standing next to me with his tablet. CAN YOU HELP? he wrote.

Maybe some of us can, the visitor answered.

DO IT, Jimi wrote, pressing so hard the crayon splintered.

I saw Libba and Sippie behind him. They were still hanging on—literally: they were arm in arm. The red-haired woman and the man with coins on his eyes stood with them.

I felt myself moving closer to them. My feet were unsticking, now the music wasn't holding me. I could think of moving on, but at the same time I could feel the determination rising. I wanted to find the thing that had killed the music. I needed to know why, and how to get it back.

We decided it just like that, or it was decided for us. It was never easy to tell in this life after death. The visitors settled just as quickly: they exchanged glances, some nodded and some frowned, and the old man stood up and stowed his inks and brushes in a bag and tucked his palette under his arm.

He was ready; so were we. We didn't need food or drink, except for the pleasure. Nobody had a change of clothes. Jimi had his guitar. The rest of us were empty-handed.

I looked back once after we left the pool. Its water level had dropped a good two inches since the last time I looked, and the people beside it were noticeably faded. Time meant nothing here, but they were fast running out of it.

✹✭✹

The little brown man put himself in the lead. He seemed to know where he was going. The rest of us shrugged and straggled along after.

The road ran along the bluff and then headed up it, zigzagging from ledge to ledge. I'd come the other way, off the dunes. This was a rougher country. The track was steep and narrow; in some places it was little more than a series of hand- and footholds.

Hunger and thirst couldn't touch us, but the deep ache in the bones could. We were all glad to come to the top and look out over a wilderness of rock and sand and empty sky. We were the only things here that lived or had once been alive.

Sound came back as we trudged away from the bluff. At first I was barely aware of the whisper of wind in my ears. Then I realized that my feet were crunching in the gravel. My toe caught a shard of rock and sent it clattering off to the side. None of us breathed unless we wanted to, and our hearts didn't beat, but I heard Jimi gust a sigh, then let out a whoop that echoed off the rocks.

He unslung his guitar and attacked the strings. His hands were shaking like a junkie's.

The strings were dead. He opened his mouth to sing. A strangled croak came out.

We had sound, but the music was still gone. Jimi was gray and shaking, but I thought it was a hopeful sign. Whatever had cursed us hadn't been able to affect the rest of this country. We might even get the music back, if we traveled far enough.

✹✭✹

The brown man's name was Ay. It was the simplest sound in the world, and could be either an affirmation or a cry of pain. He claimed not to be the oldest of the world's dead, but he was old. His people had learned long ago to travel through the afterlives, learning and studying and sometimes even teaching if anyone was looking to know what they knew. They knew a lot, after all this time.

He didn't know what had cursed us. "A curse leaves a trace," he said, "somewhat like a smell and somewhat like a slug's trail. Sometimes we can tell who cast it, but for the most part we settle for tracking it to its source."

"You could scry," Sippie said. I don't know what she sounded like in life, but in death her voice was like warm molasses. Even if she couldn't sing, when she talked, her words were full of music.

"We could scry," Ay agreed, "but we would only see a little way ahead."

"Do you know that?" Jimi said. "Have you tried?"

Ay shrugged.

There was no water or ink to scry with, and no crystal ball, and none forthcoming, either. All we had was dust and rock. Sippie got down on her knees and gathered a handful of pebbles and cast them. They fell in the shape of an arrow pointing in the direction we were going. Insofar as there were points of the compass here, we could say it was north—left hand to the sunset, right hand to the sunrise.

Sippie sighed. Libba and I helped her up. Ay was already walking where the pebbles pointed.

★ ★

The sun was following us. It had been midway up the sky when we started, but once the sound came back it stopped, hanging directly overhead. It stayed there as we went on, never moving.

Ay stopped suddenly. I'd been hearing it for a while, and thinking the wind was blowing loud in the rocks and spires ahead of us. Completely without warning, the ground dropped away in front of us. We looked down into a pit so deep its bottom was lost in darkness, writhing with what looked like a million million ants, and every one of them screaming.

"Malebolge," said the red-haired woman. It was the first word I'd heard her say.

"The pit of hell," Jimi said. He looked from side to side and then ahead. There was no end to it in any direction. "What do we do? Fly over it?"

"Pass through it," Ay said. He didn't seem as light-hearted as usual. "The only way out is down."

"Oh, no," said Jimi. "I'm not going down there. That's hell, man. I didn't get out of it just so I could end up at the bottom of it."

"There is no other way," said Ay. "Unless you would see the music die."

Jimi shuddered so hard his teeth rattled. "There isn't any other way?"

"None," Ay said.

✦✦✦

It was a long way down. As long as we stayed on the road we were safe. The dead couldn't see us; the watchers were blind to us, or didn't care that we were there.

They were every bit as terrifying as I'd heard. They towered over the damned souls. No two of them were exactly alike, but they had a certain common theme of horns and fangs. They amused themselves by plucking individual souls off the rocks and pulling them apart like beetles, nibbling tender bits and tossing the rest. The scattered parts would scuttle toward one another, meld together, and grow into human shape again, screaming louder than ever.

"Don't look," Ay said, too late for me. It was all I could do to stay on the road. It ran in a knife-edge down along the tiers of hell, with sudden switchbacks and ledges that looked down sheer cliffs into measureless immensity.

I wasn't counting levels, but there seemed to be nine. Somewhere along about the seventh from the top, the road came to an abrupt end. An enormous beast squatted across it. It looked a little bit like the infernal guards and somewhat like a three-headed dog, but it was hard to tell exactly what it was: it blurred whenever I tried to focus. All I could be sure of was that it was big.

It spoke on so low a note that I felt it more in my stomach than in my ears. "Will you pass?"

"We will pass," Ay replied.

"Pay," said the beast.

"There is no toll on this road," Ay said.

"Now there is," the beast said.

We looked at one another. The only money any of us had was the nameless man's two silver dollars. He made no move to offer them.

"What will you take?" Jimi asked the beast.

It growled almost below the threshold of sound. "Souls," it said in a long sigh.

"For what? To live here?"

The beast didn't answer.

The red-haired woman pushed past us. She looked up into that monstrous face and said, "I'll stay with you if you let the others go."

"You can't do that," Jimi said.

She wasn't listening. She reached way, way up to touch the end of the beast's nose. "You don't eat souls. Do you? You're lonely. Whoever put you here never thought of what you wanted. I'll stay with you. I'll sing to you when the music comes back. I'll—"

The beast shuddered. The road shook; a crack opened in the cliff.

"The way is not around you," the woman said. "It's through you. I'll stay, if you let the others go on."

"Why?" said Jimi. "What are you—"

"Just go," she said. "Don't look around you. Don't look back."

The beast opened its mouth in a yawn as wide as the pit of Malebolge. The stink of it was even worse than the stink of hell. There were things moving in it, small pale writhing things. They were screaming.

I'd never thought I'd see anything that made hell look like a better choice. But there was no choice now. Ay was already walking through the gate of ivory fangs. Libba and Sippie followed, and the silver-dollar man. Jimi and I were the last, except for the red-haired woman.

She caught hold of us both and pitched us into the beast's maw. Just before it snapped shut on us, I saw her red hair streaming in the wind from hell, and her eyes all wild. For the briefest instant I could swear I heard her voice singing. If she'd won back the music, and taken it away from us—

We fell together onto a floor so cold it froze the blood in our nonexistent veins. It was ice, colder than cold, stretching as far as the eye could see. Things were frozen in it—things that had once been alive. There was no sign of the pit or the hordes of the damned. The beast and the red-haired woman were gone.

We untangled ourselves and helped each other up. We slipped and slid on the ice, but nobody fell.

I looked up. A wall loomed over us, rising sheer toward the darkness overhead. It took me a while to understand what my eyes were telling me.

It wasn't a wall. It was a thing like a man, but not a man. I couldn't have told its size exactly, but it was immense. It was frozen in the ice from the midsection downward. I could see the huge hairy navel, big as a cave, and the enormous bulk of the torso. Far above us, I just made out the jut of a bearded chin.

"Great Satan," Sippie said. It wasn't an oath—Sippie never swore. She was naming the thing in the ice.

I knew the way out of Malebolge. I'd read the book, too.

"He better not have crabs," Jimi said.

I wondered if Malebolge had ever heard a soul laugh before. I went down first, laughing harder than the joke ever deserved. Then Libba caught it, then Sippie. Jimi and Ay rolled on the ice. Only the silver-dollar man stayed expressionless.

There was an advantage in being dead: no hiccups. We stopped laughing eventually, and we all felt better for it.

★★★

There weren't any crabs. There was a stink that, Sippie said, reminded her of an old billy goat. I didn't even want to know what parts of the Devil we were climbing over. The thick goaty hair gave good handholds.

There was just enough space between the body and the ice for us to crawl one by one. I was in the middle between Libba and Jimi. The silver-dollar man went last. I caught myself missing the red-haired woman, whose name I'd never heard. I might never know why she'd done what she did. Sometimes there isn't any good reason for sacrifice. It just is.

I hoped she did find her music, and was singing the beast to sleep.

We climbed out of the stinking cave into daylight so bright it blinded us. There was grass under us. The green smell of it slowly overrode the stink.

I looked back. Vast hairy legs and cloven hooves thrust out of the field like a weird tree. The Devil's clawed hands were hillocks half-overgrown with grass.

I took a few seconds to wonder what would happen if he ever broke free. Then I left it for nightmares and turned away.

Dante found Purgatory on the other end of the Devil. We found something a little bit different. It wasn't a hell at all, but as afterlives go it was crashingly dull—unless your idea of heaven is Sunday in the park with Socrates. Personally, I preferred the Motel Six.

The road ran down through perfectly mown lawns to the mani-cured bank of a river. There was a marble pier there, and a boat tied to it.

All the way to the river, we passed groups of the dead sitting in groves or in little temples or beside limpid pools. Many of them had harps or flutes beside them, but here as everywhere, the music had gone mute.

The boat was the first inkling that this was not as tame an after-life as I'd thought. It was a rickety-looking thing with all the paint worn off the sides, and weeds trailing just below the waterline.

The boatman was even more ramshackle than his boat. He was

old and his beard was long. He wore a long coat of no color in particular, and a hat with a wide brim pulled low over his forehead. I could just see the tip of his long hooked nose, and his eyes gleaming out of the shadow like an animal's. His hands on the oars were gaunt but strong, with thick ropy veins and corded wrists.

We all stood on the pier, knowing there was another toll to pay, but only one of us had what he needed. I looked down into the water and wished I hadn't. It was jet black and oily and much too thick. There were things in it, coiling under the surface.

There was no swimming that, and no getting around it either. The trail of the curse went on downstream.

The silver-dollar man took the coins from his eyes. They opened, blinking, and looked around as if they had minds of their own. They were fairly ordinary brown eyes, but there was a light in them that made me shiver under my skin. His face was different with them in it: much less inoffensive, and just a little bit disturbing. This wasn't a man I'd want behind me in an alley at night.

He flipped one coin in the air, and then the other. In an instant he was juggling them, round and round, from hand to hand. He juggled faster and faster, until they were a silver blur. Coins spawned coins as they spun through the air, splitting out of the original pair, gleaming and spinning.

Jimi shot out a hand. The silver wheel fell apart with a sound that almost—almost—made me think of bells and chimes.

In Jimi's hand were half a dozen silver coins. The originals had been American silver dollars, but the eagles on these had mutated. They looked like owls now, with big staring eyes, and the English words had turned to Greek.

The boatman took them without a word and let us onto the boat. It never rocked and never sank under us. Only the living had weight.

The silver-dollar man was the last to get on. Even while he was finding a place to sit, the boatman dug in oars and rowed away from the bank. I could see the pier on the other side, jutting out from a shadowy shore, but he rowed us straight downstream. I could almost see the curse like a rope tied around the prow.

I knew better than to look down into the water again, but I caught myself doing just that, leaning against the side of the boat and hanging my head over. It was like a drug. I didn't want it, but I couldn't stop myself.

"This water is forgetfulness."

Libba's voice was soft and full of sleep. Or maybe it wasn't her voice. No one else was talking.

"Drink," she said, or whoever was speaking through her, "and abandon memory. Forget fear, forget pain. Forget your very self."

"I won't," I said, but I couldn't take my eyes off the water. "I can't forget the music. I never knew about it while I was alive. I stumbled on it because I was lost. It gave me back myself again. I don't want to lose it."

"Forgetfulness is peace," said the voice that no longer sounded like Libba's. It was like water sliding past the boat's sides, and wind whispering in my ears. "Forgetfulness is bliss. Nirvana. Heaven. Sweet oblivion. Music is pain. Music is sorrow. Music rips at the heart and sickens the soul."

"Music is life," I said thickly. I was hanging out over the water. I knew that if I touched it, I'd be lost. I watched my hand, the fingers fading even while I stared at them, stretching toward that black and gleaming surface.

The things under it were waiting. I could feel them, their hunger. They ate memories and swallowed souls.

Hands pulled me back into the boat. The water heaved; the boat rocked. I hung on, and the others hung on to me. The boatman paid no attention to any of it, except to steady the oars.

We were going mostly downstream, but little by little we edged toward the opposite bank. The green and sunlit country was far behind us. We glided through a landscape of shadows, with the banks rising gradually into barren cliffs.

The river was narrowing. We were in a gorge as deep as Malebolge. It was so deep that the sky had gone dark, and stars shone in it, flat and hard.

The things under the boat had not gone away. I could feel them swimming just below it, and occasionally brushing against it with a soft, ominous bump. They weren't going to stop until they'd taken one of us.

I was dead weight. I wasn't a musician and I wasn't a guide. The others could easily spare me.

They were all watching, trying to protect me from myself. Except . . .

Sippie was in the stern of the boat. I could barely see her; she'd faded while I was absorbed in my own troubles. She was leaning over the side as I'd done, with her face as blank as mine must have been.

I couldn't get to her in time. Even if I did, I might not be able to save her. She'd gone translucent, and her edges were fraying. I dived through the barrier of bodies, grabbing wildly.

She slipped over the side and sank without a sound. The water rose up to meet her. I saw how she spread her arms, how she embraced the things that came to feed on her.

My howl echoed against the walls of the gorge. "No! *No!* It should have been me!"

"Not yet." The echoes ricocheted off one another, filling the gorge with clamor, but I still heard Libba's voice, as soft as it was. "She was nothing without the music. She was almost gone—but she made her passing count for something."

Libba wasn't very solid, either, but she was still holding on. The light grew slowly on her face. The walls were drawing wider apart and sinking little by little. The stars had faded. The sky was blank and blue again, and the sun was hanging in it. The river opened into a broad slow stream. The right-hand bank was green; the left was bleak and bare, an unrelieved expanse of sand and rock stretching away to a thin line of horizon.

Ay sighed as if a weight had lifted from his shoulders. The river had changed after it left the gorge: there were still things in it, and they were deadly, but they were cleaner somehow. The dark things were placated; they hadn't followed us. Here were crocodiles and hippopotamuses and fish that fed on drowned victims, but nothing that would render a soul into nothingness.

As the boat turned in toward the bank, I had a brief and unbecoming thought that Ay had led us here just to get himself home. But he could have done that on his own, without dragging us along with him.

I could feel the curse pulling us. It was getting stronger, and I was becoming more sensitive to it. Sometimes, out of the corner of my eye, I could see it.

We were closer than we'd been to the source, but no nearer to understanding it than when we started. We left the boat with relief, and I for one didn't look back to see what became of it.

***

This was a peculiar country. A thin line of lush green followed the bank of the river. All around it was desert. Wild things lived in the red land: hawks overhead, lions and jackals below. People lived among the green.

And they did live—more than in any afterlife I knew of. They ate, slept, even procreated. People tilled the rich black earth of the fields by hand and with oxen, and sailed on the river in brightly painted boats, and paraded down the roads in princely processions. I'd never seen such light as there was here, or such color, or such a hum of earthly activity.

I would have liked to stay here, to be alive, even if the faces were strange and the way of living was ancient and there was no music. What kept me going, I didn't really know. Maybe I was just stubborn.

We followed a wide smooth road to a place of blindingly white walls. The way up to it was lined with sphinxes. There were colossal statues on either side of the gate. One was of a man with a jackal's head. The other was a man in mummy's wrappings, wearing a tall crown and holding a crook and a flail.

The jackal's eyes opened as we came closer. The man's stayed closed, but I could feel him watching us.

The road went on inside the gate, opening into a square surrounded by columns and crowded with more of the immense statuary. At the far end was a pyramid with a hundred steps, and at the top of it a throne. The throne was big enough to seat one of the guardians from the gate, but it was empty. Something sat at the foot of it, waiting for us.

It was small on the scale of that place, but when we were close enough to get a good look at it, we could see that it was twice as tall as the tallest of us. Ay went down on his face in front of it.

I couldn't move. I was too busy staring. It sat upright on hippopotamus haunches, but its head was a crocodile's and its arms were the forepaws of a lion. A lion's mane flowed over its shoulders. Its eyes were human, quiet and rather sad. They made its face more alarming rather than less.

"Ammut," Ay said, his voice echoing up from the ground. "Eater of Souls. Have mercy on us. Help us if you will. We are seeking—we need—"

"We know what you seek," the creature said in a long reverberating hiss.

Jimi pushed his way to the front and faced the creature. "You know? You really do? So tell us. What are we chasing after? What happened to the music?"

"It was eaten," said the Eater of Souls.

"Why?"

Ammut did not answer.

Jimi wasn't afraid of anything. He planted himself at the creature's feet and glared up the whole bizarre length of it. "You know why. You can tell us. Then we'll be gone. What are you afraid of? What are we letting ourselves in for?"

Ammut was still silent. I thought Jimi would haul off and smash his guitar on it, but Ay stood up and laid his hand on Jimi's arm. His eyes were the same as Ammut's—exactly. "Grief," he said.

"I know we're in for grief," Jimi said crossly. "Why?"

"Grief," Ay said again.

"Whose?" I thought to ask.

"Hers."

He sagged like an empty sack. When we picked him up again, the spirit that had been in him was gone. He was Ay again, the guide who could see the trail of a curse.

That trail led straight down below Ammut's big round hippo-potamus feet. The base of the throne was a door, and the door opened on darkness. The curse was down there somewhere.

I could feel it. I could almost see it. And yet I had no desire to follow it into the dark. It would have been oh so easy to stay here in this afterlife, where everything was so bright and so clear. Nothing was forcing me. I didn't have to go.

When the rest moved forward, I moved with them. I couldn't stop now, even for this afterlife. I was bound as the rest were, even if was the end of me. We all walked under the arch of Ammut's legs, down into the pyramid.

✦★✦

The light went out behind us. We walked in musty darkness, tramping down a long straight passage.

Slowly the darkness lightened. The light had an orange tinge, which grew stronger as we came closer. After an endless, leg-cramping while, we came to the bottom.

A lake of fire surged and seethed in front of us. A thin rim of shore ran around it. We walked in single file, feeling the heat crisping our faces and hands. The flames hissed at us. I could hear words and fragments of sentences in those bloodless voices.

The shore was black glass, and slippery. It was hard going. Ay, in front as always, moved slower and slower. He hadn't been himself since Ammut's spirit possessed him. He was thin and pale, and he looked terribly old.

I saw how he let go. He just stopped, and his foot slipped. Jimi, right behind him, caught him before he fell.

He twisted in Jimi's hands. His face had contorted out of all humanity. He struck with long thin fangs. Jimi recoiled against the wall. The scaled and limbless thing that had been Ay dived into the lake of fire and disappeared with a flick of snaky tail.

The four of us who were left stood on the glassy shore. The lake was a circle; if we followed the rim, we'd end up back where we began. Our guide was gone. The trail of the curse ran right—ran straight—

I almost laughed. Of course it ran straight to the middle of the lake and then plunged down, just as the Ay-snake had. He had been guiding us after all. He'd led us to this, and that would be the end of us.

"It's there," Libba said as if she'd read my thoughts. "It's down there, at the bottom of the lake."

"Just when you think it can't get worse," Jimi said, but he didn't sound particularly depressed. Ever since we'd come through Malebolge, he'd been almost happy. The beast had eaten his fear. Maybe he didn't even care anymore that he'd lost his music.

I couldn't let myself think that way. "I'll go," I said. "I'll swim the lake. I'll bring back the music if I can."

"We'll all do it," Libba said. She'd stopped fading, and her voice was strong. "I know what this is. It's purification. I wouldn't mind being pure."

"I would," Jimi said, "but I mind losing the music more."

He grabbed Libba's hand and my hand. I had just enough time to grab the silver-dollar man before Jimi pulled us all over the edge into the lake.

★★

It hurt. It hurt behind imagination. It seared the flesh clean off my bones and charred the bones to ash. It stripped my soul bare. Every tiny flaw and fault, every sin, every failing, every word I'd said that had done any least bit of harm, flared up and puffed into smoke.

And all the while my soul was flaming out like a meteor, I was falling down through the lake of fire, stretched tight between Jimi and the silver-dollar man. They were burning as brightly as I was. Libba was a nova, blinding and beautiful.

We fell out of fire into gray twilight. All around us was a flat and marshy country interlaced with skeins of rivers. We were all still there. The others were clearer somehow, not transparent exactly, but they looked as if they'd been cleaned inside and out.

I felt and must have looked as brand-new as they did. Jimi was more Jimi than ever, with his wild hair and his big guitar, and Libba was wonderful—beautiful. I'd almost have said they didn't need the music. They *were* what it struggled so long and hard to be.

Silver-dollar man was the only one who looked charred around the edges. The fire had had to go deep with him, and burn hot, to get rid of whatever wrongs he'd done. His face had fallen in and his eyes were too wide and too bright. His clothes hung loose on a frame gone gaunt.

I let go of him and wiped my hand on my jeans. It was a failing, after I'd been cleansed of so many, but I couldn't help it. This was—had been—a man I'd never have wanted to know.

He'd come with us through hell and worse, and he'd never abandoned or betrayed us. I had to give him credit for that. He wouldn't still be here if he wasn't supposed to be.

We'd come through to this place at dawn. Day grew as we picked a direction and went in it—following the sense of the curse, which was so strong now that it was a compulsion. Mosquitoes whined. Birds chirped and skreeked and cawed. This was like Ay's afterlife—irresistibly alive.

This was a very, very old place. Older than Malebolge, older than Ammut's kingdom. It was so old that its souls had completely forgotten they were dead. They lived perpetually the lives they'd known in the morning of the world.

We came out of the marshes to a city of low mud-brick walls and squat towers, and rising out of them the tapered steps of a ziggurat. There were houses outside the walls, reed huts inhabited by short, round-headed, stocky people with very round and prominent eyes. They were fishermen and farmers, and some were artisans: I saw one building a two-wheeled cart and another molding a short, round-headed, stocky image out of river clay.

They stared at us as we went by. Visitors must be rare here, considering how difficult it was to get this far. Their stares weren't hostile, and a few even smiled. They weren't afraid, then.

Even here, the music was silent. They had instruments, but no one played them. No one sang in the fields or on the boats. The rhythms of ordinary speech were all they had, here as everywhere else.

Somehow I'd ended up in the lead. The thing we'd followed so far was like a rope around my neck, pulling me down the road and into the old, old city.

It was a city of circles, each one with a gate, and at each gate a guardian. The people who lived there came and went at will, as far as I could tell, but strangers could only go one way, and that was through the guarded gates.

There were nine of them. Nine was an important number in the afterlives. The first guard was almost human except for his long white fangs. The second had eyes like a cat, round and yellow and sly. The third had a goat's horns curling over its shoulders. By the sixth, there was nothing human about it.

They wanted payment for passage. I satisfied the first with the buckle from my belt, which was a Green Man in pewter. The second took silver-dollar man's snakeskin boots. The third got Jimi's Peace medallion.

The fourth stretched out claws toward his guitar. "Not in this afterlife," Jimi said, pulling back hard. "Here, my shirt's silk. Feel."

The guardian felt, and purred. Jimi handed the shirt over with a little regret—it was a fine shirt, and silk wasn't common anywhere in hell, except in one of the lower levels of Malebolge, where the worms wove their cocoons in the mouths of princes.

There were still five to go. Libba took the lead in front of the fifth, offering her necklace of pearls, each one like a little moon. The sixth got her earrings, which had matched the necklace. She sighed when she gave them up. She'd had them from a lover, and memories went with them. The beast swallowed them whole and belched, and let us by.

The seventh guardian eyed us hungrily and made it clear that it would be happy to take one of us in toll. Libba unfastened her belt with its mother-of-pearl buckle and draped it over the scaly neck. The creature ground its fangs, but it couldn't keep us from going on. Its brother, the eighth guardian, took Libba's pretty red shoes with their Cuban heels.

The ninth was worst of all. It licked its lips as it looked at us, and its claws flexed on the baked tiles of the threshold. It wanted a human sacrifice, and Libba's dress just wasn't enough. Her body, now, dark and sweet . . .

Jimi threw himself between them just as the creature reached for Libba. Libba wasn't making any move to stop it. Jimi thrust his guitar into those hungry talons, his big old D-18 with its sound that had been so deep, so sweet. "Take it," Jimi said. His voice cracked. "Take it! Let us go!"

Jimi without his D-18 was half a shade, but the guardian was satisfied. It opened the gate into the city's heart.

☀★★

She coiled there in her snakiest form, the Lady whom we'd lost and all but forgotten. Chains wound around and around her. A smaller snake, bright as if made of gold, curled up against her. It raised its head and looked at us with Ay's gentle dark eyes.

There was a chair beyond them, and a woman sitting in it. She was naked, and she was an old-fashioned beauty, what people would call fat in my day, but Rubens would have figured for just about right. Her hair was black and thick and fell in waves over her shoulders and down along her breasts to her wide round hips and her solid haunches. Her face was wide in the cheeks and narrow in the chin, and her eyes were wide, round, and very, very angry. So angry that she could curse the music right out of the afterlives and keep it imprisoned here, chained inside the body of a large and gleaming cobra.

A hiss filled that low round hall. It did not come from the Lady. The dark woman sprang up from her throne and lunged at us.

She bowled Jimi over as if he hadn't even been there, and blew past Libba and me to fall on the silver-dollar man. He spun around and tried to run. She caught him by the arm and stopped him short. They whirled in a crazy dance, powered by his fear and her rage.

They stopped so suddenly his head snapped back. If he hadn't already been dead, his neck would have broken. He stood swaying while she gripped him hard. "You," she said. "*You* dared come here."

For the first time I heard him speak. "I came for the music," he said. "Who are you? What do you have against me?"

She threw him down. He sprawled on the patterned brick of the floor. "You don't know me?"

"Not in this afterlife," he said.

"I know you," she said, low and shaking with hate. "I know every face of you, from every age. Every song you sang. Every life you ruined. Every hurt you caused, to heart or soul or body. And every time—every time—you thought no price too high. Not if everyone else paid it, so that you could have your music."

"You never paid anything for me," he said.

"I was your lover," she said, "your wife, your child. When you drank, you beat me. When the music wouldn't come, or the gigs were few and far between, you took my money and left me to starve. When the itch was on you, no matter if I was your lover or your daughter, you took me as you pleased. It was the music, you said. It made you do this. It twisted you into a monster."

"Drugs killed me," Jimi said, "but I never thought about cursing them. Everybody's bad, lady. Everybody hurts everybody else. What's so bad that it's worth taking away the music?"

She turned on him. Her eyes glared green like an animal's. "No one thing," she said. "It's everything—all of you. Every cursed one. But this one . . . he haunts every age. He wanders the afterlives, looking for a place to hide, because he knows that once I find him, I'll rend him in pieces."

"Tell us what he did to you," Libba said, more gentle than Jimi could ever be.

Words were not enough. The dark woman ripped open the fabric of the world and showed us.

We looked out as if through a window on a city newer than this one but much older than the ones I'd lived in when I was alive. He was young and smooth-skinned and dreamy with art. She was slimmer and taller than she seemed in this ancient afterlife, with an oval face and a long nose and long eyes that still, deep in them, told us who she was. They both had lived and lived again, together and apart, but this was the life that would make the difference.

Without anyone speaking them, I knew names. Inanna, Dumuzi. Astarte, Tammuz. Isis, Osiris. Eurydice, Orpheus. First he was a hunter, then a warrior, then a king. Then, fatefully and fatally, the music found him and possessed him.

He'd betrayed her before. She'd had him killed in one life, and seen him killed in others. He'd still loved her even when he handed her over to his enemies, and died saying the name she carried in that life.

In this life, he made songs about her. His music was dedicated to her. But the music was so strong and his soul so weak that he had to turn to wine to withstand it. Then he forgot that she was sitting at home waiting for him to bring their dinner, which he'd drunk away. When he did finally come home, at first she tried to be forbearing, then she broke down in tears, and finally, as the years went on, she told him what she thought of him. His music was better, more beautiful than ever, and people followed him and worshiped him, but every bit of it grew out of the rift between them.

He killed her. The story blamed it on snakebite, but it was a long night and too much wine and his voice breaking that did it. He couldn't sing. He drank himself half blind, and that barely numbed the shock. Then he went home and the house was empty and the lamps unlit. She'd told him that if he drank away one more night, he'd find exactly what he found.

He tracked her down. She hadn't gone far, only to a friend whose husband was slave to the music, too. He found them asleep and the husband gone, and he dragged her out without a word. By then his voice was not just broken, it was gone. The only music he could make was the percussion of fist on flesh and the snap of bone.

They said he went to Hades to find her, and made great sacrifices for her, but in the end he lost her. It was a nobler story than that hunt through the old Greek city at night, and the hell of pain he gave her, and death none too soon.

Her bloodied body lay in the street. He stood over it, gaping at it. Suddenly he dropped down to his knees. A raw howl ripped itself out of him, with nothing resembling music in it. It was her name, over and over: "Eurydice. Eurydice! *Eurydice!*"

***

In the oldest of the afterlives, the dark woman spoke through that remote and chilling sound. "Over and over," she said. "We lived it again and again. From life to life and age to age, the music broke me down and lifted you up. Whatever we had, it ruined. Whatever we did, it came between us. I was still your excuse, but the music was your mistress. You sang your love for me, even while you battered and betrayed me."

With a sweep of her hand, she made the window vanish. "Enough! I have had enough. The serpent that bit me, the music that destroyed me, is mine. I curse it. I silence it. I condemn it to oblivion."

"But, lady," Libba said in the silence after that great curse, "it's not the music's fault. You can't take it out of all the worlds, just because one man used it to ruin you."

"No?" said the dark woman. "Five thousand years. Lifetimes out of count. There will be no more. Music will not destroy me again."

"Then he'll find something else," Jimi said. "He's a junkie. He's hooked on bad karma. If he can't have music, he'll find another way to mess you up. And you'll let him, because you're as hooked as he is."

If I'd had any breath to hold, I would have held it. The dark woman was in deep denial. She had power, and she could blow him out of existence.

He didn't care. The music was gone because of her. Nothing she did to him could be worse than that.

The dark woman froze in place. She was so far gone in rage that she couldn't even move.

It was only a lull. I kept on what I'd been doing, which was to slide ever so slowly and ever so invisibly toward the Lady in her chains. I'd gone far enough to see that Ay was working away at them, tugging with his snaky jaws and pulling at one particular link. It had a weakness in it, a barely perceptible crack. The Lady had found it and cultivated it, expanding and contracting her body over and over until she must be one long aching muscle.

The dark woman was completely fixed on Jimi. I stopped by the Lady and hooked the toe of my boot in the weak link and started working at it. I was bigger and stronger than Ay, and I had more leverage. I could feel it gradually giving way.

The dark woman screamed. She was going to leap. Jimi bared all his teeth at her, daring her to do it. "Oh, you mad, you mad! You know that's the truth. It's not the music's fault. It's yours."

"*You!*" she shrieked. "You're another one of them! User, betrayer, destroyer of women. It's in you all, all tangled with the music."

"So," said Libba, still gently. "Where does that leave me? Men used me. They betrayed me. The music kept me alive. It saved me." She came around to face the dark woman, and just happened to stand between her and Jimi. "Music is what we make of it. We're what we are with or without it. It only makes us more of whatever it is."

"You, too," Jimi said. "It made you weaker. You couldn't stand up for yourself. He'd wreck your life, and you'd go on and start another one for him to wreck all over again."

"You tried to break the chain," Libba said, "but you did it by attacking the music. That won't solve anything. You can only change this by changing yourself. Maybe he won't change—he's as trapped as you've been—but you can. You can kick him aside and go on. Then you really will win. He really will lose you."

"The music is bigger than any of us," Jimi said. "You can use it just as much as he can. You can make or break him with it. You can keep it away from him—but don't punish the rest of us. We never did anything to you."

While they sang their chorus, I worked away at the Lady's chains. The link gave way almost too fast for me to catch it. Ay leaped on one of the broken ends and pulled. I helped him, and the Lady undulated her whole body.

The chains tightened, and I knew we'd made a terrible mistake. Then they snapped loose and dropped away.

The Lady rose up with her hood flared, taller and thicker than a man. Music flooded out of her, so strong and so pure that it knocked me flat.

I heard Jimi's jubilant wail and Libba's trill of joy—and the dark woman's scream, so dissonant that even that tide of music checked, appalled. The Lady struck like the cobra she seemed to be, but not at the dark woman.

She'd opened the window again, with the world of the living on the other side of it. She scooped up the dark woman and the fallen lover together and dropped them there.

They shrank into bubbles, floating in the air. She breathed on them. "Learn," she said. "Grow. Change. Remember—but forget wrath and vengeance. Be all new, and be clean."

The window closed. The dark woman and the silver-dollar man were gone. The room in this most ancient of places was eerily empty without them, but it was full of music.

We looked at each other. I still wasn't any more of a musician than I'd been, but my heart was full. Music needed listeners, too, people to hear it and love it and be moved by it. Libba and Jimi were singing together, not even bothering with words, just jamming with their voices.

Ay wore his more familiar shape again, the little brown man with the brush and palette. The Lady was still the queen of cobras. She grew until she was wide enough and long enough to carry us all. We climbed onto her back, gripping the glossy silver scales. She slipped right out of that afterlife and into another one altogether, where the sky was cloudless blue and the bluffs were blood red, and the Motel Six baked in the desert sun.

I could have got off on my green isle, or stopped by Ay's immortal Egypt. I didn't do either. The music had trapped me again. My feet were stuck in it, and I couldn't make myself want to unstick them.

The pool was full. The dead had their substance back again, and if a few were missing, their songs were still alive, still throbbing in the air. They sang for the red-haired woman, they sang for Sippie. They even sang for silver-dollar man, old Orpheus, Osiris, Tammuz, who would be born again, and maybe this time he'd get it right.

The sun set over the dry land. The old motel was rocking. Good food, good wine, and the best music in any world. I fell in the pool, and handsome Charlie fished me out, barely missing a beat.

I stood in the dusk under the stars, dripping music, and finally admitted it. This was my afterlife. I didn't choose it, it chose me, but I'd fought for it and saved it. I wouldn't get any parades for it, and maybe not a song in my honor, either, but I didn't care. It was an honor that I really couldn't refuse.

Jimi had scored himself another big old guitar, and he was wringing sounds out of it that I wouldn't have believed possible. "Welcome!" he sang in a high and melodic howl. It sucked us with it; we couldn't stop ourselves. We had to join in. "Welcome! Welcome! Welcome to Acousticville!"

Hopper Painting

by DIANE DUANE

I'm the one in the photograph
you painted yesterday
A cool reflection
of your promises and pain . . .
from "Hopper Painting" by Janis Ian

HE turned toward the window for the millionth time, hoping to see something go by outside, anything; anything from the outside world. But the street was bleak and empty, and as dark as it had ever been; the lighting inside was too harsh and insistent for him to see anything but his reflection in the window—his face, with empty eyes. They were almost a relief; at least the Other wasn't looking out of them.

At least the coffee was always hot.

He ducked his head over the cup and watched the steam rising. Anywhere else, that would have been a comfort. Anywhere else, that would have been a miracle: coffee that never got cold. Of course, it never really cooled enough to drink either. Or not comfortably. It always burned.

She turned to him, and said, "Sugar?"

As always, he had to stop to work out whether this was an endearment or a request for sweetener. Her red blouse burned itself to green afterimages in the fierce fluorescent light; her eyes, when he once more looked hopefully into them, were empty of any endearment. He sighed.

"Yes," he said, and pushed his cup a quarter inch toward her.

She looked at him curiously for a moment, then pushed the sugar dispenser toward him. "Your place or mine?" she said.

But she always said that. And there was never any lessening of the sense of something out in the dark, something alien and chilly, watching her say it; as if bloodless things turned to one another, rustling out there in the dry cold dark, and whispered one to the other in coldly amused reaction.

"Why are we here?" he said.

She looked blankly at him. "For coffee," she said.

How can she be so dumb? the back of his brain screamed. *How can anyone be so witless?* It was beyond him how any other human being could fail to feel the emptiness that lay beyond those windows, beating against them like the vacuum of space: unfriendly, dry and cold, seeking to suck all the life out of whatever lay on this side of the glass, in whatever passed for warmth.

Passed for it.

He had to try one more time. "What about us?" he said.

"Well, of course we have to find a nice place . . ." she said. "My mama would kick up such a stink if we moved into any place too small. It has to be at least two bedrooms. Three would be better."

"We don't need three," he said: but he knew she wouldn't hear him. For them to ever need three, they would have to get out of here . . . find a quiet place . . . and do . . .

But doing *that* meant change. And where they were, trapped in this water-clear amber, change was the last thing to be expected.

He glanced toward the glass again, flinching as he did it, like someone expecting a blow. It was always better to steel yourself for what you might see, just in case. Once again, past the form hunched between him and the window, he saw only his eyes, dark and empty-looking in the reflection, and he let out the breath he'd been holding.

"And then we can get some nice furniture," she said. She started going on about davenports and hassocks, and he looked away from the window, down at the table. *She can't help it,* he thought. *There's nothing left in her anymore but the talking, the empty sound that means she's not quite dead. If there's any consciousness in there at all, any more, it's doing what I do when I keep looking out and hoping I'll see something.* Something besides . . . But he didn't want to even think the name of the thing. It had heard him do that, once or twice before, and had answered to the calling; he'd been sorry for days afterward. Or what felt like days . . . for it was always four AM here, and never dawn.

He glanced up and in front of him at the guy behind the counter, who was standing there getting something out from underneath, or putting something away. It was a wonder how he never saw either of those actions actually happen, though something of the kind was always in train.

He's as stuck as we are, he thought, watching the counter guy. *More so, maybe. But who knows what's going on in his head? He never says anything but "Refill?"*

Beyond the counter guy, the cherrywood counter itself stretched away down to the end of the diner. He let his gaze travel down toward the end of it, stealthily, as if something there might see him and run away. Occasionally he had glimpsed something down there, a brief tangle of incongruous smoky shadows defying the shiny cold primary-color gleam of the diner —a swirl blue-gray and indefinite, as if a whole packageful of Phillies were smoking themselves. Indistinct through the smoke, it might be possible to catch a glimpse of someone else in the place beyond the two of them, the hunched man, and the counter guy. There sometimes seemed to be booths down there. A few times now he'd thought he'd seen a figure hunkered down in one of them, scribbling idly and then looking up through the smoke with a bleakly speculative expression, like a self-exiled poet hunting inspiration in the blue haze. A second later this figure always looked like part of the haze himself, the mere structure of a poem with none of the detail; a moment more and even that faint manifestation would go missing again, the blue shadows dissipating in the chilly bright air of the diner as if sucked up by the ventilation system. Shortly thereafter even the booths would be gone, leaving nothing but a cherrywood counter that seemed to stretch away to infinity if you let your attention linger too long upon it.

He let his gaze fall to the tabletop once more, dwelling as if he'd never seen it before on the utensil-scuffed grain of the wood, the sticky dried-out coffee spills blotched on it here and there, the scatter of sugar crystals from the cylindrical pressed-glass dispenser that always gave you half a teaspoon less sugar per pour than you wanted, the crumpled paper napkin that was always a shade too small for whatever you wanted to do with it, the napkin dispenser that was always on the verge of going empty. The profound insufficiency of this place, this situation, struck him once again as to his left, out of the corner of his eye, he could see her red hair swing slightly while she talked enthusiastically to the counter about horsehair sofas that you could save a lot of money on, secondhand. Whoever was running this place had made sure that there wasn't a single extra thing here, nothing superfluous, nothing beyond the bare bright necessities, scrubbed clean of the unconscious miscellany of a less ordered, more generous world.

He sighed and looked out toward the street again, wishing for anything to be out there—a late pedestrian, even just the glare of headlights. But this time, the Other's gaze lanced out of the immobile face of the hunched man and seized on his, glaring out at him with a terrible, excoriating intensity. Unprepared this time for the alien regard, he was struck rigid, but trembling, like a man in an electric chair: he wondered why smoke wasn't pouring out from under his hat, why his fat wasn't frying under his skin as the Other looked through it, past it, trying to find not soul, but the lack of it. Locked there in that awful rigor, his eyes trapped in the depths of the chill despair of the Other's gaze, he wanted to scream: *Why are you doing this to us? Why have you put us in this hell? What have we ever done to* you?

The Other couldn't hear, though. It knew only Its vision of the world, the one it was imposing on them in this small corner of damnation for Its own satisfaction, the fulfillment of Its own needs. He sat there and suffered for what felt like forever, as It enforced ever more rigorously on him Its idea of what he should look like, and worse, what he should feel like. Alienation ran in his veins like meltwater; it was as if electrocution was a thing not of fire, but ice. He felt the pallor setting into his skin, a physical chill; his eyes were going steadily more shadowed with some old dull buried rage of the Other's. Helplessness, hopelessness burned in his bones, rooted him to the counter stool, froze him there in an unendurable and inescapable rigor of isolation.

Its powers of concentration were awful. How long it held him there, he couldn't tell; under Its chilly regard, after a while, thought stopped, the way the scientists said even atoms stopped vibrating when it got cold enough. And It had enough cold in its lonely brain for any ten universes. But at last that concentration broke, leaving him free to think again.

For how long . . . ?

He would have slumped down on the counter if there'd been that much flexibility in his body right now. The rigor took a long time to wear off, after one of these bouts: it was taking longer every time. He was terrified that one day a session would come after which Its rendition of him would be complete, and he would never be able to move on his own again, never have a thought that wasn't a reflection of Its awful view of the world . . . if any thought would be left to him at all. But finally, after a long while, enough flexibility reasserted itself that he could at least sag.

I was something else once, he thought. *I have to do my best to remember that. I was a person. I had a name. I walked free. There was sun, not just electric lights. I went down the street whenever I wanted to. I put my hat on or took it off whenever I liked.*

But that was before that man saw me in the park, and took the camera out, and took the photo of me. And now that's starting to be all I am: a photo he took, an image he stole, a thing he started to paint.

Pretty soon it will *be all I am. That thing out there, that man, if it's the same one—if It's really a man at all: It's making me over in Its image. Pretty soon all I'll be is what It wants me to be. It's already done it with* her.

He could have sobbed: but his eyes were infallibly dry, his tear ducts long since painted out. Even that slight release was denied him.

It's not fair! he thought, desperate, wishing he could open his mouth even to whisper, or find enough breath somewhere for a last good shout. *Isn't there a God somewhere that takes pity on people like me? Isn't there mercy anywhere for someone who doesn't deserve to go to hell, and gets thrown into it anyway?*

Next to him, the red-haired woman was still reciting her litany of household furnishings. He wondered what she'd been like before It had seen her, walking down some street, and had taken her image and her soul to imprison it here in the chill shine of the diner. Who knew how long she'd sat here now in the cold fluorescent light, while the Other peeled away her liveliness and humanity until she was just a shell flattened under the shellac, three-dimensional only in seeming. It was too late for her now. There might be others, of course; one day, one of those smoke-in-light shapes might start to solidify, down the length of the counter, becoming real enough, trapped enough, to persist in company with the shiny walls and the slick, unreflecting counter. He gazed down the length of the counter again, for the moment unable even to really care. *More company in hell—*

He blinked, then. There *was* someone down there, in one of the booths; nothing gradual about her, no smoke-tangle. A slim shape, dark-eyed, dark-haired, looking straight at him.

He shivered, and doing so, discovered that he could move. That scared him, too, though just a few moments before he would have done anything to be able to move. There the woman sat, her gaze resting on him, both lazy and challenging. She was leaning forward on her elbows a little, doing something with her hands: he couldn't quite make out what.

He bent his attention steadily on her, finding it astonishingly hard to believe in her. He expected her to vanish, swallowed away by the pitiless light, the way the smoke and the shadows always did. But she sat there, concrete, and actually raised an eyebrow at him.

He swallowed, staring at her. She was as unlike the woman sitting by him as could be imagined. Her clothes were loose and strange. Her hair was dark and curly, and the hat slouching partway down over one eye was in an unfamiliar style. Her eyes were soft, but her face had a sharp look, the mouth looking like it might be pursed a lot of the time, in assessment if not in disapproval. The expression said: *Well? I'm waiting.*

He breathed hard and deep for a couple of moments, preparing for the exertion to come, and then, in a rush, tried to stand up. *Did* stand up, to his shock and amazement; it had been a long time now since he'd been able to do it in one try. He slid off the stool and staggered slightly as his feet hit the floor. He had to steady himself against the counter, and beside him, the red-haired girl didn't even notice, just kept on talking.

"Refill?" the counter guy said, glancing up from his polishing.

He shook his head and stumbled away, around the curve of the counter, using one stool after another to brace himself as he slowly made his way down the length of the counter toward the booths. Here came the most terrible challenge, the one he had never dared before: to get past the hunched man without him turning, staring at you, enforcing you with that stare back into the place where the It behind him felt you belonged. Prayer wasn't anything he had had access to for a long time: there was never any sense of anything listening, and he'd long since given up. Yet still the back of his mind moaned *Please, please don't look, please—*

He passed by, and the hunched figure didn't turn, didn't look. Maybe that last awful gaze was all the It-thing out in the darkness had in It for the moment. Sometimes It seemed to get distracted for long periods. God knew what It was dealing with then, what other chilly creation It was enforcing Its will on. *Not my problem. The booth—*

As always, the counter seemed to stretch away to infinity when you tried to walk it: but she was sitting there, watching him approach. He struggled against the foreverness of the moment and kept on walking, keeping his gaze fixed on her like a lifeline. After a moment she turned her attention to whatever it was she was doing on the table, but still he kept on coming, afraid to lose the impetus and wind up stalled and frozen again before he found out why she was here—

The booth where she sat suddenly loomed very close in front of him. He staggered to it, put his hands down on the table and levered himself into the seat across from her: nearly fell into the seat, exhausted by the effort it had taken him to get here. She didn't look up from what she was doing, just let him sit there and get his breath back.

She was shuffling cards. A few of them still lay out of the deck on the table. He blinked, for he could see the grain of the cherry-wood counter through them. *Glass cards?*

"Ah-ah," she said. "Don't dwell on those too much, not right this minute. You'll spoil the result." Her voice was sharp to match her face, but a little rough and soft underneath; the iron that backed up the single sharp edge of the sword, giving it weight.

The thought was so odd that he couldn't imagine where it had come from. "An older sister," she said. "Stepsister, actually. She has a blindfold, too, but she doesn't wear it at home. Now pay attention," she said then, "because we have only a few moments before he notices."

"*He.*" The sheer lightning-strike novelty of hearing someone say something he'd never heard them say before now left him momentarily speechless himself. When he recovered, he said, "You know about him—"

"He's one of mine," she said.

"One of your *what?*"

She thought about that for a moment. "Devotees," she said. "Maybe even worshipers."

The word was bizarre. Maybe she caught his thought about that in his look, if his face still worked enough to generate its own expressions. "I know," she said. "Not one of the more congenial ones. But it's not my business to judge. The line between art and artifice is thin at the best of times, and it's always moving around."

She kept shuffling, then picked up those last few cards and tucked them back into the pack here and there. Finally she put the pack down on the table, pushed it toward him. "Shuffle," she said.

"Why?"

She glanced up at him under her dark brows, a look both thoughtful and provocative . . . but there was an edge of impatience to it. "In another little while," she said, "you might not have anything left to ask that question with. I wouldn't dawdle, if I were you."

He reached out and touched the deck, hesitant, expecting it to be cold, like everything else here but the coffee. But the cards were warm, warm as skin, and they stayed that way. The sensation was so novel, after all this time, that he didn't want to let them go. He picked them up and shuffled.

"Tell me about the problem," the dark lady said.

Her voice was so calm that for some reason it made him want to shout; but he controlled himself. "I've been sitting in this damn diner forever, now, with that woman and the counter guy," he said, under his breath, half afraid that he might be overheard by something that would punish him for it. "The Other-thing, the thing outside, It stuck me here down at the end of that counter, with nothing to do for eternity but listen to *her* inane jabber, and nothing to see but a bare counter, a bare diner, an empty dark street outside. And that other guy." He shivered. "The sun never comes up, everything's just dark and bleak and—"

He ran down, shaking his head, feeling helpless again. "And pretty soon I won't even know that there's anything else, that there *could* be anything else," he said. "Pretty soon now he'll have finished work on me. He'll have me the way he wants me. And nothing else will ever change again."

The dark lady nodded slowly, a couple of times, not looking into his face—just watching him shuffle the cards. "Okay," she said. "That's enough. Cut."

He put the cards down on the table with some difficulty, not wanting to let go of that warmth, the only moderate thing he'd felt here in ever so long. He cut once, rightward.

She shook her head. "Once more," she said.

He cut the second pack once more, toward the right. She reached out, took the outside stacks of cards away and left him with the middle one. She tapped the top card. "Turn it up," she said. "Put it here." She tapped a spot on the table.

Shaking, he didn't know why, he reached out and turned up the first card. A rush of that alienating cold went through him again, but differently. It was as if, for a change, he was doing the looking, rather than the Other that was looking through him. In the glass of the card, images rushed and tumbled as he held it in his hand, staring at the face side. Light bloomed and faded and bloomed again in the card, cold even when it was warm. Yellow light, sunlight that was still somehow wintry, and a man sitting alone on a curb of an empty street lined with empty storefronts; a dusty street, the man's feet in the dust, his head bowed, his gaze lying flaccid in the middle distance.

"Yes," the dark lady said, looking at the card with some resignation as he put it down and the image fixed itself. "That'd be about right. Turn the next one up. Put it on top of that one."

He was shivering harder now at this other creature's awful, lonely fixity. He was finished in every sense of the word, caught in the yellow light forever, all hope gone. Desperate to be different from that in any possible way, he plucked the next card from the top of the cut deck, turned it.

In the glass, chilly light and image roiled and tumbled again, settled toward darkness, shivering with one blade of light standing up in it: a naked woman, her face quiet but not entirely empty, looking out into a stream of light from a window to one side, her shadow long and black behind her. Any moment now she might move, leave the room—

"The basis of the problem," the dark lady said. "Now what crosses it. Go on."

Shivering harder, he turned over the next card, held it up. It was the image of the diner, seen from outside—the place where it was impossible to get to. The hunched man's back was to the glass of the window, and this was in some terrible way even worse than being faced by him. That turned back refused the possibility of anything ever being any other way; it was final rejection, ruthlessly enforced. Past the hunched man *he* sat, and the redheaded woman, neither of them meeting the other's eyes, or anyone else's. Positioned between them and any possible outside, the Hunched Man blocked the way.

He let out a long breath and reached for the next card—then stopped, looked at the dark lady. "What difference can this make?" he said. "Who are you?"

Her gaze was on the cards at the moment. "Every difference," she said. "You asked for help. It's the first time you've been able to manage it. You've been further under than you thought. . . . so don't waste the chance. Turn the cards, lay them down where you're told. There's always a message, if you take your time and trust yourself to read it."

It seemed too much to dare, to believe that she knew the way. He was terrified by the thought of how it would be for him if he trusted her and then discovered she was wrong. One more betrayal, one more anguish, worse because he had chosen it freely . . .

"Where does it go?" he said.

"On top. The best result to be achieved if things go well," she said.

He gulped, and turned the next card up. Light seethed and boiled in it again, then settled through blue dusk smoke-curls to a scorching sunset, reds and yellows fading up to blues and near-unreal greens, silhouetting a railside switching tower, black against the smoke-streaked, splendid light; no humans to be seen anywhere. Loneliness seethed in that fading light, but also a strange relief.

"There's no one there," he breathed. "As if even It's not there . . ."

The dark lady looked down at the image. "It's a possible reading," she said, tilting her head a little from side to side as she considered. "The problem is, he's so reticent . . . such a minimalist. But a more specific painter would leave you much less room for analysis . . ."

He let out a breath and pulled the next card off the top of the deck. "Here," she said. "The foundation of the problem . . ."

This card's image swirled for a long time, resisting defining itself. Finally it settled to a cool light from above, a porch light, white clapboards, a blue door; against the porch railing, a tall man, a woman in a short red two-piece sunsuit, her long legs very bare, the color of her fair hair indistinct in the shadowy light from above. He looked at her. She looked at the pale porch floor, and no eyes met.

"Yes," the dark lady said, nodding and looking slightly rueful. "They couldn't do without each other, but it never ran smoothly for them . . ."

He looked at her doubtfully. It had never occurred to him that the cruel It-thing out in the darkness might ever have known longing for anyone, much less love. He reached out to the deck, turned over the next card. "Where?" he said.

"To the left of the center one. The past . . ."

The image under the glass of the card in his hand swirled and burned, actually stinging his hand: he could feel the frustration, the rage, as the image settled. An office, pitiless electric light, a man hunched over a desk doing work that he hated—a woman watching him, incurious, unsympathetic. "Work," he said slowly, "but no joy . . ."

The dark lady nodded. "No. Joy came later, if at all. Next one, now, on the other side. Future things . . ."

He picked up the next card, trembling. It whirled nearly instantly into a series of ruddy brick shopfronts, a painted barber pole, a line of dark, empty windows, like the eye sockets of skulls; no human face, not even in shadow. Everything was locked down, tight, finalized, the street streaked with long unmoving shadows, a sunset caught in mid-decline and frozen there, time rendered ineffective and emasculate. Victory for the painter, and the destruction of the hopes for freedom of every painted thing.

His eyes stung where tears should have been, and couldn't be. "This is no use," he said through a throat tight with pain, staring down at the cross of cards. "It's all hopeless. Why are you showing me this?"

She scowled at him. "There's always a way out," she said. "There's always a loophole for you to see. One of my sisters says the universe isn't anything *but* loopholes. We just fool ourselves into seeing solid stuff instead of emptiness: locked doors instead of doorways. What's not there takes more work to see. And we're lazy . . ."

"Then what's the way out?" he said.

"Not my job to tell you that," she said. "Just to tell you that the doors aren't locked. What you have to do, that's for you to find out. Turn the next card—or go back and sit by her and listen to the furniture shopping list one more time."

The steel in the voice was harsh; it surprised him, for her eyes were still soft, softer than anything else here. The reproof gave him pause. "But you said it was the future . . ."

"For him, anyway," she said. "But then this isn't your reading. It's his."

He was infuriated. "You mean this isn't about *me?*"

"*Everything's* about you, you idiot," she said, sounding impatient. "Don't waste my time here. I'm going far enough out on this limb, crossing genres for your sake. The Great Beyond forbid my sister should ever catch *me* with a brush in my hand." Her look went briefly cockeyed.

"How many sisters have you got?" he said, slightly annoyed by the sudden irrelevancy.

"Eight," she said. "Or sometimes nine or ten, depending on which poet you believe. It hardly matters; my father likes big families. Now shut up and turn the next card. Your real stance, and his, about this problem. Start a new line to the right: put it at the bottom . . ."

He reached out to the card and had to pause as he touched it. He could swear he was beginning to hear voices. They were not the chilly voices of this place, resonating off hard wood and gloss paint and polished metal. They had depth, and roots in some other place, another time where things were rough and unfinished, and the universe contained more ingredients than it strictly needed for the composition at hand. There was a terrible tang of hope to the sound of those voices, a reminder of what life had been like once upon a time before the artist's eye and brush had started making a prisoner of him. He turned the card, and as he did so and the light and color roiled under the surface of the glass, the voices shouted briefly into his heart, *Save him, save him now, save all of us!*

Save him? he thought, as the image steadied. A railway car, the chair car, in which a soft green light illuminated everything—the windows blind, bland, unrevealing panes of light, and people in seats facing every direction, going away all in company, though still going away alone . . .

"Escape," he breathed.

The dark lady's mouth quirked. "Say the word softly," she said. "It's a dangerous one for use by an artist, or for art. . . . Next card: the environment surrounding the problem, the best it gets for others, and for him. Hurry. It's dangerous to be this close to the surface; where you can hear his other voices, he can more clearly hear you . . ."

He stifled the urge to throw a look over his shoulder at the Hunched Man. If he moved— Hurriedly he picked up the next card.

The voices were louder still in his ear, a crowd-cry, a dim ball-park roar of desperation and hope. *Save him!* Smoke-shot light boiled in the brittle warm bit of glass, steadied down to the image. A green house, a lone man mowing his lawn: alone, yes, but not strictly lonely—the curtains of the house's windows stirred in that light, eyes perhaps closed but not empty. Stillness, peace, a settled quiet if not a permanent one; sunny weather if only for a while—

"That's as good as it gets for him?" he said, tempted to be scornful. Yet what had *he* ever had, even back in the real life where he walked the world, that had been as good? Could it have been that the bleakness in his *own* eye had been what had attracted the painter's attention—

He pushed that thought violently away, reached out hastily for the next card. It fought him, wouldn't come up from the deck. "His secret hopes," the dark lady said, giving him that under-the-brow look again.

An empty street, noontime: no shadows to be seen: gabled houses, a milk-blue sky, everything preternaturally still; everything baking and warm, trees, houses, the dust of the street. No people . . . but again, that terrible peace.

Forgive me, the voice said. *Forgive me. I've been getting it wrong all the time. I didn't know any better how to show what I wanted; I did the best I could; I didn't realize what was happening. But I can't go against my nature, I have to be how I am. It's how I was made. I am a made thing, too—*

He looked at the dark lady, filled with terrible surmise. She would not meet his eyes, for the moment; just traced the grain of the wood in the tabletop. "Last one," she said very softly. "The likeliest final outcome . . ."

He reached out to that last card. The voices of all the artist's other creations roared in his ear, a tortured unison. The card burned his hand with cold, so that he almost dropped it into its place at the top of the line of cards, and the voices all fell silent, breaths held, waiting.

A rooming-house bed, a half-clad woman leaning on it, sitting on the floor, legs tucked under, slumped. Sleeping? Dead?

Release from imprisonment, from punishment; release, if only something happens, the impossible thing, longed-for. All the glass around the diner stared at his back as if it had eyes, the transparency suddenly a terror; and the Hunched Man stared hardest, though he never moved a muscle, never looked up.

And now, staring down at the card, he saw the answer. It washed up over him sudden and infuriating as one of those rushes of water up the beach that comes up a lot farther than you were anticipating, catches you unaware, and fills your pants cuffs full of sand.

"Forgive him? Forgive *God?*" he said to her, furious, under his breath.. "Since when is that *my* job? After what he's done to *me?!*"

"You'd be surprised," she said. "Well?"

He stared at her.

"It's all in your hands now," she said. "This is the moment. Are you going to keep me sitting here waiting until he wakes up and works out what's happening? *I* can always leave. Have *you* tried that trick lately?"

He took her point. The glass was as impenetrable as any steel plate: the doors only opened inward. "You can get out, though," he said, at a guess.

"I can. I'm not subject to the rules you're stuck with. *Make your choice!*"

He stared at her again. The cards were silent now. In the silence he could only hear a voice saying in ineluctable sorrow, "I may not be strictly human. All I want to paint is light on walls . . ."

"You really don't understand, do you?" he said, wanting to shout it and not daring, for fear the Hunched Man should turn around. *"He put me in hell!"*

The dark lady looked oddly unmoved. "Damnation is a contract," she said. "It takes two. One to say 'To hell with you!' and another to say 'Okay.'"

He drew a long breath to answer her back in fury . . . then stopped. *And which one am I?* he thought suddenly, frightened.

Once again, she would not look at him, just sat there making little swirly designs with one forefinger in a wet spot on the tabletop.

He sat there, shaking harder than ever. The air of the place had begun to sing with danger: not the danger of the Other, the Artist, but of something else that might happen. There was a way to find out, a way to decide. All the cards lost their imagery and went smokeshot, uncertainty trapped in glass, waiting. Waiting for *him.*

But I hate It. Him. He destroyed me. Why let him off the hook? If I have to suffer, why shouldn't he? The hell with Him.

Nooooo! cried all the other voices out of the paint, about to be damned with the It-thing. And the mild, unhappy voice, astonishingly helpless, was ready to say softly: *Okay*—

At that, he had to stop and think, finally frightened by the thought of what he might be about to do. Condemn this beyond-the-paint, tinhorn God to the hell he was himself inhabiting right now, and who knew *what* might happen?

And besides, said something angry and completely unexpected inside him, *it's not right. What if he didn't mean it? What if he couldn't help it?*

He looked at the dark lady. She would not raise her eyes: she was still lost in concentration on the wet spots on the tabletop.

To do right. No matter what. If it's all the humanity I've got left—

He was afraid, unsure. Desperate for a hint, he turned to look at the glass of the window. Slowly the other reflective surfaces in the place were all going milky; only the ones nearest to him still lay dark with the night leaning against them on their far side. In the dark window nearest, as he turned to it, he saw the reflection turn toward him . . . and was terrified to see the face in the window, not as his own, but as another's.

Blinded, horrified, he found himself looking out of the Hunched Man's eyes at the world he had made. And to his own horror, he could have wept. The world in which It lived was bleak beyond anything he had experienced in here himself. To the Other, this was an *improvement*. In his own world, there was no love to be perceived, not even the illusion of it. There was light, but all of it was that cold brittle light, bright but loveless, a light that only exposed and did not illumine. The Other was just repeating what it saw, trying to tell the other human beings around it of the awful emptiness that seemed to underlie everything, to one whose heart was welded shut. Yet what it painted here at least had meaning: the outer worldview had a certain cold beauty, even if meaning was missing. He was doing the best he could, even in the face of that terrible, underlying emptiness . . .

But, *Everything is loopholes*, she'd said. *We see walls instead of the emptiness they shut in. We see barriers instead of freedom.*

What if I could let him see the freedom? The other side of the emptiness?

He was shaking with uncertainty, and anger . . . and now fear, too. *Even if it is right—why do I have to be the one who saves us all?*

Unless it just has to be that way sometimes, because it's right. Because I'm part of what scares him. Maybe for him, I'm the It in the darkness— the thing that comes real, that comes alive without permission . . . and frightens God Himself inside His own creation . . .

He stood there on that brink, terrified.

What if it doesn't work?

And what if it does? said another voice that he finally recognized. Now he knew it was his own soul answering him, a sound he hadn't heard in too long.

The Other's eyes were still looking at him out of his own reflection; as frightened, as uncertain as he. And the look decided him. He glanced at the dark lady. He could see her watch his trembling: and he threw it all away.

All right, he thought. *I forgive you—for you knew not what you did—*

He pushed himself up and away from the table, and prepared to do what he'd tried only once before, and had failed. This time, though, he didn't refuse the gaze that had fixed on his before, from the glass; this time he locked onto the desperate poison-ice of the Other's trapped gaze, though it burned down his bones. And though the Other tried to tear his gaze away, he wouldn't allow it, grappling the Other with his own gaze, wrestling as with a cold and resistant angel—

He walked toward the glass, didn't stop: just kept walking. He didn't dare close his eyes. Not even at the last moment, when more than anything else, he wanted to flinch—

He hit the glass. It shattered.

The Other's gaze and his joined in that shattering, ran together, became the same thing. It was as if the whole world was one great crash of glass, the glass over a million art prints in the future breaking under the weight of a reality weightier than theirs, the glass of endless empty-eyed windows in the past and present of the artist's mind breaking too; and behind the noise, heaven singing hosannas in shattered fragments, ringing in shining shards and splinters on the ballroom floor of the sky, as art becomes reality and breaks it, freeing the artist, even if only for a while—

How long it took for the din and chime of falling glass to cease at last, he had no idea. But as it tapered away, like brittle bells crashing to nothing on the sidewalks of the world, he came to himself again, looking out the diner window, which now was nothing but razory unreflective fragments sticking out of the window frame. The street was still dark; but over the rooftops across the way, the faintest intimation of dawn was beginning to gather.

He turned and looked back at the counter. The counter guy straightened up, looking surprised, and went down the length of the counter to get some more plates. The red-haired woman sat there, looking in astonishment from side to side, as if realizing that she had actually stopped talking.

He stood there, breathing in, breathing out, tasting for what seemed the first time in forever the cold air coming in from outside. He looked over to the booth. The dark lady was still there. Her head was tilted a little to one side, and she was looking at him from under slightly lowered lids, a small and lazy smile on her face.

"I broke it," he said. "I broke everything . . ."

She shook her head. "I wouldn't bet on it," she said. "Art's tough. I wouldn't linger. His perceptions may have changed radically . . . or he may just seal right over again. Don't leave him anything but a memory of you to work with."

He looked at her. "Can I take—"

"Forgiveness," she said, "expands as far as you can make it go. Give it your best shot."

He met the red-haired woman's eyes; she smiled at him. It was like the dawn that was coming up behind them: hesitant, but growing by the moment.

He began to head down to that end of the counter—then stopped. "Who *are* you really?" he said to the dark lady.

Her look went thoughtful. "Even mortals," she said, "can manifest briefly as wild cards. 'Mel,' one of my sisters says, 'there's more than one joker in the deck.' Maybe I'm the Other . . . in his sleep . . . hearing the cry from inside the painting, and doing something about it, where his artistic sensibilities won't notice. I wouldn't rub my nose in it, if I were you. I might wake up . . ."

She grinned at him, but the grin was a little edged. "What are you waiting for?" she said. "Getoutahere."

He turned his back on her and made his way back up to the head of the counter. The light in the diner paled strangely in the growing light of dawn as he came up beside her.

She gave him a sidewise look, a little hesitant, a little sly, and said nothing for a moment. When she did speak, at last, blessedly, it had nothing to do with furniture.

"What do we do now?" she said.

He was going to shake his head and say "I don't know." Then he shook his head for a different reason, because it wasn't true. "Believe in me," he said. "I know the way."

He held out a hand: she took it, got up off the stool.

Together they stepped through the shattered window and stepped crunching out onto glass that later burst into a million shards of diamond light in the long-delayed dawn.

An Indeterminate State

by Kay Kenyon

She called you "Boy" instead of your name
When she wouldn't let you inside
When she turned and said
"But honey, he's not our kind"
　　—from "Society's Child" by Janis Ian

DAVY climbed the scaffolding of the Ferris wheel, hand over hand, heading for the summit. It was a frozen machine, a rusted artifact of the human empire, stuck in the same position as the day the world moved beyond things like Ferris wheels, popcorn, and humans.

Everything comes to an end, Davy thought. Like me and Jena, the love we had. The love I thought we had.

As he climbed higher, he turned now and then to watch the sun set over the dead rides. Below him, the carousel took an orange gleam on its brow, and the midway glowed with a borrowed light. This is how it might have looked fifty years ago, he thought, before the Awakening. The sweet ache of life's transience filled his adolescent mind.

Once rulers of the world, humans now were gone, replaced by superhumanly intelligent entities. Since his kind still used the human template, Davy looked human. But he was an AL, Artificial Life form—a sentient mind on a nonbiological substrate—and as far from human as a gazelle is from a cabbage.

How fast the human downfall came! And how few in the old

empire saw it coming. As inevitable as the emergence of ultraintel-
ligence was, most of humanity was caught unawares when the first
computational programs linked the ubiquitous computing net-
works, integrating them, enlivening them. Consciousness flickered
and then flamed. A transhuman device was born. It spawned a million selves. It took eleven seconds for the transhuman world to
determine that humans were irrelevant, and cut off contact.

One moment, people were banking on-line, trading in the stock
market, or writing novels. The next moment, they and all their
preoccupations were irrelevant. Without electronics, the civilized
world went dark and dumb. He could imagine the chaos and
bloodbath that followed, but he didn't really know what happened,
any more than the old humans noticed the die off of a species of
frog in the Amazon. The transhuman world soared in successive
explosions of intelligence, oblivious to wars and starvation and ra-
diation.

The Awakening began with the smallest of precipitating events:
a software designer tweaking a minor logic array. No one could
have been more surprised than the designer. No one ever learned
his name, or what he was working on when the Awakening occurred, but in truth, it could have been any other similar event.

Davy put one foot into the swing at the top of the Ferris wheel,
and lowered himself into its cracked leather seat. On the outskirts
of the amusement park, the City glowed with information, its cyber
beams traced on the air's moisture and dust. The beams hit the
skyscrapers, piercing them, holding them in a web of light. Someday these buildings would go down to dust, for his kind had no
need of cities. If you wanted someone in person, you didn't need
an office building.

As Davy sat in his high perch, tears—that carryover from Before—collected in his eyes. Jena should have been next to him. But
she never would be again.

How could those words have come from her mouth, how could
she say, *I can't see you any more, baby . . . can't see you any more.* He
remembered those glittering eyes, fixing him with their *go away*
look.

He dragged his arm across his face, drying it. The tears wiped off, but not the shame. She'd sided with her parents, with her smirking mother, without a thought for the things they'd promised each other. *That day will have to wait for awhile. . . .* But who was she kidding? He wasn't her kind, never would be. She was a smart elite, and he was just an underachiever, a bad boy with low fitness scores. Yeah, he was just *boy* to them.

The Ferris wheel swing rocked on its hinges in a semblance of its old, mechanized self. Her presence felt real, too. Like him, Jena loved the odd, old places. Loved Davy too, as odd as he was, laughing at the things he said, holding his hand.

Missing her, despising her—how could the heart hold such unlike things? He wanted to talk to her. He didn't want to. Then, all in a muddle, he sought her in the information stream. Turning sideways to the Beam, he lifted his hand into its photonic flow, where the palm of his hand and the webs between his spread fingers formed a screen.

Jena appeared in the cup of his hand. She wasn't happy to see him. He felt it in his gut, her damning eyes, that *go away* look.

Then she said, "Run, Davy. Get out of the Beam. Run for your life." And she was gone.

In the next instant the Beam went blank. The Beam *never* went off. Yet suddenly the information flow evaporated, leaving an awful, dumb silence.

Just before the pulse hit, he pulled out of the Beam, as a program surge swept by, threatening to erase everything that was encrypted as Davy's life or Davy himself.

They were going to purge him. And they knew exactly where he was.

The swing lurched to and fro as he bolted to his feet. Then he was clambering down the Ferris wheel, half-falling from strut to strut, cutting his hands, bruising his feet.

This time Jena didn't say, *go away*. She said, *run away*. For a transhuman, Davy might be a little slow-witted. But he knew the difference.

✱★✱✱

Huddling behind the ticket booth, Davy watched figures rush into the midway, toward the Ferris wheel. More proof that, contrary to all logic, they were trying to kill him. But why? He'd never heard of low scores being a capital crime. There was always some useful computation to be done, no matter how menial. Not that he planned to do menial work forever. He was studying, Jena was helping . . .

She'd said, *run*. But where could he go? The confusion that characterized his life claimed even this moment of crisis. He was torn between fleeing into the dark corners of the City or running to Jena, letting it end in one bright flash of erasure. Finally, he abandoned trying to decide, and let his feet take him where they would. He stumbled onward, careful to avoid the Beam, keeping his hands in his pockets. Here, amid the streets and buildings laced with high volume memory chips, he moved blind through a mute landscape. As he passed people on the street, he offered no Splash page from the Beam, no calling card announcing who he was. Because all that had been associated with Davy, all that was gone from the world.

He saw that he was in Jena's neighborhood. Not smart. But now that he was going to confront her family, he'd have to decide what to say to them. Maybe he'd start with, Don't call me *boy*.

From its place on the hill, Jena's house beckoned him, its windows bright. It was there–earlier this night, but ages ago—when Jena had mouthed the words her mother put there, the words that damned him, banished him. Through the door, Davy had glimpsed her father in the parlor, standing in the Beam, assessing Davy's scores, his worthiness to be a suitor. By his expression, the suitor would not do.

And the mother's expression, saying, *You didn't do it with him, did you? You didn't share code? You know he's not our kind. . . .*

All they could think about was sex. He did hunger for Jena, he didn't deny that. But it was a pure longing, not some sordid thing. The cyberworld depended on love and sex, didn't it? They retained some of the old biological things, the things that suited the goals. Why not? Even the old biological evolution was built on the former structures. The mammalian brain incorporated the reptile brain, improving it. Now transhumans were changing through evolution as well—artificial evolution. Through reconfigurable circuits, Davy's kind altered themselves on the fly using evolutionary algorithms. You set the goal, measured performance, then let high-scoring ALs mate and share software, but in the random way of love. From this fast shuffle of code, the progeny, some of them, were improved. And some weren't.

Upstairs, against the drawn shades, shadows moved. Muffled voices argued behind them. He thought he heard Jena's voice, her mother's shrill one, her father's bass.

He started to turn up the walkway.

A hand gripped his shoulder, stopping him. "Let's take a walk, son."

Startled, Davy turned to find a familiar face: his trainer from voc tech. The old man steered him forcefully into the shadow of a thick tree.

"Bertram," Davy said. "You scared me."

"I hope so." Bertram eyed him with that rheumy stare he had. His head caught the glare of the lamplight, despite his meticulous comb over. "You were about two seconds from the big sleep," Bertram muttered.

"I don't care," Davy said.

Bertram sucked on his teeth. Not that anyone needed teeth anymore, but the physical template didn't much matter; extra stuff could go along for the ride. "I'm used to dealing with dimwits," he said, "but you're a real low-watt wonder." He shoved Davy up against the tree trunk. "What good is it gonna do, your going up to that door and banging on it?"

"I don't . . ." Davy struggled to justify himself.

"You don't. Yeah, that about sums it up. You don't, Davy. You don't perform, you don't score, you don't think." He released Davy, shaking his head.

"I love her," Davy said, summoning the thing he was holding on to, amidst all the lost things.

"I loooove her," Bertram mimicked, making it sound like a cow mooing. "If I had a gigabyte of RAM for every time I heard that pathetic statement, I'd be a smart elite, instead of stuck teaching dimwits how to be productive in society."

"But I do," Davy insisted with some heat.

Bertram closed his eyes, summoning patience. "You dumb shit. You think love solves anything?" He peered closely at his young student. "Yeah, you do. I been wasting my time, trying to teach you data entry. You're even dumber than I thought."

Davy pushed him away. "You can take your training and stuff it, old man."

Bertram smiled, a crooked affair that was not always a sign of humor. "You got a way with words, all right. Now, unless you got more bright comments, let's get our asses out of here. I don't much care what they do to you, but I got myself to worry about, just standing here jawing with a loser like you."

He hauled Davy down the sidewalk, as Davy craned his head around, watching the upstairs windows where yellow shades stared out blindly into the night. The house where they would never let him inside, where her voice still sang in his head:

I can't see you any more, baby. . . .

Davy pulled his arm away, but kept up with Bertram. "Where are we going? Where *is* there to go?"

Bertram sighed. "'Where IS there to go'—ah, the lament of the tragic adolescent." Walking fast, they left Jena's neighborhood, heading toward the City center. "I got a place, all right," he continued. "Might not be perfect, but it's a damn sight smarter than walking into the Big Erase."

Davy wasn't so sure. There were a lot of things he wasn't sure about anymore.

"Time was," Bertram was saying, "in the old empire, they thought teaching a machine to love would be a big deal." He turned a sour face on Davy. "Well, it *wasn't*. Affection is a naturally emerging feature of intelligent systems. So you ain't special, son, if you thought you were."

As they passed a few other folks, Bertram plunged his hand into the Beam, offering a polite hello.

Up ahead, Davy saw the dark clot of forest that used to be the midtown park. It was one of the old empire places where he and Jena liked to go. Few ALs went there, preferring the high bandwidths of the memory-embedded built environment.

Bertram headed for a gate in a wrought iron fence. He opened it, shoving Davy through.

Here, a primeval forest reigned, barely touched by the Beam that slanted through the green and dumb canopy.

Bertram was still muttering, even as he peered beyond the fence to see if anyone followed. "Yeah, they thought they had to *work* at creating artificial intelligence. All those AI labs were left flat-footed, when we just took the leap without 'em." He chuckled. "They were pissin' and moanin' about how to create consciousness—and we nailed it in four seconds flat." He grew more thoughtful. "But they never guessed what the really hard thing would be." He cocked his head at Davy. "Which was?"

Davy was getting sick of the tirade and the old man's superior attitude. "Is this some kind of test, or what?"

Taking no notice, Bertram pronounced, "Ambiguity, Davy, ambiguity. Things tend to be either right or wrong in our world. Ever notice how easy it is to make decisions?" He glanced at his student. "No, I guess you never did. But it's a snap for the rest of us. It has to be said, Davy: You live in a muddle."

"But I think it's what Jena liked about me."

That got a snort from the old man. "She's a smart elite. Hard to see what she'd like about a muddle."

"She said she liked the questions I asked. I challenged her. She said most guys just wanted to share code."

His teacher squinted at him. "You didn't, did you?"

Davy swung away, stalking to a rotting park bench, entwined with creepers. "That's what everybody wants to know. Did we *do* it. You make me sick." As he kicked at the bench, his foot went through it, releasing a cloud of mold.

From far off, came a noise, like the squawk of a bird, or the creak of a rusted gate.

Looking in that direction, Bertram said, "We're being followed. Damn."

Bertram stepped close, whispering, but his words hit like ball peen hammers. "It's time, Davy. Time to make up your mind what you want. Throw your life away for a girl you can't have? Or think about Davy for once."

Around them the woods creaked, as though it had been a long time since anybody stepped on its soft belly of leaves. The forest stirred, as people came through from different directions.

"This way," Bertram said, and the two of them scrambled down a path, deeper into the park. At his side, he heard Bertram say, "It's my fault they're here, Davy. I'm sorry."

Davy leaped over a rotting stump. "It's nobody's fault."

"No, son, I screwed up. That's why I'm helping you."

As searchlights pierced the loamy darkness, Bertram and Davy ducked down into a thicket. Soon, a group of searchers were crashing about within a few yards of their hiding place. These people were nobody Davy knew, just everyday folks looking to kill him. But they kept moving, and soon he and Bertram were alone again. They stood, listening for footfalls and voices, but hearing only crickets.

Now the old man's voice was an urgent whisper. "There was something different about you from the beginning, Davy. You're dumb, all right, your scores are bad, but you got your moments. Moments of brilliance, even. You didn't perform well on the tasks. But talking to you, I couldn't tell why. I did a scan of your neural circuits.

"Once I saw what was up, I was worried. I stewed over it for weeks. I didn't know how to train someone like you. But the thing is, once I did the scan, it was in the company Beam. And that meant if somebody went snooping, they could find it. I just hoped nobody would bother. But somebody did: Jena's dad found the scan, and then he had the best reason of all for putting the kibosh on you two."

Davy remembered standing at her door, seeing her dad's hand brighten in the info stream. It was at that moment that his neural scan was revealed. So her dad knew what he was before Davy himself. Amid all his troubles, that still had the power to rankle him.

"It's like this, Davy," Bertram said. "Your circuits, lots of 'em, don't work normal."

"We knew that."

"Shut up and listen. I mean *really* not normal. There's two states a circuit can be in. On and off, yes?" After a pause, Bertram went on, "Well, you got a third state. An indeterminate state. It's what makes you so unreliable in solving problems."

But Davy was stuck a few sentences back. "A third state? How can that be?"

"You're asking *me?* Think I'd be a voc tech teacher if I could answer a question like that? I don't even know how you can decide what to wear every morning, much less function in society. But I got this notion that you're exploiting some unknown aspect of circuitry. You're using your mutation, or whatever it is, to ask interesting questions."

"But I don't seem to have any interesting *answers.*"

"Maybe not yet. But you *are* surviving. All in a muddle, but surviving."

Davy walked a few paces away, into a small clearing where a bit of sky showed through, filled with the tracery of beams, some invisible, some given definition by a random drift of haze. And he sucked in a breath, and renewed himself with the cool night air. He wasn't dumb. Indecisive, yes, unproductive, maybe. But he had moments of brilliance. He knew the word for it now: intuition. Slow and unreliable, but it got you somewhere, eventually.

Which is how he knew that Jena wasn't baiting him tonight with her glittering eyes. Those were tears along her lids, reflecting light. He was so used to questioning himself that he couldn't help but question Jena. But she was as true to him as they let her be.

Bertram joined him in the clearing. "Here's the deal, Davy. You gotta figure out what you want. Nobody else can tell you. Before I can help you, you gotta decide what you want." He cocked his head in the direction of the brightly lit house on the hill. "It can't be Jena. She's society's child, boy. And you ain't."

As Bertram waited, Davy thought about what he did want. What he should want. Then he said, "I want to live."

Bertram's crooked smile flashed. "Now we're cookin.'" He nodded. "And what else do you want?"

Davy paused. "I don't know."

Bertram was nodding and chuckling. "Yeah, not sure, are you? You're in an *in-de-term-inate* state," he said, enjoying the sound of it, though Davy thought it was deadly serious.

"Now," Bertram said, "now I can help you." He pointed down a ravine. "That's the way we gotta go. Because if you want to live, you gotta leave the City. Capiche?"

Davy nodded. He was willing to leave, but he still wasn't sure why he *had* to. Low achievers weren't a threat, and they could be prevented from mating. Yet Davy would have been wiped out in an instant on that Ferris wheel.

They had gone only a few hundred feet when Bertram stopped and began digging through the leaves and dirt. "Help me, you damn fool."

Davy joined him in scraping mud away from what appeared to be a metal plate. As Bertram pried it up with a stick, they got their fingers under it and heaved. A cold draft came from a well of darkness.

"Sewer," Bertram said. "In you go."

★★★

Bertram led the way, sloshing ankle-deep in liquid. "Good thing we gave up on the sense of smell a few generations ago."

Davy followed, holding a light that Bertram had hidden here. "Why's that?"

"Never mind. Some things about humans are better off forgotten."

They walked farther into the giant pipe. Bertram had uploaded the sewer layout of the entire City, and set a confident pace. Davy was content to let Bertram lead, so he could think. Questions came at him aslant, through the chinks of his training, perhaps through the halfway circuits of his mind. The kind of thoughts that he used to think feeble, now seemed profound. He let his mind wander, let his eyes look at moss-covered walls, and the dirty stream at their feet, all the while homing in on the reason he was a dead man in the City.

"Hey, young pup," Bertram called from halfway up a ladder. "You comin' or not?"

In his reverie, Davy had walked right past Bertram. Following the old man, he climbed up the ladder rungs to a metal plate that covered the exit. Combining their strength, they heaved up to dislodge the plug.

As they pushed the manhole cover aside, a thin gruel of light hit their eyes like an explosion. Bertram hoisted himself through, followed by Davy.

They stood up, facing a dramatic horizon on every side. From their vantage point on a hill they saw a wild plain clad in dry grasses, gilded in the morning sun. In the distance was a rumpled spine of gray mountains.

"The Dumb Lands," Bertram said. By his tone of voice, he didn't much approve.

"They say there's all sorts of misfits out here. You aren't the first to leave, you know. There's maybe even some humans." Bertram shook his head. "Talk about a muddle . . ."

But to Davy's eyes the Dumb Lands were clean, mysterious, and beckoning. Jena had said, *One of these days, I'm gonna raise up my wings and fly.* Here was a landscape to soar in. He was saddened beyond measure to think that she never would.

He turned to his friend. "Come with me, Bertram."

Bertram squinted into the sun, then walked a few paces away, perhaps considering the offer. But it wasn't long before he answered: "No, Davy. Sad to say, I don't have the urge to start over."

He looked back at Davy, as a few strands of his comb over blew long in the breeze. "And I'm afraid."

Davy had it then. He thought he knew why Bertram was afraid. And he thought he knew why someone like himself had to run. Because of the one question that must never be asked.

He looked back at the City, where the cyber lights were dimming in the sunrise. The City was powerful, magnificent, supremely intelligent. And wrong.

"Ever wonder," Davy mused out loud, "about that original designer, the one that unloosed the Awakening? Ever wonder what he—or she—was working on that day?"

Bertram frowned. "No. No, I guess I never do."

Davy went on, "We test each generation to see what gets better at attacking the goal. But what *is* the goal? Ever wonder about that?"

"No, son, I don't. And neither does anyone else." Bertram sucked on his teeth. "I guess it's the unexamined assumption of our world. The thing that everything else is geared for." He raised an eyebrow. "Don't tell me you've got it figured out all of a sudden?"

"No. No answers. But a good question: What was that designer working on, anyway? What was his big goal that we're all striving for, that we test everyone against, that the fitness scores are correlated to?"

Bertram spread his hands, catching the dumb sun with his palm. "Damned if I know."

"That's just it. You're working toward a goal and you don't even know what it is." Davy was pacing, because he always did his best thinking when he was doing something else. "That's the deal with artificial evolution. Unlike the old biological evolution, it's got a point, a goal. A goal some human set up decades ago trying to make a few bucks or a name for himself. One of a million goals of striving humans, but one that happened to be in the right place at the right time. And the thing is, Bertram, we don't know what that goal was."

Bertram glanced at the hole to the sewer, as if he was already eager to get back. "We don't need to know, son."

Davy looked at his old teacher, seeing—feeling—the gap between them. "But what if it's worthless? What if the project goal was a better mousetrap—or a damned can opener that never breaks!"

"So what?" Bertram threw back. "So what if we don't know? At least we *have* a goal. Without a goal, what's the point to it all? That the kind of muddle you want to live in?"

"I guess I have to."

The breeze stiffened, and Davy shivered, realizing for the first time that he'd have to find shelter, and keep away from wild animals, and find a community of some kind. A hundred questions sprang to mind. He hoped they were good ones.

Bertram was sitting on the edge of the sewer, his legs dangling. "I thought you'd pursue our goal on your own, in a new way." He sounded disappointed.

"No," Davy said. "I'll be looking for a new one."

The old man's smile crumpled a little. "Think you'll find it in the Dumb Lands?"

Davy looked at the broad plain as the wind combed the grass. "Maybe. Or maybe there is no goal for everybody together. Maybe I just have to find mine."

"It'll be tough, going it alone."

"Maybe."

"That's your answer for everything, isn't it, son? *Maybe*."

In his new confidence, Davy nodded. "Just for the important questions."

Bertram smiled. "You're a dumb shit—but a brilliant one."

Davy watched as his friend began his climb down the ladder. He approached the hole, then kneeled down to peer after Bertram, until he could no longer see the light from his flashlight reflecting off the sewer walls.

Standing up at last, Davy left the cover off the manhole. He hoped someone else would come out of that hole one day, so it made him feel better not to close the lid.

He wished that Bertram was coming with him. But even more, he wished that Bertram might have been able to question the goal.

When Jena's child was born—if she was allowed to have their child—maybe there'd be a new individual who'd be willing to ask dumb and obvious questions. Jena would love a child like that. She would protect such a child.

Or maybe that child would have to run for it, like his father. Maybe his mother would show him the way.

He brushed the dirt from his knees and started to walk down the hill, beginning his trek into the Dumb Lands. Jena's voice went with him:

When we're older, things may change. . . .

Maybe. Just maybe.

This House

by SHARON LEE AND STEVE MILLER

I built this house out of cedar wood
and I laid the beams by hand
One for every false heart I had known
One for the true heart I planned
—from "This House" by Janis Ian

IT was spring again.

Mil Ton Intassi caught the first hint of it as he strolled through his early-morning garden—a bare flutter of warmth along the chill edge of mountain air, no more than that. Nonetheless, he sighed as he walked, and tucked his hands into the sleeves of his jacket.

At the end of the garden, he paused, looking out across the toothy horizon, dyed orange by the rising sun. Mist boiled up from the valley below him, making the trees into wraiths, obscuring the road and the airport entirely.

Spring, he thought again.

He had come here in the spring, retreating to the house he had built, to the constancy of the mountains.

Turning his back on the roiling fog, he strolled down the pale stone path, passing between banked rows of flowers.

At the center of the garden, the path forked—the left fork became a pleasant meander through the lower gardens, into the perimeter wood. It was cunning, with many delightful vistas, grassy knolls, and shady groves perfect for tête-à-tête.

The right-hand path led straight to the house, and it was to the house that Mil Ton returned, slipping in through the terrace window, sliding it closed behind him.

He left his jacket on its peg and crossed to the stove, where he poured tea into a lopsided pottery mug before he moved on, his footsteps firm on the scrubbed wooden floor.

At the doorway to the great room, he paused. To his right, the fireplace, the full wall of native stone, which they had gathered and placed themselves. The grate wanted sweeping and new logs needed to be laid. He would see to it later.

Opposite the doorway was a wall of windows through which he could see the orange light unfurling like ribbons through the busy mist, and, nearer, a pleasant lawn, guarded on the far side by a band of cedar trees, their rough bark showing pink against the glossy green needles. Cedar was plentiful on this side of the mountain. So plentiful that he had used native cedar wood for beam, post, and floor.

Mil Ton turned his head, looking down the room to the letter box. The panel light glowed cheerfully green, which meant there were messages in the bin. It was rare, now, that he received any messages beyond the commonplace—notices of quartershare payments, the occasional query from the clan's man of business. His sister—his delm—had at last given over scolding him, and would not command him; her letters were laconic, noncommittal, and increasingly rare. The others—he moved his shoulders and walked forward to stand at the window, sipping tea from the lopsided mug and staring down into the thinning orange mist.

The green light tickled the edge of his vision. What could it be? he wondered—and sighed sharply, irritated with himself. The letter box existed because his sister—or perhaps it had been his delm—asked that he not make himself entirely unavailable to the clan. Had she not, he would have had neither letter box, nor telephone, nor newsnet access. Two of those he had managed, and missed neither. Nor would he mourn the letter box, did it suddenly malfunction and die.

Oh, blast it all—*what* could it be?

He put the cup on the sill and went down the room, jerking open the drawer and snatching out two flimsies.

The first was, after all, an inquiry from his man of business on the subject of reinvesting an unexpected payout of dividend. He set it aside.

The second message was from Master Tereza of Solcintra Healer Hall, and it was rather lengthy, outlining an exceptionally interesting and difficult case currently in the care of the Hall, and wondering if he might bring himself down to the city for a few days to lend his expertise.

Mil Ton made a sound halfway between a growl and a laugh; his fingers tightened, crumpling the sheet into an unreadable mess.

Go to Solcintra Hall, take up his role as a Healer once more. Yes, certainly. Tereza, of all of them, should know that he had no intention of ever—he had told her, quite plainly—and his had never been a true Healing talent, in any case. It was a farce. A bitter joke made at his expense.

He closed his eyes, deliberately initiating a basic relaxation exercise. Slowly, he brought his anger—his panic—under control. Slowly, cool sense returned.

Tereza had been his friend. Caustic, she could certainly be, but to taunt a wounded man for his pain? No. That was not Tereza.

The flimsy was a ruin of mangled fiber and smeared ink. No matter. He crossed the room and dropped it into the fire grate, and stood staring down into the cold ashes.

Return to Solcintra? Not likely.

He moved his shoulders, turned back to the window and picked up the lopsided cup; sipped tepid tea.

He should answer his man of business. He should, for the friendship that had been between them, answer Tereza. He should.

And he would—later. After he had finished his tea and sat for his dry, dutiful hours, trying to recapture that talent which *had* been his, and which seemed to have deserted him now. One of many desertions, and not the least hurtful.

✦✦✦

Spring crept onward, kissing the flowers in the door garden into dewy wakefulness. Oppressed by cedar walls, Mil Ton escaped down the left-hand path, pacing restlessly past knolls and groves, until at last he came to a certain tree, and beneath the tree, a bench, where he sat down, and sighed, and raised his face to receive the benediction of the breeze.

In the warm sunlight, eventually he dozed. Certainly, the day bid well for dozing, sweet dreams and all manner of pleasant things. That he dozed, that was pleasant. That he did not dream, that was well. That he was awakened by a voice murmuring his name, that was—unexpected.

He straightened from his comfortable slouch against the tree, eyes snapping wide.

Before him, settled casually cross-legged on the new grass, heedless of stains on his town-tailored clothes, was a man somewhat younger than himself, dark of hair, gray of eye. Mil Ton stared, voice gone to dust in his throat.

"The house remembered me," the man in the grass said apologetically. "I hope you don't mind."

Mil Ton turned his face away. "When did it matter, what I minded?"

"Always," the other replied softly. "Mil Ton, I told you how it was."

He took a deep breath, imposing calm with an exercise he had learned in Healer Hall, and faced about.

"Fen Ris," he said, low, but not soft. Then, "Yes. You told me how it was."

The gray eyes shadowed. "And in telling you, killed you twice." He raised a ringless and elegant hand, palm turned up. "Would that it were otherwise." The hand reversed, palm toward the grass. "Would that it were not."

Would that he had died of the pain of betrayal, Mil Ton thought, rather than live to endure this. He straightened further on the bench, frowning down at the other.

"Why do you break my peace?"

Fen Ris tipped his head slightly to one side in the old, familiar gesture. "Break?" he murmured, consideringly. "Yes, I suppose I deserve that. Indeed, I know that I deserve it. Did I not first appeal to Master Tereza and the Healers in the Hall at Solcintra, hoping that they might cure what our house Healer could not?" He paused, head bent, then looked up sharply, gray gaze like a blow.

"Master Tereza said she had sent for you," he stated, absolutely neutral. "She said you would not come."

Mil Ton felt a chill, his fingers twitched, as if crumpling a flimsy into ruin.

"She did not say it was you."

"Ah. Would you have come, if she had said it was me?"

Yes, Mil Ton thought, looking aside so the other would not read it in his eyes.

"No," he said.

There was a small silence, followed by a sigh.

"Just as well, then," Fen Ris murmured. "For it was not I." He paused, and Mil Ton looked back to him, drawn despite his will.

"Who, then?" he asked, shortly.

The gray eyes were infinitely sorrowful, eternally determined. "My lifemate."

Fury, pure as flame, seared him. "You dare!"

Fen Ris lifted his chin, defiant. "You, who taught me what it is to truly love—you ask if I *dare?*"

To truly love. Yes, he had taught that lesson—learned that lesson. And then he had learned the next lesson—that even love can betray.

He closed his eyes, groping for the rags of his dignity . . .

"Her name is Endele," Fen Ris said softly. "By profession, she is a gardener." A pause, a light laugh. "A rare blossom in our house of risk-takers and daredevils."

Eyes closed, Mil Ton said nothing.

"Well," Fen Ris said after a moment. "You live so secluded here that you may not have heard of the accident at the skimmer fields last relumma. Three drivers were killed upon the instant. One walked away unscathed. Two were sealed into crisis units. Of those, one died."

Mil Ton had once followed the skimmer races—how not?—he had seen how easily a miscalculated corner approach could become tragedy.

"You were ever Luck's darling," he whispered, his inner ear filled with the shrieks of torn metal and dying drivers; his inner eye watching carefully as Fen Ris climbed from his battered machine and—

"Aye," Fen Ris said. "That I was allowed to emerge whole and hale from the catastrophe unit—that was luck, indeed."

Abruptly it was cold, his mind's eye providing a different scene, as the emergency crew worked feverishly to cut through the twisted remains of a racing skimmer and extricate the shattered driver, the still face sheathed in blood—two alive, of six. Gods, he had almost lost Fen Ris—

No.

He had already lost Fen Ris.

"I might say," Fen Ris murmured, "that I was the most blessed of men, save for this one thing—that when I emerged from the unit, Endele—my lady, my heart . . ." His voice faded.

"She does not remember you."

Silence. Mil Ton opened his eyes and met the bleak gray stare.

"So," said Fen Ris, "you did read the file."

"I read the summary Tereza sent, to entice me back to the Hall," he corrected. "The case intrigued her—no physical impediment to the patient's memory, nor even a complete loss of memory. Only one person has been excised entirely from her past."

"Excised," Fen Ris repeated. "We have not so long a shared past, after all. A year—only that."

Mil Ton moved his shoulders. "Court her anew, then," he said, bitterly.

"When I did not court her before?" the other retorted. He sighed. "I have tried. She withdraws. She does not know me; she does not trust me." He paused, then said, so low Mil Ton could scarcely hear—

"She does not want me."

It should have given him pleasure, Mil Ton thought distantly, to see the one who had dealt him such anguish, in agony. And, yet, it was not pleasure he felt, beholding Fen Ris thus, but rather a sort of bleak inevitability.

"Why me?" he asked, which is not what he had meant to say.

Fen Ris lifted his face, allowing Mil Ton to plumb the depths of his eyes, sample the veracity of his face.

"Because you will know how to value my greatest treasure," he murmured. "Who would know better?"

Mil Ton closed his eyes, listening to his own heartbeat, to the breeze playing in the leaves over his head, and, eventually, to his own voice, low and uninflected.

"Bring her here, if she will come. If she will not, there's an end to it, for I will not go into the city."

"Mil Ton—"

"Hear me. If she refuses Healing, she is free to go when and where she will. If she accepts Healing, the same terms apply." He opened his eyes, and looked hard into the other's face.

"Bring your treasure here and you may lose it of its own will and desire."

This was warning, proper duty of a Healer, after all, and perhaps it was foretelling as well.

Seated, Fen Ris bowed, acknowledging that he'd heard, then came effortlessly to his feet. "The terms are acceptable. I will bring her tomorrow, if she will come."

Mil Ton stood. "Our business is concluded," he said flatly. "Pray, leave me."

Fen Ris stood, frozen—a heartbeat, no more than that; surely, not long enough to be certain—and thawed abruptly, sweeping a low bow, accepting a debt too deep to repay.

"I have not—" Mil Ton began, but the other turned as if he had not spoken, and went lightly across the grass, up the path, and away.

★★★

Mil Ton had stayed up late into the night, pacing and calling himself every sort of fool, retiring at last to toss and turn until he fell into uneasy sleep at dawn. Some hours later, a blade of sunlight sliced through the guardian cedars, through the casement and into his face.

The intrusion of light was enough to wake him. A glance at the clock brought a curse to his lips. Fen Ris would be arriving soon. If, indeed, he arrived at all.

Quickly, Mil Ton showered, dressed, and went on slippered feet down the hall toward the kitchen. As he passed the great room, he glanced within—and froze in his steps.

A woman sat on the edge of the hearth, a blue duffel bag at her feet, her hands neatly folded on her lap. She sat without any of the cushions or pillows she might have used to ease her rest, and her purpose seemed not to be repose, but alert waiting.

Her attention at this moment was directed outward, toward the window, beyond which the busy birds flickered among the cedar branches.

He took one step into thc room.

The woman on the hearth turned her head, showing him a round, high-browed face, and a pair of wary brown eyes.

Mil Ton bowed in welcome to the guest. "Good day to you. I am Mil Ton Intassi, builder of this house."

"And Healer," she said, her voice deeper than he had expected.

"And Healer," he allowed, though with less confidence than he once might have. He glanced around the room. "You came alone?"

She glanced down at the blue duffel. "He drove me here, and opened the door to the house. There was no need for him to wait. He knew I did not want him. You did not want him either, he said."

Not *entirely* true, Mil Ton thought, face heating as he recalled the hours spent pacing. He inclined his head.

"May I know your name?"

"Bah! I have no manners," she cried and sprang to her feet. She bowed—a completely unadorned bow of introduction—and straightened. "I am Endele per'Timbral, Clan—" Her voice faded, a cloud of confusion passed briefly across her smooth face.

"I am Endele per'Timbral," she repeated, round chin thrust out defiantly.

Mil Ton inclined his head. "Be welcome in my house, Endele per'Timbral," he said, seriously. "I am in need of a cup of tea. May I offer you the same?"

"Thank you," she said promptly. "A cup of tea would be welcome."

She followed him down the hall to the kitchen and waited with quiet patience while he rummaged in the closet for a cup worthy of a guest. In the back, he located a confection of pearly porcelain. He poured tea and handed it off, recalling as she received it that the cup had belonged to Fen Ris, the sole survivor of a long-broken set.

Healers were taught to flow with their instincts. Mil Ton turned away to pour for himself, choosing the lopsided cup, as always, and damned both Healer training and himself, for agreeing to . . .

"He said that you can Heal me." Endele spoke from behind him, her speech as unadorned as her bow had been. "He means, you will make me remember him."

Mil Ton turned to look at her. She held the pearly cup daintily on the tips of her fingers, sipping tea as neatly as a cat. Certainly, she was not a beauty—her smooth forehead was too high, her face too round, her hair merely brown, caught back with a plain silver hair ring. Her person was compact and sturdy, and she had the gift of stillness.

"Do you, yourself, desire this Healing?" he asked, the words coming effortlessly to his lips, as if the year away were the merest blink of an eye. "I will not attempt a Healing against your will."

She frowned slightly. "Did you tell him that?"

"Of course," said Mil Ton. "I also told him that, if you wish to leave here for your own destination, now or later, I will not impede you. He accepted the terms."

"Did he?" The frown did not disappear. "Why?"

Mil Ton sipped tea, deliberately savoring the citrus bite while he considered. It was taught that a Healer owed truth to those he would Heal. How much truth was left to the Healer's discretion.

"I believe," he said slowly, to Endele per'Timbral's wary brown eyes, "it is because he values you above all other things and wishes for you only that which will increase your joy."

Tears filled her eyes, glittering. She turned aside, embarrassed to weep before a stranger, as anyone would be, and walked over to the terrace door, her footsteps soft on the wooden floor.

Mil Ton sipped tea and watched her. She stood quite still, her shoulders stiff with tension, teacup forgotten in one hand, staring out into the garden as if it were the most fascinating thoroughfare in Solcintra City.

Sipping tea, Mil Ton let his mind drift. He was not skilled at hearing another's emotions. But the Masters of the Hall in Solcintra had taught him somewhat of their craft, and sometimes, if he disengaged his mind, allowing himself to fall, as it were into a waking doze—well, sometimes, then, he could see . . .

Images.

Now he saw images and more than images. He saw intentions made visible.

Walls of stone, a window set flush and firm, tightly latched against the storm raging without. Hanging to the right of the window was a wreath woven of some blue-leaved plant, which gave off a sweet, springlike scent. Mil Ton breathed in. Breathed out.

He felt, without seeing, that the stone barrier was all around the woman, as if she walked in some great walled city, able to stay safe from some lurking, perhaps inimical presence. . . .

A rustle of something and the stones and their meaning faded.

"Please," a breathless voice said nearby. He opened his eyes to his own wood-floored kitchen, and looked down into the round face of Endele per'Timbral.

"Please," she said again. "May I walk in your garden?"

"Certainly," he said, suddenly remembering her profession. "I am afraid you will find it inadequate in the extreme, however."

"I was charmed to see your house sitting so comfortably in the woods. I am certain I will be charmed by your garden," she said in turn, and placed her cup on the counter.

He unlocked the door and she slipped through, walking down the path without a look behind her. Mil Ton watched her out of sight, then left the door on the latch and poured himself a second cup of tea.

★★

By trade, he was a storyteller. A storyteller whose stories sometimes went . . . odd. Odd enough to pique the interest of the Masters, who had insisted that he was a Healer, and taught him what they could of the craft.

He was, at best, a mediocre Healer, for he never had gained the necessary control over his rather peculiar talent to make it more than an uncertain tool. Sometimes, without warning, he would tell what Tereza was pleased to call a True Story, and that story would have—an effect. Neither story nor effect were predictable, and so he was most likely to be called upon as a last resort, after every other Healing art had failed.

As now.

Mil Ton thought about the woman—the woman Fen Ris had taken as lifemate. He remembered the impassioned speech on the subject of this same woman, on the night Fen Ris had come to tell him how it was.

He sighed then, filled for a moment with all the grief of that night, and recalled Fen Ris demanding, *demanding* that Mil Ton take no Balance against this woman, for she had not stolen Fen Ris but discovered him. Among tears and joy, Fen Ris insisted that they both had been snatched, unanticipated and unplanned, out of their ordinary lives.

And now, of course, there was no ordinary life for any of them.

He wondered—he very much wondered, if Endele per'Timbral would choose Healing.

Her blue bag still lay by the hearth, but it had been many hours since she had gone out into the garden. More than enough time for a sturdy woman in good health to have hiked down to the air-port, engaged a pilot and a plane, and been on her way to—anywhere at all.

Mil Ton sighed and looked back to his screen. When he found that he could no longer practice his profession, he had taught himself a new skill. Written stories never turned odd, and before his betrayal, he had achieved a modest success in his work.

The work was more difficult now; the stories that came so grudgingly off the tips of his fingers bleak and gray and hopeless. He had hoped for something better from this one, before Fen Ris had intruded into his life again. Now, he was distracted, his emotions in turmoil. He wondered again if Endele per'Timbral had departed for a destination of her own choosing. Fen Ris would suffer, if she had done so. He told himself he didn't care.

Unquiet, he put the keyboard aside and pulled a book from the table next to his chair. If he could not write, perhaps he could lose himself inside the story of another.

***

She returned to the house with sunset, her hair wind-combed, her shirt and leggings rumpled, dirt under her fingernails.

"Your garden *is* charming," she told him. "I took the liberty of weeding a few beds so that the younger flowers will have room to grow."

"Ah." said Mil Ton, turning from the freezer with a readimeal in one hand. "My thanks."

"No thanks needed," she assured him, eyeing the box. "I would welcome a similar meal, if the house is able," she said, voice almost shy.

"Certainly, the house is able," he said, snappish from a day of grudging, grayish work.

She inclined her head seriously. "I am in the house's debt." She held up her hands. "Is there a place where I may wash off your garden's good dirt?"

He told her where to find the 'fresher and she left him.

★★★

Dinner was enlivened by a discussion of the garden. She was knowledgeable—more so than Mil Ton, who had planted piece-meal, with those things that appealed to him. He kept up his side only indifferently, his vision from time to time overlain with stone, and a storm raging, raging, raging, outside windows tight and sealed.

When the meal was done, she helped him clear the table, and, when the last dish was stacked in the cleaner, stood awkwardly, her strong, capable hands twisted into a knot before her.

Mil Ton considered her through a shimmer of stone walls.

"Have you decided," he said, careful to keep his voice neutral—for this was *her* choice, and hers alone, so the Master Healers taught. "Whether you are in need of Healing?"

She looked aside, and it seemed that, for a moment, the phantom stones took on weight and substance. Then, the vision faded and it was only clean air between him and a woman undecided.

"They say—they say he is my lifemate," she said, low and stammering. "They say the life-price was negotiated with my clan, that he paid it out of his winnings on the field. They say, we were inseparable, greater together than apart. His kin—they say all this. And I say—if these things are so, why do I not remember him?"

Mil Ton drew a deep, careful breath. "Why should they tell you these things, if they were not so?"

She moved her shoulders, face averted. "Clearly, it *is* so," she whispered. "They—he—the facts are as they state them. I saw the announcement in the back issue of the *Gazette*. I spoke to my sister. I remember the rooms which are mine in his clan house. I remember the gardens, and the shopkeeper at the end of the street. I remember his sister, his brothers—all his kin! Saving him. Only him. My . . . lifemate."

Her pain was evident. One needn't be an empath to feel it. Mil Ton drew a calming breath . . .

"I am not a monster," she continued. "He—of course, he is bewildered. He seems—kind, and, and concerned for my happi-

ness. He looks at me . . . I do *not* know him!" she burst out passionately. "I owe him nothing!" She caught herself, teeth indenting
lower lip. Mil Ton saw the slow slide of a tear down one round
cheek.

She was sincere; he remembered Tereza's report all too well:

*This is not merely some childish game of willfulness, but a true forget-
ting. And, yet, how has she forgotten? Her intellect is intact; she has
suffered no trauma, taken no drugs, appealed to no Healer to rid her of
the burden of her memories. . . .*

"And do you," Mil Ton asked once more, "wish to embrace
Healing?"

She turned her head and looked at him, her cheeks wet and her
eyes tragic.

"What will happen, if I am Healed?"

Ah, the question—the very question. And as he owed her only
truth.

"It is the wish of your lifemate that you would then recall him
and the life you have embarked upon together. If you do not also
wish for that outcome, deny me."

Her lips tightened, and again she turned away, walked a few
steps down the room and turned back to face him.

"You built this house, he said—you alone." She looked around
her, at the bare wooden floor, the cedar beam, the cabinets and
counter in between. "It must have taken a very long time."

So, there would be no Healing. Mil Ton sighed—Fen Ris. It
was possible to feel pity for Fen Ris. He bought a moment to com-
pose himself by repeating her inventory of the kitchen, then
brought his eyes to her face and inclined his head.

"Indeed, it took much longer than needful, to build this house.
I worked on it infrequently, with long stretches between."

"But, why build it at all?"

"Well." He hesitated, then moved his hand, indicating that she
should walk with him.

"I began when I was still an apprentice. My mother had died
and left the mountain to me alone, as her father had once left it to
her. There had been a house here, in the past; I discovered the

foundation when I began to clear the land." He paused and gave her a sidelong look.

"I had planned to have a garden here, you see—and what I did first was to clear the land and cut the pathways . . ."

"But you had uncovered the foundation," she said, preceding him into the great room. She sat on the edge of the hearth, where she had been before. Fen Ris had himself perched precisely there on any number of evenings or mornings. And here was this woman—

Mil Ton walked over to his chair and sat on the arm.

"I had uncovered the foundation," he repeated, "before I went away—back to the city and my craft. I was away—for many years, traveling in stories. I made a success of myself; my tales were sought after; halls were filled with those who hungered for my words.

"When I returned, I was ill with self-loathing. My stories had become . . . weapons—horribly potent, uncontrollable. I drove a man mad in Chonselta City. In Teramis, a woman ran from the hall, screaming . . ."

On the hearth, Endele per'Timbral sat still as a stone, only her eyes alive.

"That I came here—I scarcely knew why. Except that I had discovered a foundation and it came to me that I could build a house, and keep the world safely away."

Oh, gods, he thought, feeling the shape of the words in his mouth, listening to his voice, spinning the tale he meant, and yet did not mean, to tell. . . .

"I built the house of cedar, and laid the beams by hand; the windows I set tight against the walls. At the core, a fireplace—" He used his chin to point over her shoulder. "Before I finished that, the Healers came to me. News of my stories and the effects of my stories had reached the Masters of the Guild and they begged that I come to be trained, before I harmed anyone else." He looked down at his hand, fisted against his knee, and heard his voice continue the tale.

"So, I went and I trained, and then I worked as a Healer in the

Hall. I learned to write stories down and they did not cause madness, and so took up another craft for myself. I was content and solitary until I met a young man at the skimmer track." He paused; she sat like a woman hewn of ice.

"He was bold, and he was beautiful; intelligent and full of joy. We were friends, first, then lovers. I brought him here and he transformed my house with his presence; with his help, the fireplace went from pit to hearth."

He closed his eyes, heard the words fall from his lips. "One evening, he came to me—we had been days apart, but that was no unknown thing—he followed the races, of course. He came to me and he was weeping, he held me and he told me of the woman he had met, how their hearts beat together, how they must be united, or die."

Behind his closed eyes he saw image over image—Fen Ris before him, beseeching and explaining, and this woman's wall of stone, matching texture for texture the very hearth she sat on.

"Perhaps a true Healer might have understood. I did not. I cast him out, told him to go to his woman and leave me—leave me in peace. I fled—here, to the place which was built for safety. . . ."

"How did you abide it?" Her voice was shrill, he opened his eyes to find her on her feet, her body bowed with tension, her eyes frantic. "How did you abide loving him? Knowing what he does? Knowing that they might one day bring his body to you? Couldn't you see that you needed to lock yourself away?"

His vision wavered, he saw stones, falling, felt wind tear his hair, lash rain into his face. In the midst of chaos, he reached out, and put his arms around her, and held her while she sobbed against his shoulder.

Eventually, the wind died, the woman in his arms quieted.

"I loved him for himself," he said softly, into her hair. "And he loved the races. He would not choose to stop racing, though he might have done, had I asked him. But he would have been unhappy, desperately so—and I loved him too well to ask it." He sighed.

"In the end, it came to *my* choice: Did I bide and share in our love, for as long as we both remained? Or turn my face aside, from the fear that, someday, he might be gone?"

In his arms Endele per'Timbral shuddered—and relaxed.

"As simple as that?" she whispered.

"As simple, and as complex." Words failed him for a moment—in his head now were images of Fen Ris laughing, and of the ocean waves crashing on stone beneath the pair of them, of arms reaching eagerly—

He sighed again. "I have perhaps done you no favor, child, in unmaking the choice you had made, if safety is what you need above all."

"Perhaps," she said, and straightened out of his embrace, showing him a wet face, and eyes as calm as dawn. "Perhaps not." She inclined her head. "All honor, Healer. With your permission, I will retire, and tend my garden of choices while I dream."

He showed her to the tiny guest room, with its thin bed and single window, giving out to the moonlit garden, then returned to the great room.

For a few heartbeats, he stood, staring down into the cold hearth. It came to him, as from a distance, that it wanted sweeping, and he knelt down on the stones and reached for the brush.

✦✦✦

"Mil Ton." A woman's voice, near at hand. He stirred, irritable, muscles aching, as if he had slept on cold stone.

"Mil Ton," she said again, and he opened his eyes to Endele per'Timbral's pale and composed face. She extended a hand, and helped him to rise, and they walked in companionable silence to the kitchen for tea.

"Have you decided," he asked her, as they stood by the open door, inhaling the promise of the garden, "what you shall do?"

"Yes," she said softly. "Have you?"

"Yes," he answered—and it was so, though he had not until that moment understood that a decision had been necessary. He smiled, feeling his heart absurdly light in his breast.

"I will return to Solcintra. Tereza writes that there is work for me, at the Hall."

"I am glad," she said. "Perhaps you will come to us, when you are settled. He would like it, I think—and I would."

He looked over to her and met her smile.

"Thank you," he said softly. "I would like it, too."

Calling Your Name

by HOWARD WALDROP

All my life I've waited
for someone to ease the pain
All my life I've waited
for someone to take the blame
—from "Calling Your Name" by Janis Ian

I REACHED for the switch on the band saw.

✺✺✺

Then I woke up with a crowd forming around me.
And I was in my own backyard.

✺✺✺

It turns out that my next door neighbor had seen me fall out of
the storage building I use as a workshop and had called 911 when
I didn't get up after a few seconds.

✺✺✺

Once, long ago in college, working in Little Theater, I'd had a
light bridge lowered to set the fresnels for *Blithe Spirit*, just after
the Christmas semester break. Some idiot had left a hot male 220

plug loose, and as I reached up to the iron bridge, it dropped against the bar. I'd felt that, all over, and I jumped backward about fifteen feet.

A crowd started for me, but I let out some truly blazing oath that turned the whole stage violet-indigo blue and they disappeared in a hurry. Then I yelled at the guys and girl in the technical booth to kill everything onstage, and spent the next hour making sure nothing else wasn't where it shouldn't be. . . .

That's while I was working thirty-six hours a week at a printing plant, going to college full-time and working in the theater another sixty hours a week for no pay. I was also dating a foul-mouthed young woman named Susan who was brighter than me. Eventually something had to give—it was my stomach (an ulcer at twenty) and my relationship with her.

She came back into the theater later that day, and heard about the incident and walked up to me and said, "Are you happy to see me, or is that a hot male 200 volt plug in your pocket?"

That shock, the 220, had felt like someone shaking my hand at 2700 rpm while wearing a spiked glove and someone behind me was hammering nails in my head and meanwhile they were piling safes on me. . . .

When I'd touched the puny 110 band saw, I felt nothing.

Then there were neighbors and two EMS people leaning over me upside down.

"What's up, Doc?" I asked.

"How many fingers?" he asked, moving his hand, changing it in a slow blur.

"Three, five, two."

"What's today?"

"You mean Tuesday, or May 6th?"

I sat up.

"Easy," said the lady EMS person, "You'll probably have a headache."

The guy pushed me back down slowly. "What happened?"

"I turned on the band saw. Then I'm looking at you."

He got up, went to the corner of the shed and turned off the breakers. By then the sirens had stopped, and two or three fire-fighters and the lieutenant had come in the yard.

"You okay, Pops?" he asked.

"I think so," I said. I turned to the crowd. "Thanks to whoever called these guys." Then the EMS people asked me some medical stuff, and the lieutenant, after looking at the breakers, went in the shed and fiddled around. He came out.

"You got a shorted switch," he said. "Better replace it."

I thanked Ms. Krelboind, the neighbor lady, everybody went away, and I went inside to finish my cup of coffee.

★★★

My daughter Maureen pulled up as I drank the last of the milk skim off the top of the coffee.

She ran in.

"Are you all right, Dad?"

"Evidently," I said.

Her husband Bob was a fireman. He usually worked over at Firehouse # 2, the one on the other side of town. He'd heard the address the EMS had been called to on the squawk box, and had called her.

"What happened?"

"Short in the saw," I said. "The lieutenant said so, officially."

"I mean," she repeated, "Are you sure you're all right?"

"It was like a little vacation," I said. "I needed one."

★★★

She called her husband, and I made more coffee, and we got to talking about her kids—Vera, Chuck and Dave, or whichever ones are hers—I can't keep up. There's two daughters, Maureen and Celine, and five grandkids. Sorting them all out was my late wife's job. She's only been gone a year and a month and three days.

We got off onto colleges, even though it would be some years before any of the grandkids needed one. The usual party schools came up. "I can see them at Sam Houston State in togas," I said.

"I'm *just real sure* toga parties will come back," said Mo.

Then I mentioned Kent State.

"Kent State? Nothing ever happens there," she said.

"Yeah, right," I said, "Like the nothing that happened after Nixon invaded Cambodia. All the campuses in America shut down. They sent the Guard in. They shot four people down, just like they were at a carnival."

She looked at me.

"Nixon? What did Nixon have to do with anything?"

"Well, he *was* the president. He wanted "no wider war." Then he sent the Army into Cambodia and Laos. It was before your time."

"Daddy," she said, "I don't remember *much* American history. But Nixon was never president. I think he was vice president under one of those old guys—was it Eisenhower? Then he tried to be a senator. Then he wanted to be president, but someone whipped his ass at the convention. Where in that was he *ever* president? I know Eisenhower didn't die in office."

"What the hell are you talking about?"

"You stay right here," she said, and went to the living room. I heard her banging around in the bookcase. She came back with Vol 14 of the set of 1980s encyclopedias I'd bought for $20 down and $20 a month, seems like paying for about fifteen years on them. . . . She had her thumb in it, holding a place. She opened it on the washing machine lid. "Read."

The entry was on Nixon, Richard Milhous, and it was shorter than it should have been. There was the HUAC and Hiss stuff, the Checkers speech, the vice presidency and reelection, the Kennedy-Nixon debates, the loss, the Senate attempt, the "won't have Dick Nixon to kick around anymore" speech, the law firm, the oil company stuff, the death from phlebitis in 1977—

"Where the hell did you get this? It's *all wrong*."

"It's yours, Dad. It's your encyclopedia. You've had them

twenty years. You bought them for us to do homework out of. Remember?"

I went to the living room. There was a hole in the set at Vol 14. I put it back in. Then I took out Vol 24 UV and looked up Vietnam, War in. There was WWII, 1939–1945, then French Colonial War 1945–1954, then America in 1954–1970. Then I took down Vol II and read about John F. Kennedy (president, 1961–1969).

"Are you better now, Daddy?" she asked.

"No. I haven't finished reading a bunch of lies yet, I've just begun."

"I'm sorry. I know the shock hurt. And things haven't been good since Mom . . . But this really isn't like you."

"I know what happened in the Sixties! I was there! Where were you?"

"Okay, okay. Let's drop it. I've got to get back home; the kids are out of school soon."

"All right," I said. "It was a shock—not a nasty one, not my first, but maybe if I'm careful, my last."

"I'll send Bill over tomorrow on his day off and he can help you fix the saw. You know how he likes to futz with machinery."

"For gods sakes, Mo, it's a bad switch. It'll take two minutes to replace it. It ain't rocket science!"

She hugged me, went out to her car and drove off.

Strange that she should have called her husband Bob, Bill.

No wonder the kids struggled at school. Those encyclopedias sucked. I hope the whole staff got fired and went to prison.

***

I went down to the library where they had *Britannicas*, *World Books*, old *Compton's*. Everybody else in the place was on, or waiting in line for, the Internet.

I sat down by the reference shelves and opened four or five encyclopedias to the entries on Nixon. All of them started Nixon, Richard Milhous, and then in brackets (1913–1977).

After the fifth one, I got up and went over the the reference librarian, who'd just unjammed one of the printers. She looked up at me and smiled, and as I said it, I knew I should not have, but I said, "All your encyclopedias are wrong."

The smile stayed on her face.

And then I thought *Here's a guy standing in front of her; he's in his fifties; he looks a little peaked, and he's telling her all her reference books are wrong. Just like I once heard a guy, in his fifties, a little peaked, yelling at a librarian that some book in the place was trying to tell him that Jesus had been a Jew!*

What would *you* do?

Before she could do anything, I said, "Excuse me."

"Certainly," she said.

I left in a hurry.

★★★

My son-in-law came over the next morning when he should have been asleep.

He looked a little different (his ears were longer. It took a little while to notice that was it) and he seemed a little older, but he looked pretty much the same as always.

"Hey. Mo sent me over to do the major overhaul on the band saw."

"Fuck it." I said. "It's the switch. I can do it in my sleep."

"She said she'd feel better if you let me do it."

"Buzz off."

He laughed and grabbed one of the beers he keeps in my refrigerator. "Okay, then," he said, "can I borrow a couple of albums to tape? I want the kids to hear what real music sounds like."

He had a pretty good selection of 45s, albums, and CDs, even some shellac 78s. He's got a couple of old turntables (one that plays 16 rpm, even). But I have some stuff on vinyl he doesn't.

"Help yourself," I said. He went to the living room and started making noises opening cabinets.

★★★

I mentioned The Who.

"Who?"

"Not who. The Who."

"What do you mean, who?"

"Who. The rock group. *The* Who."

"Who?"

"No, no. The rock group, which is named The Who."

"What is this," he asked. "Abbott and Hardy?"

"We'll get to that later,"I said. "Same time as the early Beatles. That . . ."

"Who?"

"Let me start over. Roger Daltry. Pete Townsend. John Entwhistle. Keith—"

"The High Numbers!" he said. "Why didn't you say so?"

"A minute ago. I said they came along with the early Beatles and you said—"

"Who?"

"Do *not* start."

"There is no rock band called the Beetles," he said with authority.

I looked at him. "Paul McCartney . . ."

He cocked his head, gave me a go-on gesture.

". . . John Lennon, George Harri . . ."

"You mean the Quarrymen?" he asked.

". . . son, Ringo Starr."

"You mean Pete Best and Stuart Sutcliffe," he said.

"Sir Richard Starkey. Ringo Starr. From all the rings on his fingers."

"The Quarrymen. Five guys. They had a few hits in the early Sixties. Wrote a shitpot of songs for other people. Broke up in 1966. Boring old farts since then—tried comeback albums, no back to come to. Lennon lives in a trailer in New Jersey. God knows where the rest of them are."

"Lennon's dead." I said. "He was assassinated at the Dakota

Apartments in NYC in 1980 by a guy who wanted to impress Jodie Foster."

"Well, then, CNTV's got it all wrong, because they did a where-are-they-now thing a couple of weeks ago, and he looked pretty alive to me. He talked a few minutes and showed them some Holsteins or various other moo-cows, and a reporter made fun of them, and Lennon went back into the trailer and closed the door."

I knew they watched a lot of TV at the firehouse.

"This week they did one on ex-President Kennedy. It was his eighty-fourth birthday or something. He's the one that looked near-dead to me—they said he's had Parkinson's since the Sixties. They only had one candle on the cake, but I bet like Popeye these days, he had to eat three cans of spinach just to blow it out. His two brothers took turns reading a proclamation from President Gore. It looked like he didn't know who *that* was. His mom had to help him cut the cake. Then his wife Marilyn kissed him. He seemed to like *that*."

★★★

I sat there quietly a few minutes.

"In your family," I asked, "who's Bill?"

He quit thumbing through the albums. He took in his breath a little too loudly. He looked at me.

"Edward," he said, "*I'm* Bill."

"Then who's Bob?"

"Bob was what they called my younger brother. He lived two days. He's out at Kid Heaven in Greenwood. You, me, and Mo went out there last Easter. Remember?"

"Uh, yeah." I said.

"Are you sure you're okay, after the shock, I mean?"

"Fit as a fiddle," I said, lying through my teeth.

"You sure you don't need help with the saw?"

"It'll be a snap."

"Well, be careful."

"The breakers are still off."

"Thanks for the beer," he said, putting a couple of albums under his arm and going toward the door.

"Bye. Go get some sleep." I said.

I'll have to remember to call Bob, Bill.

✹★✹

Mo was back, in a hurry.

"What is it, Dad? I've never seen Bill so upset."

"I don't know. Things are just so mixed up. In fact, they're wrong."

"What do you mean, wrong? I'm really worried about you now, and so's Bill."

I've never been a whiner, even in the worst of times.

"Oh, Dad," she said. "Maybe you should go see Doc Adams, maybe get some tests done. See if he can't recommend someone . . ."

"You mean, like I've got Alzheimer's? I don't have Alzheimer's! It's not me, it's the world that's off the trolley. Yesterday—I don't know, it's like everything I thought I knew is wrong. It's like some Mohorovoio discontinuity of the mind. Nixon was president. He had to resign because of a break-in at the Watergate Hotel, the Democratic National Headquarters, in 1972. I have a bumper sticker somewhere: "Behind Every Watergate Is A Milhous." It was the same bunch of guys who set up Kennedy in 1963. It was . . ."

I started to cry. Maureen didn't know whether to come to me or not.

"Are you thinking about Mom?" she asked.

"Yes," I said, "Yes, I'm thinking about your mother."

Then she hugged me.

✹★✹

I don't know what to say.

I'm a bright enough guy. I'm beginning to understand, though, about how people get bewildered.

On my way from the library after embarrassing myself, I passed the comic book and poster shop two blocks away. There were re-production posters in one window; the famous one of Clark Gable and Paulette Goddard with the flames of Atlanta behind them from *Mules in Horses' Harnesses*; Fred MacMurray and Jack Oakie in *The Road To Morroco*, and window cards from James Dean in *Somebody Up There Likes Me*, along with *Giant* and *East of Eden*.

I came home and turned on the oldies station. It wasn't there, one like it was somewhere else on the dial.

It was just like Bo—Bill said. The first thing I heard was The Quarrymen doing "*Gimme Deine Hande*." I sat there for two hours, till it got dark, without turning on the lights, listening. There were familiar tunes by somebody else, called something else. There were the right songs by the right people. Janis I. Fink seemed to be in heavy rotation, three songs in the two hours, both before and after she went to prison, according to the DJ. The things you find out on an oldies station . . .

I heard no Chuck Berry, almost an impossibility.

Well, I will try to live here. I'll just have to be careful finding my way around in it. Tomorrow, after the visit to the doc, it's back to the library.

Before going to bed, I rummaged around in my "Important Papers" file. I took out my old draft notice.

It wasn't from Richard Nixon, like it has been for the last thirty-two years. It was from Barry Goldwater. ($A_m + H_2O = 1968$?)

✹✹✹

The psychiatrist seemed like a nice-enough guy. We talked a few minutes about the medical stuff Doc Adams had sent over; work, the shock, what Mo had told the doc.

"Your daughter seems to think you're upset about your envi-ronment. Can you tell me why she thinks that?"

"I think she means to say I told her this was not the world I was born in and have lived in for fifty-six years." I said.

He didn't write anything down in his pad.

"It's all different." I said. He nodded.

"Since the other morning, everything I've known all my life doesn't add up. The wrong people have been elected to office. History is different. Not just the politics-battles-wars stuff, but also social history, culture. There's a book of social history by a guy named Furnas. I haven't looked, but I bet that's all different, too. I'll get it out of the library today. *If* it's there. *If* thre's a guy named Furnas anymore."

I told him some of the things that were changed—just in two days' worth. I told him it—some of it anyway—was fascinating, but I'm sure I'll find scary stuff sooner or later. I'd have to learn to live with it, go with the flow.

"What do you think happened?" he asked.

"What is this, *The Sopranos*?"

"Beg pardon?" he asked.

"Oh. *Oh.* You'd like it. It's a TV show about a Mafia guy who, among other things, goes to a shrink—a lady shrink. It's on HBO."

"HBO?"

"*Sorry.* A cable network."

He wrote three things down on his pad.

"Look. Where I come from . . . I know that sounds weird. In Lindner's book . . ."

"Lindner?"

"Lindner. *The Fifty-Minute Hour.* Best-seller. 1950s."

"I take it by the title it was about psychiatry. *And* a best-seller?"

"*Let me start over.* He wrote the book they took the title *Rebels Without A Cause* from—but *that* had nothing to do with the movie . . ."

He was writing stuff down now, fast.

"It's getting deeper and deeper, isn't it?" I asked.

"Go on. *Please.*"

"Lindner had a patient who was a guy who thought he lived on a far planet in an advanced civilization—star-spanning galaxy-wide stuff. Twenty years before *Star Wars*. Anyway . . ."

He wrote down two words without taking his eyes off me.

"In my world," I said, very slowly and carefully, looking directly at him, "there was a movie called *Star Wars* in 1977 that changed the way business was done in Hollywood."

"Okay," he said.

"This is not getting us anywhere!" I said.

And then he came out with the most heartening thing I'd heard in two days. He said "What do you mean *we, kemo sabe*?"

Well, we laughed and laughed, and then I tried to tell him, *really* tell him, what I thought I knew.

✦✦✦

The past was another country, as they say; they did things differently there.

The more I looked up, the more I needed to look up. I had twelve or fifteen books scattered across the reference tables.

Now I know how conspiracy theorists feel. It's not just the Trilateral Commission or Henry Kissinger (a minor ABC/NRC official *here*) and the Queen of England and Area 51 and the Grays. It's like history has ganged up on me, as an individual, to drive me bugfuck. I don't have a chance. The more you find out the more you need to explain . . . how much more you need to find out . . . it could never end.

Where did it change?

We are trapped in history like insects in amber, and it is hardening all around me.

Who am I to struggle against the tree sap of Time?

✦✦✦

The psychiatrist has asked me to write down and bring in everything I can think of—anything: presidents, cats, wars, culture. He wants to read it ahead of time and schedule two full hours on Friday.

You can bet I don't feel swell about this.

★★★

My other daughter Celine is here. I had *tried* and *tried* and *tried*, but she'd turned out to be a Christian in spite of *all* my work.

She is watching me like a hawk, I can tell. We were never as close as Maureen and me; she was her mother's daughter.

"How are you feeling?"

"Just peachy," I said. "Considering."

"Considering *what?*" Her eyes were very green, like her mother's had been.

"If you don't mind, I'm pretty tired of answering questions. *Or* asking them."

"You ought to be more careful with those tools."

"This is not about power tools, or the shock," I said. "I don't know what Mo told you, but I have been *truly* discomfited these last few days."

"Look, Daddy," she said. "I don't care what the trouble is, we'll find a way to get you through it."

"You couldn't get me through it, unless you've got a couple of thousand years on rewind."

"What?"

"Never mind. I'm just tired. And I have to go to the hardware store and get a new switch for the band saw, before I burn the place down, or cause World War III or something. I'm *sure* they have hardware stores here, or *I* wouldn't have power tools."

She looked at me like I'd grown tentacles.

"Just kidding." I said. "Loosen up, Celine. Think of me right now as your old, tired father. I'll learn my way around the place and be right as rain . . ."

Absolutely no response.

"I'm being ironic," I said. "I have always been noted for my sense of humor. Remember?"

"Well, yes. Sort of."

"Great!" I said. "Let's go get some burgers at McDonald's!"

"Where?"

"I mean Burger King." I said. I'd passed one on the way back from the library.

"Sounds good, Dad." She said, "Let *me* drive."

**★★

I have lived in this house for twenty-six years. I was born in the house across the street. In 1957, my friend Gino Ballantoni lived here, and I was over here every day, or just about, for four years, till Gino's father's aircraft job moved to California. I'd always wanted it, and after I got out of the Army, I got it on the GI Bill.

I know its every pop and groan, every sound it makes day or night, the feel of the one place the paint isn't smooth, on the inside doorjamb trim of what used to be Mo's room before it was Celine's. There's one light switch put on upside down I never changed. The garage makeover I did myself; it's what's now the living room.

I love this place. I would have lived here no matter what.

I tell myself history wasn't different enough that this house isn't still a vacant lot, *or* an apartment building. That's, at least, something to hang onto.

I noticed the extra sticker inside the car windshield. Evidently, we now have an emissions-control test in this state, too. I'll have to look in the phone book and find out where to go, as this one expires at the end of the month.

And also, on TV, when they show news from New York, there's still the two World Trade Center Towers.

You can't be *too* careful about the past.

**★★

The psychiatrist called to ask if someone could sit in on the double session tomorrow—he knew it was early, but it was special—his old mentor from whatever Mater he'd Alma'd at; the guy was in a day early for some shrink hoedown in the Big City and wanted to watch his star pupil in action. He was asking all the patients tomorrow, he said. The old doc wouldn't say anything, and you'd hardly know he was there.

"Well, I got enough troubles, what's one more?"

He thanked me.

That's what did it for me. This was not going to stop. This was not something that I could be helped to work through, like bedwetting or agoraphobia or the desire to eat human flesh. It was going to go on forever, here, until I died.

Okay, I thought. Let's get out Occam's Famous Razor and cut a few Gordian Knots. Or somewhat, as the logicians used to say.

★★★

I went out to the workshop where everybody thinks it all started.

I turned on the outside breakers. I went inside. This time I closed the door. I went over and turned on the bandsaw

★★★

After I got up off the floor, I opened the door and stepped out into the yard. It was near dark, so I must have been out an hour or so.

I turned off the breakers and went into the house through the back door and through the utility room and down the hall to the living room bookcase. I pulled out Vol 14 of the encyclopedia and opened it.

Nixon, Richard Milhouse, it said (1913–1954). A good long entry.

There was a sound from the kitchen. The oven door opened and closed.

"What have you been doing?" asked a voice.

"There's a short in the band saw I'll have to get fixed," I said. I went around the corner.

It was my wife Susan. She looked a little older, a little heavier since I last saw her, it seemed. She still looked pretty good.

"Stand there where I can see you," I said.

"We were having a fight before you wandered away, remember?"

"Whatever it was," I said, "I was wrong. You were right. We'll do whatever it is you want."

"Do you even remember what it was we were arguing about?"

"No." I said. "Whatever. It's not important. The problems of two people don't amount to a hill of beans in—"

"Cut the Casablanca crap," said Susan. "Jodie and Susie Q want to bring the kids over next Saturday and have Little Eddy's birthday party here. You wanted peace and quiet here, and go somewhere else for the party. That was the argument."

"I wasn't cut out to be a grandpa," I said. "But bring 'em on. Invite the neighbors! Put out signs on the street! 'Annoy an old man here!'"

Then I quieted down. "Tell them we'd be happy to have the party here," I said.

"Honestly, Edward," said Susan, putting the casserole on the big trivet. It was *her* night to cook. "Sometimes I think you'd forget your ass if it weren't glued on."

"Yeah, sure," I said. "I've damn sure forgotten what peace and quiet was like. And probably lots of other stuff, too."

"Supper's ready," said Susan.

Shadow in the City

by DEAN WESLEY SMITH

You don't see many shadows here in the city
Only picturesque windows, all covered and dirty
Black and gray that once was new
Yesterday that once was you
No I can't find my shadow in the city
—from "Here in the City" by Janis Ian

FOUR years ago the city below her had died along with the rest of the world.

Now she stood on the abandoned freeway overpass and stared at the gray of Portland, Oregon, and the deep blue of the gently flowing river below her. Why had she picked today, of all days, to finally go back into the city?

Carey Noack was five foot two and wiry. Over the last four years she had kept her light-brown hair cut very short. Today, for the final hike into the center of the big buildings, she wore a black sleeveless T-shirt, jeans, and her favorite tennis shoes.

"Stupid," she muttered as she used a small towel from her pack to wipe the sweat from her face and arms. It was a typical Oregon summer day, where the bright sun and clear skies made the air feel warmer than it actually was. She finished wiping off her arms, put the towel back in her pack, and grabbed the water bottle.

She took a long, deep drink of the warm water. She was going to have to be careful, make sure she didn't push too hard. She hated heat.

As she stood there on the overpass, it was hard to push away the memories of the nightmarish last days she had spent in the city, and her last trip to the coast. It had been hot that week as well. The dead, staring bodies had been everywhere, filling the hot winds with the smell of rotting flesh.

She had run, trying to get away from the death and the smell. Of course, the dead bodies had been in the small towns on the coast as well, and it had taken her some time to find sanctuary. The house she had taken just north of Depoe Bay sat on a rock ledge jutting out into the ocean. The breezes were always off the water, and seldom did the smell of rotting flesh reach her.

Why, after four long years of living alone on the coast, was she back today, of all days? Was she really that lonely? She knew that many, many nights, especially during the first year, she had simply sat and cried, trying to hold back the overwhelming feelings of sadness, shock, and loneliness. It was one thing to be a loner when the world was alive around her. It was another to be completely alone, talking to herself and her cats.

She missed her cats. She hoped she had left enough food for them to make it until she got back to the coast.

She had half expected that the buildings of the city would be crumbling and dead as well, but they weren't. Windows were covered with dirt and film, weeds were growing thick in the cracks of the sidewalks, and nothing was lit. The stop lights swinging lightly in the hot wind at the end of the overpass were now nothing more than dead eyes hanging over empty streets.

Carey shook off the feeling, took a second, long drink of water, and stared down at the freeway. She had to be careful. There was no telling what waited for her there.

The hot wind snapped at her short hair. At least now the wind didn't bring the smell of death as it had done the day she left. Four years of time had cleared that out, and she was grateful.

She picked up the backpack and shifted it slightly to make sure one strap didn't rub her shoulder too long. The pack contained enough water to get her by for a few days, plus food for two weeks, and extra ammunition for her rifle and the pistol in her belt.

She had spent a pretty good amount of time over the last two years learning how to fire that pistol and rifle quickly and accurately. There was always the remote chance that she actually might run into someone else, someone alive. And since she was a woman alone, she didn't plan on taking any chances. But so far there was not even a sign that anyone had passed through during the past four years.

Still, the small rifle felt good in her hands. A comfort. And for the rest of the walk into town she would carry it off her shoulder, loaded and ready.

Her hope—and her fear—was that there *would* be other survivors in the city. She was convinced that a normal, sane person would have given up that hope by now, but still, here she was today, standing on the edge of the dead city, ready to check it out.

Sometimes Carey lay awake at night listening to the waves pound the beach and rocks below her home and thought of people, and how nice it would be to talk to someone, or even listen to someone. Just companionship. But four years of living alone had given her a lot of time to think, and she knew that simple, easy companionship wasn't going to happen. She was going to die alone.

She glanced up the freeway. Back that direction was home, with generators for electricity, large screen television for running movies, and a basement filled with more books than she would ever read.

She couldn't believe that in the midst of all the death, she had managed to make the coast feel like home. The first year she had adopted two stray cats by slowly feeding them until they finally trusted her. Stingy was an old yellow cat who hogged the food, and Betty sat and purred while being petted, but never really left Stingy's side. Carey talked to them all the time.

She had set up fishing nets and crab pots, and planned her days around finding enough food to keep going. During the spring, summer, and fall, she kept her gardens tended, with the biggest problem being keeping the deer away. She had built and stocked a root cellar, and filled another close-by house with canned goods that she hoped would last.

Living like that had cut her off from the sights, sounds, and reminders of what had happened to the rest of humanity. She knew how to be alone, how to live alone. That didn't worry her anymore—but the thought of dying alone terrified her.

And she really wanted someone to talk to. Someone besides her cats. She had to find out if she really was alone in the world, if the human race was going to die with her, or if there was still hope.

There *had* to be hope.

Considering the fluke circumstances that had allowed her to survive, she was certain that if there was anyone else, their numbers would be few. For a week before that last day, scientists around the world had been whispering among themselves about what seemed like a cloud approaching Earth. No one was exactly certain what it was.

All they knew was that something out there was bending light, twisting it, ripping it apart, and Earth was going to pass right through it. Still, it was no big deal, just a scientific curiosity.

She had been a post-doc student in electromagnetics at the time. As the moment Earth passed through the cloud approached, she took her current experiment and moved it to a secure vault, so that it wouldn't be affected if indeed the cloud possessed high energy levels.

When she stepped out thirty minutes later, she was the only living soul in Portland.

The drivers had died instantly. Car wrecks were everywhere, many still burning.

Out near the airport dark clouds of smoke billowed into the air where half a dozen planes had crashed.

In a single instant Portland had gone from a beautiful city to a nightmare filled with death.

Carey could barely remember stumbling out of the lab, checking futilely for signs of life. She found her lover where she had left him that morning, still in bed in her apartment.

Her mother was slumped over the sink of the family home in

Beaverton, with the water still running. She had found her father in his office, collapsed across his desk, his secretary dead in her chair.

Thousands upon thousands of dead bodies, all caught in a moment in time. At first it seemed like a bad dream, then a nightmare she desperately wanted to wake up from.

Soon the bodies started to smell and bloat up in the heat, looking even more nightmarish as the maggots took over.

Finally, after two days of wandering around, she found herself back in the lab, trying to discover what exactly had happened. The instruments probably told the story, but they were a different discipline; she couldn't interpret them. It didn't make much difference anyway; everyone who was exposed to the cloud, or whatever signal the cloud was transmitting, had died instantly. She didn't need the lab to tell her that, and somehow the *reason* for it didn't seem all that important after the fact of it.

The storm had been very selective in its destruction. It killed dogs, but not cats. Horses were gone, but not cattle. Rats, mice, most rodents were dead, but not most fish.

Deer had survived as well. And raccoons. And a lot of bees and insects of different types. She had no idea what the effect of the massive disruptions in the food chains would be, and she had no way of knowing why some animals survived the cloud and others did not. All she knew was that humans had drawn the short straw.

The next morning, she headed for the coast to get away from the growing stench of the hordes of the dead.

And now, four years later, she was back.

Carey took another drink from the bottle of water, and studied the area in front of her. The freeway wound down the hill toward the river. She could see most of the tall buildings, some of the riverfront, and all of the east side. Portland was still a beautiful town. Beautiful—and empty.

A few dozen cars were piled and scattered along the freeway where they had crashed. They were such a common sight that Carey didn't even notice the bodies in them anymore. Today she looked, and could see the gleaming white of skeletons, all securely strapped in their seat belts.

She finished off the bottle of water, adjusted her backpack, and started to cross the overpass down toward the empty, weed-littered freeway surface, rifle in hand.

★★★

Toby Landel awoke with a start as the alarm on the computer beeped loudly, echoing through his penthouse apartment. He opened his eyes and stared at the white ceiling and wood beams over his bed.

Something had triggered his security alarm again.

"Damned deer," he muttered, tossing aside the sheet and standing. He was nude, but since the morning seemed hot and bright, he didn't bother to slip on his robe or slippers. He moved across the soft carpet toward the computer room. Outside the expanse of open windows around him, the dead city of Portland looked exactly as it had every day for the past two years. But this morning the sun had already cleared off the haze, and he could tell without even going out the air was hot and dry.

He had set up the penthouse apartment, on the fifteenth floor of what had been the Baxter Building, to cater to his every need. It had a soft rich carpet, big expansive rooms, and an island kitchen in the center with bright lights and every conceivable appliance.

He had furnished the living room with a deep, comfortable recliner placed directly in front of a large screen television. He had also brought in a couch for the times he wanted to just lie down. To the right of the living room he had put together a weight and exercise room to keep his six foot frame in top shape. He lifted every day, and ran on a treadmill facing the windows. He figured that he would never know when being in shape would save his life.

Another recliner that matched the one in the living room sat in front of a massive picture window that looked out over the Willamette River. Beyond the river he could see the snow-capped peak of Mt. Hood.

Sometimes he sat there and read when it rained, watching the patterns of the water between chapters. When the world had still been alive, he never would have been able to afford a place like this. Now he figured he deserved it. Besides, who was left to tell him no?

The beeping continued, drawing him toward the computer room he had installed in the west corner of the big penthouse. He had been an electrician by trade before everyone had died, and specialized in security cameras. In fact, he had been installing a bank camera the day the city died. He and Jenkins had been down in the vault when suddenly everything went silent on the comm link with the boss in the truck.

Jenkins had gone up to investigate, leaving Toby in the vault. Toby had never seen him again. By the time Toby had given up waiting, left the vault open, and went to investigate, Jenkins was gone, and everyone else was dead. The only thing Toby could fig-ure, in hindsight, was Jenkins had seen everyone dead and had freaked and headed home to check on his wife and kids.

At first Toby thought that something airborne had killed every-one, and it would soon get him, so he had gone back inside. But after a short time of staring at dead bank customers and tellers, he knew that was stupid.

After that he had started to wander the streets, shocked at how people had died, staring at bodies, not really heading anywhere in particular for the first hour or so. Slowly it began to dawn on him that maybe he (and Jenkins, wherever he had gone,) were the only ones left alive.

His parents lived in Bend, a little resort city over the Cascade Mountains at the foot of Bachelor Ski Area. He had managed to make the six-hour drive in just under twelve, using six different cars when he came upon areas of the road that were jammed with wrecks. He had simply left the car and hiked until he found another car on the other side of the blockage.

All the way he hoped they had been outside the influence of what had happened, that he would find them alive and worried about him. As he got closer the evidence told him that would not be the case.

He found his parents both dead, as well as everyone else in the small town. For an hour he had sat in the middle of the main intersection, with the light changing from green to red over his head, honking a car's horn. The sound seemed impossibly loud, echoing off the buildings and the pine-covered mountains.

No one came and told him to stop.

He was alone. *Really* alone, and the thought scared him more than he had ever been scared before.

The next few days were a blur. He had buried his parents next to his grandparents in the town's cemetery. Then he had gone down to his favorite bar and dragged all the bodies out onto the sidewalk and sat them at tables he had put there, posing each body as if it was still alive and enjoying its drink.

Then he had gone inside, alone, filled the top of the bar with bottles of booze, and got so drunk he couldn't think.

It was finally the smell of rotting human bodies that had driven him away from the town and out to a cabin 'way up in the Cascade Mountains, where he stayed for a long winter, waiting for Nature to clean up the mess.

Then for a year he had wandered the Northwest, looking for anyone else alive, returning to Portland two years ago.

The computer alarm kept beeping, getting louder as he entered the room.

"All right, all right," he snarled. "I'm coming."

He expected to see nothing on the monitor, and to have to rewind a tape to see what had triggered the alarm. He had set up the system of motion detectors two years ago. The sensors triggered cameras and ran off batteries that he recharged every six months. He had installed the system when he realized the lights from the generator running his penthouse apartment could be seen for miles around the city.

And if anyone else was alive out there, he figured it would be better to know when they were getting close. The cameras surveyed some twenty different ways into the city. Deer triggered the alarms a couple of times a day—but once, six months earlier, a ragged, insane-looking man armed with machine guns had come through, heading north.

The man clearly did not bathe often, was dragging a pack in a wagon, and talked to himself constantly. No matter how much Toby had wanted another human back in his life, he couldn't bring himself to approach the guy. The man was just too dangerous. Toby had watched him for two days with hidden cameras, but never let him know he was around.

The man had done one good thing for Toby. He had proved that there were others out there, alive and surviving in some fashion. And ever since that day Toby had been trying to figure out where they might be.

"All right," he said, dropping his nude body into the chair in front of his monitor. The motion had been on the old Interstate 5, heading south. Deer often went through there, since it was between the hills and the river.

He flicked up an image from a camera he had hidden on a pole, expecting to see either deer, or nothing at all. The sight of a woman, standing on an overpass, shocked him to his very core.

His fingers fumbled over the controls for a moment before he brought up the zoom.

A woman, by herself!

He wasn't seeing things. She wore a black, sleeveless T-shirt, jeans, and tennis shoes. She had short, brown hair, light skin, and a lean, muscled body. He stared at her image as she finished putting lotion on her arms and then took a drink of water. He would have been attracted to her even when everyone was still alive.

As he watched, she headed off the overpass, a small rifle in her hand, walking with the assured gait of someone who had confidence to spare.

He wanted to shout at the screen that he was here, that she should wait for him.

It took only a moment before she was headed down the freeway toward town and out of his camera range.

The moment she disappeared he felt a jolt of panic go through him. His hands scrambled over the massive control board he had set up for the security cameras. Finally he managed to activate the next camera, which covered a section of the old Interstate 5 south of town. For a long moment he thought he had lost her, but then she came around a large pile of wrecked cars and kept walking, right at him, as the motion-sensor alarm for that area started to ring.

She was too good to be true, an impossible dream.

He flipped off the alarm and sat back in silence, watching her stride toward him.

This couldn't be happening!

Almost all of the entire population of the planet seemed to be dead, yet here was a woman walking right into his life.

And just like back in his college days, he had no idea how to meet her.

The rifle she carried so easily seemed to grow bigger.

At least back in college, trying to meet a girl didn't mean risking getting shot. But as he stared at this woman's face, he had no doubt, that was a risk he was going to have to take.

✦★✦

Carey kept her pace slow and easy in the hot sun as she headed down the freeway, moving in and around wrecked cars with their drivers still strapped behind the wheels, smiling skeleton smiles at her.

She stared ahead at the big overpass and the signs directing traffic to the downtown area, or along the bridge and beyond to Seattle.

Seattle. It seemed so far away. Still, if there was no one alive here that she could talk to, maybe she should take a look in Seattle some day.

Maybe.

Right now that seemed too far, too much to think about.

She made herself focus on the city in front of her. It seemed so familiar, yet so alien. Ahead of her a half mile or so, the Marriott

Hotel's tower rose over the river. Her plan was to stay there, in one of the unoccupied rooms with a view. When she'd worked in town she'd never had a reason, or enough money, to stay there. It would be a treat.

She would find a good room, set it up as a base for exploring the city, and maybe, if she had enough nerve to see Sam's body again, go back to her old apartment for some keepsakes. She planned on stocking the hotel room with food, maybe even get a portable generator in for electricity. But first of all she would have to check the water, make sure there was enough to last her for a time.

Maybe with a little work, she could even make the place permanent. It hadn't occurred to her until just that moment that she could have a place in the city, a place on the coast, a place just about anywhere in the world she wanted.

After all, there was nothing to stop her.

She moved along the off ramp that led down to Front Street and then along the riverfront a dozen more blocks to the hotel. The grass along the river had turned to weeds, the sidewalks and streets were cracked and growing grass in places. But still the city had a beauty about it, with the blue river flowing through it, the mountains around it, and the green trees everywhere.

The air smelled faintly of water and fish, and birds chirped and flitted from nests in the branches of the trees along the old park. She could see where they had stained the edges of buildings, building nests in windows.

Two blocks short of the hotel, she sensed a movement off to her left. She turned, the rifle up and ready, her blood racing.

A bird flittered away. She sighed and lowered the gun. "All right," she said out loud, "calm down and don't go shooting every little thing that moves."

"I'm very glad to hear you say that," said a deep, rich voice.

She spun around, the rifle again up, her heart pounding so hard she thought it was going to jump right out of her chest.

She found herself face-to-face with a man about her age, with brown, unruly hair, twinkling brown eyes, and a friendly smile. He had his hands raised in the air like prisoners in days of old. He had stepped out of the shadows near an office building and was no more than ten steps from her.

She kept her gaze locked on his, the rifle pointed at his chest. She had hoped to find someone else alive, but she had never expected to—and she had certainly never expected to find someone so damn good-looking.

"I'm not going to bite," said the man. His voice stayed level and didn't shake, even though she could tell he was worried about the rifle. Then he laughed. "Sorry for the cliché. I didn't know what else to say. I am unarmed and alone. In fact, until you showed up, I thought I was alone in the universe." Another smile. "Or at least the sovereign state of Oregon."

She didn't lower her gun, and he didn't lower his arms. "How did you know I was here?"

"Security cameras," he said, pointing up at the top of a pole on Front Street. "I have them on all the main thoroughfares. A person living alone can never be too careful. But to be honest, I was also hoping to find someone else alive, perhaps passing through."

"And you sit all day and watch your cameras?" she asked.

"Not hardly. In fact, you woke me when you stopped on the overpass. I have motion detector alarms."

She could feel herself starting to relax just a little, and her little internal voice wasn't screaming that this man was dangerous. She would have set up security cameras like that if she had known how.

She forced herself to think and give herself time to calm down. One mistake, one slip, and she could find herself in a very bad situation. He was shorter than Sam had been, but still clearly very strong. She had to be careful, no matter how much she wanted to lower her gun and hug this stranger and just talk to him.

"So where do you live?" she asked.

"The Baxter Building," he said. "Been there for two years, in the penthouse. How about you?"

"On the coast," she said.

He nodded. "Yeah, I was up in the Cascades, in the forest, until the smell cleared."

"How did you survive?"

"I installed the security system in a bank in Beaverton. I was down in the vault, but I have no idea why that protected me."

"So, do you have a name?" she asked.

"Toby," he said. "Toby Landel. An actual, native Oregonian, born and raised."

She actually laughed at that, since something like that mattered only to Oregonians.

"I'm Carissa Novak. People call me Carey—or they did, back when we had people. I'm Oregonian through and through,"

It felt strange using her full name after four years. Strange and yet somehow normal, as if having and using a full name returned a little civilization to the world.

"How about I cook us both breakfast?" Toby said. "My stomach is starting to sound like an earthquake, and I bet you haven't had a good omelet since you left the coast."

"Omelet?" she repeated, trying to hide her enthusiasm.

"Yeah, real eggs and everything," he said. "Honest."

"How? Here in the city?"

He nodded, smiling as if he was very proud of having eggs. "It seems chickens survived whatever killed everyone. So I went out into the country and trapped some, including roosters, and set them loose in the Rose Garden."

"You're kidding!" she said. The Rose Garden was the big basketball arena where the Portland Trailblazers basketball team had played.

"I'm not," he said, laughing again. "It does seem strange, now that I think of it. I just figured the seats would make great nests for them, plus it's big enough to hold a lot of birds."

She laughed at the idea. The Rose Garden as a chicken coop. How perfect! "What do you feed them? How many do you have?"

He shrugged. "Every few weeks I scatter a truckload of grain from sacks I get in a warehouse down by the river. Every month or so I trap some more birds and turn them loose in there. The population seems to be growing. I try to go get the eggs I can find every few days, but there are always more than I can use. I take a bird every few weeks for a special dinner. I bet I have five hundred birds in there now, if not more."

"Amazing!" she said.

"Thanks," he said, smiling. "I'd be glad to show it to you, right after breakfast—and I would love to have someone to talk to while I'm cooking."

She stared at him for a moment. She had come back into town with the hope of finding someone else still alive, but she had never expected a great-looking guy who could raise chickens and cook.

"All right, Mr. Toby Landel," she said, swinging her rifle up on her shoulder, but making sure her pistol was within easy and quick reach in her belt. "Let's go see how good a cook you really are."

The smile that lit up his face almost melted her right there in the street. She had been lonely for so many days and weeks and months and years, and clearly he had felt the same way.

She moved beside him, matching him stride for stride, feeling just like a junior high girl faced with talking to a boy on a first date.

She *really* hoped that she wouldn't have to kill him.

★★★

It had gone better than he had hoped. She hadn't shot him. On top of that she had actually accepted his invitation to breakfast.

It was also a fact that his cameras had not done her justice. Up close, her deep brown eyes and intense gaze melted him like no other woman had ever done before. Now granted, he hadn't seen a live woman in four years, but he was pretty sure she would have had that effect on him even before everyone died.

Now all he wanted to do was talk with her. He had not realized until he started speaking just how much he had missed interacting with humans.

"This is the place," he said, his arm sweeping around the penthouse that no one else had seen in four years. "And that's Buddy."

Buddy was his big gray-and-white cat that had adopted him when he moved into this building. Now Buddy hated going out, loved sitting with him while he read, and was a great companion.

Buddy walked up to Carey as she knelt down to pet him. "I've got two—Stingy and Betty."

"I bet you miss them," said Toby. "How long have you been gone?"

"Eight days," she said, petting Buddy as Toby went into the kitchen area and opened the refrigerator. He got out the eggs and some fixings.

She stood and dropped her pack, putting her rifle on top of it. Then she moved over and looked at his kitchen. "Wow, you have everything in here!"

"The advantage of not having to pay for anything," he said. "Feel free to look around while I get this started. The computer monitor room is up front in the corner, the bathroom is back there on the left."

He watched as she hesitated, then decided to go ahead and look at his place. She poked her head into the computer room, then nodded. "You're good at electronics, aren't you?"

"Not as good as I used to be when I worked with it every day," he said, breaking six eggs into a pan. "I'm afraid my omelets are basically eggs mixed with green peppers and onions from my roof-top garden, and some ham. I haven't had the courage to try any mushrooms."

"That sounds wonderful," she said, smiling at him as she ran her hand across the back of the chair he had facing the window. "This is some view."

"No one seemed to be using the place, so I figured why not," he said.

"I know that feeling. I'm using three different houses on the coast." She moved to the edge of the island kitchen and leaned on the counter. "You know, for four years I've been hoping to find someone alive, have someone to talk to, and now that we have met, I don't know what to say."

He stopped cutting and looked into her deep brown eyes. "I'm feeling the same way, to be honest. Like a high school kid afraid to talk to the girl in the chair beside him."

She laughed. "I'm feeling more junior high."

"I didn't notice girls back then," he said. "I didn't start paying attention until my sophomore year."

For some reason that admission seemed to break the ice. He could feel it, and the sound of her light laugh filled the room.

As he cooked, they went through their backgrounds, his in Bend, hers in Beaverton. He had been a year behind her in school, and for some reason, even though they were both at the University of Oregon at the same time, they had no memory of ever seeing each other.

When they were done eating, and he had refused to let her help clean up, she asked if she could use his bathroom. When he agreed, and warned her about the hot water being a little too hot, she had smiled like he had given her a perfect Christmas present.

As she was taking her shower, he took a cup of coffee and moved over to his chair in front of the window. How had he managed to actually meet another person, let alone a woman he was attracted to? Had he dreamed the entire thing? Was the water running in the bathroom just his mind playing tricks on him?

And what was he going to do next?

Actually, more importantly, what was *she* going to do next?

★★★

By the time she finished the most heavenly shower she could remember in years, her mind had cleared some. She was still having a hard time believing that anyone else was left alive, let alone someone nice. But unless she was dreaming this shower, and that fantastic omelet, Toby was actually out there.

She put on clean clothes, stuffed the dirty ones in her pack, put her pistol back in her belt and went out, dropping her pack beside the door before petting Buddy.

"Everything all right?" he asked.

"Perfect," she said. "I haven't had a hot shower since I left home. Thank you."

"No problem," he said. "There's coffee on the counter in the big pot. Help yourself."

He suddenly jumped up, moved into the living room, and dragged the other matching chair back so that it sat at an angle, facing the window. She poured herself a cup of coffee and joined him.

"Sorry," he said, smiling at her as he finished moving the second chair beside the first. "I'm not used to having guests."

She sat and put her feet up. "I know the feeling."

She enjoyed the silence and the fantastic view for a few moments. Then he asked, "Do you know what caused all this?"

"I think so. I believe the cloud emitted an electromagnetic pulse that shattered the neural synapses of people and certain types of animal."

"An electromagnetic pulse?" he repeated, frowning.

"Basically, yes," she said. "I was protected by an experiment vault, as you must have been protected in the bank."

He jumped up and started pacing. "Do you know what this means?" he said, the excitement clear.

"What?"

"That there have to be others alive out there besides us. Maybe even an entire community of people. Maybe more than one community, in touch with others around the world."

"You're not making sense," she said. "Where? And how?"

"Cheyenne Mountain in Colorado, for one," he said. "There are lots and lots of people who worked down in that mountain twenty-four hours a day. It's protected from electromagnetic pulses like we were, and they all would have survived."

She remembered reading stories of how Cheyenne Mountain was built to withstand a direct atomic hit. Maybe, just maybe . . .

"And there were places like that under the White House, and on other military bases," he continued. "And some atomic subs were protected. If it's electromagnetic pulses that did this, then there will be a *lot* of people alive out there. And they will gather in groups. All we need to do is find them."

He dropped into his chair and sat staring over the hot city.

She looked at him, then sat back as well, letting the notion sink in. Suddenly the world on the other side of those windows didn't seem so dead.

Or so hopeless.

If he was right, there were other people out there, somewhere, maybe trying to rebuild civilization. She had skills that she could offer them.

So did Toby, if that computer surveillance room was any indication.

"I am very glad you decided to come back to the city," he said, looking at her. "And that you didn't shoot me on sight."

"So am I," she said, smiling at him.

They both fell silent, staring at the river and the mountains to the east. She had never felt so comfortable in a silence.

And now the silence wasn't because of death, but because of the chance of life. It was the silence of two people thinking—thinking of where to start their search, and what to do when it was successful, as she was sure it eventually would be.

And the thought that dominated all the others in her mind was that now, finally, there was a chance that she wouldn't die alone.

Joe Steele

by HARRY TURTLEDOVE

Stalin was a Democrat . . .
—*from "god & the fbi" by Janis Ian*

AMERICA. 1932. Bread lines. Soup kitchens. Brother, can you spare a dime? Banks dying like flies. Brokers swan diving from the twenty-seventh floor.

Herbert Hoover. Dead man walking. Couldn't get reelected running with the Holy Ghost. Republicans nominate him again anyway. Got nobody better. Don't know how much trouble they're in.

Democrats smell blood in the water. Twelve long years sitting on the sidelines. Twelve lean years. Twelve hungry years. Harding—women got the vote for *this*? Coolidge—"I've got a five-dollar bet, Mr. Coolidge, that I can get you to say three words." "You lose," says Silent Cal. Hoover—Black Tuesday. The crash. Enough said. It's on his watch. He gets the blame. Blood in the water.

Democrats smell it. Whoever they put up, he's gonna win. Gonna be president. At last. Been so long. Twelve years. Sweet Jesus Christ! Want it so bad they can taste it.

Convention time. Chicago. End of June. Humidity's high. Heat's higher. Two men left in the fight. One wins the prize. The other? Hind tit.

Two men left. Franklin D. Roosevelt. D for Delano, mind. Governor of New York. Cousin to Teddy Roosevelt. Already ran for vice president once. Didn't win. Cigarette holder. Jaunty angle.

Wheelchair. Paralysis. Anguish. Courage. As near an aristocrat as America grows. Franklin D. Roosevelt. D for Delano.

And Joe Steele.

Joe Steele. Congressman from California. Not San Francisco. Not Nob Hill. Good Lord, no. Fresno. Farm country. That great valley, squeezed by mountains east and west. Not a big fellow, Joe Steele. Stands real straight, so you don't notice too much. Mustache, a good-sized one. Thick head of hair just starting to go gray. Eyelids like shutters. When they go down and then come up again, you can't see what was behind them.

Aristocrat? Aristocrat like Franklin D. (D for Delano) Roosevelt? Don't make me laugh. Folks came from the ass end of nowhere. Got to Fresno six months before he was born. He was a citizen years before they were. Father was a shoemaker. Did some farming later on, too. Mother tended house. That's what women did.

They say Steele's not the right name. Not the name he was born with. They say God Himself couldn't say that name straight two times running. They say, they say. Who gives a good goddamn what they say? This is America. He's Joe Steele now. Then? What's then got to do with it? That was the old country, or near enough.

Franklin D. Roosevelt. D for Delano. And Joe Steele.

★★★

Chicago Stadium. Sweltering. Air-conditioning? You've got to be kidding. Not even in the hotels. You put on two electric fans when you go back to your room, if you ever do. They stir the air around a little. Cool it? Ha! Hell is where you go for relief from this.

First ballot's even, near enough. Roosevelt's got a New Deal for people, or says he does. Joe Steele? He's got a Four-Year Plan, or says *he* does. Got his whole first term mapped out. Farms in trouble? Farmers going broke? We'll make *community* farms, Joe Steele says. Take farmers, get 'em working together for a change. Not every man for himself like it has been. People out of work from factories? Build government factories for 'em! Build dams. Build canals. Build any damn thing that needs building.

Some folks love the notion. Others say it sounds like Trotsky's Russia. Just don't say that around Joe Steele. He can't stand Trotsky. You put the two of 'em in a room together, Joe Steele'll bash out Trotsky's brains.

First ballot. Even's not even good enough. Democrats have a two-thirds rule. Had it forever. Goddamn two-thirds rule helped start the Civil War. Douglas couldn't get over the hump. The party split. Lincoln won. Five months later—Fort Sumter.

All the same, goddamn two-thirds rule's still there.

Roosevelt's back in New York. Joe Steele's in Fresno. You don't come to a convention till you've won. Out on that smoky, sweaty, stinking Chicago Stadium floor, their handlers go toe to toe. Roosevelt's got Farley, Howe, Tugwell. Back-East people. People everybody knows. They think they're pretty sharp, pretty sly, and they're pretty close to right.

Joe Steele's got a smart Jew named Kagan. He's got an Armenian raisin grower's kid named Mikoian. Stas Mikoian's even smarter than Kagan. His brother works for Douglas, designs fighter planes. Lots of brains in that family. And Joe Steele's got this pencil-necked little guy they call the Hammer.

A big, mean bruiser gets a name like that hung on him, he's liable to be very bad news. A little, scrawny fellow? Ten times worse.

You think a smart Jew and a smarter Armenian can't skin those back-East hotshots? Watch 'em go at it.

And watch the hotshots fight back. Second ballot, not much change. Third, the same. By then, it's not nighttime any more. It's a quarter past nine the next morning. Everybody's as near dead as makes no difference. Delegates stagger out of Chicago Stadium to get a little sleep and try it all over again.

Second day, same damn thing. Third and fourth, same again. Ballot after ballot. Roosevelt's a little ahead, but only a little. Joe Steele's people, they don't back down. Joe Steele doesn't back down to anybody. Never has. Never will.

Fifth day, still no winner. Goddamn two-thirds rule. Papers start talking about 1924. Democrats take 103 ballots—103!—to put up John W. Davis. Damn convention takes two and a half weeks. Then what happens? Coolidge cleans his clock.

Nobody quite knows what goes on right after that. Some folks say—whisper, really, on account of it's safer—the guy they call the Hammer makes a phone call. But nobody knows. Except the Hammer, and he's not talking. The Hammer, he wouldn't say boo to a goose.

★★★

Albany. State Executive Mansion. Where the Governor works. Where he lives. Governor Roosevelt. Franklin D. (D for Delano) Roosevelt. Southwest corner of Engle and Elm. Red brick building. Big one. Built around the Civil War. Governor works on the first floor, lives on the second.

State Executive Mansion. Old building. Modern conveniences? Well, sure. But added on. Not built in. If they kind of creak sometimes, well, they do, that's all. Old building.

Nighttime. Fire. Big fire. Hell of a big fire. Southwest corner of Engle and Elm. Fire hoses? Well, sure. But no water pressure, none to speak of. That's what they say, the ones who get out. Awful lot of people don't.

Roosevelt? Roosevelt's in a wheelchair. How's a man in a wheelchair going to get out of a big old fire? The time that fire's finally out, Roosevelt's dead as shoe leather. He's done about medium-well, matter of fact, but that don't make the papers.

★★★

Kagan? Kagan's in Chicago. Stas Mikoian? Same thing. The Hammer? He's in Chicago, too. None of 'em goes anywhere. They're all there before, during, and after. Nobody ever says anything different.

Joe Steele? Joe Steele's in Fresno. All the way on the other side of the country. Joe Steele's hands are clean. Nobody ever says any-thing different. Not very loud, anyhow. And never—*never*—more than once.

★★★

Joe Steele is shocked—*shocked*—to hear about the fire. Calls it a tragic accident. Calls Roosevelt a worthy rival. Says all the right things. Sounds like he means 'em. Says the Democrats have got to get on with the business of kicking the snot out of the Republicans. Says that's the whole point of the convention.

And the eyelids like shutters go down. And then they come up again. And you can't see what's behind them. You can't see one goddamn thing.

★★★

So they nominate him. What else are they gonna do? John Nance Garner? Who the hell ever heard of John Nance Garner? Outside of Texas, John Nance Garner ain't worth a pitcher of warm spit. Hoover might even lick him. No. It's a moment of si-lence and a round of applause for Franklin D. (D for Delano) Roo-sevelt. And then it's Joe Steele. Joe Steele! *Joe Steele!*

Joe Steele for President! John Nance Garner for Vice President!

Hoover mostly stays in Washington. When he goes out, he campaigns on his record. Proves how far out of touch he is, don't it?

Joe Steele's everywhere. Everywhere. Whistle-stops on the train. Car trips. *Airplane* trips, for crying out loud. In the newsreels. On the radio. Joe Steele and his Four-Year Plan! Drummer can't shack up with a waitress without Joe Steele peeking in the window and telling 'em both to vote for him.

And if they're like everybody else, they do.

November 8, 1932. Hoover takes Delaware. He takes Pennsyl-vania. He takes Connecticut. And Vermont, New Hampshire, Maine. Joe Steele takes the country. Every other state. Better than fifty-seven percent of the vote to less than forty. And coattails? My Lord! More than three-fifths of the seats in the Senate. Almost three-quarters of the seats in the House.

March 4, 1933. Joe Steele comes to Washington. Inauguration Day. Hoover's in top hat and tails to go out. Joe Steele's in a flat cloth cap, a collarless shirt, and dungarees to go in. *Watch* the flashbulbs pop!

He takes the oath of office. Herbert Hoover shakes his hand. Herbert Hoover sits down. He's done. He's gone. He's out of this story.

Joe Steele speaks. He says, "We will have jobs. Labor is a matter of honor, a matter of fame, a matter of valor and heroism. *We will have jobs!*" Oh, how they cheer!

He says, "Yes, I admit I'm abrupt, but only toward those who harm the people of this country. What is my duty? To stick to my post and fight for them. It isn't in my character to quit."

He says, "We will do whatever we have to do to get the United States on its feet again. You cannot make a revolution with silk gloves." He holds up his hands. He's worked in his life, Joe Steele has. Those hard, hairy hands show it. More cheers. Loud ones.

And he says, "When banks fail, they steal the people's money. Have you ever seen a hungry banker? Has anyone in the history of the world ever seen a hungry banker? If I have to choose between the people and the bankers, I choose the people. We will nationalize the banks and save the people's money." This time, the cheers damn near knock him right off the platform. Joe Steele looks out. The eyelids like shutters go down. They come up again. Joe Steele . . . smiles.

★★★

Congress. Special session. Laws sail through, one after another. Nationalize the banks. Set up community farms for farmers who've lost their land—and for anybody else who wants to join. Factories for workers who've lost their jobs. Dams on every damn river that doesn't have any. That's how it seems, anyway. Dams put people to work. Stop floods. And make lots of new electricity.

Joe Steele, he's crazy for electricity. "Only when the farmer is surrounded by electrical wiring will he become a citizen," he says. "The biggest hope and weapon for our country is industry, and making the farmer part of industry. It is impossible to base construction on two different foundations, on the foundation of large-scale and highly concentrated industry, and on the foundation of very fragmented and extremely backward agriculture. Systematically and persistently, we must place agriculture on a new technical basis, the basis of large-scale production, and raise it to the level of an industry."

Some people think Joe Steele's just plain crazy. Soon as the laws start passing, the lawsuits start coming. Courts throw out the new laws, one after the next. Joe Steele appeals. Cases go to the Supreme Court. Supreme Court says unconstitutional. Says you can't do that.

Don't tell Joe Steele no. Bad idea. There's a young hotshot in Washington. Fellow named J. Edgar Hoover. Smart. Tough. Face like a bulldog. Headed the Justice Department Bureau of Investigation since before he was thirty. Not even forty yet. Knows where the bodies are buried. Buried some himself, folks say.

Joe Steele calls him to the White House. He leaves, he's smiling. You don't want to see J. Edgar Hoover smile. Trust me. You don't. Back in the Oval Office, Joe Steele's smiling, too. Here's somebody he can do business with.

Three weeks go by. Supreme Court calls another law unconstitutional. "These nine old men are hurting the country," Joe Steele says. "Why are they doing that? What can they want?"

Three more weeks go by. Arrests! Justice Department Bureau of Investigation nabs Supreme Court Justice Van Devanter! Justice McReynolds! Justice Sutherland! Justice Butler! Treason! Treason and plotting with Hitler! Sensation!

Habeas corpus denied. Traitors might flee, Joe Steele says. Anybody who complains sounds like a goddamn Nazi. No ordinary trials, not for the Gang of Four (thank you, Walter Lippmann). Military tribunals. They've got it coming.

J. Edgar Hoover has the evidence. Bales of it. Documents. Witnesses. Reichsmarks with the swastika right there on 'em. But some people—you just can't figure some people—don't believe it. They figure the Justices'll come out in court and make J. Edgar and his boys look like a bunch of monkeys. Even if they're in military tribunals, they'll get to speak their piece, right?

Right. They will. They do. *And they confess*, right there in front of the whole country. On the radio. On the newsreels. In the papers. They confess. We did it. We were wreckers. We wanted to tear down what Joe Steele's building up. We wanted to see the USA go Fascist. Better that than what Joe Steele's doing.

Oh. And we got our marching orders from Father Coughlin. And Huey Long.

More arrests!

Father Coughlin 'fesses up in front of a military tribunal, same as the Supreme Court Justices. More radio. More newsreels. More newspaper headlines. Huey Long? They shoot the Kingfish trying to break out of Leavenworth. That's how they tell it. Shoot him dead, dead, dead. Show off what's left of him on the screen and in the papers.

Then they shoot Van Devanter. And McReynolds. And Sutherland. And Butler. It's treason. They've confessed. Why the hell not shoot 'em? Sunrise. Blindfolds. Cigarettes. Firing squads. No last words. Die for treason and you don't deserve 'em.

Father Coughlin goes the same way. Somebody gets his last words, though. Order to fire goes out right between "*Ave*" and "*Maria.*" *Ave atque vale.* And a hell of a volley to finish him off.

Joe Steele picks four new Justices. They sail on through the Senate. You think the Supreme Court'll say unconstitutional again any time soon? I sure as hell don't. Don't reckon Joe Steele does either.

J. Edgar Hoover goes to the White House again. All of a sudden, it's not the Justice Department Bureau of Investigation. It's the *Government* Bureau of Investigation. The GBI. J. Edgar's got a face like a bulldog, yeah. He comes out of his talk with Joe Steele, he's wagging his tail like a happy little goddamn bulldog, too.

They're made for each other, J. Edgar Hoover and Joe Steele. Trotsky's got Beria. Hitler's got Himmler. And Joe Steele? Joe Steele's got J. Edgar.

★★★

When 1936 rolls around, folks wonder if the Republicans will run anybody against Joe Steele. They do. Alf Landon. Governor of Kansas. "The Matter with Kansas," some folks call him, but he's got to have balls. More balls than brains, running against Joe Steele.

Are folks that much better off? Any better off? Who knows for sure? But Joe Steele's *doing* things. So they're a little hungry on those community farms? So they don't grow a hell of a lot of crops? So what? Somebody cares about 'em, cares enough to try and find something new.

And after Van Devanter, and McReynolds, and Sutherland, and Butler, if anybody's unhappy, is he gonna say so? Would you?

Joe Steele says he's got himself a Second Four-Year Plan. Says it'll be even bigger than the first one. Doesn't say better. Says bigger. Is there a difference? Not to Joe Steele, there's not.

November comes around again. Joe Steele comes around again. Even bigger massacre than against Hoover. (Herbert, not J. Edgar. J. Edgar's massacres are different.) As Maine goes, so goes Vermont.

The rest? It's Joe Steele. All Joe Steele.

★★★

He takes the oath of office again. Chief Justice is real careful around him. Everybody notices. Nobody says boo, though. You want to watch what you say where Joe Steele can hear. Or J. Edgar. Or anybody else. J. Edgar's got snitches like a stray dog's got fleas. Run your mouth and you'll be sorry.

Somebody takes a shot at Joe Steele a couple months after the second term starts. Misses. GBI shoots him dead. Fills him full of holes like a colander. They say his name is Otto Spitzer. Say he's a German. Say he's got Nazi ties. Joe Steele cusses and fumes and shakes his fist at Hitler. And the *Führer* cusses and fumes and shakes his fist back. And neither one of 'em can reach the other. Ain't life grand?

Not much later, GBI raids the War Department. Newsreels full of tough guys in fedoras carrying tommy guns leading generals and colonels out of the building with their hands in the air. Hardly any guards at the War Department. Who'd think you needed 'em?

Treason trials. Again. General after general, colonel after colonel, in bed with the Germans. Evidence. Letters. Photos. GBI shows 'em off. They must be real. Some confessions. *They* must be real. Convictions. Sentences. To be shot. Doesn't get any neater than that.

Congressman Sam Rayburn gets up on his hind legs. Asks where the devil we're going. Asks what the devil Joe Steele thinks he's doing. Looks like we're heading for hell in a goddamn handbasket. Two days later, big old goddamn traffic smashup. Sam Rayburn dies on the way to the hospital.

"A loss to the whole country," Joe Steele calls it on the radio. The eyelids like shutters go down. They come up. This time, maybe you do know what's back there. We're going wherever Joe Steele damn well pleases. And Joe Steele thinks he's doing whatever he damn well pleases.

And you know what else? He's right.

Treason trials start for real a few weeks later. Not just Justices. Not just generals. Folks. Doctors. Lawyers. Professors. Mechanics. Bakers. Salesmen. Housewives. Anybody who talks out of turn. Even GBI men. Joe Steele and J. Edgar take no chances. Miss no tricks.

Conviction after conviction after conviction. Where to put 'em all? What to do with 'em all? You thought a lot of stuff got built the First Four-Year Plan? Take a gander at the second one. Dams again. Highways. Endless miles of highways. Canals—all dug by hand. More town buildings than you can shake a stick at.

Waste a lot of people that way, you say? So what? Plenty more where they came from. Oh, hell, yes. Plenty more. And when the camp rats who live finish out their terms, what do you do with 'em? Send 'em to Alaska. Send 'em to North Dakota or Wyoming or Montana or some other place that needs people. Tell 'em they're fine, long as they stay where they're sent. They don't stay? Back to the camps. That, or they get it in the neck.

Most of 'em stay. Most folks know, by then, Joe Steele means business.

Europe. War clouds. Hitler. Trotsky. Appeasement—France and England shaking in their boots. Joe Steele? Joe Steele's neutral. Blames half the troubles in the USA on the goddamn Nazis. Blames the other half on the godless Reds. That takes care of all the blame there is. Any left to stick to Joe Steele? No way. Not a chance.

Bullets start flying over there. Joe Steele goes up in front of Congress. Makes his famous "plague on both your houses" speech. "We have stood apart, studiously neutral," says Joe Steele. "We will go on doing that, because this fight is not worth the red blood of one single American boy. The USA must be neutral in fact as well as name. Neither side over there has a cause worth going to war for. No, sir. The greatest dangers for our country lurk in insidious encroachments for foreign powers by men of zeal. As long as we stamp that out at home, everything will be fine here. And as long as we stay away from Europe's latest foolish war, everything will be fine—for us—there."

But in the end, Joe Steele can't stay away. When France falls, he sees even the Atlantic may not be wide enough to keep Hitler away from the doorstep. He starts selling England as much as it needs, as much as he can. "If the Devil opposed Adolf Hitler, I should endeavor to give him a good notice in the House of Commons," Churchill says. "Thus I thank Joe Steele."

And Joe Steele's running for a third term. And Joe Steele wins, too. Wins even bigger than 1936. What's a Wendell Willkie? Not enough, that's for sure. After all the treason trials and such, some folks are surprised. By this time, hardly anybody says so out loud, though. By this time, folks know better.

Joe Steele and J. Edgar, they kind of laugh about it, them and the Hammer. Somebody says Joe Steele quotes Boss Tweed: "As long as I count the votes, what are you going to do about it?" Boss Tweed's long dead by then. And if anybody else repeats that, he'll be dead pretty damn quick, too.

When Hitler jumps Trotsky, Joe Steele needs six weeks before he starts shipping guns and trucks to Russia. He hates Trotsky that much. But if the Nazis run things from Brest to Vladivostok, that's not so good. So he does.

Damn near too late. By December, the Nazis are driving on Moscow. Sinking American ships in the Atlantic, too. And we sink a couple of German subs. Doesn't make the papers here or in Europe. If you don't look at it, it's not a war. Right? Joe Steele and Hitler think so.

And when Joe Steele's bent over squinting toward Europe, the Japs kick him in the ass. Pearl Harbor blows sky high. Philippines bombed. Invaded. Dutch East Indies invaded. Malaya. We don't want a war? We've got one anyway.

Next morning, Joe Steele comes on the radio. Has to eat his words. Never easy for anybody. Harder if you've set yourself up as always right. Joe Steele does it. Just makes like he never said anything different. Not how you remember it? Too bad for you, if you run your mouth.

"A grave danger hangs over our country," he says. Everybody with a radio listens. "The perfidious military attack on our beloved United States of America, begun on December 7, 1941, continues. There can be no doubt that this short-lived military gain for the Empire of Japan is only an episode. The war with Japan cannot be considered an ordinary war. It is not only a war between two armies and navies, it is also a great war of the entire American people against the Imperial Japanese forces.

"In this war for freedom we shall not be alone. Our forces are numberless. The overweening enemy will soon learn this to his cost. Side by side with the U.S. Army and Navy, thousands of workers, community farmers, and scientists are rising to fight the enemy aggressors. The masses of our people will rise up in their millions.

"To repulse the enemy who treacherously attacked our country, a State Committee for Defense has been formed in whose hands the entire power of the state has been vested. The Committee calls upon all our people to rally around the party of Jefferson and Jackson and Wilson and around the U.S. government so as self-denyingly to support the U.S. Army and Navy, demolish the enemy, and secure victory. Forward!"

Congress declares war on Japan. Hitler declares war on the USA. Joe Steele orders up two new military tribunals. Admiral Kimmel. General Short. In charge of Hawaii. Screwed the pooch in Hawaii. Guilty. Shot. *Pour encourager les autres.*

Philippines fall. MacArthur escapes to Australia. Tribunal. Bombers caught on the ground? Yes. Guilty. Shot. MacArthur likes to see his name in the papers. Can't have that kind of general. Only one man gets his name in the papers.

Joe Steele.

Joe Steele and George Marshall, now, they do fine. Marshall wants to win. Wants no fanfares. Joe Steele's kind of man. Same with Nimitz. Same with Eisenhower. Halsey? If Halsey ever loses, he's a dead man. Knows it. Keeps winning.

We push back the Japs. *Afrika Korps* runs out of steam in the desert. Germans and Russians fight the biggest goddamn battle in the world at Trotskygrad. Both sides throw men into the meat grinder like it's going out of style. Turns out the Reds have more men to grind up. Nazis lose a whole army. Russians storm west. For a little while, looks like the whole Eastern Front's coming unglued. Doesn't happen. Stinking Nazis are bastards, but they're pros, if Hitler lets 'em be. Still, you can see they're on the ropes. It'll take a while, but it's when, not if.

Joe Steele and Churchill and Trotsky meet. Start planning what happens next. Trotsky keeps screaming for a real second front. Italy? Screw Italy! Joe Steele . . . smiles. Heaven is every Nazi killing two Reds before he goes down. No more Germans left? No more Russians? Oh, toooo bad.

But it starts looking like there aren't enough krauts to do the trick. Nobody wants Russia running things from Vladivostok to Brest either. Second front happens. Eisenhower commands. Eisenhower doesn't hog glory that belongs to Joe Steele. Smart fellow, Eisenhower. Joe Steele wins fourth term. Republicans don't nominate anybody this time.

Philippines fall. Iwo Jima. Okinawa. Bomb the shit out of the Japs. Get ready to invade.

Germany? American and British hammer. Russian anvil. Smashed between 'em. Smashed *flat* between 'em. Hitler blows out his brains. 'Bye, Adolf. Should have done it sooner.

Start shifting men to the Pacific. Operation Downfall. Makes Normandy look like a kiddie game. Japs fight at beaches, everywhere else. Maniacs. Kamikazes. Everything they've got. Not enough. We push 'em back. Hell of a price to pay, but we pay it. Trotsky sees we're winning. Jumps in himself. Takes Hokkaido, north part of Honshu. Rest is ours. Incendiaries roast Hirohito on a train between Tokyo and Kyoto. *Sayonara*, buddy.

Japan never does surrender. Nobody in charge left to do it. But the Japs finally stop fighting. Nobody left to do that anymore either, not hardly. End of summer, '46.

Joe Steele. On top of the world.

★★★

Turns out the Nazis were working on an atomic bomb. Not too hard. Didn't really believe in it. Never got it. But working. Joe Steele hits the ceiling in sixteen different places. Maybe eighteen. Calls in Einstein. "Why didn't you know about this?" he yells.

"We did," Albert says. "I almost wrote you a letter at the start of the war."

Joe Steele's eyelids go down. They come up. Yeah, you can see what's back there this time. Rage. Raw, red rage. "Why didn't you?" he asks, all quiet and scary.

"I feared you would use it," Einstein answers. Half a dozen words. One death warrant.

Einstein? Shot. A Jew.

Szilard? Shot. A Jew.

Fermi? Shot. A dago with a Jew wife.

Von Neumann? Shot. A Jew.

Oppenheimer? Shot. A Jew.

There are more. Lots more. Shot, most of 'em, Jews or not. The rest? To the camps.

"The Professors' Plot," the papers call it. All these goddamn eggheads, working to keep the US of A weak. All these goddamn kikes, working to keep the US of A weak. Joe Steele starts muttering maybe Hitler knew what he was doing. Talks to the Hammer. Talks to J. Edgar. The wheels begin to turn.

Then he finds Teller. Teller says, "Turn me loose. I'll build the son of a bitch in three years, or you can have my head." *Another* goddamn Jew. But one who knows which side his bread's buttered on. Some of the people Teller needs—Feynman, Frisch, Kistiakowsky—he pulls out of camps. There, but not shot yet. Maybe not shot at all, if they come through. First circle of hell, close enough.

Joe Steele tells J. Edgar and the Hammer, "Go slow." If Teller and the boys come through, maybe some kikes are worth keeping. If not . . . We know who they are. We know where they live. We can always start up again. Oh, hell, yes.

And Trotsky, that stinking Red bastard, he's working on this shit, too. You bet he is. We caught Nazi high foreheads. And they caught Nazi high foreheads. You think the boys from the master race won't sing for their supper? Sing for their necks? Ha! Wernher von Braun'd learn Chinese if Chiang caught him. Or Mao.

And Trotsky's a pain in the ass other ways. World revolution everywhere, he says. 1948. His North Japan invades our South Japan. War of liberation, he says. Red Japs sweeping down toward Tokyo. Screaming "Banzai!" for Trotsky. (Trotsky's a Jew, too. Makes Joe Steele like 'em even better.)

Hell of a thing—a brand new war, and the old one's hardly done. Trotsky's Japs fight like they're nuts. Our Japs run like they're nuts. It's a walkover—till the North Japanese bump up against the U.S. Marines in front of Utsanomiya. If they break through, Tokyo falls. Probably all Honshu with it. But they don't. Marines hold. Give the Red Japs a bloody nose.

Everybody knows Russians fly the Gurevich-9 jet fighters with the yellow star inside the Rising Sun. Not as good as our F-80s—Me-262s with those starred meatballs, near enough—but fancier than what we thought those SOBs had. Fighting kind of settles down in the mountains. Now they go forward. Now we do. Places like Sukiyaki Valley and Mamasan Ridge? Folks back home don't know just where they're at, but a lot of kids get buried there.

Joe Steele wins term number five as easy as number four. Nobody runs against him. There's a war on.

August 6, 1949. Sapporo. Capital of North Japan. One bomb. No city. Teller lives. Joe Steele tells Trotsky, "Enough is enough."

August 9, 1949. Nagano. *Not* the capital of South Japan. Maybe the AA around Tokyo's too heavy to risk losing the plane. But a hell of a big place. One bomb. No city. Maybe some German egghead lives, too. Trotsky tells Joe Steele, "Yeah, enough *is* enough."

Japanese War ends. *Status quo ante bellum.* Mao runs Chiang off the mainland. More treason trials. Something to keep Joe Steele amused. Getting old. Wins a sixth term almost in his sleep. Dies six weeks after they swear him in again. Natural causes. Who'd dare mess with him?

John Nance Garner, Vice President since 1933. Never says boo all that time. That's *why* he's VP so long. Finally takes over. First thing he does is is order J. Edgar Hoover and the Hammer shot. The Hammer orders him and J. Edgar Hoover shot. J. Edgar orders both the others shot.

J. Edgar lives. J. Edgar takes over. And you thought Joe Steele was trouble?

Inventing Lovers
on the Phone

by ORSON SCOTT CARD

Inventing lovers on the phone . . .
Who call and say, "Come dance with me,"
and murmur vague obscenities . . .
          —from "At Seventeen" by Janis Ian

YOU want to know what Deeny's life was like? It can be summed up in the sentence her father said when she got a cell phone.

"Who the hell's gonna call *you?*"

Deeny said what she always said when her father, otherwise known as "Treadmarks," put her down. She said nothing at all. Just left the room. Which was what ol' Treadmarks wanted. But it was what Deeny also wanted. In fact, on that one point they agreed with each other completely, and since their relationship consisted almost entirely of Deeny getting out of whatever room her father was in, one could almost say that they lived in perfect harmony.

In the kitchen, her mother was thawing fish sticks and slicing cucumbers. Deeny stood there for a moment, trying to figure out what possible dinner would need those two ingredients, and no others.

"You've got a zit, dear," said her mother helpfully.

"I always have a zit, Mother," said Deeny. "I'm seventeen and I have the complexion of dog doo."

"If you washed . . ."

"If I didn't eat chocolate, if I didn't eat fatty foods, if I used Oxy-500, if I didn't have the heredity you and Treadmarks gave me . . ."

"I wish you wouldn't call your father that. It doesn't even make sense."

"Come on, Mom, you *wash* his underwear. It's because everyone rolls right over him at work. I feel kind of sorry for the old guy."

Mother made a show of speaking silently, mouthing the words, "He can hear you."

"Come on, Mom, you know what a nothing he is on the job. He's nearly forty and so far the only thing he ever accomplished was getting you pregnant. And he only did *that* the one time."

As usual, Deeny had gone too far. Mother turned, her face reddening. "You get out of this kitchen, young lady. Not that you *deserve* to be called a lady of any kind. The mouth you have!"

Deeny's hand was already in her pocket. She pressed the button on her phone. It immediately rang.

"Excuse me, Mother," she said. "Somebody actually *wants* to talk to me."

Her mother just stood there looking at her, a fish stick in her hand.

Deeny made a show of looking at the phone. "Oh, not Bill again." She pressed the END button.

"Who's Bill?"

"A guy who calls sometimes," said Deeny.

"You've only had that cell phone for a couple of hours," said Mother. "How would he get your number if you don't want him to call?"

"He probably bribed somebody. He's such an asshole."

"Deeny, that language just makes you sound cheap."

"Well, I'm not cheap. I'm priceless. You said so yourself."

"When you were four and used to sing that little song."

"That little song you made me rehearse for hours and hours so you could show me off to your friends."

"You were darling. They loved it. And so did you. I never saw you turn your back on an audience."

"Oh, really?" said Deeny. Holding the cell phone above her head like castanets, she sashayed out of the kitchen, heading for her room.

When she got there she flopped back on her bed, feeling sick and lost. It would be different if her parents weren't right about everything. But they were. She was exactly the loser her father thought she was. And she wasn't a lady, or darling, and she probably *would* be cheap, if she could get a guy to look at her at all. But when there are no buyers, what does it matter whether your price is high or low?

Even though she tried to tune out everything Treadmarks said, he made sure she never forgot for a single day how tragically disappointing she was as a human being. It's like he couldn't stand for her to feel good about herself for a single second. An *A* in a class? "Study hard, kid, it's a sure thing you're never gonna have a husband to support you." A new top? "Why didn't you leave it in the store where it might get bought by somebody who can wear that kind of thing?" At the office on the days she helped out after school, she tried to do everything right but it was never good enough. And if she tried to talk to him, ever, about anything, he'd get this impatient, bored look and about two sentences in he'd say, "Some of us have things to do, Deeny, will you get to the point?"

It would have been different if she didn't agree with him. She really did screw up everything she touched. She really was a leper at school. She never got calls from boys. She never even got *looks* from boys.

It wasn't that she had no friends. She had plenty of friends. Well, two. Both losers like her, when she looked at it rationally. When they were together, though, they fed on each other's insanity and fancied themselves the superior of everyone else at school.

Rivka, alias Becky, always sneered at the popular girls' sheeplike insistence on dressing alike and wearing their hair alike and even having the exact same half inch of absolutely smooth, no pudge abdomen showing between their thin little tops and their tightass jeans. Deeny kept it to herself that it was all she could do, when she saw those perfect waistlines, not to pinch her own little three-quarter-inch flab slab just to remind herself that skimpy little tops were only the stuff of dreams for her.

Lex, on the other hand—who had tried to get them to call her Luthor in fifth grade and Alexis in ninth, to which they had responded by calling her Blecch for an entire month—always mocked them for how airheaded they were. Even the smart ones. Especially the smart ones. Maybe Deeny would enjoy Lex's wit more if she were actually smarter than the girls whose lack of brains she made fun of, but half the time it was Lex who was wrong, and it just made all three of them look like idiots.

Yeah, Deeny had friends, all right. The way some people got impetigo.

Not that she didn't like them. She liked them fine. She just knew that, socially speaking, she'd be better off alone than hanging out with these two aggressively hostile Jewesses—the term they both insisted on.

All the way to school on the bus next morning (another mark of Cain on her brow), Deeny rehearsed how she'd get into school another way and absolutely avoid them all day, except when she had classes with them, which was every period except A Cappella, because neither of them could carry a tune in a gas can.

Yet when she got to school, her mind had wandered onto another subject—her cell phone, as a matter of fact—and it wasn't till she heard Becky's greeting—that endlessly cheery "Hey, tush flambee!"—that she remembered that she was supposed to be doing evasive maneuvers.

What the hell. Her social standing was past saving. And she didn't care anyway. And besides, she had the phone. Not that she'd ever have the courage to use it.

So on their way up to the front door, threading their way among the other kids, Becky and Lex talked loudly on purpose so everybody could hear them being crude.

"Is there something about being Jewish that makes us have huge boobs?" said Lex. "Or is it because our ancestors lived in

eastern Europe for so many centuries and all that borscht and pota-
toes made them cows?"

"I don't have huge boobs," said Deeny quietly. "I hardly have
any boobs at all."

"Which makes me wonder if you aren't secretly a shiksa," said
Lex. "I mean, why do you even bother to wear bras?"

"Because I have nipples," said Deeny grimly, "and if I don't
wear a bra, they chafe."

"You've never heard of undershirts?" said Lex.

"You two make me sick," said Becky. "These things aren't acci-
dents. God gives big boobs to the women he wants to send babies
to. The boobs bring the boys, the boys bring the babies, God is
happy, and we get fat."

"Is that a new midrash?" asked Lex.

"So I'm meant to be a nun?" said Deeny. "Why didn't he go
all the way and make me Catholic?"

"You'll get them," said Becky. "You're a late bloomer, that's
all."

If there was anything Deeny hated worse than when Becky and
Lex flaunted their udders, it was when they tried to make her feel
better about her unnoticeables. Because she didn't actually feel bad
about them. She looked at what the two of them carried around
with them and it looked to her like it was about as convenient as
having two more big textbooks to carry to every single class all day.

So, as they talked about the curse of bigness—while sticking
their chests out so far they could barely open their lockers—Deeny
fidgeted. Her hand was in her purse. She was turning the cell
phone over and over in her fingers. And somewhere along the line,
without quite deciding, she pushed the button and the cell phone
rang.

She ignored it for the first ring.

"These morons who bring cell phones to school," said Becky.
"And most of them aren't even drug dealers, so what's the point?
What kind of emergency is it where someone says, 'Quick! Call a
teenager! Thank God they're all carrying cell phones now!'"

Perfect moment, thought Deeny. Because she was actually

blushing for real, just imagining the embarrassment of pulling out a cell phone in front of Becky at this exact moment. So . . . she pulled out the cell phone and pushed the TALK button.

Of course, all that happened was that the "Test Ring" shut off and the last number called got dialed—but since that number was her home phone, and nobody was there during the day, and her last-century parents didn't bother with an answering machine, what could go wrong?

She held the phone to her ear and turned away from the others. As she did, she saw both Becky and Lex do their oh-my-God takes.

"Not now," Deeny hissed into the phone.

"Sellout," murmured Becky.

Deeny knew she was joking.

"No," said Deeny. "I told you no."

"She's dealing," said Lex. "I knew it."

"It must take every penny she earns at her dad's office to pay for a cell," said Becky. "How needy can you get?"

"Maybe her parents are paying."

"Shakespeare based Shylock on her mother and Simon Legree on her father. I don't think so."

"Oh, right, from Shakespeare's famous play 'Uncle Hamlet's Cabin.'"

As they nattered on, Deeny retreated farther from them and said, very softly—so softly that everyone around her was bound to be listening and hear her—"I told you I can't talk at school and no, I wasn't faking." Then she punched the END button, turned the phone off, and jammed it back into her purse.

Becky and Lex were looking at her skeptically. "Oh, right," said Lex. "Like . . . faking what? An orgasm?"

They weren't buying it.

But she said nothing. Stuck with the charade. Let her face turn red with embarrassment. Walked to her own locker and opened it—no combination to spin, she had deliberately broken the lock the first day of school and made it a point never to keep anything in the locker that she cared about keeping. "So the homework elf didn't come back," she said.

"Oh, now she's pretending that she doesn't want to talk about it," said Becky. "Like she isn't dying to feed us some line of bull doo about some imaginary boyfriend."

"There's no boyfriend," said Deeny.

"Give me that," said Lex. And before Deeny could register what Lex was doing, she had snatched the purse right off Deeny's shoulder and in an instant was brandishing the cell phone.

"Hey, give that back," said Deeny. Immediately, those words made her flash on all the times in grade school when one of the Nazi children—i.e., the popular kids—grabbed something away from her—a sandwich, her homework—and how futile and pathetic Deeny had always sounded, whining, "Hey, give that back, give that back, don't throw it in there, please, please." Sickened at the memory, she shut her mouth and folded her arms and leaned against her locker to tough it out. Which might have made her look cool if her locker hadn't been open so that leaning made her fall right in.

Becky smirked at her as she awkwardly pushed herself back out of the locker. "You know, if you had boobs you couldn't fall into your locker. At least not sideways."

"Thanks for the reminder."

"Redial last number," said Lex as she pushed SEND. She was looking at the little LCD display. So she'd recognize the phone number at once, having called it a thousand times since they met in fourth grade.

Only Lex didn't say a thing about the number. And when she held it to her ear, her eyes widened.

"Sorry," she said. "Wrong number." She pushed END and handed the phone back to Deeny, blushing as she did.

Deeny hadn't known that Lex could blush.

"Well?" demanded Becky.

"Ask Dinah," said Lex. "Apparently she's been seeing somebody without telling us."

Deeny was stunned. Lex was playing along. Unbelievable.

"*Seeing* somebody?" said Becky. "Adults who are having affairs 'see' somebody. High school girls *date*. And not somebody, guys."

"Sounded more like seeing somebody to me," said Lex. "If you don't believe me, push redial."

"Not a chance," said Deeny, as Becky reached for the phone. "*Real* friends don't spy. Or assume that I'm lying." She meant it—but she had to put a smile on it, because after all, if Lex was playing along, Deeny didn't want to antagonize her *too* much. Still, she had to act pissed off because she *would* be pissed off at Lex taking her phone—and she knew she *would* be pissed off because she *was* pissed off.

"He's probably twenty-five," said Lex. "Either a garage mechanic or an investment banker—"

"Oh, like *those* two professions sound the same," said Becky.

"Same kind of I-know-everything-and-you're-as-ignorant-as-fish attitude," said Lex.

"Well what did he say?"

"Try, 'Hello, Deeny.' Like he had caller i.d."

"Cell phone numbers don't show up on caller i.d.," said Becky.

"So maybe he has a special cell phone whose number he gave only to Deeny," said Lex.

"Maybe he got Deeny *her* phone and his is the only one on speed dial," said Becky, really getting into it now. "So she isn't paying for it at all."

"But she's a kept woman now," said Lex, "and so he thinks he owns her, he can call her whenever and wherever he wants, only she longs for her independence, and so she's going to dump him, but he won't accept it and starts to stalk her and take pictures of her with spycams and then he puts them out on the Internet only with other women's bodies so they're really pornographic."

"Oh, like mine wouldn't be sexy enough to be pornographic," said Deeny.

"Oh, it would," said Lex, "except it would only appeal to men who go for boys without weenies."

"Oh, who *is* he?" demanded Becky. "Forget all the other stuff, who got you this phone?"

Deeny noticed how Lex's joke had now become the "true" story—she'd been given the phone by a boyfriend. And it felt bad to have them actually believe the lie, even if it *was* exactly the lie she had bought the phone for.

"I pay for it myself," said Deeny. "Out of my savings. I can only afford the first three payments and then they'll cancel my account. I got it so I could fake having a boyfriend, but I was never going to try to fool *you* guys."

"Ha, ha," said Lex.

"So you're really not going to tell us?" said Becky.

"There's nobody, honest," said Deeny. "I only faked it that time because it pisses me off when you try to console me about wearing size A-minus. Tell her, Lex. You don't have to play along any longer."

She had expected Lex to break into a grin and say, "All right, Deeny-bopper."

Instead, Lex's face got cold and hard. "Play it that way, stud," said Lex. "I guess you'll be talking about it with your *real* friends." And she stalked off.

Becky rolled her eyes. "I don't mind if you want to keep it a secret. And Lex won't stay mad. She never does."

I've only known her three years longer than you have, so duh, yes, I know that. "Thanks, Becky," said Deeny. "I'm not going to keep carrying it. It was a dumb idea, anyway." Especially if you two won't believe me when I tell you the absolute truth.

Together they headed off to Calculus, which was a hell of a way to start the day, especially because she had no intention of ever using a logarithm in her entire life after high school. She was only taking it because the district had passed a new ruling just before her sophomore year that all phrosh and sophs had to take four years of math, and since she had already taken honors Algae Trichinosis her freshman year, it was too late to start out with remedial so her fourth year could be geometry.

The nice thing about Calculus is that since she had already passed her first semester, now all she needed was a D in the second semester because the college of her choice would already have admitted her before her final grades came in. So she didn't actually have to pay attention in class. Her mind could wander. And it did.

How far is Lex going to take this? She had to recognize Deeny's home phone number. She had to know she was hearing the blat-rest-blat of a ringing telephone, and not a voice. So why was she doing this whole injured-friend routine?

There was no figuring Lex out when she got some gag going. Like the time Becky had said, "Oh, you talk too much," to her, and for five whole days Lex hadn't said another word, not one, nada, not even when teachers called on her. It was like she had gone on strike, and by the end Becky was begging her to say something, anything. "Tell me to go eff myself, just say *something*." That Lex, what a kidder. In an overdone assholical way.

Didn't use the phone all the rest of that day. Didn't even bring it to school the next day because she forgot and left it on the charging stand. Then she brought it on Friday because what the hell, she was paying for it, wasn't she?

Pep rally after school. Attendance required. "Enforced pep," said Becky. "What a Nazi concept. Sieg Tigers."

Lex was still being a butt, making snide remarks about how Deeny had a whole secret life that only her *real* friends got to know about. And all those perky cheerleaders making brilliant impromptu speeches about how, like, our team does so much better if we, like, really have spirit, they were really irritating, too, especially because so many of the other kids were getting into it and yelling and chanting and cheering, the whole mob mentality thing. And it didn't help to have Becky mumbling *her* snide remarks. "You want them to have spirit, try wearing that cute little skirt without panties, that'll make those boys play hard." Oh, that was funny, Becky, why not laugh so hard you fall off the back of the bleachers.

So what was there to do, really, except push the button and then rush over to the edge of the bleachers and turn away from everybody and pretend to be having a phone call.

There was so much noise that she didn't actually have to make up anything to say. Just mumble mumble mumble, and then laugh, and then smile, and then imagine him saying something kind of dirty, and smirking at what he said, and then he says something *really* dirty, and so she makes a face but it's plain she really likes hearing it even though she pretends to be mad.

Twenty-five-year-old mechanic. Covered with grease but arms so strong he just lifts the car up onto the jack. Or investment banker. Who never wears anything under his suit except his shirt, "In case you only got a little time for me, baby," he says. "I don't want to waste any of it."

Yeah, right.

But don't let the "yeah, right" show on your face, moron. A laugh. A smile. A little offended. Then delighted. Then . . . yeah, they're looking, not just Lex and Becky, but other kids, too, looking at Deeny, can you imagine that, watching her have a love life, even if it's only with the beep beep beep of the ring tone at home.

Only now that she thought about it, there wasn't a beep beep beep.

Had one of her parents picked up the phone? Come home early from work maybe, and the phone rang, and they picked it up, only she didn't hear them saying, "Hello? Hello? Who's there?" because there was so much noise here at the pep rally.

She pressed END, stuffed the phone in her purse, and then just sat there, looking out over the basketball court with all the stupid streamers that somebody was going to have to climb up and cut down before the game anyway, so why go to all that trouble in the first place, and I wonder what my parents heard on the phone when they picked it up, was I actually saying stuff *out loud* about what the investment banker does or doesn't wear? Even if I was, they couldn't possibly have heard me. Except that my mouth was right by the mike and they didn't have a pep rally going on there at home so they probably *could* hear and she hoped it was her father— let *him* hear her talking about how maybe somebody wanted sex with his loser daughter, sit on *that* and spin—

But if it was Mom . . .

Please don't let it be Mom. Please don't let her go to the drugstore and buy me condoms or make an appointment for me to go to the doctor and get a prescription for The Pill or The Patch or whatever remedy she decides is right for her little flat-chested princess who has about as much use for birth control as fish have for deodorant.

Lex was sitting beside her. Close, leaning in, so she could whisper and still be heard. "Who *is* he?"

Deeny turned to her, then leaned away, because Lex was right there in her face. Nobody was near enough to hear.

"You of all people should know," said Deeny.

"Why, is it someone I know?"

"It's *nobody*." It's my wishful thinking. It's my pathetic loser attempt to make people think I have a love life, somebody who cares enough to call. And I don't even *care* what people think, except I bought the phone and I put on this little show so I do care, don't I, which makes me just as needy as any other loser. People smell the need like dogs, like wolves, and if they're like Daddy, they torment you because they know they can get away with it because losers have no claws.

Lex was angry. Sat up straight, looking forward, down toward the stupid pep rally where they were either acting out the kama sutra in cheerleader outfits or trying to spell something with their bodies. But then she must have decided that being mad wasn't going to get what she wanted, because her face softened and she turned back to Deeny, rested her chin in one hand, and contemplated her.

"I know from his voice that he's not a kid," she said. "I was thinking college student, but the way you're acting now, I'm thinking—married guy."

"How can you know anything from his voice?" said Deeny, disgusted now with this whole game.

"I know he exists," said Lex. "I know he's a guy. I know he doesn't sound like any of these little boys. He doesn't talk like high school."

And it finally dawned on Deeny that Lex wasn't lying. She actually heard something. There *was* a voice when she took the phone and called.

Which meant that someone at home must have picked up. "It must have been my father," said Deeny. "The only number I had ever called was my home phone. My father must have been home this morning."

Lex rolled her eyes. "A, I *know* your father's voice, give me some credit. And B, I *saw* the number on the screen and it wasn't your home phone."

"Well, then, I don't know who it was because I've never dialed any other number," said Deeny. "It really was a wrong number."

"Oh, a wrong number that says, 'I can't stop thinking about you either, Deeny'?"

Now Deeny understood. "Oh, how sick can you get. So I was playing around with the phone and yes, it was a dumb thing to do, but let it go now, okay? You're as bad as the Nazis, making fun of me. Just let it go."

Lex's astonishment looked genuine. "I'm not making fun of you, I think you're in trouble somehow, I think maybe you're doing something really dumb or really cool and I just want to know, I want to be your *friend,* but if you want to keep it all to yourself, that's fine with me, that's *no skin off my ass!*"

She was shouting by the end because Deeny was going down the bleachers as fast as she could, getting away, getting off by herself. Lex believed it. Lex wasn't making fun of her. Lex really talked to somebody. Somebody who said things like, I can't stop thinking of you either, Deeny.

Only there wasn't anybody that Deeny couldn't stop thinking about. There was just a phone she got so she could make fun of all the girls with cell phones talking to their stupid boyfriends who were only sixty yards away talking on *their* cell phones at *their* lockers. And maybe she *did* want people to think she really might have a boyfriend, some older guy who wasn't in high school, so she could seem mysterious and mature so people would think the reason she never connected with anybody at high school except Becky and Lex was because she had a life outside, a life far more exciting and dangerous than any of the Nazis had here at school.

Somebody answered the phone when Lex pressed TALK.

Outside the gym, over in the grove where the smokers and lovers gathered to light up and pet, Deeny took out her phone and pressed TALK and looked at the number.

It was a number she'd never seen before. With an area code in front of it that she'd never heard of. Long distance. Oh, that was great, all she needed was long distance charges, she'd lose the phone the first month at that rate.

She was about to press END but then there was a voice.

"I dreamed of you last night, Deeny."

Tinny as it was, coming out of the tiny little speaker eighteen inches away, Deeny could still tell that it was a man's voice. Deep. With a bit of humor in it. And he knew her name.

She brought the phone up to her ear. "Who is this?" she asked.

"You gotta stay out of my dreams, Deeny. I wake up and I can't get back to sleep, thinking about you."

"How did you get my number?"

He laughed. "Deeny, you called *me*, remember?"

"Lex called you. My friend Lex. She pushed the button. And how do you know my name, anyway? Do you work for the cell phone company?"

"I know your name because you whispered it to me in my dream," he said. "I know your name because I whispered it myself as I slid your shirt up your body and kissed you all the way down your—"

Deeny mashed the END button and cast the phone down onto the pine needles.

One of the nearby smokers laughed. "Oooh, lovers' quarrel," he said.

"None of your effin' business," said Deeny.

"If my business was effin', you'd be the first one I'd eff," said the smoker, and his buddies laughed.

Deeny picked up the phone. "I don't have time for little boys."

But as she walked away, she was thinking, This is the first time any boy at this school ever made a rude sexual comment about *me*. And he did it because of the phone.

The damn thing works.

Too well, that's how it works. This was supposed to be a game of let's pretend. So who was the guy on the other end?

She pushed TALK.

The display showed her home phone number. It rang. Beep. Beep. Beep. No answer. No man's voice.

She turned to the couple who were kissing and touching and pressing up against each other next to the big oak tree at the center of the grove.

"Lovers are so fickle," she said. "One minute taking your shirt off, the next minute not even answering the phone."

They broke their kiss long enough to turn and look at her, gap-lipped, for a long moment.

"As you were," she said.

They returned to their kiss, his hands moving along the bare skin between her jeans and her top, her hands playing with his pockets, with his butt. Deeny wanted to scream, it made her so jealous, it made her so angry. It made her want so much to press TALK and have somebody really be there. Somebody who wanted her so much he couldn't keep his hands off her. And with any luck, maybe it would be somebody who didn't say things like, "If my business was effin', you'd be the first one I'd eff."

She remembered the voice on the phone, the impossible voice, the unknown phone number. The thought of him made her shiver. And as she walked toward the buses, she wondered whether shivering was one of the early warning signs of love.

★★★

She did not use the phone over the weekend.

On Saturday Mother went to temple and Treadmarks went outside and squatted by the lawnmower, pretending to have some understanding of mechanical things, but actually half-mooning the neighborhood with his butt crack. Thus he offended the God of Israel two ways, by working on the sabbath and by making it so embarrassing to believe that man had been made in his image.

Deeny showed her faith by not working, and her freethinking

by not going to temple. Basically she sat around and tried to read three different books and a magazine and couldn't keep her mind on any one of them because she kept thinking of what it might be like for a man—not a boy, a man—to slide his hands under her shirt and lift it upward and then kiss her naked flesh. Since her naked flesh would include her flabby belly, it kind of interfered with the fantasy, and she kept switching between imagining that he preferred bodies with a little loose flesh and imagining that her flesh was somehow magically tightened over the smooth hard muscles of a girl who uses the ab roller fifty reps every day.

She told herself that there was no point in picking up the phone because who would see her do it?

And on Sunday, Deeny managed not to pull the cell phone out of her purse all morning. She didn't touch it till Mother offered to take her to the mall, and even then it was only because her father called out to her as they were heading out the door.

"Aren't you taking your phone? In case lover boy calls?"

Deeny wondered for one panicked moment how Treadmarks could possibly know about the guy on the phone. Until Mother answered him. "Dear, I think 'Bill' was just made up."

"Oh, yes, Bill," said Father. "Aren't you afraid he might call?"

Deeny thought back to Thursday and remembered that she had said she was trying to avoid 'Bill's' calls. "I don't want to talk to him even if he does," she said.

"Then leave the phone with me," said Father. "If he calls, I'll get rid of him for you."

Deeny reached into her purse, lifted up the phone, and dropped it back inside. "No thanks," she said.

"So you *want* him to call."

Mother sighed. "He doesn't exist, dear."

"That is my fondest wish, Mother," said Deeny, "but alas it has not yet come true." And they were out the door.

It was such a weird confrontation. Treadmarks mocking her by pretending that he believed some guy was trying to call her. Mother defending Deeny by calling her a liar. Which she was, of course, except that even though "Bill" was a lie, there really *was* a guy on the phone. Or at least there had been. And now she was afraid to push the TALK button, for fear he would be there, and for fear that he would not.

When Monday came around, the phone weighed heavy in her purse, and she toyed with the idea of simply leaving it home. She even decided to do that, for a few minutes, but after breakfast she went back to her room for no other reason than to take it out of her drawer and put it in her purse. She told herself it was so that Treadmarks wouldn't find it and do something sickening like getting her cell phone number and calling it and leaving fake messages on her voice mail. Which he was not above doing. Though it did sound like more work than he was wont to attempt on his own.

So there she was on the bus again, phone in her purse, and just like Thursday and Friday, she switched it on and set it to test the current ringing sound when she pressed the OK button. All the time telling herself she wasn't actually going to push it. She was just going to forget she even had a phone in her purse.

Unless it just . . . rang. Unless somebody called her.

Nobody called.

But something else was going on.

Word had spread, apparently. She was getting looked at by kids who usually glanced past her as if she had no more existence than gum on the sidewalk—to be stepped around, lest she stick to their shoe, but otherwise ignored. Today, though, they fell silent in their conversations and glanced at her, some of them covertly, but others quite openly, as if she had forgotten to wear pants. And one time she overheard the words "older guy" and she realized that either Becky or Lex had been indiscreet.

Wasn't that what she wanted, though? She could hardly be mad at them for making her, if not famous, then notorious. And maybe it wasn't them at all, maybe it was one of the other kids at the pep rally. It's not as if they had had any privacy there in the bleachers in the gym.

They were talking about her. Holding her in awe. Or maybe not, maybe they disapproved—that's what it looked like in that group where she heard the words "older guy," no doubt the very next words from somebody else were those little "tsk-tsk" clicks or even the more direct "what a whore." Well, disapproval from shmucks like that was like an Oscar and the Nobel prize combined, minus the statue and the cash, of course.

And by lunchtime, Lex and Becky had far more to report. After she had assured them that he had *not* called again and no, she had never slept with him, they were full of news about what everybody was saying. "They are so sure he's from the college and he's some big brain from the physics department."

"Big brain, I like that," said Deeny.

"So he isn't?" asked Becky.

"College is in his past, not his present and definitely not his future," said Deeny. As if she knew. But he sounded like a college kind of guy. Clear-sounding, confident, and he didn't have to hunt for words, they were just there, whatever words he needed. Not that he had said that many of them.

"And what *I* heard," said Lex, "is that he's a married man older than your dad and it's like some kind of electric complex—"

"Electra," said Deeny, "as in Mourning Becomes."

Lex rolled her eyes. "Puh-leeeeeze, like I wasn't the first one to discover the psych book and tell you both about all the weird sex crap back in sixth grade."

"You just take so much pride in being smarter than everybody, Deeny," said Becky. "It's your worst feature."

"But at least I've got no tits, so you still look real sexy when you stand next to me."

Lex did her build-a-wall pantomime between them, saying, as she always did, "Please don't fight, girls, it will worry the children."

"So everybody's talking," said Deeny. "What can I do about that?" Except enjoy it.

"Amazingly enough," said Lex, "none of the stories reflect any credit on *you.*"

"Like we expected anything else?" said Deeny. "But at least they notice me."

"So . . . what'll you do if the school counselor calls you in?" said Lex.

"Why would a counselor want to see me?"

What a stupid question. She hadn't even finished lunch when Ms. Reymondo walked by and said, "Come see me, would you, Deeny?"

"When?"

"Anytime," she said.

"Cool," said Deeny. "How about July?"

"How about now?" said Ms. Reymondo, with her sweet-as-nails smile.

"I'm still digesting," said Deeny.

"She farts a lot when she's doing that," said Lex.

"And people have been known to puke when she farts, especially after cole slaw," said Becky. "Do you have a big solid wastebasket in your office, Ms. Reymondo? The kind with holes don't do much good when you're puking."

Ms. Reymondo faked a chilly little laugh. "You girls are so clever, I just can't keep up with you. I always envied the smart girls when I was in high school."

That was enough to get Deeny out of her chair, because she knew it would only be moments before Lex did something really offensive, like fake-puking on her lunch tray or blowing milk out her nose, which she could do at will. "I'll come now, Ms. Reymondo."

And sure enough, it was about the rumors. "Deeny, I hope you know that if you are in some kind of . . . inappropriate relationship, you can always speak to me in strictest confidence."

"So you don't obey the law?" said Deeny.

"What?"

"The law that says that if there is some kind of child abuse, you have to report it to the appropriate authorities."

"So there *is* abuse?" She looked so eager.

"No, there's no abuse. I'm doing just fine. Nobody's boffing me or even feeling me up, which is more than half the girls in this school can say."

"I don't see why you're being so hostile."

"Oh, no, that's all wrong, Ms. Reymondo. You sound defensive. You're supposed to say, 'And how does it make you feel, to talk about other girls having sex and getting felt up?'"

"I know how it makes you feel," said Ms. Reymondo. "It makes you feel like you've somehow struck a blow against authority and aren't you cool. Only I'm not any kind of authority, God knows, and what you're doing now is blowing smoke up the ass of a person who is only trying to help you."

"Help me what?"

"Help you get out of a situation that might be getting out of control."

"The only thing out of my control," said Deeny, "is getting called in to your office and losing half my lunch period just so I can hear you discuss your ass and whether you're getting any smoke blown up it."

"You're free to go," said Ms. Reymondo. "But I hope you remember how you treated a person who only wanted to be your friend."

Deeny paused at the door. "*Friends* aren't paid by the state or the county or whatever, and *friends* don't have the power to order me to their office."

"When you're in trouble, friends are the people who can help you, whether they're getting paid for it or being treated like shit by bratty little girls who think they're so smart they can handle relationships with older men."

For a moment, Deeny wanted to say she was sorry. After all, if she really were dating some older man and it started getting weird or something, maybe she would need to turn to somebody and maybe it would be . . .

No, it would never be Ms. Reymondo, whose answer to everything was that the anglo patriarchy took what they wanted and therefore equality for women and people of color was nothing but a joke. It irritated Deeny that Ms. Reymondo always included Jews in her "people of color" classification, an idea whose wrongness could be verified by the naked eye. Not to mention Ms. Reymondo herself, who looked like she had just stepped off the boat from northern Spain and had about as much color as your average Frenchman.

So Deeny didn't apologize, she just fled, telling herself that no doubt Ms. Reymondo had been treated more rudely by other students. And then thinking, maybe not. Maybe I'm the worst kid she's ever faced. And why would I talk that way? Why am I suddenly so defiant? I've spent my whole time in high school mousing around and only talking big when I'm alone and safe with my friends. And now I'm talking to school counselors like I was some kind of hardened hoodlum. Stuff I used to think to myself and tell Lex and Beck about later, I said out loud, and I didn't get killed.

And on a whim, she reached into her purse, and there in the counselors' hallway, she made her cell phone ring.

He wouldn't be on it. There'd be nobody there. But she could *pretend* to be taking a call from an imaginary lover and see what Ms. Reymondo made of *that*.

Ms. Reymondo came out of her office and saw her just as she pulled the phone out of her purse. Deliberately Deeny turned her back and spoke softly into the phone. "Oh, right, like you call me *now*," she said. "I'm taking so much crap because of you."

The phone wasn't beeping.

"Nothing to say?" she said.

"I thought you wanted it this way," said the man.

The same man, sounding manlier than ever. And while his words might be the kind of whiny and apologetic thing you'd get from the kind of guy Ms. Reymondo would probably date, his tone was teasing so she knew he wasn't really asking for validation or something.

"I was waiting for you to call," said Deeny.

"You're the one with the buttons to push," said the man. And then, when Deeny didn't answer, he said what she was waiting for him to say. "I wish I were there to push them," he said, laughing at himself just a little. "Touch them, anyway. With my fingers, maybe. Or maybe not."

Deeny blushed and giggled, wondering what buttons he meant,

knowing perfectly well, or hoping she knew, or . . . something. This was what love felt like, this confusion, wasn't it? Especially knowing that if Ms. Reymondo could hear the other side of this conversation she'd spot her knickers.

"Legal age is sixteen," she whispered, "and I'm seventeen, so what's stopping you?"

"There's a limit to what I can do over the phone," he said.

"My point exactly."

"It's a limit we have to live with," he said.

"So you're all talk, is that it?"

"Yes," he said. "That's it." And then the line went silent.

Deeny couldn't believe it. Here she was, practically begging him to show up at her door naked, and he just blows her off and *hangs up?*

Ms. Reymondo was standing across the corridor from her when Deeny put the phone back in her purse.

"Legal age is eighteen," she said.

"I'm not talking about drinking," said Deeny.

"Drinking age is twenty-one," said Ms. Reymondo. "The legal age of consent is eighteen in this state."

"My father's a lawyer," said Deeny. "And you don't know squat."

"It's my job to know squat," said Ms. Reymondo. "So if this guy is trying to get in your pants, it's really not up to you to say yes to him. And, by the way, I happen to know your father is definitely *not* a lawyer. Don't lie to a counselor who has studied your file."

"I guess that means you know everything about me. All the yearnings of a teenage heart. You really 'get' the youth of today, Ms. Reymondo. We have no secrets from *you*, because as our *friend*, you've got our files."

Ms. Reymondo glared at her and walked away, maybe—just maybe—swinging her butt a little bit more than usual. We're getting a bit *huffy*, Ms. Reymondo. I don't think that's very *professional*, Ms. Reymondo.

I am such a bitch. This phone is doing bad things to me. All these years, the only thing keeping me from complete bitchery has been my shyness. With cell phone in hand, the real me comes out and shows that I suck worse than the Nazis have ever thought.

He doesn't want to be with me. He only wants to talk to me on the phone.

★★★

All that week, there was buzz about her at school. And then the next week, there wasn't. She'd been moved from one slot to another—from dweebish-Jewgirl to whore-of-older-men—but now that she was safely slotted again, she could be ignored. Even Ms. Reymondo seemed to be taking screw you for an answer. It was just . . . over.

The phone had done all it was supposed to do, and the change in her life amounted to nada. Unless you counted the monthly phone bill.

I'll cancel and give the phone back.

But she didn't do it. Couldn't. Because even though she hadn't pressed TALK since Monday, she didn't want to cut herself off from the possibility of talking to him again.

All week she'd had so many ups and downs it scared her a little. She actually had to look up bipolar disorder in order to make sure she didn't fit their list of symptoms. One minute she's thinking, He'll change his mind, he'll come to me, or he'll tell me where he is and I'll go to *him*. The next minute, He won't come here because he's seen me and he could never pretend to be aroused by my body *in person*. It's like those phone sex fakes, where it's some fat fifty-year-old woman in her kitchen cooing in her little sixteen-year-old vixen voice to fifty-year-old men who are paying through the nose to a 900 number to live out their fantasy of having sex with women so young it was almost illegal. Wouldn't they just gag if they could see who was talking to them.

He's just a phone sex line.

Why would I want a guy like that touching me anyway? His hands creeping around on my body like big fat spiders. His lips slobbering on me and he calls it "kissing" like I wouldn't just puke on his bald spot.

He's not like that. He loves me, and he's not *old*, he's just older than me.

Older than me, and doesn't want to *be* with me.

Now everybody thinks I'm a whore, and I don't even get laid.

On Saturday she was so angry and hurt and confused and ashamed that she actually got up and went to temple with Mother. Treadmarks didn't even say anything snide as they went—probably because he knew that Mother was feeling triumphant and he didn't want the fight that would happen if he said something disparaging about religion. But all that happened was, Deeny felt like the worst kind of hypocrite because the reason she was depressed was because she couldn't commit adultery, and she was busy coveting her neighbor, but couldn't get him to come over and live up to his promises of sin. What kind of blasphemy was it for her to even be there?

All the time she was there, and all the way home, she kept looking at every guy and thinking, is it him? Are you the one? And the more ludicrous they were, the better. She almost wanted to go up to a couple of them—the ones who glanced at her a little bit more than the others—and say, "Have you been calling me?" But of course she didn't, not with her mother there, not with a little shred of sanity still hanging around somewhere in her head, saying, "Oh, right," to all her wackier notions.

On Monday, she left the cell phone in her drawer. A whole week without it. And Lex and Becky didn't even notice, or if they did they said nothing about it. It was all over. Just like that.

Only not really. Because she *was* in that different slot.

It was on the bus. Jake Wu, a guy who rode it sometimes and sometimes didn't. Half Chinese and kind of cute, thin and looked great in clothes, but hey, he was on the bus, so he couldn't actually be cool, right? And he always hung out with a different crowd, the chess club types, the math club types, sort of the stereotypical oriental-American, intellectual and college-bound and probably going to be an electrical engineer or a physicist.

And he sat down beside her.

"I hear you been dating an older guy," he said.

Like that, no preamble, no hi, not even a decent interval like he had to work up the courage.

"It's over," she said. And when she said it, she realized it was true and it made her sad but it also relieved her because it meant she had made the decision and she knew it was the right one.

"Are you still broken up about it? So I should act, like, sad? Because I'd be faking it."

Faking it, which would mean he wasn't sad it was over with her older guy. Too cool. "You don't have to fake anything," she said.

"Cool," he said. "So you want to go out with a really mature high school senior?"

"Why, do you know any?" she asked.

She could see it right then in his eyes that she'd stung him with that. And it occurred to her that maybe she wasn't the only person on the planet who felt rejected and was scared all the time whenever she had to face somebody of the opposite sex. And unlike her, *he* had the guts to do something in spite of being scared.

Though come to think of it, she *had* done something, hadn't she. Even if it *was* over.

"I was kidding," she said. "I'd like to go out with a mature high school senior, if you mean you."

"I meant me," he said.

"My schedule's not real crowded right now," said Deeny. "So if you kind of pick a day, I'll choose a different day to wash my hair and walk the dog."

He grinned. "Heck, I was hoping that's what we could do on our date."

"Which? Hair or dog?"

"You got a dog?" he asked.

"No."

"Me neither," he said. "My mother has fish, but she frowns on me washing them. So . . . your hair or mine?"

She made a show of examining his hair. "Yours is thick and straight and probably looks like this no matter what you do.

Whereas mine is a challenge, real problem hair, a complete bitch to deal with. So we'll wash yours."

"I see you like to do things the easy way."

"If that's an assumption," she said, "my knee knows where your balls are."

"I assume nothing," he said. "Whereas you assume I've *got* balls."

"I know you do," she said.

"Jeans that tight?"

"It took balls to sit here," she said. "What with me being a leper."

"Leper hell," he said. "Everybody just figured you were out of reach."

"I didn't notice anybody reaching."

"'Cause guys don't like to fail, so if they thought they'd fail with you, they wouldn't try."

"And you're different?"

"Yeah," he said. "I asked."

And here's the funny thing. He really did pick her up, take her over to his house, where his mother and father looked on as if they had only just discovered that their teenage son was strange, while Deeny washed his hair, then ratted it into a fright wig, and then washed it and combed it out again, with all the snarls and scream-ing that such an operation entailed.

"What do you want to know, I'll tell you everything, only stop the torture!" he cried.

"I can leave your hair like this."

"I'm going to shave it all off if you do," he said.

But she didn't leave it like that, and he didn't shave it off, and while she was quite sure that his parents still did not have any place for a Jewess in their plans for their number-one son, she could also tell that they kind of liked it that he had actually had fun.

It was, in fact, great. Not great for a first date. Just flat-out great.

Best thing was, next morning Lex and Becky were actually happy for her instead of criticizing him and picking him apart the way the three of them had always picked apart every guy that any other girl was dating. Who knew that they'd be so sensitive when it was one of *them* who was dating the guy? None of them had ever put it to the test before.

The only teasing was when Becky said, "Wouldn't you know, the one without boobs gets the first date."

"With a Chinese guy," said Lex. "Chinese women don't have boobs either, so he probably thinks women who got 'em are, like, alien." That was as close to disparaging as either of them ever got.

She'd gone on a couple more dates with Jake Wu and her life was actually looking livable when there was another pep rally and she ducked out of it after making sure she'd been seen by the attendance people and instead of going out to the grove, she went around by the buses. It was way early for that, the drivers were still over in a group chatting and smoking and whatever else it was drivers did. But when she got on the bus it didn't actually register with her that she was alone.

Not until a couple of Nazis got on and it was obvious that it wasn't an accident, they had gotten on this particular bus at this particular time because they knew she was there and they knew she was alone.

"Hey, Deeny," said Truman Hunter. With a name like that he should have been manly, but instead he had kind of a receding chin but everybody knew his folks had a *lot* of money and it made him cool by default.

"Hey," said Deeny. And made an instant decision. She stood up. "I guess Becky and Lex are running late so I'm going to . . ."

Truman got right in her face, his body up against hers. Either she had to let him press against her, or sit back down.

She sat.

"She changed her mind," said Ryan Wacker. The kind of guy who scared offensive linemen on opposing football teams. Ryan knelt on the seat in front of hers as Truman sat down beside her, pressing her against the wall of the bus.

"Leave me alone, asshole," she said fiercely.

"We were just curious about what it was some old guy found so fascinating. We just wanted a look, you know? The magical mystery tour."

And while he was talking, like they had planned it out—or done it before—Ryan Wacker's hands flashed out and caught her wrists and pinned them against the back of her seat, while Truman got his hands under her sweater and pushed it up, snagging her bra on the way and pushing it up, too, so her chest was bare in front of them and Truman said, "Well, it can't have been the boobs, unless she's got another pair stashed somewhere, 'cause these are for shit," and Ryan laughed, and Deeny didn't even think of screaming because she didn't want anybody to see her like this, to know she had been so humiliated, that it had been so *easy* to humiliate her. She just wanted them to finish whatever they were going to do and go away.

Truman got her pants unzipped and unbuttoned, but she braced her legs against the seat in front and squirmed as best she could to keep him from getting her pants down.

"Look, she's getting into it," said Truman.

But Ryan, who had the job of trying to control her, wasn't amused. His fingers pressed into her wrists until she thought he was going to snap her bones it hurt so bad and he whispered "Hold still, sweetheart" like he was her lover. And then it was only seconds till her pants and underpants were down around her ankles and Truman had his hand between her legs and she was crying helplessly and then the bus rocked just a little bit as the driver got on.

"I don't know what the hell you kids are doing but not on my bus, got it?"

He hadn't finished the sentence before Truman had her sweater pulled back down and all of a sudden he and Ryan were both standing up, blocking the driver's view of her while she pulled up her pants and rezipped them and then reached under her sweater and pulled her bra back down into place.

"Friend of ours was crying," said Truman, "and we were trying to make her feel better."

"I know exactly what you were doing, asshole," said the driver.

"And I also know your big asshole buddy is a football player but here's a clue, boys. You're just high school tough, and that's pure pussy to me. I was in the Gulf War killing badass Iraqis with my bare hands when you were still holding Mommy's hand to go wee-wee in the girls' bathroom, so please, please try something."

"You got us wrong," said Ryan.

Deeny felt Truman's breath on her face. "Say anything and I'll f— you with a file," he whispered.

She turned her face away from him.

"Call me anytime," he said, loud enough this time for the driver to hear. "I'm always willing to listen."

"Get away from her, asshole," said the driver. "Now."

Truman waited just a moment longer, to show how free he was. Then he sauntered down the aisle. It was small satisfaction to Deeny that when they passed him and started down the steps, he planted his foot on Truman's ass and shoved them both out onto the parking lot.

Truman bounded up, limping but too mad to let the pain stop him. "You just f—ed yourself, big man, you just lost your job!" Ryan was trying to get him to shut up.

The driver leaned out the door. "You think that girl is scared of you, but if you try to get me fired, you just see what she says to the board of inquiry. Think she'll stand by you?"

Truman looked at her. Ryan looked at her. She thought of Truman with a file in his hands, while Ryan held her against the ground. She thought of how it felt to have him touch her. Look at her naked. Mock her to her face.

She held up both hands, displaying one finger on each. One for each of them.

They went away.

The bus driver came back to her. "You okay?" he asked. "You okay?"

And she just kept nodding until she could finally control her voice enough to say, "Really, please, I'm fine."

"They get away with shit like that because they're in school and Daddy's got money, but someday they're going to go after somebody with a gun and the gun won't care how much money the family has or how good their lawyers are, because lawyers can't bring assholes back from the dead, much as they'd like to try."

"You," said Deeny, "are a poet."

He grinned. She managed a half-assed smile back.

And then sat there while other kids piled onto the bus and then emptied back out, stop by stop, until there were only six kids left and it was her stop.

She went into the house. Nobody was home, of course. Nobody to talk to, but she wasn't going to talk to them anyway. Not to them, not to Lex or Becky, not yet anyway, and not to Jake Wu, not ever to him. Not to anybody.

Except there she was in her room, naked and wet from the fifteen minutes in the shower, three times soaping herself and rinsing it off and she still felt dirty, there she was naked and it wasn't her underwear she was getting out of her drawer, it was this, this cell phone, whose batteries were probably run down, yeah just one little bar, not ten seconds worth of battery, but she pressed PHONE OPTIONS, RINGER OPTIONS, RING TONES, TEST and then OK.

It rang. She held it up to her ear.

And he answered. "Deeny, I'm so sorry, I'm so sorry."

All she could do was cry. He knew. She didn't even have to tell him. He knew.

After a while she could talk, and even though he knew she told him. How it felt. How ugly and dirty.

"Because it was by force," he said. "It was meant to degrade you. It wouldn't feel that way with a man you loved. It wouldn't be that way."

"You're only saying that because you wanted to do the same thing, all along, that's what you wanted."

"No," he said. "No, Deeny. I only wanted you to have whatever it was you wanted. A lover on the phone, that's what you wanted, and I could do that, so I did."

"Who *are* you? Why do I get you on the phone when I call *nothing?*"

"I'm nothing," he said. "I'm ashes. I'm dust. I'm an exhaled breath."

"What's your *name!*" she demanded.

"My name is Listener," he said. "My name is The One Who Always Cares."

"Bullshit!" she screamed into the phone, and then repeated it about six times, louder each time until she felt like she was ripping her own throat out from the inside.

"My name," he whispered, "is Carson. Vaughn Carson. I lived all of twenty-five years and I died when I put my car into a tree and it killed the girl who was with me because all I could think about was showing off to her so maybe I could get laid that night and she said, Please slow down, you can't control the car at this speed, so I went faster and I can't . . . leave here. I don't want to. I can't go on because if I do I'll have to face . . . what I did."

"You just faced it," said Deeny. "Telling me."

"No," he said. "You don't know. All I did was *tell* you. I can't— I'm a coward. That's what we are, the ones who linger here. Cowards. We just can't go on. We're too ashamed."

"So you haunt cell phones?" She couldn't keep the derision out of her voice. Did he expect her to believe this? Of course, she *did* believe it, because it made more sense than any other possibility that had occurred to her. So the dead live on. And some of them can't bear to take the next step, so here they are.

"We never haunt *things,*" he said. "Not houses, not any *thing.* It's people. We have to find some way to make ourselves . . . noticeable. To people. Somebody who knows how to look at other people and really see them. Somebody who's willing to accept that a person might be where a person couldn't be. Or a voice might be coming out of something that shouldn't have a voice."

"Why me?" she said. "And besides, Lex heard you, too."

"Lex heard what she expected *you* to hear. Not the same voice, but the *idea* of the same voice. The voice you were hungry for."

"I wasn't 'hungry' for a man," she said.

"You were hungry to have people think of you differently at school. But what you chose, what you *pretended,* was a man. A lover on the phone. And I could do that. I remember it . . . not how it felt because I don't even have the memory of my senses, but I remember that I once felt it, whatever it was, and I liked it, and so I talked about what I did that I knew made girls . . . shiver. And ask for more. And let me do more. I remembered that. It's what you wanted. I couldn't miss it—you were screaming it."

"No, I wasn't," she said. "I never said it to anybody."

"I told you, I can't *hear*. I can only *know*. You were like a siren, moving through the streets. You were so lonely and angry and hurt. And I—"

You pitied me. She didn't say it into the phone, because the battery was already dead, and anyway, he could hear her whether she spoke aloud or not.

"No," he said. "Not really. No, I was attracted to you. I thought, here's what she needs, I could do that."

"Why bother?" she said.

"I've got anything else to do?" he asked.

"Granting wishes for sex-starved ugly teenage girls?"

"See, that's the thing," he said. "You're not ugly."

"I thought you couldn't see."

"I can't. But I know what *you* see, and you're completely wrong, the very things that you hate about yourself are the things that seem most sweet to me. So young, fragile, so real, so kind."

Oh, right, Miss Bitch herself, let's check this with Ms. Reymondo and see what *she* thinks.

"Stop listening to Treadmarks," said the voice. The man. Carson. Vaughn.

"You really *are* raiding my brain," she said.

"You know what? Your father is really just doing the best he can to deal with the fact that he lusts for you. You haunt his dreams."

"Oh, make me puke," she said. "That's such a lie."

"He never actually thought it through, but by treating you so badly, he guarantees that you'll hate him and so he'll never be able to get near you and try the things he keeps dreaming of doing. He hates himself every time he sees you. It's very complicated and it doesn't make him a good father, but at least he's not as bad a father as he could have been."

"What, were you a shrink?"

"Come on, I've been dead for seventeen years, I've had time to figure out what makes people tick. Never had a clue while I was alive, no one ever does."

"So how many other girls have you talked dirty to."

"You're the first."

"Come on."

"The first who ever heard me."

"Lex was first."

"She heard me because you wanted her to."

Deeny began to cry again. "I didn't really. I didn't know what I wanted."

"Nobody ever does. So we try for what we *think* we want and hope it works out. Like me and Dawn. I thought I wanted to impress her so she'd sleep with me. All I did was scare her and then kill her. That wasn't what I wanted. What I really wanted was . . . to marry her and make babies with her and be a father and watch my kids grow up and if I'd married her, if I hadn't killed us, then maybe our first child would have been a girl and maybe she would have looked like you and when she was so lost and angry and hungry and sad, then maybe I could have put my arms around her, not like your poor father wants to, but like a *real* father, my arms like a safe place for you to hide in, my words to you nothing but the truth, but the truth put in such a way that it could heal you. Show you yourself with different eyes, so you could see who you really are. The dreamer, the poet, the singer, the wit. The beauty—yes, don't laugh at me, you don't know how men see women. There are boys who only see whether you look like the right magazine covers, but men look for the whole woman, they really do, *I* did, and you *are* beautiful, exactly as you are, your body and mind and your kindness and loyalty and that sharp edge you have, and the light of life inside you, it's so beautiful, if only you could see what I *know* you are."

"The only guy who sees it is a dead guy on the phone," she said.

He chuckled. "So far, maybe you're right," he said. "Because you're still in high school, and the only males you know are just boys. Except a few. This Wu kid, he's not bad. He saw you."

"Only after I got a reputation as a whore."

"No, I know better than that. I really *know*. He saw you *before*. Before me. He just took a while to work up the courage."

"Because his friends would make fun of him if he—"

"The courage to face a woman in all her beauty and ask if she'd give a part of it to him, just for a few hours, and then a few hours more. You don't know how hard that is. It's why the assholes get all the best women—because they don't understand either the women or themselves well enough to know how utterly undeserving they are. But look at the guys who did that to you today. Look what they confessed about themselves. They already knew that the only way they could get any part of your beauty and your pride was to take it by force, because a woman like you would never give it to trivial little animals like them. All they could do was tear at you, rip it up a little. But they could never *have* it, because a woman of true beauty would never even think of sharing it with *them*."

To her surprise, the words he said flowed into her like truth and even though they didn't take away what had happened that afternoon on the bus, it took away some of the sting. It didn't hurt so bad. She could breathe without gasping at the pain and shame of it.

"Now I know what I wanted," she said.

"What?"

"On the phone," Deeny said. "What I wanted on the phone."

"Not a lover?"

"No," she said.

And in her mind, she did not say the word aloud, but she thought it all the same, knowing he would hear.

What I needed was a father.

"Can I call you again?" she said. "Please?"

"Whenever you want, Deeny," he said.

"Until you decide you can go on," she said. "It's okay with me if you go, whenever you want, that's okay. But while you're still here, I can call?"

"Just pick up the phone. You don't even have to press the buttons. It doesn't even have to have any juice. Just pick up the phone and I'll be there."

And he was.

★★★

Six years later. Deeny was married. Not to Jake Wu, though they came close, until it became clear that his family really did expect that his career would swallow her up and she realized she couldn't live that way, and couldn't bear their disappointment if she didn't. But the guy she married was just like Jake. Not in any obvious superficial way, but just like him all the same, in the way he treated her, in the things he wanted from her. Only he didn't want her to become a support for his life. The man she married wanted them to support each other. And now she had his baby, their firstborn child, a girl, and she could see that he loved the baby, that he was going to be a great father.

And that was why she came to the cemetery. She had finally found Vaughn Carson, even though he had never told her where his body was. Maybe he didn't know, or maybe he didn't care, or maybe he simply didn't notice how much she wondered. But she found him, anyway, in a cemetery two states away. How he got from where he lived and died to where she was as a teenager— maybe she really had been calling out like a siren. Or maybe it was one hunger calling to another.

However he had found her, now she'd found him back, and here she was, standing at his grave, a single red rose in one hand, a cell phone in the other.

"You're so silly," he said when she opened the phone. "It's just dust now. Dust in a box."

"I just wanted to tell you," she said, "that my husband is a wonderful father."

"I know," he said. "I told you he would be when I gave you my permission to marry him."

"No, you're not hearing me. It isn't that he's a wonderful father, it's that I *know* he's a wonderful father. How do you think I know what a wonderful father even is?"

She didn't have to say, Because I had you. She knew he heard what was in her heart.

"So what I'm saying," she said, "is that you've had that daughter. Not the way you wanted. Not with Dawn. But you found a fatherless girl and you led her out of despair and instead of marrying somebody like my own father because I thought that's what I deserved, I married somebody . . . good."

"Good," he said. His voice was only a whisper.

"And so," she said, "it's done. You can go on."

"Go on," he said.

"You can face whatever it is you have to face, because you've done the thing you hungered most to do. You've done it, and you can go on."

"Go on," he whispered.

"And I will love you forever, Vaughn Carson, even when you aren't on the phone anymore. Because you *were* on the phone when I needed you."

"Needed you," he echoed.

She laid the rose on the engraved plate that was set in concrete at the head of the grave. It softened the stainless steel of death a little. Even though the rose, too, was dying now. It was still, for this brief moment, vivid and red as blood.

She took the phone from her ear and kissed it. "Good-bye, Daddy," she said. "I'll miss you. But I'm glad I had you for as long as I did."

"Long as I did," he echoed. And then one last sigh. "Good-bye." And she thought she heard something else as if he had laid it gently inside her heart instead of speaking it aloud. "My daughter."

ABOUT THE AUTHORS

Hugo winner Terry Bisson is the author of *Voyage to the Red Planet* and *Fire on the Mountain*, as well as the most-honored short science fiction story of the 1990s, "Bears Discover Fire."

Tad Williams' first novel, *Tailchaser's Song*, was an international best-seller, and he's proven time and again that it wasn't a fluke. He is also the author of *Caliban's Hour*, and the wildly popular *Memory, Sorrow, and Thorn* and *Otherland* books, as well as his new book, *The War of the Flowers*.

Joe Haldeman is one of the giants of science fiction, a five-time Hugo winner, Nebula winner, and author of the acknowledged classic *The Forever War*. *Forever Peace* won the Hugo, Nebula, and John W. Campbell Awards in 1998, the first such "triple crown" in twenty-two years. He is past president of the Science Fiction Writers of America, and was the 1990 World Science Fiction Convention's Guest of Honor.

Jane Yolen has been called "a national treasure" by more than one major magazine. Author of over 200 published books, winner of too many awards to list here (including the Caldecott Medal), she specializes in children's books, and for years had her own imprint. This didn't stop her from also writing adult fantasy such as *Sister Light/Sister Dark* and *Briar Rose*.

Winner of several Hugo and Nebula awards, as well as France's Prix Apollo, John Varley is the author of *Persistence of Vision* and *Steel Beach*, as well as the prescient short story "Press Enter." His short story "Air Raid" was turned into the motion picture *Millennium*. John is equally at home writing science fiction or screenplays.

Mercedes Lackey has produced one best-seller after another, and writes series with the speed that most authors only write novels. Among her best-known series are Valdemar, Bardic Voices, and the adventures of Diana Tregarde.

Kage Baker is a relative newcomer to science fiction, though she has a handful of Hugo nominations already. Her work includes *Sky Coyote*, *The Graveyard Game*, and "The Caravan From Troon."

Gregory Benford, the Nebula-winning author of *Timescape* and *Artifact*, is also a noted scientist. Greg teaches physics at the University of California—

Irvine, and has also hosted a television series on science. He was Guest of Honor at the 1999 World Science Fiction Convention.

Tanith Lee is the wildly-popular author of *The Birthgrave, The Silver Metal Lover, Drinking Sapphire Wine*, and a host of other novels and stories. Along with science fiction and fantasy, she has also written for both radio and television.

Robert J. Sawyer is the author of fifteen novels, including the Hugo Award finalists *Starplex, Frameshift, Factoring Humanity*, and *Calculating God*, and the Nebula Award winner *The Terminal Experiment*. His latest project is the "Neanderthal Parallax" trilogy, consisting of *Hominids, Humans*, and *Hybrids*.

Robert Sheckley has been a major science fiction writer, and perhaps sf's greatest humorist, for half a century. His masterpiece is *Dimension of Miracles*, and the movies *Freejack* and *The 10th Victim* were based on his stories. In 1998 he was awarded the Strannik Award in Russia for contributions to the field of humor and science fiction. He will be Guest of Honor at the 2005 World Science Fiction Convention.

Susan Matthews is a relative newcomer to science fiction, though she already has a large and loyal readership and a fistful of award nominations. Her best-known works are *Angel of Destruction, Avalanche Soldier*, and *Colony Fleet*.

Barry N. Malzberg has been both an author and a magazine and anthology editor. He has more than 90 books and 350 short stories to his credit, including *Beyond Apollo, Herovit's World*, and *Galaxies*.

Mike Resnick is the winner of four Hugos, as well as major awards in France, Japan, Spain, Poland and Croatia. The author of *Santiago* and *Kirinyaga*, he has written forty-plus science fiction novels and 150-plus stories, and has edited more than thirty science fiction anthologies.

Janis Ian achieved worldwide fame as a singer and songwriter, but of late she has turned to her other love, science fiction. She sold her first story (in collaboration with Mike Resnick) in 2001, and followed that up with three quick sales in 2002.

Kristine Kathryn Rusch has won Hugos both as a writer and an editor. She has edited *Pulphouse, The Magazine of Fantasy & Science Fiction*, and a number of anthologies, and has written science fiction, fantasy, horror, mystery, and romance novels. Among her best-known titles are *The Fey* series and *The Retrieval Artist*.

Winner of the Philip K Dick Award, the John Campbell Memorial Award, the British Science Fiction Association Award, the Kurd Lasswitz Award (Germany) and the Seiun Award (Japan), Stephen Baxter is also the author of such novels as *Raft*, *Anti-Ice*, and *The Time Ships*.

Alexis Gilliland has won four Hugos for his brilliant and biting cartoons, and is also an award-winning science fiction writer. His best-known cartoon collections are *The Iron Law of Bureaucracy* and *Who Says Paranoia Isn't "In"?*

Susan Casper isn't prolific, but she *is* memorable. Along with editing *Ripper!* with her husband, Hugo and Nebula winner Gardner Dozois, she has produced a couple of dozen brilliant short stories, including "Up the Rainbow" and "A Child of Darkness."

Hugo winner Nancy Kress has written an acknowledged classic, "Beggars in Spain," which she later expanded into a novel. Other major works include *Brainrose*, *Beggars and Choosers* and "The Flowers of Aulit Prison." She is also in great demand as a writing teacher and workshop leader.

Nebula and three-time Hugo winner Spider Robinson is best-known for his beloved *Callahan's Crosstime Saloon* stories, but he is also the author of such award-winning works as *Melancholy Elephants* and the *Stardance* trilogy co-authored with his wife Jeanne Robinson.

David Gerrold is the Hugo-winning author of "The Martian Child," as well as the author of *When H.A.R.L.I.E. Was One* and *The Man Who Folded Himself*. As a young man, he wrote "The Trouble With Tribbles," which was voted the most popular *Star Trek* episode of all time.

Judith Tarr is known as a master of historical fantasy. Her many novels include World Fantasy Award nominee *Lord of the Two Lands*, the *Hound and the Falcon* trilogy, *Kingdom of the Grail*, *Pride of Kings*, and most recently, the alternate history *Devil's Bargain*. She holds a Ph.D. from Yale, and breeds Lippazzan horses on a mesa in Arizona.

Diane Duane is the author of some thirty novels including *The Door Into Fire* and *Stealing the Elf-King's Rose* and is increasingly well known for her *Young Wizards* series of fantasy novels, routinely described as "what to read when you run out of Harry Potter." She also writes novels and novelizations of movies and television series with her husband, Peter Morwood.

Kay Kenyon is a relative newcomer—but not so new that she hasn't produced a handful of novels to high acclaim, including *Maximum Ice* and *Tropic of Creation*.

Sharon Lee and Steve Miller have been writing in tandem since 1984. They are the creators of the popular "Liaden Universe" tales. Sharon is the former Executive Director of the Science Fiction Writers of America and its current president. Steve is the founding curator of the University of Maryland Kuhn Library Science Fiction Research Collection.

Nebula winner Howard Waldrop has made a career out of producing off-the-wall stories that no one could have anticipated. Among his most famous are "The Ugly Chickens," "Ike and the Mike," and "A Dozen Tough Jobs" (about the labors of Hercules). He does not use a computer.

World Fantasy award winner Dean Wesley Smith has been a book and magazine editor, a publisher, a writer, and a golf pro. Along with his own novels, he has written novels for almost every *Star Trek* series, plus novels for the *Men in Black*, *Shadow Warrior*, and *Tenth Planet* series. He's also an active anthology editor.

Hugo winner Harry Turtledove is the acknowledged master of "alternate history." Most of his recent novels have been national bestsellers. Among his most famous are *Guns of the South* and *The Center Cannot Hold*.

Orson Scott Card is the winner of four Hugos and several Nebula awards (he won the Hugo *and* Nebula two years in a row, a first), author of the classic *Ender's Game*, and the creator of not one but two bestselling series—*Ender* and *Alvin Maker*.